LIPS LIKE SUGAR

A BLUEBIRD BASIN ROMANCE

JESS K HARDY

PRAISE FOR JESS K HARDY

LIPS LIKE SUGAR

"Every once in a while, a book reminds me why I love romance so much, and Lips Like Sugar is that. I couldn't put it down!"
-SARAH MACLEAN, *author of the Hell's Belles series*

"So full of hope: hope for second chances and new beginnings and even more than that, hope for laughter and butterflies and passion even as we walk through some of the hardest human moments of life."
-KATE CLAYBORN, *author of The Other Side of Disappearing*

"A gorgeous, thoughtful, soft, and sexy book - everything I love about Jess Hardy!!!"
-SARAH T. DUBB, *author of Birding with Benefits*

"Cole and Mira's love story made my heart swell so much I almost cracked a rib. A triumph of a novel."
-ANITA KELLY, *author of Love & Other Disasters*

"Only Hardy could make Tiger Balm sexy and teach me more about menopause, all in a beautiful romance about two people who find each other at just the right time."
- ALICIA THOMPSON, USA Today bestselling author of Love in the Time of Serial Killers

"A sweet, sexy knockout of a romance. Mira is fiery but relatable, while Cole is the cinnamon roll grandpa I didn't know I needed. Jess K. Hardy is giving us the grown-up Gen-X romance we've been craving. This forgotten generation might also be the hottest generation."
- REGINA BLACK, author of The Art of Scandal

"A romance brimming with real heart and soul. I couldn't have rooted harder for Cole and Mira's happy ending!"
- KAREN BOOTH, author of Gray Hair Don't Care

"...A love song to GenX - aging, changing, and falling in love, and still sexy as hell at 50."
-L.B. DUNBAR, USA Today Bestselling Author

COME AS YOU ARE

"...the older protagonists are refreshing—and their sex scenes are hot as hell. This is a winner."
- PUBLISHERS WEEKLY

"Cozy & sexy. This was a win."
-KATE CLAYBORN, Author of Love Lettering and Georgie, All Along

"A charming and heartfelt romance."
-ALICIA THOMPSON, Author of Love in the Time of Serial Killers

"...a hot cider, snow, slobbery rescue dog, fireplaces, cabins with rocking chairs, and mix tapes novel."
-*MARIA VALE*, author of the Legend of All Wolves series

"I loved this...A very sweet & steamy romance with a very good dog."
-*ANITA KELLY*, author of Love & Other Disasters and Something Wild & Wonderful

A NOTE TO MY READERS

This book includes discussions of and experiences with drug and alcohol abuse, addiction, relapse, divorce, and living with a parent with mild cognitive impairment.

For Shane and Joe,
and the people who leave us too soon.

CHAPTER ONE

MIRA

PEERING DOWN through cotton so faded it was transparent, Mira stepped into the only pair of clean underwear left in her drawer, pulling them up carefully so they didn't disintegrate on their way over her thighs. While she hooked her last clean bra behind her back —a bright yellow disaster that could double as caution tape—she tried to remember where she'd bought it. And, more importantly, why? Halloween maybe? That year she'd gone all in as a Minion because Ian had wanted to be Gru?

She frowned at her reflection in the full-length mirror, but she only had herself to blame. This was what happened when she slept in instead of doing laundry—she spent the day in the Mummy's panties with a Minion's tits.

Taking a black tank dress out of her closet, she slipped it on, smoothed it down over her hips, and shoved her feet into a pair of red canvas flats. "Ian! You up?" she shouted, walking down the hall while slinging her hair up into a ponytail. "You need to leave in—"

"Five minutes," he grumbled, a spoon of Golden Grahams in suspended animation on the way to his mouth. "School's started at the same time all year long, Mother."

Ignoring her son's general fourteen-year-old grumpiness, she kissed his head through his curls and said, "Sorry, I slept in."

"Neat," he slurred, mouth full.

"I was up late making tarts." She opened the fridge and pulled out the OJ. "For Madigan and Ashley's wedding."

"Tarts? I thought you were making their cake."

"I'm making both. Is Mimi up?"

He shook his head. "I heard her walking around in the middle of the night again." Standing from the table, he shuffled into the kitchen, rinsed his bowl in the sink, and put it in the dishwasher before she had to remind him. *Miraculous.* Hoisting his backpack over his shoulder, he said, "Gotta go."

She'd borne witness to every single day of Ian's existence, but it still shocked her, the way he'd miraculously transformed overnight into a tall, deep-voiced man-child with an Adam's apple budding from his throat, hair sprouting on his upper lip, and an occasional 'tude that made her want to check his skin for devil marks.

"Wait!" She skirted around the counter, intercepting him before he could bolt down the stairs, spreading her arms wide. "Hugs?"

With a tight, obliging smile, he leaned in for the most perfunctory single-arm non-hug hug in the history of humankind.

Pulling back, she studied him for the brief moment he allowed it, noticing the way his shoulders drooped, the shadows smudged under his hazel eyes. "You okay, buddy?"

"I'm fine," he replied flatly.

"You sure?"

"Yep."

"I'd know if you weren't telling me the truth," she said, arching a brow. "Because you came from me. I grew you—"

"Mom."

"—inside my body."

He palmed his forehead. "Seriously, could you, like, not be so weird all the time?"

Taking a moment to straighten his backpack strap, she said, "I could try, but I think I'd be setting us both up for disappointment."

After watching him roll his eyes at her for the millionth time before he jogged down the stairs, she sighed the eternal sigh shared by mothers of quiet teen boys, poured juice into two glasses, cracked four eggs into a pan, and walked to the back room to wake up her mom.

"Mira!" her mom called out from the kitchen. "Is it granulated or brown sugar for the snickerdoodles? I can't remember."

Three years ago, Linda Harlow could have recited every single Glazed and Confused recipe backward and forward, especially since she'd written most of them. But every day, something new slipped through the cracks. Today, it was the snickerdoodles.

"Did you check the binder?" Mira asked, pushing the kitchen door open, finding her mom with a wooden spoon in one hand, a measuring cup in the other, an empty bowl in front of her, and her salt and pepper hair looking unwashed, unbrushed. At least it was shower night.

"The binder..." Her mom glanced to her left, then her right, then frowned, confused, lost in that way that gave Mira's heart an express ride down to her stomach. Because it wasn't only forgetting. It was *knowing* she was forgetting. That this was something she should remember but couldn't.

"Sorry, Mom." Mira grabbed the binder she always took the blame for moving, even though she never did. "I must have left it next to the sink."

Swiping a hand across her brow, leaving an irritated smear of flour behind, she said, "Don't make excuses for me, Mira. I know you didn't move it. What good is a recipe book if I can't remember where it is?"

"It's just like Jen said." Mira placed the binder next to the empty bowl. "No strategy is perfect. If one doesn't work, we—"

"Try another, I know." Pointing her spoon in Mira's direction, she said, "I used to change Jen's diapers, and now she's making labels and laminating signs to remind me where the forks go. It's not right."

"We can always find a different speech therapist. Maybe someone who hasn't been my best friend since we were two years old. There must be someone around here whose diapers you didn't change. Maybe in Bozeman? Missoula? Spokane?"

"You're very funny."

"Seriously, though," Mira said, meeting her mom's stare, tiptoeing along the tightrope between concern and keeping things light, solving problems while trying not to make new ones. "If it's weird seeing Jen, I'll drive you wherever we need to go. I think the therapy is helping, but I don't want you to be uncomfortable."

The lines around her mom's mouth, between her brows, softened. "I know you would. But you already do too much for us. Besides, I love Jen, you know that. It's just..." When she looked around the kitchen, at the shiny signs taped up on every wall, the labels pasted on every drawer, the lines returned. "These are the signs of our lives."

Mira had to admit the signage was getting a little out of hand, but —"If they allow you to continue doing the things you want to do without me hovering over your shoulder all the time, they're worth it, right?"

While her mom's attention swiveled back to the mixing bowl, her mouth opening for a reply, the bell Mira's grandfather had hung above the bakery door nearly seventy-five years ago went *ding*.

"Hold that thought," Mira said, flipping to the *Snickerdoodle* page in the binder.

"Is that a memory joke?" Her mom's hand landed on her hip, her fingers pointing to the *Confused* in the Glaze and Confused logo on her apron. "Because I've already forgotten if it was funny."

Mira snorted. At least it wasn't so bad yet. At least they could still laugh about it. At least her mom could still bake, even if she needed signs and binders to do it. She slid the glass container of granulated sugar across the counter, kissed her mom's cheek, and said, "You know none of my jokes are funny."

Switching the playlist from the indie mix they'd been listening to all day to late '80s/early '90s alternative, Mira pulled her ponytail tight while the first few drumbeats of REM's "It's the End of the World as We Know It" played over the speakers. Not realizing the significance of the song, the obvious cosmic warning going *rat-a-tat-tat*, she walked down the hall, rounded the corner into the bakery, and froze in place like she'd hit concrete. Spinning on her heel, plastering herself against the wall, she hissed, "Shit!"

"Mira? What's wrong?" her mom called to her down the hallway, her preternatural skill of hearing any swear word uttered within a country mile fully intact. "Is it a mouse?"

No, it wasn't a mouse. A mouse would have been great. Compared to the ex-boyfriend who'd bailed on her, then married another woman two minutes later, currently perusing her pie rack, a mouse would have been a goddamned delight!

"Mira?" Paul said, his deep, familiar voice triggering a painful neck spasm. "Are you back there?"

Fuck, fuck, fuck!

"Uh, just a second," she said, louder than she probably needed to. "I...had to pee." *Fantastic.*

"O-kay," Paul said slowly, probably running a hand through his dark brown hair, probably looking slick and handsome and completely put together while she had a neon yellow bra strap sliding down her arm.

With a deep breath, she slid the strap back up, finger-combed her bangs, groaned as quietly as she could, then stepped into the bakery.

"Hi, Paul," she said woodenly. She looked at the floor, then at the clock on the wall, and finally, awkwardly, at his face. She blinked fast, protectively, like if she stared at him too long, her retinas would detach—which was something her optometrist had warned her about just last week after she'd started having floaters. "How can I help you today?"

"Did you get something in your eye?" His head tilted in a way that made his soft hair swoop over his smooth forehead. Paul was one of those fifty-year-old men who barely aged—no gray hairs, only enough wrinkles to be charming, retinas likely firmly attached.

"Must be some flour." Mira rubbed her eyes, then forced herself to look at him like a normal person. "What are you doing back in town?"

"We're here for the wedding."

"Oh, right." She mashed her lips together. "Of course." Of course he was going, because, for some unknowable reason, the entire populace of Red Falls invited anyone they'd ever known to their weddings. "Welcome back, I guess."

"How've you been? I've been meaning to call—"

A scoff launched out of her. Because if he was about to say he'd been meaning to call her, she was about to tell him he was full of shit. He hadn't reached out to her once in the two years since her mom moved in, and he hightailed it back to Bozeman.

His expression fell, almost wounded, throwing her off balance the way raindrops did when the sun was still shining. "Mira, please."

"Don't." She held up a hand. "Don't *Mira, please* me, okay? We're good. Everything's great. Mom's great. Ian's great. I'm super great." It was almost true. True enough. True adjacent.

"Oh." He cleared his throat. "Okay. That's...great."

They stared at each other, lapsing into an awkward silence, until something clanged to the tile in the kitchen, and her mom yelled out, "I'm fine! Just dropped a beater!"

"Are you looking for donuts?" Mira asked him. "Cupcakes? Perhaps a brioche or two?"

"It's...Chrissy. She wanted a—"

"Pauly! I can't believe this town still doesn't have a Starbucks!"

Mira clutched the counter with both hands as Paul's wife

breezed in through the door. With wavy strawberry-blond hair and a smile like a literal ray of sunshine, Chrissy was radiant in head-to-toe green satin. Paul, Mira thought, could not have picked a woman more precisely, perfectly, specifically, not her.

Chrissy gasped, her freshly French-manicured hand landing on her chest. "You must be Mira! I have heard so much about you!"

Mira, at that moment, wished she was a turtle. How lucky they were, always having a place to hide. "I've heard so much about you too," she said, trying to sound believable, trying to beat back the bitterness turning her stomach. It wasn't Chrissy's fault Paul had broken her heart. "What can I get for you?"

"I'd give my right arm for a decent Americano," Chrissy moaned, throwing said arm dramatically onto the counter. "Pauly promises me you have the best in town."

"Does he?" Mira raised a brow. "What a kind thing to say, *Pauly*."

Closing his eyes for a long, tight-jawed blink, he said, "Make mine a decaf, please."

Why was he here? Why was he in her bakery complimenting her coffee? Their breakup had been terribly amicable in the way adult breakups were, like the most devastating business transaction—they'd even shaken hands. Maybe she should have, but she'd never held it against him that he'd left. He'd never taken a blood oath to help her care for her mom while her mind slowly deteriorated. They'd only been together for a year. Plus, his toes were freakishly long, and he snored. *Whatever*.

"Two Americanos, one decaf," she assured him with a raised finger. "Coming right up." When she turned around, scooping grinds into the portafilter, Chrissy asked, "Are you going to the wedding too?"

Grounds scattered like dark-roasted snow onto the counter. She *was* going to the wedding, but unlike Chrissy and Paul and probably everyone else on the guest list, she was going alone, solo, sans date. Unless you counted the cake.

She didn't want this to be happening. She didn't want to be this person—this sad, single, fifty-year-old woman about to tell her ex and his gorgeous wife that she'd be going stag to the biggest wedding Red Falls had seen in years.

But, she thought, clicking the portafilter into the machine a little too hard, *what if I don't have to be that person?*

What if she did have a date lined up? But maybe he'd get sick? Maybe he'd come down with food poisoning so he couldn't actually go to the wedding? Paul and Chrissy would both be gone in a couple of days. Nobody would have to know her date wasn't real. No harm, no foul.

"I'm going to the wedding." Her lie dripped faster than the espresso. "With...my boyfriend." It felt wrong coming out of her mouth, but right and wrong were only mental constructs. Survival was what mattered here.

"You are?" Paul asked while she poured their drinks. "Who is he? When did you meet? How long have you been—"

"We, uh, met a few months ago." She set their to-go cups on the counter, avoiding eye contact with either of them. "He's great. You'd like him."

"That's... Wow."

Wow? That was his response? Why *wow*? Why was it *wow*-worthy that she had a boyfriend, even if he wasn't real? "It's not that groundbreaking, Paul. People meet new people every day."

"That's not what I meant," he said in the calm, level way he said nearly everything. Like when he'd said *I don't think this is working anymore.* "I'm just happy for you."

"Thanks?" she offered, not sure how else to respond.

Abruptly, he perked up, an idea lightbulb blinking into existence above his head. "We should sit together at the wedding."

Her eyes popped at the jump-scare. "Oh, uh," she hedged, trying to come up with some plausible excuse as to why that could never happen. "He doesn't actually like...sitting." *Jesus Christ.*

"Sweetie, I'm sure she'll be too busy." Chrissy moved in closer, clinging to Paul like moss to a tree. "You're making the wedding cake, right, Mira?"

"I am. But after I set it up, I'll just be a wedding guest too," Mira said, for some inexplicable reason. Why wasn't she using Chrissy's question as the obvious slam-dunk out it was? "I think sitting together sounds great." What were the words coming out of her mouth and why wouldn't they stop? "It'll be great to catch up."

The real Mira, the reasonable, rational Mira, disconnected from her body, floating above the counter in baffled mortification as the bizarro Mira below her continued making plans for her perfect ex-boyfriend to meet her nonexistent new one.

"That's great," Paul said, and when he added "it's a date," her soul crashed back into her body, her heart pounding, her brain screaming *What the fuck?*

What had she done? What madness had her Minion tits bewitched her into? There was no boyfriend, no date. Not unless she ran back into the kitchen and made one out of snickerdoodle dough.

The silence descending while Mira slowly melted down shattered as the bell above the door dinged. Even though she'd heard that sound so often it was ingrained in her psyche, this ding was different. This ding trilled. It sang. It tinkled over her like sound confetti as a perfectly timed dream come true walked into her bakery.

The man's movements were lithe as an alley cat's, his hair a soft, silvery-blond tousle. He wore a Cure T-shirt that looked like he'd scored it at one of their concerts in the eighties—faded jeans pulled straight from Cobain's closet, and dark sunglasses that reflected her shocked expression when he turned to look at her.

Thank you, she offered up to the universe for this rare act of benevolence. Girding her loins, she said, "Oh, here he is now," while flashing the stranger her best *please play along* eyes. "Hey, baby." Her guilty warble was less than ideal. "I've missed you."

Michael Stipe's voice faded out. No one moved. No one breathed. The planet stopped spinning while Mira waited for her savior to call her bluff. After a pause seismic enough for tectonic plates to inch away from each other and create new continents, he slid his sunglasses up into his hair, set his brown-eyed stare on her, and with a smirk worthy of an academy award, said, "I've missed you too, sugar."

CHAPTER TWO

COLE

SMALL TOWN HOSPITALITY *is massively underrated,* Cole thought, barely keeping his feet under him while this beautiful woman with sea-green eyes and jet-black hair reached across the counter, grabbed his shirt in both hands, and yanked.

"I am *so* sorry," she said softly into his ear. *Damn,* she smelled delicious, like lemon-flavored icing. "But can I kiss you?"

When Madigan had asked him to stop by this bakery on his way to Bluebird to "pick up some tarts," Cole highly doubted this was what he'd had in mind. But semantics had never been his strong suit. Besides, this was hardly the first time a person he didn't know had asked him for a kiss. A lifetime ago, when he'd drummed for the Makers, it happened several times a night. Even though he was supposed to be older and wiser now, some things never changed. Things like his response, which was the same now as it had always been then—an instinctual, enthusiastic "hell yes."

The words barely made their way out of his mouth before her lips cut them off.

Her lips. *Hot damn,* her lips. They were so impossibly full and soft against his that, after the exhausting eight-hour drive from Seattle, a coherent corner of his short-circuiting brain wondered if he'd fallen asleep at the wheel. But then her fingers curled around his neck, long and delicate and trembling, and reality shook him back to his senses. Not only was the kiss definitely happening, but whoever she was putting on this show for, it definitely wasn't him.

Behaving himself, not giving in to the temptation to tilt his head a single degree, Cole waited to see what might happen next. As soon as her lips parted from his, she tugged him into an embrace so tight the countertop dug into his hip, and whispered, "Thank you."

Grinning against her ear, he whispered back, "Anytime."

"I'm Paul." The tall man who'd uttered these words materialized out of thin air, sprouting like a weed from the black and white tiles to stand beside him. Or Cole just hadn't noticed him. How could he notice anything aside from the way her thick bangs curtained her big green eyes? Or her long raven layers cascading from a high ponytail down her back, the silver glinting in the crisscrossed patterns she'd shaved into the hair above her ears? Or her heart-shaped face, her straight nose, the bow of her upper lip, the curve of her lower lip—

"Babe," she said, angling her head sharply toward the man. "Say hi to Paul."

"Hi, Paul." Cole held out his hand to the side without taking his eyes off—he squinted at the name embroidered on her apron—*Mira*. "Name's Cole."

While he shook Paul's hand, Mira's eyes flared in recognition, her face paling. "C-Cole? Madigan's Cole?"

If subterfuge was the name of the game, she wasn't necessarily nailing it. "Nah, sugar. I'm *your* Cole. Remember?"

"Ha!" she barked. "Ha ha. You're so funny. Isn't he funny?"

"You're Cole Sanderson, aren't you?" Paul asked, deeply skeptical.

"Last I checked," Cole replied, only then realizing there was another woman in the bakery.

"I'm Chrissy," the woman with blond hair said, reaching out a hand for a brief shake.

"Hi, Chrissy. Good to meet you."

Leveling Mira with his still-skeptical gaze, Paul said, "You're dating Cole Sanderson? You're dating the drummer from the Makers?"

Cole was dying to hear her answer, but her wide, pleading eyes had him in a chokehold. "I love it when you wear your hair up like that," he told her, leaning forward, resting his elbows on the counter. "Did you just get it shaved again?"

Running her fingers over the checker-patterned fuzz above her right ear, she said, "Just yesterday."

When he told her "I love it," her lips parted and slid into a smile, and Cole's neck felt a little crispy from the heat of Paul's glare.

"I was suggesting to Mira that we should all sit together at the wedding," Paul said through a jaw so tight Cole heard his teeth grinding.

"And *I* was suggesting that Mira would probably be too busy with the cake to worry about us," Chrissy said, the wedding ring encircling her finger making Cole wonder if the waters he'd just waded into ran deeper than he'd thought. Not that he'd thought of much after Mira had hauled him across her counter. It wasn't necessarily his forte, thinking, considering, looking before leaping.

"Well, Mira," he said, because he was up to his waist in it now whether he should have looked first or not. "What do you think? *Are* you too busy?"

As dazed as a deer in the headlights of an oncoming semi, she swiveled her head from side to side.

"It's settled then." Cole slid his hands into his pockets, pivoting to meet Paul's flat stare. "It'll be fun."

"Right, fun," Paul repeated, not meaning it even in the most generous sense. He nodded once in Mira's direction. "Thanks for the coffee."

While a wall of tension so thick Cole could knock on it slammed between Paul and Mira, Chrissy—likely sensing it too—tugged her man toward the door. "We should go, Pauly," she said. "I'm tired from the drive."

Acquiescing, Paul took the to-go cups from the counter, dropped a twenty-dollar bill in their place, and followed Chrissy to the door. Turning around one last time, giving Mira the same look a person might give a house they'd lived in for years, but for one reason or another had to sell, he said, "See you tomorrow?"

"You bet," Mira chirped, waving and watching them leave. Once they were halfway down the block, she finally exhaled.

"Sooo," Cole drawled. "Wanna tell me what that was all about?"

"You... You're Cole Sanderson."

He laughed. "I think we've established that. The more important question is, who are you?"

"Shit." She wiped her hand on her apron, then held it out. "I'm Mira. Mira Harlow."

It was a perfect name, considering she looked exactly like a golden-age movie star, all big eyes and pouty lips. "Nice to meet you, Mira Harlow. I'm here to pick up—"

"The tarts!" Those big eyes popped. "Madigan said he might be sending someone to get them."

Waving a hand down his torso, Cole said, "That would be me."

"I should have recognized you. But with Paul and Chrissy, and the whole—"

"Thing where you kissed me?"

Her eyes slammed shut, her hand flying over her mouth. "I can't believe I did that," she said between her fingers. "I'm so sorry."

"Don't be." He meant it too. "I came to pick up some baked goods and walked away with a wedding date. That's the definition of a win."

She groaned, burying her face in her crossed arms on the counter. "What the fuck is *wrong* with me?"

Wrapping his hand gently around her ponytail, he pulled just enough to raise her head and said, "I'm sensing you're having a moment."

"Paul's back in town for five seconds, and I completely lose it." Her gaze met his dead-on. "Thank you for not blowing my cover, but you do *not* have to be my date to your best friend's wedding just so I don't have to look pathetic in front of my now-happily-married ex-boyfriend. I'll figure something out or come clean or—"

"But what if I want to be your date at my best friend's wedding?"

The corners of her lips sank. "Are you being serious right now, or only being nice?"

"I suppose you could say I'm being nice. But you could also say I'm being an opportunist. You need a date, and I'm more than happy to play Vivian to your Edward. Besides, I am a *blast* at weddings."

"Yeah, but Edward at least paid Vivian. I can barely pay my bills."

He shrugged. "I've always been more of a pro-bono pretty woman anyway."

"You've done this sort of thing before?" Her eyes sparkled under the bright pink pendant lights suspended above her head.

"Show up in a random small town in my hot car and wind up scoring a date with a beautiful woman at the bakery? At least once a week."

"Hot? Really?" Leaning across the counter to squint through the window at his car, she said, "You drive a Volvo station wagon."

"What? You don't find safety a turn-on?"

When her cheeks turned as rosy as a sunset over Elliott Bay, Cole said, "I do have one requirement for taking a stranger to a wedding, though."

"Is this about to get weird?" she asked, pulling up short. "I was joking about the whole *Pretty Woman* thing."

He held up his hands. "Like you said, I drive a Volvo. How weird could I be?"

She laughed. "Okay, fine. What's your requirement?"

"That they appreciate Richard Linklater films. It's a fantastic name for a bakery, by the way—Glazed and Confused. Did you come up with it?"

While her eyes narrowed, she backed away slowly from the counter, crossing her arms over her chest.

"What?" he asked, wilting a little under her suspicious glare.

"I forgot you were a drummer."

"Hey, what's wrong with being a drummer?"

"Nothing, aside from being the worst flirts on the planet."

He winked. "I think you pronounced *best* wrong."

"Who's a drummer?" someone shouted from the back room. "Drummers are bad news, Mira."

"Who's that?" Cole asked, peeking around the corner.

"My mom."

"Gah." He winced, placing a hand over his heart like she'd just shot him with an arrow. "Why do all moms hate us?"

"It's just a friend of Madigan's," Mira called back. "Not to worry, Mom." For the very first time, she gave him a true, genuine smile. He'd never seen anything like it. "We *all* know to stay far away from drummers."

Well, this was more fun than he'd had in about a million years. "Good luck with that. We're irresistible."

She rolled her eyes.

Straightening, doing his best to ignore the twinge in his lower back from driving all day, he said, "All right, Mira. If I'm going to be your little drummer boyfriend tomorrow, I should probably know more about you."

"You have a point," Mira conceded as a group of young women burst through the door, waving at her before beelining it for the scones.

"But you're obviously busy," he said. "And I need to get the tarts to Madigan before he sends out a search party."

"Oh, hang on." She disappeared into the back room, returning with three pink boxes decorated with the Glazed and Confused logo —the bakery name nestled in the center of an even pinker donut with blue sprinkles. Setting the boxes on the counter, she said, "You seriously don't have to do this. In fact, we can pretend none of this ever happened. Like it was just"—she gestured vaguely at nothing—"a shared hallucination."

Psh. Was she kidding? He was all in now. "I *want* to do this. Actually, I can't wait to do this."

Shaking her head, her blush blooming brighter than the boxes on the counter, she plucked one of her cards from the plastic holder next to the cash register. "My cell is on the bottom."

When he took the card, he let his fingers brush over hers. It was a move he'd perfected once upon a time to make seem accidental, and he was thrilled his rusty ass could still pull it off. "When's a good time to call?"

"We close in an hour," she said, curling the fingers he'd touched toward her palm. "Then I have to drop my mom off at therapy, then take my kid to piano. So maybe around six?"

"The rehearsal dinner is at seven, so that's perfect. I'll call you then." He held out his hand, because a finger-brush wasn't enough, not by half. "Nice to meet you, Mira Harlow."

When her hand slipped into his, her grip was somehow soft and strong at the same time. "You too, Cole Sanderson."

Giving her hand a shake, he slid his sunglasses back into place, picked her tarts up off the counter and, with a crooked smile, said, "Here's to an interesting weekend."

CHAPTER THREE

COLE

SLIPPING on the icy lodge stairs, not dropping the tarts only by the grace of a solid metal handrail, Cole wondered how Ashley and Madigan felt about their mountain being covered in what looked like four fresh inches of snow the day before their wedding. They were, he guessed, probably not pleased.

A booming *woof!* preceded thunderous galloping paws, and Cole braced himself. "Whoa, Murphy!" he warned, angling his body away from the enormous Saint Bernard charging toward him like a fur-covered wrecking ball. "No jumping! I've got tarts! Very special tarts!"

"Murph! Hold up!" The deep-voiced shout from the lodge pushed Murphy's pause button. "That you, Cole?"

"Yo, Mad!" Cole called out, breaking into a grin when Madigan—the man, the myth, the legend—came into view at the top of the stairs. His beard, those piercing crystal-blue eyes, his shoulders stretching the seams of a dark gray Henley, pushed Cole's pause button too. He looked even bigger than he'd been at Flannelfest four months ago, and he'd been so big then that Cole had fallen into a lumberjack TikTok spiral for a solid week afterward.

"How much wood do you chop up here?" Cole asked while Murphy panted beside him. "You're huge!"

"A lot. Especially lately." Madigan tugged at his collar. "Helps blow off steam. Here, let me get those for you."

Handing over the boxes of tarts, Cole followed Madigan and Murphy into the dining hall. After he set the tarts on the counter, Mad wheeled on him, hauling him into an almost painfully tight hug.

"Hi," Cole croaked, feeling something pop. "I think you cracked my back."

Letting him go, taking him in, Madigan said, "You look good. Really good. How the hell do you always look so good?"

"Must be that PNW glow," Cole said. "You look good too. Maybe we should start a band or something. I bet we'd make out."

Madigan barked a laugh. "No doubt. Take a load off," he said, waving Cole over to the bar.

While Madigan took the tarts into the kitchen, Cole climbed onto one of the well-worn leather barstools that were probably never empty during ski season. He looked up, following the dark wood beams spanning the vaulted ceilings down to the old-fashioned skiing advertisements hanging on the walls in paint-chipped frames, the huge windows overlooking the deck, the mountain reaching for the sky behind them. It was light, spacious, warm, the world Madigan lived in now, and a grateful pang shot through Cole's chest.

When Madigan had told him he wanted to move to a tiny town in Montana to start a sober living home, Cole had hidden it well, but he'd been worried. He'd watched his best friend, his brother for all intents and purposes, struggle for years to get clean, with so many setbacks, and he'd wondered if moving away from his friends, his family, his entire support system, was the right choice. Even though he'd never been happier to have been proven wrong, sometimes Cole missed him so much it cored him out, like there was a Madigan-shaped hole in his life that no other friend could fill. And not only because he was so huge.

"Hot cocoa?" Mad asked, setting a steaming mug in front of Cole before walking behind the bar.

Frowning at the tiny white blobs bobbing in the foam while Murphy thumped to the ground beneath his stool, Cole asked, "You put marshmallows in this?"

"*I* didn't put them in there. The mix comes with them. But"—he scratched his head, ruffling curls that had definitely gone a bit grayer since the last time Cole had seen him—"I specifically order this mix because I like the marshmallows."

"Do you remember how much Andy loved marshmallows?" Cole asked. Andy, the Makers' original lead singer, had a sweet tooth that rivaled any five-year-old's.

Madigan's fingers curled around his mug. "I do. He used to pour half a packet of hot chocolate mix into his coffee every morning."

Cole nodded. "Seriously think he did it just for the marshmallows."

Raising his mug, Madigan said, "To Andy."

"To Andy," Cole agreed. While they clinked mugs, toasting the friend they'd lost nearly thirty years ago to an accidental overdose, Cole tried hard not to think about how close he'd come to losing Madigan the same way.

After taking a sugary sip, Cole set down his mug and said, "Speaking of sweet things, I scored a date to your wedding."

"Really?" Madigan's dark brows crowded over his blue eyes. "Did they come with you? Where are they?" His lips pulled tight beneath his beard. "It's not Nancy, is it?"

Cole couldn't fault him for his concern. His relationship with Nancy had been the definition of unhealthy. It might have taken him most of his life to finally break free of it, but it wasn't because he didn't know how bad they were for each other. "You don't need to worry about Nancy," he said. "We're over for good this time. But my date? It's kind of a funny story."

"Uh-oh," Mad said. "Your 'funny stories' have a tendency to end with somebody winding up in jail—usually me."

Cole laughed, remembering all the times they'd bailed each other out during the Makers' debauched touring days. "This one's completely above board," he said, then reconsidered. "Except for the part where she kissed me."

Bringing his mug back to his lips, Madigan said, "Now you've got my attention."

"She's that woman who owns the bakery you sent me to. Mira."

Mad coughed on his cocoa. "Mira? Glazed and Confused Mira?"

"Unless there's another bakery owner named Mira in this town."

"Mira?" he repeated, wide-eyed. "Mira kissed you? Mira Harlow? Who you just met today?"

"Yes." Reaching out, Cole righted the mug dangling from Madigan's fingers before he spilled his cocoa. "Are you okay?"

"What? How? When?" He blinked. "How?"

"You asked that already."

"Well, it bears repeating. How in the hell did Mira Harlow wind up kissing you?"

"You know what I think it was?" Cole said, glancing wistfully up at the ceiling. "I think it was one of those serendipitous right-place-right-time situations. She was trying to not appear single in front of her ex-boyfriend, and I showed up to...help her with that."

"By kissing a total stranger?"

"No," Cole replied calmly. "By letting a total stranger kiss me. I was merely an innocent bystander."

"Oh, I see," Madigan said, entirely unconvinced. "So you walked into her bakery, and Mira Harlow just...kissed you. That's what you're trying to get me to believe?"

Raising his right hand, Cole declared, "It's the truth, the whole truth, and nothing but the truth. So help me god."

"*Shiiit.*" Madigan tugged on his beard. "And now she's your date to our wedding?"

"She is. I have a phone appointment with her later today."

"I'm sorry," Madigan said, not appearing sorry at all. "Did you say you have a phone appointment with her? Are you planning on going over your taxes? Discussing your credit score? Comparing and contrasting each other's love languages?"

"Maybe that last one. Never underestimate the power of knowing your partner's love language. Do you know Ashley's?"

"I was joking, Cole."

"I'm serious, Mad. Why didn't you tell me you had a gorgeous bakery goddess in your town?"

"Ashley's love language is Acts of Service. And when would that have come up? It's not like I send out a monthly newsletter listing all the eligible single people in Red Falls."

Cole snapped his fingers. "Now there's an idea. It's rough out there for single fifty-three-year-olds. Help us out."

"It's just so hard to believe," Mad said, and when Cole scoffed, he explained, "Look, I realize you're very handsome and charming, and you've always had the best game out of any of us—"

Cole waved him off. "Your game was flawless. I just had twice as many options."

"But I've known Mira for years. She's wonderful. But she is *not* the kiss-a-perfect-stranger type."

"Mira kissed a stranger?" Ashley asked, wandering into the dining hall before stalling out to glare at her phone, her thumbs moving furiously across the screen.

"Hey, Ashley," Cole said.

She lowered her phone, and a smile lit her face. "Cole! When did you get in?"

"Just now." He stood to give her a hug. "Haven't even gotten my bags out of the car yet."

"He picked up the tarts for us," Madigan said, adding, "and that's not all," under his breath.

Taking Cole by his shoulders, Ashley fixed him with a profoundly grateful yet somehow also frantically exhausted look, and said, "Thank you."

"The pleasure was all mine," Cole replied as she rounded the bar to collapse against Madigan's side. While Mad wrapped her up in his arms and kissed her head, Cole's swagger fizzled. It wasn't jealousy weighing him down, not entirely. It dug deeper than jealousy. This was envy.

Cole was envious of Madigan and Ashley. Nobody would ever doubt they were in love. It was obvious. Ashley didn't constantly force Madigan to fight for her affection. She didn't only love him when she was lonely or bored or push him away when he tried to get close. She didn't leave him behind the second something or someone more interesting came along.

Suddenly profoundly tired—because thinking about his life with Nancy often had that effect on him—Cole ground the heels of his palms into his eyes.

"Long drive?" Ashley asked, and when he dropped his hands, he almost laughed at the worried-parent stares they gave him.

"The baby got me up at four," he said, a plausible explanation, even partially true. "Then I decided to hit the road. I'm wrecked."

"How is Ruby?" Mad asked. "I still can't believe you're a grandpa."

The primal, reflexive need to share every picture he'd ever taken of his granddaughter fully triggered, Cole reached into his back pocket for his phone. "She's amazing." After finding his favorite recent picture of Ruby—sitting in Becks's lap, her dark hair sticking straight up after a nap, her grin so wide she looked completely unhinged—he spun his phone around on the counter.

"Aw," Ashley cooed, taking his phone and bringing it close. "She's so cute!"

"How old is she now?" Mad asked. He grinned at the picture. "Cole, she's precious."

There was self-pride, there was parental-pride, and then there was grandparental-pride. It was next level, and it blazed through him like a solar flare. "Five months."

Ashley passed his phone back, and Madigan asked, "They're living with you now, right?"

"Yep." Though he wanted to, Cole did not kiss his daughter and granddaughter on his screen before locking it. Nobody needed to know how often he did that sort of thing. "Becks is going through some shit with Ruby's dad. He flaked after the baby was born, disappeared for three weeks. So they moved in with me. Josh eventually came to his senses, but Becks feels like she already has enough on her hands to manage his immaturity crisis too. Don't get me wrong, it's been amazing having Becks and Ruby under my roof, but I hope they can work it out. He's a good kid. Shit, they're both just so damn young."

Shaking his head, Madigan said, "Babies having babies."

Cole huffed a laugh. "Becks is twenty-six, which is pretty much how old Nancy and I were when we had her. And we didn't know anything about anything."

"I was even younger when I had Davis," Ashley said, her honeyed eyes going distant. "You're right. We knew nothing."

"I'm sure they won't stay with me forever, but I also don't want them to leave. It's nice not being all alone in that big house."

Thrust into a sudden uncomfortable silence while Ashley and Madigan stared at him, giving him the looks people who were settled and happy gave to their unsettled friends—the expressive equivalent of *you poor thing*—Cole blurted out, "How about all this snow, huh? Seattle's in full spring, flowers everywhere. But it's still, like, winter... here..."

Finally noticing Mad's wide eyes, his tattooed fingers cutting across his also tattooed neck in the universal sign for *Shut up, dude!* Cole stopped talking, but not before adding, "It's really beautiful, though. And maybe it'll all melt tonight."

Ashley's shoulders fell. "We were supposed to have the wedding outside. Shannon and Tex spent weeks building this beautiful trellis, and Sam just finished painting it for us two days ago. It was supposed to be perfect."

"It's already perfect, babe," Mad told her. "Only now there won't be bugs."

"Solid upside," Cole agreed enthusiastically. "Bugs in the wedding cake is never a good look."

Ashley exhaled a pained little laugh, and while Madigan consoled her, telling her something that made her cheeks flush and her shoulders shake with laughter, Cole gripped his phone and squeezed. For reasons he couldn't entirely explain, he felt the need to pull up his calendar and double check that he'd set his call with Mira for the right date and time, triple check the alerts, making sure he wasn't on silent mode, wondering if he should set a special ringtone only for her—

"Wanna go get your bags?" Mad asked, interrupting his scheduling spiral. "Then I can show you to your room. I've got group with the guys in about an hour, so you can rest up"—his chin jutted toward Cole's phone, his lips curling into a shit-eating grin—"until your *appointment*."

SETTING his bag down on the bed, Cole walked to the guest room window and pulled the curtains back, revealing the ski hill rising like a snow-covered wave toward a bright blue sky. "What a view."

"It's great, isn't it?" Madigan joined him at the window. "Changes every day too. For example," he said with a heavy sigh, "last week the slopes were bare, with little patches of bright green grass. Perfect for an outdoor wedding. We thought mid-May would be safe, but it's Montana."

Clapping a hand on his shoulder, Cole said, "Sorry, Mad. I hope I didn't upset Ashley by bringing up the snow."

"No worries, man. Sure, we would've preferred having the wedding outside, but Ashley says a ski hill owner should never complain about snow on her mountain, even if it's on her wedding day."

Cole laughed. "That makes sense. She's amazing, Mad. I'm so happy you two found each other."

Turning to face him, his eyes glassy in the sunlight, Madigan said, "I'm so happy you're here. I know the wedding was short notice, and I know you're busy—"

"Hey," Cole said, cutting him off. "I wouldn't miss this for the world."

It was hard to tell, but Cole thought Madigan's chin wobbled under his beard. "I'm trying to hold it together, but I'm an emotional mess right now. I never thought I'd be this happy."

"What you have, it's what we all want," Cole told him, and it was true. Despite what most of his romantic life suggested, Cole didn't actually want to keep settling for brief moments of happiness perched between long stretches of heartache and loneliness. "And nobody deserves it more than you."

After another bone-cracking hug, Mad looked him dead in the eye, and said, "We *all* deserve it."

Cole nodded, wanting to believe him.

"Get some rest," Mad said. Then, on his way to the door, he added, "And since I know from experience that waking you up is like trying to reanimate the dead, do you want me to set an alarm for your *appointment* too?"

Slowly, giving Mad the most innocent smile he could muster, Cole extended the middle finger of his right hand, earning a laugh before Madigan closed the door behind him with a *snick*.

CHAPTER FOUR

MIRA

MIRA USUALLY SAT in her car and updated Glazed and Confused's QuickBooks during Ian's piano lessons. Today, however, completely shirking her financial responsibilities, she'd spent the entire hour stalking Cole Sanderson's Instagram. Cole charismatic-punk-drummer-for-90s-grunge-band-the-Makers Sanderson. Cole Seattle's-most-eligible-bisexual-bachelor-over-fifty Sanderson. Cole plays-drums-on-his-YouTube-with-kids-all-over-the-country-to-fundraise-for-music-programs-in-public-schools Sanderson. Cole *I-can-still-feel-your-hand-wrapped-around-my-ponytail* Sanderson—

"Wasn't that our exit?"

"Shit!" Mira slammed on the brakes, the tires on her Honda Element squealing as she made the exit to Red Falls by the skin of her teeth.

"Language, Mother," Ian reprimanded in a bored monotone.

Setting her jaw, she cut her eyes to her son. *Mother*. It was new, the designation. And she hated it. "How'd your lesson go?"

"Fine."

"That's good."

"It is good," he agreed, raising his phone to take a weird closeup of his face to snap to his friends.

"Really good," she said, tapping her fingers on the steering wheel.

"What's with you?" He scowled at her. "You're all...fidgety."

Turning right onto Main Street, she said, "I have a call with someone in"—she checked the dashboard clock, her nerves accelerating faster than the car—"fifteen minutes."

"A call?"

"An important call," she clarified, stopping at one of the two traffic lights in town.

"With whom is this important call?"

She cleared her throat. "It's with, uh, a man."

"A man?"

"Yes."

"A human man?"

"As far as I know."

Ian's brows slid together. "Do I know this man?"

Pausing at the stop sign, rolling through it because the streets were empty, she said, "You might, actually. He's a musician. Cole Sanderson. Have you heard of him?"

"He was the drummer for Madigan's band, right? The Breakers, or something?"

"Makers." She turned into the narrow gravel alley behind Glazed and Confused.

"Doesn't he have that YouTube channel where he plays drums with kids?"

"Huh, I don't know. Maybe," Mira said, playing it off that she hadn't just watched twenty of those videos. Pulling into the garage, she killed the engine, faced her son, and said, "I met him this morning, and now he's going to be my date to the wedding."

Nodding once, Ian said, "Nice."

It was as close to encouraging as teenage Ian ever got, and Mira decided to take it and run.

"W<small>HAT ARE YOU WATCHING</small>?" her mom asked, emerging from her bedroom to sit beside Ian on the couch. "*Adventure Time?*"

"Yep," Ian said.

"Can I watch with you?"

"Sure."

While Ian made room on their small couch for her mom, Mira ground her teeth together. Ian wasn't a kid anymore. He needed his own space, but space in their three-bedroom apartment above the bakery was in short supply, especially since her mom had moved back in. But that was one of many problems for tomorrow Mira, because today Mira's phone buzzed.

Nearly spilling the contents of her purse all over the floor trying to get at it, she said, "I'll be in my room for a few minutes if you need me for anything." Taking advantage of the fact that neither Ian nor her mom paid her a lick of attention, she snuck into her room, tossed her purse on her dresser—after finally locating her phone in the bottomless chasm of gum and receipts and hair thingies—and crawled into her bay window.

It was an out of state number. It had to be him. And she needed to answer, preferably before he went to voicemail. *Be cool. Be cool. Be cool.*

"Hello?" she said, asking it like it was a question, like she'd just learned the word, like she'd never answered a phone before and had no idea what would happen next. Would it explode? Melt through her fingers? Morph into a bird and fly away?

"Mira?"

"Speaking." *Speaking?* She never said *speaking*.

"It's Cole."

"Oh. Hi, Cole."

"Is this still a good time?"

"It's... Yes, it's a fine time. Thank you."

"Well, you're welcome," he said with a small laugh, and then—before she died of embarrassment—he admitted, "I've been nervous about making this call all afternoon."

"I've been nervous about answering it." When he didn't respond, she screwed her eyes shut. *And the Oscar for most awkward woman in the northern hemisphere goes to...*

"Glazed and Confused has fantastic vibes. It's classic, but also very cool. How long have you owned it?"

It was a conversational bone; one she was more than happy to fetch. "Thank you," she said, again, then winced at the unbearable awkwardness. Muting the call, she shook out her hands, rolled her neck, and pulled herself together. She was a grown woman. She'd talked to men before, she was sure. Many times, in fact. She could talk to this one too. "My grandfather bought the bakery back in the fifties. Then he passed it to my mom. And a few years ago, she passed it down to me."

"Generations of ownership. I love that."

Her lips, responding to his genuine enthusiasm, curved. "We all live above it now. Me, my mom, and my son, Ian."

"How old is your kid?" He sounded relaxed, like he was lying on his bed with a hand behind his head, maybe with his feet crossed at his ankles.

"He's fourteen."

"Oof." He laughed. "Tough age. I have a daughter, Rebecca—we call her Becks. She's twenty-six now."

"I know."

"You...know?"

Mira jolted like she'd been stung by a bee. Yes, she knew. She knew he'd been in a long-term on-again-off-again relationship with Nancy Hayes from the all-female 90s alt rock band Asyd Nancy. She knew they'd had a daughter together. She knew he owned a recording studio and liked sunsets and had a sailboat. She knew what T-shirt he'd worn last Wednesday, and that he'd stopped in Wallace, Idaho, for a bite to eat on his drive in from Seattle. "I...may have spent some time on your Instagram."

"Ahh, honesty. I like it. Especially since I may have done the same. Your Insta made me hungry." Was that a purr? Did he just *purr* at her? "So many cookies."

Definitely a purr. *Fucking drummers.*

"Anyway," he went on. "When Becks was fourteen, it was a *time*. Fifteen was worse, though, I think."

"It gets worse?"

"I'd tell you it doesn't, but I don't think our relationship should be based on lies."

"Definitely not," she said with a laugh. And when he chuckled too, she grasped her neck, squeezing at the shiver trying to race up her spine. "Ian's a great kid, but fourteen is such a shift. It's like overnight he's just...gone quiet. I swear, only a few months ago we were super close, and now I'm just Mom. No, not even that. I'm *Mother*."

"Mother?" He whistled. "That's an attack."

"Right? And he puts so much stink on it too. Might as well add *fucker* behind it."

"He'll come back to you eventually," he told her. "But until then, thoughts and prayers, Mira. Thoughts and prayers."

She grinned, leaning forward to push the window open, suddenly too warm.

"That man in the bakery, Paul, is he Ian's dad?"

Gathering her hair over her shoulder, she said, "No. Paul and I were only together for a while a couple of years ago. But that's over, and now he's happily married."

"To the woman who was with him today? Chrissy, was it?"

"Yep."

After a beat, he surmised in brutal fashion, "So, Paul's in town for the wedding with Chrissy, and you don't want to look single in front of them, even though you are? Am I getting it right?"

"Pretty sad, huh?"

"I'm not judging you. At all. Believe me. Just getting the story straight so I know what to tell other people."

Other people? Reality, the way it loved to do when things started to feel even slightly good, reared its ugly head. "Ashley and Madigan are going to know we haven't been dating." If anyone asked them, if *Paul* asked them, she'd be exposed. A dog barked in the distance, and her shoulders slumped in defeat. "This isn't going to work."

"Oh, that," he said. "Well, let's say, hypothetically, that Madigan already knew. Would that make you feel better? Or worse?"

A surge of adrenaline kicked at her ribs. "Madigan already knows?"

Cole sucked in a breath across the line. "I'm realizing now that I probably shouldn't have said anything to him before I talked to you about it. It's just, Mad and I have always told each other everything, and I might not have been thinking clearly after the long drive and then getting jumped in a bakery by a beautiful stranger."

Mira groaned, leaning back against the wall to stare up at the ceiling. "I really don't do things like kiss strangers every day. Or ever. I swear."

"I'm honored to be your first."

She palmed her forehead.

"But I am sorry about telling Mad."

"Don't be sorry," she said. "It's not you. It's me. I'm the one who put you in this position in the first place. Let's just call it off—"

"And lose my date to the wedding? No chance. We've got this. I trust Mad's discretion with my life. But we do have some details to iron out. What would you think about getting together later? I can pick you up after the rehearsal dinner. It would be like...research."

"Research?" she repeated as a gentle breeze stirred the hairs at the base of her neck.

"If by the end of the night I haven't convinced you we can pull it off, then we'll at least have had fun trying."

Half her brain still wanted to hop off this ride before the brakes stopped working, but the other half was already trying to figure out what to wear—black skirt, silky red top, kitten heels. "What time?"

"Is nine too late?"

"Nine is perfect."

"Good. Looking forward to it. And I'm not only saying that because you're a fantastic kisser."

"Cole, please stop," she said through a laugh. "I'm already embarrassed enough."

"And I've never been embarrassed a single day in my life. We're perfect for each other. See you soon."

When he ended the call, Mira held her phone over her still-racing heart. This was probably a terrible idea, but he was right. It would, without a doubt, at least be fun.

CHAPTER FIVE

MIRA

W<small>HEN HIS BLACK</small> Volvo wagon pulled up, Mira attempted a sophisticated saunter to the curb in her favorite outfit and only pair of un-scuffed heels.

"Hey, there," he said after rolling his window down, leaning over his stick shift to peer up at her. "You look amazing. Hop in."

"It's not far," she said as the spring breeze lifted her hair off her shoulders. "We could walk."

"Sounds perfect." He gave her a smile, and she felt it everywhere, tiny bubbles popping over her skin like diving headfirst into a glass of champagne.

He parked, then swung his door open, his long legs emerging before the rest of him. He still wore his suit from the rehearsal dinner, dark gray pants and jacket, a black tie. Every piece fit him like someone had sewn the fabric around him, like he was a famous person walking the red carpet at an awards show. Which he had been, several times. *Thank you, Google.*

She suddenly felt underdressed, too casual when paired with his bespoke famous-person's suit. As if reading her mind, he slid his jacket off and undid his tie with a swift tug, slipping it from around his neck. Tossing both his tie and his jacket onto the passenger seat, he closed his door and turned to face her.

Now he was headed to the afterparty. Now he was casual, loose. Now they matched.

"Nice night," he said, strolling her way while he undid his cuffs and rolled his shirtsleeves up with a practiced efficiency, one arm at a time, revealing muscles, veins, skin. "You really do look amazing."

"Thank you," she said, wondering if she could fry an egg off her cheeks. "You look amazing too. How was the rehearsal dinner?"

Stepping up onto the curb, he ran a hand through his hair, leaving it tousled. Pristinely messy. "Emotional. Conor, Madigan's dad, gave this incredible speech. There wasn't a dry eye in the room. Even the restaurant staff teared up. It's fine, though. I only have to follow it with the best man's toast tomorrow. No big."

She tilted her head to the side, indicating the way to the bar. "Have you written it yet?"

"Not yet," he said, falling seamlessly into step beside her before amending. "That's not entirely true. I've written and rewritten the speech ten times, but it's still off. It's ironic, too, because if Mad knew how tied up I've been over it, he'd be the first person to tell me to go easier on myself. But I can't. It has to be right. It's Madigan."

"I get that." And she did. Matthew Madigan had touched countless lives in Red Falls since he'd moved to town, hers included. Most recently, when he hired her to make their wedding cake.

"Mad and I have been friends most of my life. I lived with him through high school after the Madigans took me in. He's like a brother. I can't mess this up."

"So much pressure," she said.

"Loads," he agreed.

"Did you know that studies show pressure can actually boost performance?"

"I did, actually," he said with a smirk she caught from the corner of her eye. "And at my age, I'll take all the help I can get."

She laughed while her skin hummed.

"So, where are you taking me tonight?"

"I thought we'd try Jimmy's."

"Jimmy's?" He toed at a pebble in her path, clearing it from the sidewalk. "Is that a bar?"

"It's technically a pub. Its full name is Jimmy O'Callaghan's Irish Public House. But everyone calls it Jimmy's. It's usually not as crowded as Randy's."

"Randy's?" The string lights from the Herron's Home Décor awning twinkled in his rich brown eyes as he turned to face her. "Let me guess, it's actually Randall Fitzsimmons's Old English Tavern and Gastropub?"

"How did you know?" When he smiled, she explained, "Randy's is where the young, single people go. It's more of a shouting-at-each-other-while-your-shoes-stick-to-the-floor than a scheming-with-your-impromptu-wedding-date kind of place."

"Ah, well, Jimmy's it is." He turned, and they started walking again. "Although Randy's sounds like a good time."

A memory of a particularly sloppy make out session with Andrew Grant in one of Randy's back booths emerged from the blurry depths of her twenties. "When I was younger, it definitely was."

With a soft bite on his lower lip that made her bra shrink two sizes, he said, "That sounds like a story I want to hear."

In that moment, Mira appreciated the evening. She even appreciated the dim, vacant storefront where the Candy Station used to be. Because in the darkness, he couldn't see how easily he'd made her blush.

"Lots of these places are for sale, aren't they?" He pointed to the for-sale sign in the Candy Station's window, then across the street at the string of empty stores that used to be a photography studio, a boutique, and a Mexican restaurant.

"Small towns," Mira said, like that would explain everything. But he was from the city, so maybe it didn't. "It's hard to make a living in Red Falls. It's even harder to keep young people from leaving once they graduate from high school. A lot of these stores had been owned by the same families for generations, just like Glazed. But taxes keep increasing as wealthy, out-of-state people move to Montana. Costs rise every year, consistent staff is harder and harder to find, and as younger people inherit these businesses from their parents and grandparents, they see the expenses and the difficulties, and it's just not worth it compared to the money they could make somewhere else. And believe me"—she kicked at her own little pebble, imagining it was her last bank account statement—"I understand why they make that choice."

"That's too bad," he said, and seemed to mean it. "Have you ever thought about leaving?"

Breathing in the evening air, the freshness of pine and sweetness of just-bloomed lilacs, and glancing up at stars she always felt closer to here than anywhere else, despite her own expenses and difficulties, Mira said, "No. Not once."

JIMMY'S WAS HOPPING by Red Falls standards, couples in cowboy boots two-stepping on the dance floor, every barstool occupied, most of the tables jam-packed with pitchers and pints. It wasn't that Mira was surprised half the town was there, but part of her had hoped it would have been a slow night. That way she might have avoided the awkward joy of introducing Cole to Bud from the hardware store while he shared a mountain of nachos with his husband, Brad, and asked way too many questions. Or the barely sensical conversation they'd struggled through with an absolutely tanked Jules and Malcolm while they gushed about the eight-month-old triplets they were finally taking a night off from. Or the overly persuasive Carl and Carrie from the gas station who'd tried so hard to get them to do tequila shots, Cole had to fake an incoming call so they could make a break for it.

But it wasn't until Jen flagged them down, her red hair braided over her shoulder, her blue eyes already scheming, that Mira set her jaw and crossed her fingers behind her back. She'd given Jen the run-down on Cole when she'd dropped her mom off for therapy earlier in the day, but that in no way meant Jen wouldn't...Jen.

"Hi," Cole said to Jen and the two other therapists from her rehab facility sitting with her. "I'm Cole."

"We know who you are," a very millennial therapist said. Mira thought her name was Taylor. "My fiancé subscribes to your YouTube."

"Nice. Tell them thanks for the support."

"I'm Jen." Jen's hand whipped out across the table. "Mira's best friend. It's nice to meet you."

"Nice to meet you too, Jen," Cole said smoothly, shaking her hand before turning it over in his, studying it, pulling it in for a closer look. "Love the nails."

While the therapist who might have been named Taylor said, "Sa-*woon*," under her breath, Jen took her hand back, stared down at her sunset and palm trees manicure, then blinked up at Mira. Her expression was unreadable, and Mira bit her cheek, waiting for Jen to do something like call Cole a "charming devil" or tell them they looked hot together. Because while she was one of the most infec-tiously vibrant people on the planet, Jen was also brutally honest and had no filter whatsoever. So when she only smiled and said, "Have fun, you two," Mira wondered if she was coming down with something.

"Jen seems nice," Cole said, sliding into a dim corner booth once they'd finally made it through the gauntlet of a small-town bar meet and greet.

"She's great," Mira agreed, pulling her buzzing phone out of her purse while she took her seat, because she never missed a buzz, not a text, not a call, in case Ian or her mom needed her. This buzz, however, was not from either of them. This buzz was from the Jen she knew and loved.

> Jen: Mira. MIRA!! That man is gorgeous! Like Johnny Knoxville and Timothy Olyphant had a sexy baby. And he noticed my mani. Who does that? If you don't fuck him, I will.

Deleting the text faster than an unsolicited dick pic, Mira shoved her phone back into her purse and looked across the table at Cole. Jen's description, she realized, had been devastatingly accurate.

"All right," he said, unbuttoning the top button of his dress shirt, getting comfortable while her nerves shot a hole through the ceiling. "Tell me everything about you."

"Ha! Ha ha!" she blurted out. "I might need a drink first." *Or three.*

He was on his feet in a heartbeat, his crisp white shirt, black belt, and flat stomach moving directly into her line of sight. "What's your poison?"

Johnny Knoxville lookalikes. "Vodka cran?"

"Coming right up."

As Cole walked to the bar, Mira yanked her phone back out of her purse and typed feverishly.

> Mira: Help. I'm dying.

> Jen: That smolder of his is fairly fatal.

> Mira: What am I doing?

> Jen: Hopefully getting laid within an inch of your life.

> Mira: JEN! Everyone will know we aren't actually together tomorrow. You should have seen the look Bud gave me tonight. He knew I was full of shit. I'm a terrible actress.

> Jen: Yeah, but something tells me Cole's not. Terrible. At anything.

> Mira: Be serious. I need you to tell me what to do.

Mira chewed on her thumbnail, waiting for dots to turn into words.

> Jen: Take a breath. Have a drink. And maybe try to trust him. He's Madigan's best friend. He agreed to do this for you when he didn't have to. His public persona is spotless. Oh, and whatever you do, don't forget to FUCK HIM!

> Mira: I'm not fucking someone I just met. I'm not twenty anymore.

> Jen: That's the hill you're dying on? In this economy?

> Mira: haha

> Jen: Besides you didn't just meet. You've been long-distance dating for months, right? Lol.

> Mira: FML

> Jen: Heads up. He's on his way back to your table. Live the dream!

Jen's laughter rang through the bar as Mira turned her phone face down on the table and Cole slid into his seat, placing her drink in front of her.

"Thank you," she said, grasping her straw and sucking down a sip big enough to give her brain freeze.

"So..." He met her stare.

"So..." She did her best not to look away.

Clasping his hands loosely around his beer while she took another sip, he said, "I think what we need here is an icebreaker. Maybe we should play a game."

Coughing on vodka was surprisingly painful. "A game?"

She must have looked scandalized, because he raised his hands and said, "A purely PG game, promise. I'll ask you a question, then you ask me a question. Back and forth, to get to know each other. Quid pro quo."

"Like *Silence of the Lambs?*"

His easy laughter loosened her shoulders. "Exactly."

"Okay, but only as long as I get to be Hannibal."

"Mira"—his thumb swept languidly up the side of his glass and back down again—"you can be whatever you want."

Still staring at his thumb, wondering what it might feel like sweeping along her wrist or her neck or her lips, she said, "Can we pass? If a question is too personal, or the answer is too embarrassing?"

"Of course. You aren't actually behind bars, Dr. Lecter." After taking a sip of his beer, he said, "You can even go first."

"What a gentleman."

Wiping his hint of a smile with the back of his hand, he said, "Only sometimes."

Her internal temperature spiked, and while some old country song she couldn't remember the name of but had always liked started playing on the jukebox, she crossed her legs tightly and asked, "Are you single right now?"

He looked at her like she'd brandished a cream pie she intended to smoosh into his face. "*That's* your first question?"

"What?" she asked, laughing. "It's a fair question. I'm not trying to devise an elaborate wedding date scheme with someone else's man."

"I just figured you'd ask me something easy first, like what's my favorite color or do I like ponies."

"Do you? Like ponies?"

"Are you switching your question?"

She pinched her straw, stirring her drink. "No."

Looking up from her fingers, he said, "I'm single. I've never been married. In recent years, I've had a few short-term things, two boyfriends, a girlfriend. But as far as serious, long-term relationships go, there was only ever one."

"Nancy Hayes?" she guessed. When he raised a wary brow, she winced. "Along with stalking your socials, I may have googled you. Also, I used to love Asyd Nancy."

"Yes, Nancy Hayes, you sneaky googler," he scolded, and she probably shouldn't have liked it so much. "And so did I. Great fucking band." He took another sip, his forearm muscles flexing, his long throat bobbing through a swallow. Setting down his glass, he leveled a look at her and said, "Your turn."

"I'm ready."

"What drew you to Paul?"

The question was as jarring as the blare of a car horn when she spaced out at a green light.

"Mira?" he asked, amused lines inching from his eyes. "Did I break you?"

"I'm just wondering what happened to ponies."

"You can always pass. Although I think it might help me understand what you're into."

There was something about the word *what*. Not *who* she was into, but *what*. Like there was some menu out there of all the different things a person could want, desire, need, and Cole was trying to figure out what she might order. "It's fine," she said. "But the whole thing is kind of embarrassing."

He only waited, his head tilted like he was already listening.

"I had one of those intense can't-eat, can't-sleep crushes on Paul in high school. Back then he was this tall, brooding, quiet boy who journaled in the courtyard and listened to Joy Division. I didn't just love him. I loooved him," she said, drawing out the word. "I drew sketches of him. I made these horrible abstract sculptures inspired by him and titled them things like *The Depths of his Eyes* or just *Pain*."

He covered his mouth, at least trying to hide his amusement at her expense.

"I wrote poems about him. Lots of poems."

"Do you still have them? Can I see one?"

"God no," she said with a laugh. "Nobody ever did or ever will see them, because I burned them all like any self-respecting emo chick. But no matter how many balls of clay I tortured or how many overdramatically sad ashes I collected in my wish jar—"

"You had a wish jar?"

"Still do," she admitted. "Somewhere. In my closet maybe. Either way, it didn't matter. Paul wasn't into me."

"Too much woman for him?" he guessed, and she wasn't sure if his gaze flashed to her throat, across her collarbone, dipping down to the curves of her breasts, or if she only imagined it. It was dark in Jimmy's, and he did have very long lashes.

"When Paul went off to college, I figured he'd be like most of the kids from Red Falls, gone forever, never looking back. But a few years ago, he left his special effects business in Bozeman and came back to help his dad sell their house after his stepmom died. I'm not a religious person, but I'd been single for a while and pretty much thought I'd stay that way. So the first time Paul walked into the bakery, I'd thought for sure some divine force had intervened, putting all my teenage dreams into a pretty little box, tying a bow around it, and telling me, 'Don't say I never did anything for you.'"

Cole grinned, then took a sip of his beer.

"Turned out, it wasn't divinity. It was only that Paul had been too shy in high school to tell me he actually liked me. We got serious pretty quickly, and things were really good with him at first, and I thought..." She laughed at herself, at the way things turned out. "I thought maybe we could make it, beat the odds, live happily ever after. I actually believed it." Even though she knew better. Even though she knew exactly how easily things went wrong, how quickly really good could become really over.

"What happened?"

"Nope." She raised her hand, giving him a gestural stop sign, grateful for the rules of the game so she didn't have to say out loud that Paul had decided being with her was more trouble than it was worth. "It's my turn, Clarice."

Sitting back, he stretched his arms out to rest on the back of the booth, the movement tugging his shirtsleeves even higher, exposing his forearms up to his elbows. "Do your worst."

"How old are you?"

"Ouch," he grunted. "Low blow."

"You told me to do my worst."

His lips quirked, and Mira blanked for a moment, losing her train of thought in that quirk. "I suppose I did," he said. "But didn't you find out how old I am in your googling?"

She probably had, but she couldn't remember because that one video of him shirtless and drumming along to Beyonce's "Crazy in Love" had been far more interesting. "I guess I'm not very good at googling."

With a grim set of his jaw, he said, "Here's the thing. Every time I answer this question, I feel like there's so much more to the story. It's like I'm a weatherman in Alaska reporting on the windchill." He dropped his voice. "Cole Sanderson is only fifty-three, but today he'll *feel* more like sixty-seven."

A laugh loud enough to turn heads burst out of her. "It's so true." She lowered her voice, trying to match his. "Mira Harlow recently turned fifty, but with this cold front coming through, grab your Tiger Balm and prepare for the joints of an eighty-year-old."

"Tiger Balm." He groaned, his head falling back. "I love that stuff."

"Me too. Can't sleep without it."

When he leaned toward her again and asked, "Where do you rub it?" the bar went silent, the screeching kind of silence after someone jerked a needle off a record.

"Where...do I—"

"Rub it?" There was no doubt that he was staring at her throat now, even through the veil of his lashes. "The Tiger Balm?"

Her eyes burned, likely because she'd forgotten how to blink.

"On my neck." She trailed her fingers from just below her ear to the tip of her shoulder, and his eyes followed the path they made. "And... my low back."

He hummed, and never had the application of a beloved topical counterirritant felt so pornographic, like they'd unlocked some secret level of old people foreplay.

"Where do you"—she could not believe she was about to ask Cole Sanderson—"rub it?"

His voice was quiet, a little gravelly, like he was already in bed. "My shoulders. Sometimes my wrists and fingers after drumming." When he blinked, something dazed and heavy cleared from his eyes. "But you gotta be careful when you have that stuff on your hands."

"Right," she said in a rush. "It's not a good idea to touch certain—"

"Body parts," he finished for her.

Then they stared at each other, her heart pounding, her lips parting, time slowing. She'd nearly forgotten they were in public before the jukebox switched to the Cowboy Junkies' version of "Sweet Jane," and he asked, "When's your birthday?"

Birthday? What's a birthday? Working much harder than someone should ever have to work to remember their own birthday, she eventually said, "February seventeenth."

"Aquarius." A corner of his mouth tipped up. "That makes sense."

"It does?"

"Sure. Aquarians are passionate, thoughtful, ambitious." Just then, she noticed the tiniest freckle under his left eye. "And perfect matches for Geminis."

"You're a Gemini?"

Tapping the fingers of his right hand to the languid beat of the song, he said, "Tragically."

The only specifics Mira knew about the zodiac signs were the ones she'd learned from watching YouTube videos with Ian when he was nine and in an astrology phase. If anyone had told her she'd someday use that information to flirt with a famous musician in a corner booth at Jimmy's... "Then I guess that makes sense too."

His fingers stilled. "Don't tell me you've already figured out that I'm impulsive, can't stop talking, and hate being bored. And here I was, at least trying to look cool."

"I doubt you've ever had to try." Her throat spasmed when his eyes locked on to hers, going coffee-dark. "But what I meant," she said tightly, "if I remember Angie's Astrology correctly, is that Geminis are funny, creative, loyal, and...they're also—"

"Yes?" he pressed. "Don't leave me hanging. Geminis need constant reassurance, or we develop complexes."

Tempted to hold her cold glass up to her suddenly scalding cheeks, she said, "Charming. Geminis are notoriously charming." She slipped her feet out of her shoes so she could wiggle her toes. "Wait, if you're a Gemini, that means you have a birthday coming up."

"In a couple of weeks." His lips twisted. "Fifty-four seems so much older than fifty-three somehow. Like sixty is right around the corner."

"Well, you look phenomenal."

"Thank you, Mira." After another silence so electric it buzzed under her skin, he asked, "Have you ever been to Seattle?"

"Once," she said. "I was sixteen, and my mom took me and Jen to a Depeche Mode concert over spring break. It was a *huge* deal."

"When?" He leaned his elbows on the table, a storm-like intensity gathering in his eyes.

"When was the concert?"

He nodded.

Counting the years in her head, she said, "I was a sophomore, so it must have been in '88."

"I was at that concert."

She gasped. "Shut up! You were not!"

Sitting back again, he said, "I've seen them four times, and that show was one of the best. The Makers weren't big then, and I remember it was one of the last concerts where I was able to just be a fan in the crowd without having to wear a hat and sunglasses."

"I can't believe we were at the same concert. You were really there? You're not messing with me?"

"I was there, Mira. We might have sat right next to each other, bumped into each other at the merch table, and we never even knew it."

The space between them stretched and shrank all at once, time flickering from then to now and back again, until he said, "I think it's your turn."

She twirled her glass while the music, changing to something more upbeat, inspired her to ask, "What's your favorite song?"

He straightened. "That's a very complicated question."

"I wasn't going for complicated," she said, bringing her straw to her lips. "Otherwise, I would have asked if you knew how magnets worked."

He made a dismissive sound. "Nobody knows that. It's a miracle."

She smiled around her straw. But when he sucked his lower lip into his mouth, when it came back out slightly wet, her sip took a sharp left down the wrong pipe.

"I'm going to tell you my favorite song."

Clearing her throat, she slid her feet back into her shoes and said, "Okay."

"It's 'Straight to Hell' by the Clash."

"I have a poster of Joe Strummer smoking a cigarette above my bed."

"Mira," he said, deadly serious, his gaze penetrating. "Marry me."

She snorted, then replied with "Okay." As a joke, of course, obviously. "Wait, how was that question complicated? You answered it like a champ."

"Ah!" He raised a finger. "Allow me to explain. While 'Straight to Hell' is my brain's favorite song, we all have a second favorite song. The song that lives in our heart. The song we belt out in the car or in the shower with tears streaming down our faces. The song we never admit to loving as much as we do because nobody else would understand."

"Our heart song," she said.

He nodded, solemn as a priest, a decidedly hot priest.

"What's yours?"

With a *tut-tut*, he said, "I could be wrong, but I'm fairly certain it's my turn." The trap he'd set snapped shut. "You first."

"You're seriously going to make me admit this?"

He raised his glass to his lips, not letting her out of his sight.

"Fine," she said, relenting. "But before I embarrass myself with my heart's favorite song, I'll tell you my brain's favorite. It's 'Just Like Heaven' by the Cure."

"Mmm. One of the best love songs ever written," he agreed. "But now..." His fingers played a drumroll out on the table, her attention snagging so hard on how fast they moved she barely heard him ask, "What is your heart song?"

"I can't believe I'm telling you this," she said. "But my heart's favorite song—"

"Your tears-in-the-shower song."

"—is 'Sailing.' You know, that song from the seventies?"

A hand rising to cover his heart, he said, "The rousing and evocative Christopher Cross yacht rock classic? Yes, I know 'Sailing.'"

"Don't make fun of me."

"I would never," he said with complete sincerity. "Why is it your heart song?"

"It's so hard to describe." She raised her arm off the table, showing him her pebbled skin and raised hairs. "Look, just thinking about it gives me goose bumps."

Reaching out, he brushed his fingers over her arm, settling her hairs back down, or at least trying to. "Tell me, Mira. Why do you love 'Sailing'?"

Letting him lower her arm gently back to the table, struggling to form a single coherent thought while he did, she managed, "I think it's the intro, the strings. Or maybe it's his voice. It's such a beautiful song, but it's also so heartbreakingly sad somehow, so nostalgic. It's like watching the sunset on your last day of vacation."

"That's very poetic."

"And I've always wanted to sail."

Bringing his hands back to his glass, he said, "I have a sailboat."

She gave him a remorseful grin.

"But you already know that." He tipped his glass toward her. "Because you've been on my Insta."

"What did we do before we could stalk each other over the interwebs?"

She wasn't sure if he'd realized his foot had slid forward, his shoe brushing up against the side of hers.

"Is that your next question for me?"

"Oh, no," she said. "You're not getting out of telling me what your heart song is."

He snapped his fingers, and she realized that not only were they capable of moving at the speed of light, but they were also very, very long. "Worth a shot."

"I'm waiting, Mr. Sanderson."

"Okay, but don't make fun of me either."

She drew a crisscross over her heart.

Inhaling deeply as if bracing himself, he said, "It's 'I Will Always Love You.'"

"Dolly or Whitney?"

"Dolly is a dream. But Whitney"—he kissed his fingers, then blew the kiss up to the ceiling—"she's the light and the way."

"I feel like I know you so much better now."

The way he threw his head back and laughed made her stomach swoop, nose-diving like a bird that had spotted something shiny.

"Tell me why you love it," she said. "It's only fair."

"You're right. You showed me yours." His brow rose. "I'd better show you mine."

Her brain made an unintelligible high-pitched squeak.

"I can't hit half the notes," he explained while she closed her fingers around her drink. "But when that song comes on, no matter where I am, no matter who I'm with, I'm on a stage, the lights are bright, and I am Whitney."

Picking up her glass, holding it out to him, she said, "To heart songs."

Clinking his glass with hers, he added, "And to the people we trust enough to share them with."

After several more rounds of their game, after he asked her to name the most frivolous thing she'd buy for herself if money wasn't an option—a Maine Coon cat—and she asked him what his favorite cartoon was—*Space Ghost*—she sipped the dregs of her drink, he drained his pint, and then she looked around. While they'd been talking, while time had continued to tick outside the bubble of their booth, Jimmy's had cleared out except for the regulars who sat at the bar every night until closing.

"Is it my turn?" he asked.

"I think so."

He pursed his lips, his eyes narrowing while he thought of another question. "What inspires you?"

That one was easy. "Listening to Ian play piano. Sometimes my mom and I will sit on the couch while he plays for us for hours."

"That's fantastic."

"It is," she said. "And I think it's good for Mom. Jen told us classical music can help with memory." She pulled her hair over her shoulder, tugging on it a little bit, preparing herself mentally to force the words out because making herself say them, it always took effort, like fighting the tide. "Jen isn't just my friend. She's also our speech therapist. My mom has what they call mild cognitive impairment."

His forehead creased. "Is that like dementia?"

"It's not dementia yet. But there's a good chance it'll end up there."

"What's it like now?"

She would have shrugged, but a mountain pinned her shoulders down. "Some days she seems fine. Other days she can't remember where the forks go, or that she shouldn't wear the same outfit two days in a row. Sometimes she remembers conversations we had the day before clear as a bell. Other days it's...murkier."

Taking her hand like it was the most natural thing in the world, he asked, "Do you want to keep talking about this? Because we can, but I wanted to check."

A wave of relief washed over her, through her, all around her. "I really, really don't."

He nodded, gave her hand a squeeze, then he let her go. "I just thought of a *great* question. But I think I've already asked you two in a row."

Raising her hands, she said, "I yield my time to the senator from Washington," grateful for the distraction, even more grateful he was the kind of person who knew when to let a conversation end. Because a lot of people weren't. A lot of people asked her a thousand questions about her mom she either couldn't answer or didn't want to answer because it hurt too much. A lot of people couldn't wait to offer endless advice on the newest medications or some overpriced but useless supplement they saw on the news. A lot of people thought sharing war stories about everything their grandparent with Alzheimer's went through was somehow helpful, when all Mira could handle was the day, the hour, the minute right in front of her.

"What kind of couple are we?"

His question yanked her out of her head so hard the room spun. "What?"

"We've been together for months, ostensibly," he went on. "So what kind of couple are we? Are we secret glances from across the room? Are we hand-holders? Or are we full-on PDA, nobody ever wants to invite us anywhere because we can't keep our hands off each other disasters?"

Words, every single one of them, flitted from her mind like snow.

"We can be anything," he said. "Anything you want. Imagine

your dream wedding date, your perfect night. I want to be that for you."

In some parallel universe, the unsuspecting version of Mira who lived there fell straight over, taking one for the team because this Mira in this universe was somehow able to tell him, "We're hand holders, I think."

"Is that all?"

"And maybe," she swallowed a literal bowling ball, "we dance."

His smile—the kind that got women kidnapped in all the true crime shows her mom liked to watch—lit up the entire bar. "Yes," he said. "We definitely like to dance." Looking out at the empty bar, at the empty dance floor in front of the jukebox, he asked, "But don't you think we should practice? So I don't accidentally step on your toes?"

She didn't believe he'd stepped on another person's toes once in his life. Not that it changed her answer. "That might be a good idea."

"Mira, I am *full* of good ideas." Before she could respond to that little nugget, he said, "I'll go pick us a song."

While he strode toward the jukebox with purpose, she let her gaze trail across his straight shoulders, down the lines of his back to the tiny pleat where his shirt was still tucked neatly into his pants, pants that looked soft and expensive and made her fully appreciate what a skilled tailor could do for a man's ass.

The lights from the jukebox painted him in red and blue and pink, highlighting the silver in his hair until he glowed like a neon sign. After pressing his finger to the screen, he turned to her, hooking that same finger, neon-sign Cole blinking *Come, Come, Come,* in the darkness.

She slid out of the booth, giving into his pull while "Drive" by the Cars started playing. "I love this song too," she said when she reached him, taking his outstretched hand.

"Of course you do." His fingers closed around hers, his arm sliding around her waist, palm warm on her lower back. He brought her close, but not too close, their bodies barely touching, her breasts pressing so faintly into his chest she was tempted to take a deep breath just to get more contact.

"Is this how we'd dance?" he asked, his toes nowhere near endangering hers.

"I think"—she let go of his hand to slide hers over his shoulder, curling her fingers around his neck—"we might do it like this."

Slipping his hand up her back, urging her deeper inside the circle of his arms, he said, "Sometimes we do this too."

So carefully, making sure he wouldn't notice, she turned her head and inhaled. He smelled like the sea, sunny and sweet and a little salty—

"And sometimes you sniff me."

Shit.

"And sometimes," he said, nestling his face into her neck, "I sniff you back."

When he inhaled, her eyes rolled up behind her lids, her internal moan so loud it was indecent.

"But we still haven't answered one very important question."

"The one about ponies?"

If she was only allowed one single word to describe his answering laughter, it would have been *sultry*. "No, Mira. Not the one about ponies. The one about how we met."

"I guess that is pretty important," she said, forcing her vacationing nervous system back on the clock. "Flannelfest makes the most sense."

He pulled away, his eyes wide when they found hers. "You were at Flannelfest?"

"Cole, everyone within fifty miles was at Flannelfest."

"I must not have seen you. Because if I had, I would have remembered. I would have *noticed* you."

Tiny fireworks exploded in her belly. "I noticed you."

"You did?"

"I think your hair was longer then," she said. "It curled a little under your snowcap."

"I was in my scruffy, stay-at-home grandpa era in January. I've cleaned up since then."

"I kind of liked it long."

"And I just fired my stylist."

She laughed. "I remember you wore this black Sub Pop hoodie that was a little faded and frayed at the cuffs."

Taking her hand, flattening it over his heart so she could feel it thump under her fingertips, he said, "That's my lucky hoodie."

Of course he had a lucky hoodie. Of course her brain immediately wondered what it might feel like to wear it, sleep in it.

"But how did it happen?" he asked, the song carrying them into a slow-motion sway. "How did we meet? Specifics are important with this kind of subterfuge."

"Specifics," she repeated, traveling back in time to that day in January, feeling the cold biting at her cheeks, the excitement prickling her skin because nothing as huge as that concert had ever happened in her tiny town before. "Maybe I'd been dancing in the crowd all day, but when the Makers started playing, I decided to move closer to the stage. Maybe"—she stared at her hand under his—"I thought their drummer was cute."

When she looked up again, his eyes glinted in the darkness. "Maybe," he said, "I saw you while I was twirling my stick."

She grinned. "Is that a euphemism?"

He didn't answer. "Maybe you smiled at me, like you're smiling at me now, and I thought, *Who is that gorgeous woman? I'm not leaving this mountain until I meet her.*"

Heat bloomed over her cheeks. "Maybe, after the show was over, you climbed off stage and followed me into the warming hut."

His thumb slid under the hem of her top, just barely, probably by accident. "You looked cold, so I shamelessly used my fame to cut in line and bring you a cup of hot cider."

"I was so nervous meeting you my hands were shaking," she said, a little shocked they weren't shaking now.

"I told you I loved the way you shaved your hair. I said it reminded me of Cindy Lauper in the 'Time After Time' video."

The memory didn't exist, it had never happened, but somehow it was one of her favorites. "I told you I loved your hoodie."

"We talked until the sun set, about our lives and our families and music."

"We told each other our heart songs."

His fingers curled into her hip, drawing her closer. "And we felt an instant, undeniable..."

"Spark," she heard herself say, so completely lost in his eyes she'd need a map to get out.

"Later that night, under the stars, I kissed you." After a moment, while an entire lifetime of what-ifs unspooled before her, he said, "But the next day, I had to go back to Seattle."

"And I had to go back to my life."

"Once I got home, I couldn't stop thinking about you. So maybe I found you on social media. At first, I only stalked your account like a creep. But one day, you posted a picture of these red velvet cupcakes with vampire teeth icing and the caption 'the Dracula: Red and Loving It special—'"

She'd actually done that, just last week. He had been on her Insta.

"—and it was so clever, and the cupcakes looked so good, that I couldn't resist. I liked the post."

"Maybe I squealed so loud when I saw it, I scared Ian."

His soft chuckle swirled around her like smoke. "Then maybe I said *fuck it* and followed you."

"And maybe I followed you back so fast I sprained a finger."

"Maybe we started DMing." The way he looked at her was so intense a herd of elephants could have marched into the bar to eat the peanuts in the barrel by the door and he wouldn't have noticed until he saw their reflection in her eyes. "Then you gave me your number, and we started texting."

"Maybe, after a while," she said, "I finally worked up the courage to call you."

"Then I got brave enough to FaceTime you."

"And I got brave enough to answer."

"And then," he said, "slowly, we became..."

"Us."

His thumb drew a small circle over her skin, not at all by accident, and a shiver gripped her neck. "This feels good," he said. "It feels right." And there it went, her heart, sliding between her ribs and skipping along the floor. "I think we'll have them all fooled."

Fooled, right. She swallowed something bitter, wondering if she was the first person in the world to be jealous of themselves in a relationship that had never happened. "I still can't believe we're doing this."

"Oh, come on, Mira." He pulled her close again, and she leaned in, notching her chin over his shoulder, smelling the sea on his skin. "Who ever said we couldn't do ridiculous things anymore just because we're old?"

"Young people."

He barked a laugh, then, after another verse, another chorus, he admitted, "The answer is yes, by the way."

"Yes, what?"

Solemnly, he said, "I do like ponies."

Hiding her grin in his neck while he spun her around, even though she knew it was a terrible idea, possibly the worst she'd ever had, she let herself think, if only for a second, *I wish you didn't live in Seattle.*

CHAPTER SIX

COLE

DESPITE ITS APPARENT lack of sex appeal, Cole's Volvo always gave him a smooth ride. But after he'd danced with Mira for three more songs before walking her back to her bakery, the winding road up to Bluebird might as well have been paved with feathers. His skin hummed everywhere she'd touched him, the lingering sensation of her body against his distracting him so thoroughly he'd accidentally veered onto the gravel shoulder twice.

While he drummed a random beat on the steering wheel, his headlights blazing a path between the trees, he gasped, fingers snapping between his ears as the unmistakable lightning strike of inspiration hit. Beats, rhythms, lyrics. They were right there, thrumming through his veins. He wanted to write a poem, a song, an epic space opera, a—"Best man's speech!" he said out loud.

He'd been stuck for days, but now the lines wrote themselves in his mind, everything he wanted to say to Ashley and Madigan, all his hopes for them as clear as the night sky over his head. It had been a while since he'd had a muse, but *damn* if Mira Harlow wasn't Red Falls's very own Edie Sedgwick.

Pulling into Bluebird's parking lot, he grabbed his coat and tie from the passenger seat and raced up the steps and into the lodge, words swimming in front of his eyes, his fingers itching to put them down.

"Where are you going in such a hurry?"

Wheeling around, he clutched at his chest. "Davis," he wheezed, his heart pounding. "It's dangerous to scare a man my age like that."

"I know CPR," Ashley's daughter stated calmly, sitting alone at a table, her shoulder-length blond waves curtaining her face while she stared at her phone. "And we have an AED if things get really hairy."

He dropped his hand to his side. "You do?"

She nodded. "In the kitchen. On the wall by the back door. My grandpa bought it years ago after watching a *60 Minutes* on cardiac arrest. It probably still works."

"That's...good to know," he said haltingly, his heart rate stabilizing, helped in part by the way Davis's shoulders slumped, her thumb sliding absently up and down her screen, her expression flat as lake water. He glanced around the empty dining hall, the only light coming from the EXIT signs, her phone, and the moon. "You're up late."

"It's only midnight. It's early."

"Time *is* subjective," he conceded. When he was Davis's age, the night didn't even start until two a.m. Now, he was lucky to make it past ten thirty with his eyes open. "Everything all right?" he asked, because she didn't seem all right. She hadn't seemed all right at the rehearsal dinner either, sitting quietly next to Kev, neither of them saying much to each other, or to anyone else, for that matter. He didn't pretend to know the details of their relationship, but he knew they'd been close. And it had pressed on an old bruise, watching her whisper in Kev's ear, rub his back like she was trying to coax some sort of response from him. If Cole knew anything, it was when someone was shutting their partner out. He'd been that partner more times than he could count.

"Yep, fine," she replied. "Just excited. Big day tomorrow."

Davis wasn't much younger than Becks, and maybe because

they seemed so similar to him, both take-no-shit spitfires, the second Cole had met Davis at Flannelfest, they'd just clicked. They'd stayed up for hours by the big bonfire, talking, cracking jokes, telling stories. But if she'd been a spitfire then, there was no spark in her tonight.

His speech could wait.

Pulling out a chair, he joined her at the table. "*Huge* day," he agreed, setting his coat and tie on the chair next to him. "Lots of changes."

"They never stop, do they?"

"Not until we're in the ground."

Ashley's were golden brown, Maude Alice's a pale gray, so when Davis looked up from her phone, Cole thought she must have gotten her vibrant blue eyes from her dad. He hadn't met Chuck at Flannelfest, but he'd heard all about what he'd done to the guys, to Madigan and Ashley. He also knew Davis wasn't talking to him anymore, and he wondered how much that weighed on her. "Where'd you go tonight?" she asked. "I looked for you after dessert, but you were gone."

"Oh, I just went out," he said, aiming for nonchalance and probably missing. "Trying to get to know your town a bit better."

Davis raised a brow, looking somehow exactly like Maude Alice and Ashley at once with the gesture. "Alone?"

"No. Not exactly," he admitted. "I...was with Mira."

"Mira Harlow?"

He nodded.

"How do you know Mira?"

"We, uh, met this morning. When I picked up the tarts."

"And you took her out tonight?" She whistled. "Damn, bro. You move fast."

He didn't bother denying it. He had moved fast, sprinting from not knowing Mira at all to wishing he had all the time in the world to get to know her better like he was being chased by a bear. "That's what they tell me."

Setting her stare on him, squinting, considering, she said, "You two would actually make a great couple."

He coughed into his fist, a tiny spark flickering beneath his sternum. Probably heartburn. "Do you have your toast written?" he asked her. "You have to go right before I do, right?"

Picking up her phone, she opened the notes app and flashed her screen at him. "Almost. I've never been a maid of honor before. It feels, I don't know, stressful. The speech is so much harder than I thought it would be."

"I know," he agreed. "I've been working on mine for weeks. I've been completely blocked, until tonight. Until—"

"You found some inspiration?"

At least he'd earned a smile, even if she was giving him hell. "Something like that." He sat up straighter. "I've got an idea. Let's work on our speeches right now, together. When we're done, we'll read each other's and say nothing but glowing things about them."

This smile was even more genuine. "I'm down. But we need..." She stood from the table. "Hang on. I'll be right back."

When she walked to the kitchen, Cole realized she was in her pajamas, black fleece pants decorated with tiny red hearts, fuzzy pink slippers. Maybe this was something Davis did when she couldn't sleep, sat in the dining hall by herself, in the dark. Or maybe it was something else, *someone* else, keeping her up, carving those purple half moons under her eyes.

Returning to the table with two steaming mugs of coffee in her hands, Davis set one in front of him and said, "Thanks for hanging with me, Cole."

Taking the coffee, even though he knew it would keep him up for hours, he said, "My pleasure." When he pulled his phone out of his coat pocket to start working on his toast, a grin spread across his face at the text waiting for him.

Mira: Thanks for a great fake date.

Typing—

Cole: Fake date, real feels.

—he hit send, opened his notes app, nodded at Davis, and said, "Let's do this."

"I can't believe you're torturing us like this on your wedding day," Sam grunted, reaching to the side, stretching his deeply tanned twenty-something body into triangle pose.

Reaching calmly toward his ankle, Madigan said, "Snowga is hardly torture. But we can stay in triangle for an extra minute if you'd like."

When Mad had asked him earlier in the morning if he'd wanted to come to pre-wedding yoga with the guys from Little Timber, Cole thought they'd be stretching out in the lodge like sensible, rational humans. If he'd known they'd be half-naked assuming downward dog in four inches of snow, his answer might have been different.

Bracing against a sharp pain in his side when he'd tried to touch his foot, his indignation intensifying, Cole hissed, "Shit."

"No swearing," a new resident named Thom said. Rail thin with shaggy brown hair, Thom had a tight, jittery cackle that would give a hyena a run for its money. It made Cole strangely uncomfortable, until he realized why. Madigan had laughed like that when he'd been using. "Learned that one the hard way."

"What do you mean?" Cole asked, moving gracelessly into warrior pose while goose bumps raced across his exposed chest and arms. He was fucking freezing.

"It's a rule," Kev said from his other side. "You'll get bathroom duty."

"What the hell is bathroom duty?"

Leaning in close, Thom told him, "Boss makes us scrub the bathroom floors with a toothbrush."

Cole's jaw dropped. "He does *what?*"

Both Kev and Thom snorted.

"Do you have something you'd like to share with the rest of the class?" Madigan asked, intimidating in mountain pose in nothing but his boxer briefs, tattoos, lumberjacked muscles, and a brow raised.

"If they swear," Cole said, wide-eyed, incensed, "you make them scrub the bathroom floor with a toothbrush?"

Bursting into laughter, Tex folded forward so quickly the ratty cowboy hat he almost never took off toppled into the snow.

Madigan's hands landed on his hips, his tattooed fingers flashing HOPE and FEAR in Cole's direction. "I do not make them use a toothbrush."

Patting Tex's back while his laughter morphed into a coughing fit, Sam said, "That's true. It's more like a hairbrush."

"It's a cleaning brush," Madigan insisted. "A perfectly normal bathroom cleaning brush. And I get a new one at Bud's every month, so it never gets too gross."

"Did he tell you about the bucket?" A round-bellied, middle-aged white man named Stanley asked, rubbing warmth back into his arms.

"There's a bucket?" Cole could only stare at Madigan while the rest of the men started cracking up.

"It's a perfectly normal cleaning bucket. For the soapy water—" Mad cut himself off, ran a hand through his hair. "You know what? Never mind. This concludes Madigan's Pre-Wedding Snowga." Glancing down at the still-snowy ground surrounding them, he sighed deeply. "Go get dressed. Breakfast in fifteen in the lodge."

While the men shuffled through the snow back to their cabins, stopping every so often to hurl slushy spring snowballs at each other, Cole approached the groom. "How are you holding up?"

Madigan's lips twisted. "It'll be okay, right? It'll be good. I won't have a panic attack at the altar, right?"

"Do you even have an altar?" Cole asked.

"We *had* that trellis thing. But now, we only have a..." He motioned vaguely in the air. "A spot on the floor where we're supposed to stand."

"That's good," Cole said. "Much less intimidating than an altar."

When Madigan reached out, his big fingers wrapping around Cole's arms, Cole wondered how one man could produce so much heat, like a living furnace. "You have to help me," he pleaded, his furnace hands squeezing. "I was hoping snowga would mellow me out, but it barely took the edge off."

Cole frowned. "Of your nerves? Maybe we should go for a run or something." His frown deepened. "Not like I run unless I'm being chased."

"It's not my nerves," Mad said. "I mean, it is my nerves, but mostly it's that Ashley is apparently superstitious. She's insisting we sleep in different rooms and keep our hands to ourselves until we're married."

"Ahhh," Cole said, finally understanding.

"It's only been five days, and I'm losing it! How did I go from abstaining for years to not being able to survive five days without sex? Every time I see her, every time I hear her voice, I want to tear her clothes off. I don't know if I'm going to make it until tonight. I'm dying."

"I thought blue balls being fatal was a myth," Cole said, his toes going numb.

Madigan's groan of a laugh was pure misery.

"Look," Cole said, "you're almost there. Just think about baseball or paying your taxes or—"

"Leprechauns."

"That's...a little niche," Cole pointed out, trying to stomp some feeling back into his feet, his teeth chattering. "But whatever works. Now let's go eat Mira's tarts before my dick falls off."

"You're right," Mad said, releasing Cole's arms. "You're totally right. I can do this." Closing his eyes, he inhaled through his nose and recited, "I am a calm, focused, evolved man who will not let his need for sex make his friend's dick fall off." When his eyes opened again, they were clear, crystal blue and glinting in the morning sun.

"Seriously, Mad." Cole clapped a hand over his shoulder. "You've got this."

"I'm so glad you're here, Cole."

For reasons he'd expected, and for one very important reason he hadn't, Cole replied, "Me too, Mad. Me too."

CHAPTER SEVEN

COLE

SITTING NEXT to Madigan's dad, Conor, while his three younger brothers milled around the room like gorgeous, impeccably dressed antique shoppers, Cole leaned forward, placed his elbows on his knees, and studied his best friend.

The man of the hour faced the full-length mirror in his tailored black pants and his white dress shirt, concentration sharpening his features while he struggled with his bow tie. Folding the strip of black fabric over itself, Madigan twisted, tugged, scowled, then tugged some more. There was something so deceptively ordinary about the scene—a man, a mirror, a stubborn tie. But it was Mad's expression that hit Cole in the gut, the creases branching out from his eyes, his tightly clenched jaw. It said *If I can just get this damn tie under control, everything else will fall in line.*

Pushing up from the couch, unwilling to let Madigan continue to wrestle with the literal albatross around his neck all by himself, Cole asked, "Can I help?"

"Please." Madigan dropped the ends of his tie, raised his chin. "Save me."

When Cole took the tie in his hands, he was rewarded by a

mouth-watering mixture of cedar and spice flooding his senses. "Good lord. Is that your beard oil?"

"You like it?" Madigan asked, the first smile Cole had seen on his face in hours making an appearance. "It's called Man of the Woodlands."

"You need to lead me to these woodlands, because that"—he sniffed Madigan's beard—"is delicious."

"It's Ashley's favorite."

"She has excellent taste," Cole said, then winked. "But we already knew that." He tugged the ends of the tie. "Now let's whip this bad boy into shape."

Being good at tying ties around other men's necks was one of Cole's favorite random bisexual flexes, but after wrapping and pinching and tugging while Madigan's brothers stopped whatever they'd been doing to watch, confer, then start taking bets on whether he'd pull it off, Cole huffed, releasing the still-crooked bow. "It's cursed."

"Good afternoon, gentlemen." Maude Alice floated into their makeshift dressing room—which also happened to be her office—like an angel summoned from formal wear heaven. "Don't you all look splendid."

"Maybe *they* do," Madigan grumbled.

She frowned. "I beg your pardon?"

"His tie." Cole motioned to Madigan's neck. "We can't get it straight."

"Ah." Crossing the room, her heels thudding quietly over the carpet, Maude Alice said, "Sometimes these things require a woman's touch."

When she dismissed him with a tap on his shoulder, Cole was more than happy to step aside to join Conor on the couch again, watching in awe as she made quick work of a perfectly straight bow.

"There." She smoothed down the collar of Madigan's dress shirt, her gaze going distant. "It's been a while since I've gotten to do that."

Snatching one of her slender hands in his, Madigan kissed her palm, and said, "Thank you."

Conor cleared his throat, his gray-blue eyes shining like glass. "You look good, Mattie. Real good."

"He looks like a monkey on steroids," Madigan's brother Sean quipped, ducking to narrowly avoid the couch pillow their youngest brother Brady threw at his head.

"I should have left you all at home," Conor said, whipping out a hand to snag an end of Sean's tie and tug it out of its bow.

"Nice one, Dad." Pretending to slide his hands into his pockets, Sean caught Conor sleeping and yanked his tie loose in retribution.

"No," Madigan warned, backing away with his hands raised when they rounded on him. "Nobody touches this tie and lives to tell about it."

"So touchy," Sean said, ducking another pillow hurled by Madigan's third—and usually most serious—brother, Darryn.

"Ahem!" Maude Alice's voice was a ruler slapping against chalkboard, and everyone in the room snapped to attention. "Does everyone remember their places? The ceremony starts in less than thirty minutes."

Setting the pillows back on the couch while scowling at his unruly children—as if he hadn't always been just as bad—Conor said, "I'll make sure they'll all be where they're supposed to be, Maude Alice."

"Wonderful. I'd better head back out there. Mira just arrived with the cake."

Cole's head whipped up. "She did?"

"A few minutes ago. She's setting the table up now." Staring down at her red nails, Maude Alice snuck a sideways glance in Cole's direction. "She may need some help."

"If you're good here, Mad," Cole said, slipping out of his suit jacket and hanging it back on its hanger, "I'm just going to go make sure the cake is, uh, up to your standards."

"*His* standards?" Brady asked dubiously, hooking a thumb toward Madigan. "Does it have sugar in it?"

"And frosting?" Sean added.

"Then it's up to Mattie's standards," Darryn said conclusively.

"At least I don't drink pickle juice straight from the jar," Madigan countered, magically in possession of another couch pillow, making his brothers run for cover while Brady snapped, "That is a family-only secret!"

"We're all family here," Madigan said, laughing as the pillow he'd hurled bounced off Sean's face.

Maude Alice linked her arm with Cole's. "I think we'd better get out of here before a brawl breaks out."

"Good idea," Cole replied, ushering her from the room to the sound of the Madigan clan descending into a full-on no-holds-barred pillow fight, having fun the way they always did when Cole lived with them in his teens, before everything with Madigan went so dark, before they'd all fought and endured and survived to find the light on the other side. Before they'd all taught Cole what family really meant. Shutting the door behind them, he made a mental note to call Becks later and check in, tell her he missed them.

"It's interesting," Maude Alice said as he walked with her down the stairs to the dining hall.

"What's that?"

"When I mentioned Mira, you perked right up. Reminded me of Murphy when I open a bag of treats."

He really needed to work on his poker face.

"But what was even *more* interesting," she continued, "was Mira's four-alarm blush when I told her you were busy getting into your tux. I've known Mira since the day she was born, and I'm not sure I've ever seen her blush before."

"That *is* interesting," Cole said, unable to hide his grin.

"I didn't realize you two had met." She raised a brow. "Shows how little I know."

This was laughable. Nothing slipped past Maude Alice, and she knew it as well as he did. Leaning in to kiss her cheek, he told her, "You look beautiful tonight."

She touched her silver hair, pulled back into an elegant bun at the nape of her neck, then glanced down at her dress, a classic midnight blue sheath that hit her mid-calf. Her smile was rueful, her eyes shining. "I wore this dress to my own rehearsal dinner with Max so many years ago I've lost count. Ashley wanted me to wear it today. She wanted it to be her 'something blue.'"

"It's stunning."

Clearing her throat, she regained her composure. "Thank you, dear. I'm just thrilled it still fits. But you might want to save some of that charm, because once you see our baker..."

Rounding the corner into the dining hall, Cole halted in his tracks, frozen in place, a gasp caught in his throat.

"I did try to warn you," Maude Alice said, patting his arm before striding across the room to greet the few guests trickling in.

The late day sun slanted in through the windows, centering Mira in a golden, dust-moted spotlight. She hadn't noticed him yet—too busy arranging delicate flower petals around a stunning three-tiered wedding cake with ivory frosting and intricate lace details piped around the edges. So he took his time noticing her.

She'd pinned her raven waves back, revealing a simple black helix piercing in her left ear. Her exposed neck sloped gracefully to meet her bare shoulders, and his fingers, remembering how soft her skin had been there, twitched at his sides. Was that a tattoo peeking out beneath the strapless bodice of her red dress, right over her spine? It had to be. If he released her zipper an inch or two, would he be able to tell what it was? Or would he have to pull her zipper all the way down to see the whole design?

He'd noticed her body last night. It had been impossible not to when he'd held her close on the dance floor, his hand following the dip of her waist, her breasts soft and full against his chest. But now, in that dress, the way the silky red fabric clung to her curves like it loved them, her body could make an hourglass jealous. It almost hurt, knowing he wouldn't remember this precise view of her. Maybe he could sneak his phone out for a second and—*no, that'd be weird.*

Why was he being weird? Why did he want to take a hundred pictures of a woman he barely knew and might not see again for... who knew how long? It was the wedding, the nerves and excitement and expectation buzzing through the air. Or maybe it was her tarts they'd had for breakfast. Madigan had been right. They were amazing—buttery, sweet, perfect.

Maude Alice cleared her throat loudly from across the room, and when he followed the sound, he found her tilting her head toward Mira in a very clear *get on with it* gesture. Giving her a small salute, Cole made his way to the cake table with his hands in his pockets, a swagger in his step, and a smile on his face. Once he was close enough to smell her citrus scent, he said, "Haven't you heard it's impolite to upstage the bride at her own wedding?"

Goose bumps rose across her neck, prickling down her arms, her fingers stilling in midair, a dark pink rose petal clutched between them. Placing the petal on the cake's second tier, her lips curling at the corners, she muttered, "Fucking drummers."

CHAPTER EIGHT

MIRA

*F*AKE DATE, *real feels. Fake date, real feels.*

She'd reread Cole's text so many times last night the words had left an afterimage on her retinas, an echo between her ears. She'd even dug her wish jar out of her closet, writing his words down so she could light them on fire and save the ashes forever.

It was embarrassing, how quickly he'd gotten under her skin. But it wasn't entirely her fault. She was, she realized after he'd dropped her off last night, a little starstruck. He was gorgeous, famous, and it certainly wasn't the first time she'd crushed on a drummer. They were a different breed—charming, funny, cool with not being the center of attention, ridiculously dexterous, blessed with godlike stamina...

Shaking off thoughts she definitely shouldn't be having, certainly not in public, certainly not with him standing less than an arm's length away, she finally turned around to face him. And all the air evacuated her lungs in a *whoosh.*

His brown eyes sparkling under the rented chandelier above their heads, he said, "Hi, Mira."

Her gaze sank to his bow tie, his crisp white shirt, the

simple metal clasp of his belt buckle, his sleek black pants, shiny black shoes. Two days, two suits. *Death by formal wear.* "Hi, Cole."

"You look phenomenal," he told her when she met his eyes again. "I *love* that dress."

"You look like you just stepped off a GQ cover."

He made a show of checking his cufflinks. "Mad's got this whole James Bond theme going tonight."

She nodded, coming to terms with his bow tie, a thing that had never been sexy to her before but was irrefutably sexy now. It was a fact. The sky was blue. Her shoes were too tight. Bow ties were sexy. "Major 007 vibes."

"Speaking of espionage." He glanced around the dining hall. "Are Paul and Chrissy here yet?"

She'd checked for Paul when she'd first arrived, but now, for some reason that probably had a lot to do with the number of times she'd rewatched *Casino Royale*, she could barely remember his name. "Not yet."

"Good. That gives us plenty of time to talk about this cake." Leaning in for a closer inspection, he studied the frosting lace she'd spent hours getting just right, the arrangement of rose petals and violets she'd tried to make look like a waterfall trickling over the tiers. "Ah, I understand now. I see it."

"You...what?"

He glanced sidelong at her. "You're an artist."

It was a simple statement with profound effects, like her heart forgetting to beat, her throat seizing up. Maybe these were normal responses to someone telling her something she'd wanted to hear her whole life, but she needed some water.

"This isn't just a cake. This is art. Art that Ashley and Madigan will remember for the rest of their lives." When he ran a finger softly over a rose petal, through some mysterious quirk of physics, she felt it along the shell of her ear.

"Thank you," she said, barely more than a whisper.

"Are Linda and Ian coming tonight?" he asked, turning his attention back to her.

"No. Mom wanted to, but sometimes she gets overwhelmed when she's around too many people at once. I think it's too much stimulation. She wasn't feeling up to it tonight."

"Understandable."

"And Ian was more than happy to stay home with his Mimi so he could play *Minecraft* all night instead of pretending to have fun at a wedding."

Cole laughed. "That's understandable too."

"Did you finish writing your speech?"

"I did, late last night. What can I say?" There was a wry tilt to his lips, a twinkle in his eye Mira couldn't look away from, even if her life depended on it. "I was inspired."

Breaking the charged silence crackling between them, Chrissy's wind chime of a voice rang out, "Mira! Cole! Hieeeey!"

"How about that," Cole said, not looking at them because he was still smirking at her. "They're here."

Mira's palms itched.

"Are you ready?"

"I think so," she said. But when she turned to see Paul and Chrissy stroll toward them, she wasn't so sure. They looked too happy, too perfect—Paul in a dark gray suit, his yellow tie matching Chrissy's pretty yellow cocktail dress, their hands tightly intertwined like that's just where they lived, like they probably only ever let go of each other when one of them had to use the bathroom.

Without warning, a warm hand snaked around her waist, then Cole's words were in her ear. "Act like I just said something absolutely fucking filthy to you."

A shocked laugh burst out of her.

"That's better," he said, so close his exhale brushed over her neck. "You looked sad for a minute."

"Aww, look at you two," Chrissy crooned. "So cute. Aren't they cute, Pauly?"

"Adorable." Paul's tone was stiffer than the collar of his dress shirt. Then, noticing the cake behind her, he softened. "Wow, Mira. You've outdone yourself."

Cole squeezed her hip, and she couldn't decide which felt better, Paul's compliment or Cole's hand. Only one left an imprint on her, though—a patch of warmth that lasted long after he pulled away.

"Good to see you again." Cole reached out to shake Paul's hand. "And Chrissy." His smile was polite, not the one Mira was used to. There was no teasing twist to it, no humor in the way his lips pressed together. "You look lovely."

"Oh, this old thing?" Chrissy twirled her hips, her skirt flaring. "You've got yourself a real charmer there, Mira."

She could only agree.

Running a hand through his hair, Cole said, "I'd better go get the rest of the way into my tux and make sure Madigan's remembering to breathe."

"We'll catch up later," Paul said, and Mira turned instinctively toward the stern, almost demanding tone he had no right using.

"Looking forward to it," Cole replied, unfazed. But instead of walking away, he pulled Mira close again and said, "See you in a few." Then, like it was normal, like it was something they just *did*, he brushed his soft, full lips behind her ear, and she melted straight out of her dress, through the floor, past the earth's crust to take a lap around its molten iron core.

Fighting to keep her eyes from fluttering up behind her lids, she managed a wispy "Okay." But that was it, the best she could do while she watched Cole walk away from her and tried to keep her wobbly knees from buckling. Knowing without a doubt that her face was now as red as her dress, she avoided making a single second of eye contact with either Paul or Chrissy or anyone within a twenty-mile radius and said, "We should probably find our seats."

SNIFFLES and soft sobs surrounded her, the line of family standing up for Madigan and Ashley—Davis, Maude Alice, Madigan's brothers, and Cole—all wiping their red eyes or blinking hard to keep the tears at bay. Even Murphy looked wrecked, sitting between Davis and Maude Alice, his ears drooping, his huge head hanging between his shoulders.

They'd written their own vows, which was, Mira realized, a truly unfair thing to do to your wedding guests. Ashley's had been beautiful. But the second Madigan opened his mouth, the entire guest list took a collective, shuddering gasp. While Madigan spoke—the room growing so quiet a pin would have crashed like a cymbal—Mira's gaze drifted to Cole in time to watch him pull out his pocket square and dab at his eyes.

After showering Ashley with words that redefined sincerity, Madigan ended his vows with "So many things in my life have made me strive to be a better man, but none of them have affected me as deeply as you. There was a time I didn't think I'd live past thirty. Now I want to live as long as I can so I can grow old and gray, or grayer"—this got some watery laughs—"by your side. Being with you has taught me something I'd thought I'd already learned, but I really hadn't. You taught me that life is a gift. And one of the reasons life is a gift is because there's a chance for each of us, if we want it, if we're lucky, to find a love like this one. You're the gift, Ashley. You're the love I live for now. And I will spend the rest of my life trying to give that gift back to you." When he touched his forehead to hers and said, just loud enough for everyone to hear, "All the stars in the sky shine dim," Mira recognized the lyric from one of the Makers' songs, and her chin threatened a wobble.

While she wondered what it would feel like to have someone love her the way Madigan loved Ashley, the universe, with its impeccable cosmic timing, drew her attention to Paul sitting beside her, hugging Chrissy close. And then, when she looked away, it cleared a path to Cole across the room. His eyes were clear, calm, and locked on hers.

"That is *not* funny," she told the universe under her breath.

As good as he looked, as good as he felt, as good as he made her feel, it didn't matter. None of this was real. She was still Mira from Montana with a small, messy life and too many responsibilities. And he was still Cole from Seattle, a rich and famous dream three states away from ever coming true.

The wedding was beautiful, Ashley and Madigan were made for each other, Paul and Chrissy were probably soulmates, and no matter how close to him she'd felt last night, no matter how much fun they might have tonight, tomorrow Cole would leave, and Mira would be perfectly okay.

CHAPTER NINE

COLE

COLE WAS NOT OKAY. He was nowhere near okay. He might never be okay again.

Making his way through the crowd to find Mira, needing her close for reasons he didn't care to examine, Cole fought to pull himself together. He had a job to do at this wedding, and having an emotional meltdown over the fact that he—someone who, as a boy, married his Barbie doll to his G.I. Joe action figure, and then both of them to Snake Eyes in the most epic power throuple ever—was fifty-three, still single, and might remain that way forever, wasn't it.

"Are you all right?" Mira asked when he finally reached her after stopping once to hug Madigan's parents, then a second time to become the meat in a Madigan-brothers three-way hugwich.

"Not really," he answered honestly.

Her head tilted. "You have..."

Silently, he watched her reach out to wipe a stray tear from his cheek. It was such a sweet gesture, so kind. No judgment. No rolling her eyes or calling him overly emotional.

"Thank you." Glancing up ahead to where Madigan and Ashley stood at the end of the aisle, greeting their guests, he said, "I guess we'd better go congratulate them." He gave his head a shake. "If I don't fall apart again, it'll be a miracle."

When she took his hand, squeezed his fingers, and said, "I got you," he knew it wasn't true, just something people said, but that didn't mean he couldn't pretend, only for tonight, that it was.

Across the table, Chrissy poked at her chicken breast with her fork while Paul scowled at his salmon. "You live in Seattle, right, Cole?" Chrissy asked.

"He does," Mira said, clutching her water glass so tightly her knuckles turned white around it.

"How did you two meet? Mira never told us."

Since Chrissy's question was directed at him, Cole replied, "We had that big fundraiser here last winter. And—"

"What was that called?" Paul interrupted, condescension rippling off him in waves. "Grungeapalooza or something?"

Setting down her fork, Chrissy frowned. "Paul, don't be rude."

"It was Flannelfest, actually," Mira said. "Davis named it. I thought it was clever."

Paul at least had the decency to look cowed. "Oh, right."

"There I was," Cole continued, deciding in that moment to mount a can't-lose charm offensive against Paul's petulance, "up on stage, drumming away, when I spotted this woman dancing in the crowd. She had the brightest green eyes I'd ever seen. I was so distracted, I missed enough beats in the song to make Madigan throw his guitar pick at me."

Slowly, Mira set down her glass and turned to look at him.

"As soon as I got off stage," he said, his smile so genuine even he couldn't tell if it was part of the act anymore, "I followed her into the warming hut and bought her a cider. And the rest, as they say, is history."

"Ugh." Chrissy propped an elbow on the table, then plopped her cheek into her hand. "That is so romantic."

"It really was." Mira grinned back at him, until Paul asked, "Isn't it hard, dating long distance? Never seeing each other?" with a veritable mountain of jealous-ex energy.

It raised Cole's hackles. Paul didn't own Mira, nor was he owed any explanation about her love life. With a shameless smirk, he said, "It's amazing what you can accomplish over FaceTime."

Mira coughed on her water, and Cole took full advantage of the chance to touch her again, stroking her back with an unhurried hand, letting his finger skate beneath the bodice of her dress, right over that tattoo he was dying to see. When he pinched her zipper pull and gave it the tiniest tug, he was rewarded with a sharp gasp he'd remember for the rest of his life.

"*Can I have your attention!*" Conor boomed over the mic, making Cole jump straight out of his skin until Mira slid her hand into his.

"It's time, isn't it?" she asked.

"I'm afraid so," he said, easing his nerves by brushing his thumb over the velvety skin on the inside of her wrist.

"*I'd like to invite Madigan's best man and best friend, Cole Sanderson, up for a toast.*"

Before he stood from the table, Mira pulled him close, leaned in, and kissed his cheek. "For good luck."

He stared into her eyes, and from somewhere very, very far away, Conor said, "*We're not getting any younger, Cole.*"

"Shit." He patted his pockets down for his phone, panic rising when he came up empty.

"It's right here."

Taking the phone she'd picked up from the table, despite the nerves racing through him like a thoroughbred after the bell, he smiled. "You're a lifesaver." When she smiled back, he realized they were good at pretending to be a couple. Davis was right. In another world, another time, they would probably have made a great one.

He wasn't prone to stage fright, not like Madigan. But he did have an infamously hard time keeping his emotions in check. After making his way to the head table and accepting the microphone and a hug from Conor, Cole looked at Madigan and Ashley, looked away when his throat went tight, and finally found some strength in Mira's encouraging double thumbs-up across the room.

"Good evening, everyone," he told the crowd.

The crowd, in return, stared expectantly back at him.

"If you'd be so kind, please grab a glass of non-alcoholic champagne or sparkling water, because in a few short, hopefully successful, minutes, I'll ask you to join me in a toast."

While empty-handed guests made their way to the bar, Cole used the moment to gather himself. His attention drawn to the loud, heavy panting at his side, he looked down to find Murphy staring up at him in his little doggy bow tie. Scratching the emotional support dog behind his ears, Cole said, "Do me a favor and stay right there for the next five minutes, okay?"

Murphy, strangely enough, seemed to nod.

After everyone returned to their tables, Cole opened the notes app on his phone, pulled his readers from his coat pocket, and prayed he wouldn't fuck this up.

CHAPTER TEN

MIRA

Mira's grip tightened around the stem of her glass. If she'd thought tuxedo Cole had been sexy, he was nothing compared to tuxedo Cole in black-rimmed reading glasses. It was like a professional hit on her hibernating hormones.

"We always want our friends to be happy," he said, his voice steady and resonating through the microphone, pebbling her skin. "But more than that, we want our friends to thrive. I don't know what the secret recipe is for thriving, but I know it's not an easy thing to do. Life is hard, bad things happen, we're lonely a lot of the time. We all want someone in our lives who makes the hard things easier, the bad things less painful, the loneliness less pronounced. We want that person who becomes a light for us when the world goes dark. I know this because, at one point in my life, Matthew Madigan was that person for me."

"Jesus, Cole," Madigan blurted out, already wiping his eyes with the back of his hand.

When Cole looked at his friend, smiling apologetically, Mira's heart squeezed itself into a quivering lump of feels. She'd expected his speech to be eloquent, funny, charming as always, but nothing could have prepared her for his heart-wrenching honesty. Men, in her experience, didn't do that. They didn't broadcast their emotions over a microphone to a room filled with mostly strangers.

"Madigan," Cole went on broadcasting, "was the first person in my life to make me feel like I had something to offer the world. Neither of us had any idea how much we'd go through together before I was able to convince him that he did too. But when you go through hell with someone and emerge whole on the other side, it bonds you. Watching you fight and heal and help other people heal..." He paused, blinking hard, and Mira had never wanted to hug a grown adult so hard in her life. "You're the best man I know. You're so good, I honestly didn't think anyone would ever be good enough for you. Until I met Ashley."

Ashley's hand rose, but not fast enough to cover her gasp.

Glancing down at his phone, Cole slid his thumb along the screen like he was searching for his next line. But Mira wondered if he was only buying himself time, struggling to keep it together.

After a moment, he raised his eyes again and said, "I want to thank you, Ashley. Thank you for soothing the loneliness. Thank you for making the hard things easier. Thank you for making the bad things less painful. Thank you for being the light for Madigan when the world goes dark." Raising his glass to her, he said, "Thank you for helping my friend thrive."

Mira didn't cry very often. She definitely didn't cry at weddings. Except, she thought as her vision blurred and a lump formed in her throat, for this one.

"Please join me," Cole said thickly, "in raising a glass to Ashley and Madigan." Not only did glasses rise, but guests did too, everyone standing from their chairs and turning toward the bride and groom. "We wish you love, happiness, and long lives together so you can make the rest of us unbearably jealous for the rest of ours."

Cheers erupted, echoing through the dining hall as Ashley and Madigan stood, raised their glasses back toward Cole, and took sips of their drinks. It was Madigan's father who started the *ting* of his fork on his glass, but soon it was all Mira could hear as she joined in, clanging her spoon on her glass so hard she was worried it might shatter.

More than happy to appease the crowd, Madigan looped his arm around Ashley's waist and lifted her off her feet, kissing her deeply while her fingers burrowed into his hair. As if pulled by some irresistible force, Mira's attention moved from the happy couple, not to Chrissy, not to Paul, not even to Davis as she took the microphone and told everyone to "Make some noise!" for Madigan and Ashley's first dance. The only person she saw in a room full of people was Cole, walking toward her while he tucked his glasses back into his pocket.

The kiss on the cheek she'd given him might have been for show, but the way she wrapped her arms tightly around him now as he leaned into her, that was just for them.

"That was a beautiful speech," she told him.

"It wasn't too much?" he asked into her neck. "It felt like too much."

She shook her head, her cheek brushing over the stubble softly dusting his. "It was the perfect 'much.'"

She thought he might pull away, but instead, he kissed her neck again, and a deep shiver rushed through her.

"Mira," he whispered, his lips still hovering over her skin. "You're so sensitive here."

Her chest heaved, her breasts pushing into her dress, straining seams, testing the integrity of her zipper as she dug her fingertips into his shoulders. The moment between them was intimate, private in a way it probably shouldn't have been, and she felt too exposed, too hot, like they stood under a spotlight. She needed some air, some space. *Immediately.*

"I'm...going to step outside for a minute," she said, backing out of his arms.

"Want company?" He ducked his chin. "Or was that 'much' definitely too much?"

"It's fine." She waved at the air like she was shooing away a fly. "I'm fine. My dress is just...tight."

Cole's eyes flared, but his jaw clenched tight, like he was physically trying to keep words inside his mouth. Then, as they both noticed Paul staring at them, Cole flashed his phone at her and said, "I'll take some pictures while you"—his gaze flicked over her body like the tip of a tongue—"cool off. Dance with me later?"

Already feeling the heat of his hand on her back, the press of his hips as he swayed her side to side, she chirped, "Yep. You bet."

After watching him walk away, she threaded through the crowd, resisting the urge to fan her neck while she made a break for the deck. She pushed through the door, then crossed to the railing while the brisk evening air prickled her skin. Looking up to the dimming sky, still feeling Cole's lips on her skin, she thought, *Why am I like this?*

She wasn't an idiot. She knew she had something a lot of people probably only dreamed of—a no-strings, no-expectations, nothing-but-fun night with Cole Sanderson. So why wasn't she letting herself enjoy it? Why was she holding herself back? Because she was scared? Because she was worried about what people might think? Or about making Paul feel uncomfortable?

Staring up at some oblivious star twinkling above the mountain, she said, "Well, fuck that." And a split second before she took the first deep breath she'd taken all night, someone asked, "Fuck what?"

My life, that's what, she thought, closing her eyes.

Stepping up to stand beside her, Paul swept his bangs to the side, then slid his fingers over the railing. "Nice night," he said, looking out over the mountain.

It wasn't quiet on the deck, not with the music and the laughter spilling out through the windows, but it had at least felt calm. "Yep," she replied, already missing her calm.

"The cake turned out great."

"Thank you."

"Are you really serious about him?"

Wheeling around like he'd grabbed her shoulders and spun, she spluttered, "W-what?"

"Cole? Are you serious about him?"

It was like he'd hurled a flash-bang at her, leaving her dazed and blinking. "I...I don't know. Maybe. Why?"

"He's a drummer, Mira."

Drummers really did get a bad rap. "He's a good guy," she said, because he was. She might not actually know Cole very well, but she knew that much.

"I'm sure he's fantastic." Despite the sarcasm dripping acidly off each word, under the moonlight, his pale skin almost blue, Paul's expression was unreadable.

"Why are you suddenly acting like a jealous boyfriend?" Where was this concern when he'd left her with barely a backward glance? "Why do you care who I date?"

When he looked down at her and said, "I just want you to be happy, believe it or not," she almost laughed.

"Happy? You want *me* to be happy?"

"Yes," he ground out, his jaw clenched. "And a long-distance relationship seems like it would be difficult. Even with a 'good guy' like Cole."

Nothing about this interaction made sense. Paul caring about how difficult her relationships may or may not be while he was happily married and living the literal dream in Bozeman didn't make any fucking sense. "You know how busy I am," she said, giving him an explanation he didn't deserve.

"Yeah, I know. Believe me."

She rubbed at her arms, less from the chill in the air than from the ice in his tone. "Well, thank you for your concern, but I'm great. Everything is—"

"Great, yeah. So you keep saying."

Frustration boiling over into outright anger, she threw her hands up. "What the hell do you want from me, Paul? Did you think I'd stay single forever? Is that what you wanted while you got to move on with whoever you wanted to? That's completely unfair. You were the one who decided we were over, not me."

His unfairly smooth forehead pinched tight. "I... What?"

"What do you mean 'what'? You left. Things got hard, and you left. Mom moved in, and you took off."

He looked lost, like he'd never seen her before. "Mira, I didn't... I *never* wanted—" He cut himself off with a humorless laugh, scrubbing a hand over his face. "This was a mistake. Coming out here was a mistake."

She curled her hands into fists, hiding the way they trembled from him. She'd never asked for much from Paul, but she wanted something from him now. She wanted an apology, some recognition of the awful, heartless way he'd left her. But he'd never apologize, and she refused to let him ruin her night. He'd already ruined too many. "Look, I came here to have a nice time. So how about this? I won't worry about you, and you won't worry about me. Because we're over. You've moved on, and I'd really like to do the same."

"I see." His words were clipped, cold, final.

She rubbed her arms again. "I'm going to go back inside and have some fun. I think I deserve it."

The wind picked up, whistling through the pines alongside the lodge, but when she walked past him, she thought she heard him say, "You deserve everything."

Walking back into the dining hall, she shook out her arms, shaking off the confusion and frustration she refused to let swallow her up again. Spotting her across the room, Maude Alice waved her over, dancing with an older Black man Mira recognized from when he'd flipped burgers at Flannelfest. The man had been a resident of Little Timber at the time, and she remembered he had a phenomenal laugh and a habit of using it whenever Maude Alice said anything even remotely funny.

"Mira, this is Clayton Briggs," Maude Alice said with an incandescent glow. "Clay, this is Mira. She made the cake."

Stopping his swaying to "Let's Stay Together" long enough to shake Mira's hand, Clay said, "I bake too, but nothing like that. You're a very talented young woman."

"Thank you," Mira replied, letting herself keep the grin while Paul led Chrissy out onto the dance floor.

"How's Linda?" Maude Alice asked her over the music. "I was hoping she'd come. When we talked last week, she'd been considering it."

Maude Alice and her mom had been close friends for as long as Mira could remember. Now, her visits and their weekly cribbage games were one of the few things that gave Mira time to go grocery shopping while Ian was at school. It wasn't that her mom couldn't be left alone. It was just the way it felt like that might change at any moment. And what if, when it did change, Mira wasn't there? She knew she was being overprotective, but if she didn't protect her mom and her kid, who would? "She's doing great," she said. "But she didn't feel up to it. She's hanging with Ian tonight."

Before Maude Alice could reply, Madigan swooped in, taking her hand as Allison Krauss's angelic voice filled the room. While Madigan spun Maude Alice away from them, Mira turned back to Clay, accepted his outstretched hand, and placed hers on his shoulder. It was only then, dancing with Clay while they talked about the cake, that Mira saw Cole.

He wandered the periphery of the dance floor, snapping pictures of the guests with his phone, zooming in on Madigan and Maude Alice, Ashley and Conor, Davis dancing with the cute blond kid Mira thought was named Kev. It touched her, the way he'd pulled himself out of the party to capture these memories for Ashley and Madigan, and maybe capture some for himself. Because when his phone centered on her, he kept it aimed there long enough to take several pictures. And she realized that though things hadn't worked out between her and Paul, that was life. More often than not, things didn't work out. It didn't mean that *she* no longer worked.

When the song ended and Maude Alice returned to claim her dance partner, Mira stepped away, acutely aware of Cole coming for her. "I'd better go save the top tier of the cake," she told Clay and Maude Alice. "Don't want it to"—she stalled out when he stepped up beside her, his hand sliding across her low back to rest loosely on her hip—"melt."

"We couldn't have that," Maude Alice said with a wink. "Could we?"

Feeling like she'd just gotten caught with her hand in the cookie jar—something that happened far too often when a person grew up in a bakery—Mira said, "Ha ha, right," reached back to loop her arm through Cole's, and pulled him off the dance floor and toward the cake table.

"Have I told you how beautiful you look tonight?" Cole asked. "I'm sure I did. I must have, since it's all I can think about."

Could a person hurt themselves from holding back huge smiles all night? Like a mouth sprain?

"Is everything okay?" he asked, sobering. "I saw Paul go after you when you went outside, and you looked a little shaken when you came back in."

Stopping at the cake, Mira turned to face him. "He was being weird. But I'm fine." It surprised her, how true it was. "I just need to put the top of the cake in the walk-in for Ashley and Madigan."

"The walk-in?" he said, a brow rising with interest. "That sounds hard. Need some help?"

Yep, mouth sprains were definitely a thing. "I think I've got it."

Across the room, Paul spun Chrissy out, twirled her back in, dipped her into a kiss, and Mira watched them, waiting for the ache to hit her, waiting to feel...something. But there was nothing, not until she looked at Cole again. He'd been watching them too, but the way his eyes met hers now? *That* made her feel something, a tightness at the back of her neck, a current flowing under her skin, flames licking at her throat.

He nodded once, as if coming to some sort of agreement with himself, then said, "I have an idea." While she held the top of the cake in one hand, he took her other hand in his and met her stare. "Whether you need my help or not, I am following you into that freezer."

CHAPTER ELEVEN

COLE

It only took a single sideways glance to make sure Paul noticed him following after Mira like a love-sick puppy into the kitchen. Maybe it was a dick move, but with how much it hurt *him* that Mira had no choice tonight but to watch her ex and his wife dancing together, he couldn't imagine what it felt like for her. So *fine*, he'd be a dick. Wouldn't be the first time. Wouldn't be the last.

Stepping into the freezer behind her, he closed the door and turned around in time to watch her reach up, stretching her body out long to set the cake carefully on one of the upper racks. When she pivoted to face him, her eyes wide, she asked, "So, what was your idea?" her breath making a cloud in the frigid air.

"Sometimes"—he took a step toward her, but only one, because when he did, her fingers curled nervously at her sides—"couples at weddings can get...inspired."

"Inspired?" Her throat bobbed.

He nodded. "To do things."

"What kind of things?"

Sliding his hands into his pockets, he said, "Sneak around. Disappear into dark corners or closets—"

"Or walk-in freezers?"

His lips twitched. "Or walk-in freezers."

She took a step toward him, but only one. Maybe he looked nervous too. "Is that what we're doing? Sneaking around?"

"People watched us come in here," he said. "They'll watch us come back out. They'll see us. They'll see *you*."

Her head tilted. "Paul will see me, you mean."

"I don't want to assume that you want to make him jealous."

Like a flame guttering, her gaze fell. "I don't know what I want anymore."

"But I," he said, closing the distance between them, drawing her eyes back up to his, "for some reason, do."

"You want to make Paul—"

"So jealous he can't see straight."

A tiny blue vein pulsed in the soft hollow above her collarbone. "Do you have a plan to make him jealous?"

God, he loved that question. He loved it even more that she'd asked it. Because he did have a plan. Was it risky? Was it dangerous to say what he was about to say in this tight space with her, standing so close now their breath clouds mingled? Maybe. Did he care? Nope. "I think you should take off my coat."

Her eyes flared. "You do?"

Taking his hands from his pockets, he held his arms out at his sides. "Yes."

"Okay," she said softly. Sliding her fingers up his lapels, silence enveloping them aside from the repetitive thumping of the bass beating in time with his heart, she slid his coat off over his shoulders and draped it over the shelf behind her.

"Now you should untie my bow tie," he told her next, his eye contact unwavering as her steady fingers tugged the ends of his tie until they came loose, hanging limply over his chest.

"What if I undid this?" she asked, toying with his top button, circling the smooth plastic with her fingertip. "Or would that be too much?"

His cock twitched at the low rasp of her voice. "I don't think it's too much."

After slipping the button free, spreading his collar open, she continued to hold the reins, steering them deeper into the farce that, at the moment, didn't feel like a farce at all. "What if I ran my fingers through your hair? Messed it up a little?"

Cole was pretty sure they were still in the walk-in, but he wasn't cold anymore. "I love that idea."

While her fingers slid into his hair, he moved even closer to her, the rise of her breasts meeting the plane of his chest. "What if I kissed you here?" he asked, lowering his lips to the junction of her neck and shoulder. "A small, soft kiss?"

Her fingers in his hair curled in response, guiding his mouth to her neck. "Seems"—she shivered when his lips met her skin—"realistic."

She didn't ask about rucking his shirt up in the back and slipping a hand underneath, her cold fingers dancing along his side. He didn't ask whether it was okay to suck her earlobe into his mouth.

"Holy shit," she gasped, her nails biting into his hip while he grazed his teeth along the slope of her neck.

Pulling away, he met her dazed, hungry stare. He couldn't see her like that for another second if he still hoped to keep this encounter relatively PG. So he spun her around, watching her brace herself with her hands on the rack. "I think I'd ask to see it."

"See what?" she squeaked.

Humming a laugh, he slid his lips along her shoulder, his fingers reaching for her zipper. "Your tattoo. I should probably know what it is. For full believability." He kissed the spot behind her ear, wrapping an arm around her waist when she swayed to the side. "I should know how far down it goes." He didn't press his erection into her ass, but *fuck* he wanted to. "Don't you think?"

"It m-makes sense," she stammered, one hand releasing the rack so she could hold her bodice in place.

Pinching her zipper pull between his thumb and finger just like he'd done at their table, loving moments like these—when through whatever trick of fate or destiny or luck, fantasies became realities— he lowered her zipper one tooth at a time. Slowly, drawing the experi- ence out for as long as possible, he exposed the canvas of her back, fine black lines swirling across her spine, musical notes dotting her skin.

He traced the ink decorating her body, sliding his fingertip between her shoulder blades to the swoop of her low back, the design disappearing into her underwear until he hooked his finger under black lace and pulled just enough to see it all, and maybe a little more. "It's a song."

"The first one Ian ever wrote," she said, her head falling forward, her forehead resting against the rack.

Releasing her underwear, he traced his fingertip back up her spine, following the notes while her shoulders tensed, her back arching under his light touch. Studying the tattoo from top to bottom, he hummed the melody the notes played out on her skin.

"You can hear the song? Only from looking at it?"

"I can," he replied. "It's beautiful."

"Cole," she whispered as he ghosted his lips over her neck, zipping her back up as slowly as he'd unzipped her, hating her zipper for every inch of her skin it hid from him. Just to spite it, he didn't pull it all the way up, not yet. When he was done, she spun around to face him, her hands fisting in his shirt.

Feeling the heat radiating from her skin, the need in the way she grabbed him, he said, "Kiss me, Mira. Right here," pointing to the corner of his mouth. Because if she kissed his lips, if he tasted her mouth, if he felt the softness of her tongue against his, they wouldn't leave this freezer all night, maybe not even the next day. And as real as this moment with her felt right now, as fast as his heart was beat- ing, as hard as his blood thundered through his veins, his need so hot and demanding it made him leak, this wasn't about him. This wasn't *for* him. This was for her. This was to wipe away that torn, confused look in her eyes when Paul had kissed Chrissy on the dance floor.

Mira would leave this freezer looking well served, even if it ruined him for the rest of the night.

Her tongue slipping out to wet her red lips, she leaned toward him, cupped his neck, and kissed him. At first, she only kissed the corner of his mouth like he'd asked. But he must have turned his head, or maybe she turned hers. Either way, as their lips slid dangerously close to perfect alignment, his hands dangerously close to grabbing her hips and pulling her body against his, her zipper dangerously close to being slid back down, he knew he had to stop, for his own sake if for no one else's.

He pulled away, a herculean feat, because not kissing her was like choosing not to sail on a perfect blue-sky day, and he almost laughed at how awful it felt.

While she looked him up and down, her full red lips curled into a smile. "You're kind of a mess."

He reached down for his suit coat, slinging it over his arm. "All a part of my grand plan." Messing up his hair again, he took a fortifying breath and said, "I'll leave first, give you some time to...get yourself together." His gaze dropped to her breasts, which looked one heave away from freeing themselves from her dress, and more than a small part of him wished he was still young and reckless and willing to take everything too far. "If you know what I mean."

She looked like she wanted to say something, her mouth opening for a brief moment before closing again. Instead, she reached out and pulled on one side of his tie, leaving the ends slightly uneven. "Thank you, Cole. Thank you for tonight. For everything."

"My pleasure." *Understatement.* "But you still owe me a dance."

When she nodded, he turned away from her and opened the freezer door, squinting against the bright kitchen lights. He waited until he was back in the dining hall, until he found Paul sitting at their table again, until he had the man's undivided attention, before he ran a hand through his hair, tucked his shirt back into his pants, and brushed his thumb over his lips, looking down at the hint of her red lipstick he'd swiped away. *Nice.*

He'd barely sat down at their table again when Mira emerged from the kitchen, looking far more put together than he had, except for that one secret part of her he'd kept undone. When she took her seat next to him, her cheeks indecently flushed, Cole reached behind her, said, "Oops. Must have missed this," and tugged her zipper the rest of the way up while Paul crumpled his cocktail napkin into a tiny ball and dropped it onto his plate.

"I'LL BE RIGHT BACK!" Cole shouted over the music, angling his head toward the bathrooms. After dancing with Mira for the last two hours, his feet aching in the best way even though he was pretty sure he had a blister on both big toes, he needed a minute.

"'Kay!" she shouted back. Some of her hair had come loose from its updo, wispy strands brushing over her shoulders and sticking to her neck. "I'm gonna go get us some water."

"Yes, please." When she turned toward the bar, Cole took a moment to watch her go, missing her already. On his way to the bathroom, he stopped mid stride as Madigan and Ashley tumbled out of her office, laughing like children who'd just gotten away with something very, very naughty. If Cole had thought he'd left Mira looking disheveled in the walk-in, he was getting schooled, hard. Ashley was barely in her dress, and Madigan's shirt fell open while he hopped on one foot, trying to put on one of his shoes, the other shoe nowhere in sight.

Their laughter petered out once they noticed him noticing them, and Ashley blanched as Madigan snapped, "Not a word, Cole."

Cole raised his hands. "Hey, I'm just glad the drought is over."

"Where's your other shoe?" Ashley asked, squinting down at Madigan's socked foot.

"I must have left it in there."

Grabbing his shirt and pushing him back toward her office door, she said, "I guess we need to go find it."

With a body-wide smile, Cole pushed the bathroom door open. But when his phone buzzed, his smile faded.

> Nancy: How's the wedding? I still can't believe Madigan is getting married. Are you coming into the studio next week?

Sliding his phone back into his pocket without answering the text, he stared at himself in the mirror. Even though their relationship was amicable these days, he didn't want to see Nancy next week. He didn't even want to go into the studio. He didn't want to keep doing all the things he'd been doing in his life that kept him busy but weren't making him happy. For the first time in his life, he didn't want to go back to Seattle.

CHAPTER TWELVE

MIRA

"I'M SO GLAD YOU CAME," Ashley told her, hugging her tightly. "Let's go get coffee sometime, okay?"

"I'd like that," Mira answered honestly.

"Thank you for the cake, and the tarts," Madigan said, tucking her into his side. It felt like being tucked into the side of a house. "I'm not sure I've ever seen Cole smile so much in one night," he said into her ear, his beard tickling her cheek. He smelled absolutely amazing. "So thanks for that too."

Blushing for the fiftieth time in the last six hours, Mira said, "Make sure to wrap the top tier tightly tonight before you go to bed. It should be good and frozen by then."

"What do we do with it?" Madigan asked, turning to Ashley. "Should we eat it before our trip?"

After they'd cut the cake, Madigan had surprised Ashley with a three-week honeymoon in Iceland, revealing the details with tears in his eyes and buttercream frosting in his beard.

Wrapping her arm around his waist, Ashley said, "We eat it on our first anniversary."

"That's not the only thing I'll be eating," Madigan purred.

Cole made a throaty noise, rolling his eyes while he took Mira's hand and led her to the stairs. "I think I should walk you to your car before shit gets out of hand in here."

It was after midnight, and the night air was brisk, bordering on cold. As soon as they stepped outside, Cole wrapped his suit coat around Mira's shoulders, his lingering heat and sunshine scent surrounding her as she slid her arms into his sleeves.

"Which one is yours?"

She pointed at her Honda.

"*Psh*. And you said my car wasn't hot."

She gasped. "I'll have you know that the Honda Element is a rugged, flexible, dependable sex-bomb. It's also super easy to clean."

"Is that what you want?" he asked, stepping toward her, inches away from crowding her up against her car door. "Rugged, flexible, dependable?"

"Don't forget easy to clean."

His warm chuckle ghosted over her cold cheeks. "Did you have fun tonight?"

"I had a lot of fun tonight. Maybe too much." The admission, especially with his lips so close to hers, felt dangerous, like walking into a cage with a lion and shouting, "Here I am! Kiss me!" She might have been mixing her metaphors.

"It's too bad..." He cut himself off, the unfinished thought hanging in the air while his eyes searched hers. She searched his too, both of them looking for something from the other. Permission? A reason to keep touching? A reason to stop? An answer to the unspoken question of *what now?*

"It is too bad," she said, whispering it, breathing it into the space between them, because even though neither of them said it, they both knew. *It's too bad you're not here. It's too bad this isn't real. It's too bad we don't have more time. It's too bad this is the end of something instead of the beginning.*

A corner of his mouth hitched, and he leaned toward her, placing a hand on her car, right next to her head. "I had maybe too much fun tonight too."

His body moved into her space, a magnetic pull realigning her molecules, spinning them one by one until they pointed directly at him. When his hips met hers, she wrapped her fingers around his arms, his muscles tensing as his tongue slid along his lower lip. Her brain screamed *Kiss me, kiss me, kiss me!* And like he'd heard it, the desperate screaming in her brain, he angled his head, slid a hand behind her back, tugged her close, and brought his lips to hers at the exact moment something cold and wet nudged her elbow.

"What the hell?!" she cried, while Cole leapt back like he'd been electrocuted.

A giant, furry, panting head answered, Murphy's cold nose nudging her elbow again, pushing her hand away from Cole's body, insisting she use it to pet him instead.

"Cockblocking me, Murph?" Cole looked down his nose at the Saint Bernard. "Not cool, buddy."

The dog barked, voices carried on the breeze as Bud and Brad came hand in hand down the stairs, and Mira sighed so deeply a dictionary might have insisted it was a moan. They'd almost had a moment. He'd almost kissed her. And now, unless she wanted Bud and Brad telling everyone in town she slipped the Makers' drummer some tongue at Madigan and Ashley's wedding, she needed to go. She needed to check in on Ian and her mom. She had to wake up early to start baking. She had to get back to her normal, not gazing into his gorgeous brown eyes, not getting freaky in a walk-in freezer, not almost making out against her car door like a couple of teenagers, life. And maybe Murphy's cockblocking was a blessing, because it would be a hell of a lot easier to do all of that if she didn't kiss Cole Sanderson. "I'd better get going."

Taking another step away from her, he nodded. His smile was tight, and for the rest of her life, she'd remember it as disappointed too. While his gaze swept down her body, he snapped his fingers and said, "Come on, Murph. We've got to let her go."

Her heart pumped an extra beat as Murphy dropped his head and ambled to Cole's side. Not knowing what else to say—barely trusting herself not to blurt out, "fuck it," and give Bud and Brad free tickets to an X-rated show—she turned around, opened her door, and climbed into the driver's seat. Closing the door between them, she watched him watching her, his hand resting on Murphy's head, his mouth set in a tight, resigned line.

When she'd been younger, she might have done it, rolled down her window and called him over. She might have risked her entire heart for a single kiss. But her heart was already stretched too thin, spread out in twenty different directions, none of them leading to Seattle. It had been a night she'd never forget, a bright spot, one of those memories that would always keep her warm, and that would have to be enough.

Keeping her window rolled up, she waved goodbye. When Cole waved back, his head turning slowly from side to side, an amused grin crept across his face.

She was halfway down the mountain before she finally understood why. She was still wearing his coat.

"Hey," Mira said, wrapping her arms around her waist, hugging herself in Cole's coat.

"Hey," Ian replied, still awake and playing video games.

She sat down next to him on the couch. "How was Mimi?"

"Good. She went to bed early."

"She had to have been exhausted from staying up so late the last couple of nights. I hate it when she doesn't sleep."

Ian nodded, pushing buttons frantically while his game's lights flashed across his face. "Whose coat is that?" he asked, taking a split-second break from the action to notice her outfit.

"Oh, this?" She curled her fingers around the cuffs. "It's...his."

"His?"

"Um, Cole's."

A suspicious brow quirked. "Cole Sanderson's?"

"Yeah. I'll have to mail it back to him." *Or keep it forever until they bury me in it.*

He dropped his controller into his lap. "Cole Sanderson let you have his coat?"

Lifting the lapel to her nose, she inhaled the sun and the sea. "It was cold out. And then I think we both forgot I was wearing it."

Ian's eyes rolled. "Wow. How are you so old and you don't know the 'leaving an item of clothing behind' move?"

"Hey, I'm not that old," she said, bumping her shoulder into his. "How are you so young and know any moves at all?"

"I guess I'm not that young." He almost smiled, very nearly, a smile's second cousin, twice removed. "He'll be back for that coat. Maybe not tomorrow, but someday. Dude's got game."

"No, it's not like that. Here, I'll prove it." When she pulled her phone out of Cole's coat pocket to text him, Ian snorted.

> Mira: I'm still wearing your coat. Sorry! I'll mail it to you if you give me your address.

The three dots bursting immediately onto the screen made her lungs forget their purpose in life.

> Cole: Yeah, I know. It was a move, Mira. See you in the morning.

Clutching her phone to her chest, she admitted, "Okay, fine. He definitely has game."

"You're going to, like, sleep in it, aren't you?"

She didn't dignify that with an answer, even though it was *definitely*. After kissing Ian's curls, she got to her feet. "Don't stay up too late. Sleep is important to the—"

"Growing teenage brain," he droned.

"You okay?" she asked him again, because she always asked him, because he didn't tell her anything anymore, because he was alone on a Saturday night playing video games in the dark.

"I'm fine."

There were these situations as a parent that weren't written about in a handbook. There wasn't some website she could click on to help her decipher what a fourteen-year-old kid's "I'm fine" meant. It was possible he was fine. It was also possible he was drowning in stress and expectations. It was possible that his quiet, stoic nature was actually depression. Lots of things were possible, but all she knew for certain was what he told her. Which wasn't much.

"Okay," she said, wondering if she was fucking him up by not trying harder to break through his silence, at the same time wondering if she was overreacting to it. "Love you, buddy."

"Love you too, Mom."

Walking into her room and shutting the door, she slipped Cole's coat off her shoulders and hung it on the hook on the bathroom door. After stepping out of her dress and kicking off her shoes, she turned the hot water on in her shower and let it run. In only her bra and underwear, she took her wish jar off her dresser, climbed into her window, and wrote one word on a scrap of paper. One wish. *Cole.*

After opening the window, she struck a match and held the paper above the jar, watching the flame curl the corner of his name, watching *Cole* become *ole* and then only *e* until the flames nearly burned her fingertips. And then she let it go, letting him fall into the ashes of all the other wishes she'd made but knew she'd never get.

CHAPTER THIRTEEN

COLE

It must have been the sunrise flaring pink and orange across the mountains, or the crisp morning chill making steam rise from his mug, or the way his fingertips still felt the softness of Mira's skin along her spine, but Cole had never had such a perfect cup of coffee in his entire life.

"You and Mira seemed to have a good time last night," Madigan said, sipping his coffee with one hand and petting Murphy with the other.

"When did you become a mind reader?" Cole asked, smiling into his mug. "I was just thinking about the good time I had with Mira last night."

Madigan chuckled, crossing his slippered feet while they rocked in the big Adirondack chairs on the deck.

"I'm actually surprised to see you up so early," Cole said. "I thought you and Ashley might have worn each other out once you finally got some alone time."

"Do you see Ashley out here?" Madigan asked, looking smug in profile. Cole held out his mug, and Mad clinked it with his, then said,

"But I couldn't let you leave without saying goodbye." He turned his gaze away from the view, the sunrise sparkling in his eyes. "Are you sure I can't convince you to stay a few more days?"

"I'd love to stay." *More than you know.* "But I need to get back to Becks and Ruby. And I've got a few recording gigs next week."

"I have to admit, I'm kind of jealous."

"Of me?" Cole laughed at that. "You just married your soulmate and you're getting ready to spend three weeks in Iceland to celebrate it, and you're jealous of me? Ha. Ha ha ha."

"It's true. I miss making music."

"Yeah, well. This 'music' is for a toothpaste commercial. And Nancy already told me she'd be at the studio next week so..."

"Hmm." Madigan fixed Cole with a stare that was far too thoughtful for this early in the morning. "Hard to get away from her in Seattle, isn't it?"

The wind whistled through the trees, over his skin. Cole tried not to shiver. "What are you getting at, Mad?"

He shrugged. "Nothing. Just an observation."

"An observation? Care to elaborate?"

"I think, sometimes," Madigan said, looking out at the mountain again, "it can be hard to move forward into your future while you're surrounded by your past."

Cole checked his phone for the time, opting for snagging another few minutes with Mira in lieu of spending them at Madigan's Hard Truths Coffee Hour. "I should probably hit the road."

"I'll try to get Ashley up, but Davis will literally kill me if you don't say goodbye to her before you leave."

"Maude Alice up already?" Cole asked, knowing he'd need to say goodbye to her too.

"I'm not sure that woman ever sleeps. She's in the kitchen, probably starting on breakfast despite Ashley asking her not to until she was awake to help."

"It's a pretty great world you've found for yourself here," Cole said, meaning it in a way that made him wonder if he *was* stuck in his past, either lacking the momentum or just too damn scared to ever make a break the way Madigan had.

Pushing out of his chair, Madigan held a hand out for Cole and pulled him up. "Thanks for coming, Cole. Thanks for being my best man, and my best friend." With their hands still clasped, with the sunrise bronzing his beard, he added, "And there's always a room for you here in this world too."

Coffee sloshed over Cole's mug as he wrapped his arm around Madigan's back and leaned in. "Have fun in Iceland," he said. "Send me pictures."

"Deal," Madigan said, squeezing him tightly.

"Oh, Cole." Ashley rubbed her eyes as she walked out onto the deck, a red plaid blanket wrapped around her shoulders. "Are you leaving already?"

"It's a long drive, and my night vision sucks these days."

"Seriously," she said. "Mine too."

"Same here," Madigan concurred. "Like driving with Vaseline on my windshield."

Accepting a hug from Ashley, warmed briefly by the blanket she'd wrapped around his shoulders, Cole said, "Have an amazing honeymoon, and take care of him for me," into her ear.

"Always," she replied. "But before you go, you'd better go see—"

"Davis," he said, a hand raised. "I'm on my way."

AFTER STOPPING by the kitchen to say goodbye to Maude Alice, Cole made his way down the hall to Davis's room. When he rapped his knuckles on her door, it started to swing open. "Davis?" he said, holding the knob with one hand to keep the door closed while he knocked again with the other. "You up? It's Cole."

"Are you leaving?" she asked. There was gravel in her voice, like she hadn't slept at all. "You can come in."

When he pushed the door open, he found her sitting on the edge of her bed, staring out through her window. Her room was so clean it bordered on unlived-in, her pale-yellow walls bare except for a mirror above her dresser, a blue ribbon with a mountain bike on it, and a single picture where she stood in front of Old Faithful, smiling with an older man who must have been her late grandfather. If she had lived fully in this room once, sprawling out to claim every corner the way teenagers did, she certainly didn't now. This was the room of someone who wasn't sure they were staying.

She'd seemed so much happier last night, snapping pictures, laughing, dancing with everyone and anyone, even dancing with Kev for a song. Cole had hoped it meant they'd turned a corner, but maybe there was only so much one dance could do.

"You okay?" he asked, stepping into the hollowed-out room to sit next to her on the bed.

"Oh, yeah." The smile she gave him was as forced as his sophomore yearbook picture. "I'm good. Probably just stayed up too late."

"I haven't stayed up that late since 1996."

She laughed, then turned to him, her expression brightening. "Hey, what if I came out to Seattle sometime? You could show me around, introduce me to Becks?"

"I would love that," he told her. "Anytime."

"Maybe I could even convince Mira to come with me."

At the wink in her tone, he nudged her shoulder with his. "I wouldn't complain about it."

"You two were cute together. You seemed so"—the light dimmed through her curtains—"happy."

The opening was there. He could ask her about Kev now, let her know he was here for her, just to listen if nothing else. And he would have, but she turned away, tucking her hair behind her ear and clearing her throat before he had the chance. "It's supposed to rain today," she said. "Drive safely."

"Always do. That's why I have a Volvo, even if *some* people think they're not sexy," he mumbled, mostly to himself.

She patted his hand, consoling. "Not just some people, Cole. All people. All people think Volvos aren't sexy."

He laughed at that. "Keep in touch, Davis. You have my number. I'm always around." Making sure to catch her stare, he said, "Always. For anything, okay?"

Unsurprisingly, she ducked right, then hooked left with "Are you going to see Mira on your way out of town?"

"Have to." He rose to his feet, tugged the hem of his lucky hoodie down, and winked. "She wore my coat home last night."

Davis made a *puh* sound. "That move's as old as you are."

"*Classic*, Davis. The word you're looking for to describe me, and my moves, is *classic*."

Pushing up from the bed, she gave him a quick hug and said, "I stand corrected."

BLARING Amyl and the Sniffers on his way down the mountain, Cole turned on the heat as the sky above him darkened, heavy clouds rolling in over the treetops. Pausing the music to ask his Bluetooth to call Mira, he waited, drumming his fingers on the steering wheel, pinning his lower lip between his teeth while the phone rang through his speakers.

"Cole?" She sounded sleepy, like maybe she was still in bed, the mental image increasing the tally of how many times she'd made him veer off the road by one.

"Morning. Did I wake you?"

She made a little moan while sheets rustled across the line. *Make that two.* "I'm up, just lying here pretending I'm not. Are you leaving?"

"Not without my coat."

"Riiight," she said slowly. "About your coat. It...might need to be ironed."

"Why's that?"

"I may have...slept in it."

His tires chewed up shoulder gravel.

"Was that your car? Are you okay?"

"A squirrel," he choked out, the thought of Mira in his coat and nothing else making every drop of blood in his body shoot south. "Just barely missed him."

"Lucky squirrel."

Thunder rolled in the distance. "Are you wearing it right now?"

"Yes."

"Holy hell," he wheezed.

"I'm sorry, but it's"—she paused, and he imagined her arms stretching over her head, his coat riding up the length of her thighs—"comfy."

He liked that, that something of his made her comfortable. He liked it so much he almost offered to let her keep the coat. But he was a selfish man, and he needed a reason to see her one last time before he left. "Keep it warm for me. I'll be there soon."

Putting his car in park in front of Glazed and Confused, he peered through her window. The lights in the bakery were dim, a CLOSED BUT STILL DELICIOUS sign hanging on the door. Tilting his rearview until his reflection shone back at him, he ran his fingers through his hair, making it look just the way he liked it—a touch chaotic but still on the safe side of bedhead. The perfect amount of stubble shadowed his chin, enough to look rugged, but not so much he looked sloppy. Repositioning the mirror, he killed the ignition and stepped out of his car, squinting up at the moody morning sky that already smelled like rain.

He knocked three times on her door, then, after a moment, knocked twice more. He was about to pull his phone out and text her when the sound of footsteps running down the stairs stilled his hand, whipping his head up. Maude Alice had been right. He was a dog, and Mira was definitely his treat.

She'd swept her hair up into an untidy bun, and the shade of pink flushing her cheeks was one he wasn't sure he'd ever seen before, like rose but brighter, a new color. *Mira Pink.* She was barefoot in black leggings and a loose gray sweatshirt that hit mid-thigh, the collar cut off, the frayed fabric slipping off her bare shoulder. It was the kind of outfit meant for curling up on the couch with a mug of hot tea and a movie. It was the kind of outfit meant for cuddling.

"Hi," she said, a little breathless when she opened the door. "Oh, wow." She looked up at the sky. "It's going to rain, isn't it?"

"Cats and dogs."

Stepping away from the door, she motioned him inside. "Come in, come in. I'll, um, get your coat."

While she disappeared behind the counter, he inhaled the sweet bakery scent of cookies and frosting and freshly baked bread. "Good lord, it smells amazing in here. How do you do anything but eat all day long?"

"I definitely have my moments," she called back to him. "I used to be skinny before I took over running the bakery."

"Thank fuck you did," Cole said under his breath.

She emerged from the kitchen bearing his coat in one hand, a Glazed and Confused box in the other, and a smile that made him stagger back a step. "I made you some to-go treats. For your drive."

"You did?"

She nodded, her bun bobbing up and down.

When he raised the lid, revealing two black and white cookies, a Boston cream pie, and one of those tarts she'd made them for breakfast yesterday, he tried to think of something to say, but he had a hard time finding his words. She'd put this box together for him. She'd *thought* about him. It meant more to him than it probably should have, than any sane man with a single shred of self-preservation left would let it. But he'd spent most of his romantic life being the giver of gifts, almost never the receiver. "This is amazing, Mira. Thank you."

While the clock on her wall ticked behind them in the ensuing silence, she said, "I can't believe we only met two days ago. It feels so much...longer."

It did feel longer, like time had slowed, paused, stretching itself out just for them. The way her fists had yanked him close the first time he'd walked through her door, her eyes did the same now, beckoning him behind the counter so he could take her face between his hands and kiss her while the loose strands of her hair brushed over his fingers. Back then, the electric spark of her lips against his had felt like the start of something. As badly as he wanted to, he knew if he kissed her now, it would feel too much like the end.

Maybe she felt it too, because when she blinked, folded his coat on the counter, and said, "Thank you for letting me wear this last night," the momentum shifted, and the tension between them swept out like the tide.

Taking his coat and looping it over his arm, he wondered if it would smell like her now, like citrus and sugar. If it did, he'd never wash it again. "It was my pleasure."

She stared down at her hands, twin divots sinking between her brows. She was about to tell him something, and even though he didn't know what it was, somehow he knew it would hurt to hear it. "Cole, I—"

"You know the feeling when something entirely unexpected happens to you?" he said, stopping her before she could leave a bruise. "Some monumental twist of fate uncoils at your feet, and you have no doubt that in twenty years it'll be one of your favorite stories to tell your grandkids?" Not expecting an answer—because the question he'd interrupted her with was rhetorical—he said, "I can't wait to tell my granddaughter this one."

Her eyes misted over, shining like emerald glass. Covering her face with her hands, laughing sadly, she said, "Fucking drummers."

He laughed too, then reached out, pulling her hands down one at a time to tell her, "Goodbye, Mira Harlow."

Sliding her fingers out of his, she said, "So long, Cole Sanderson."

With regret already filling his shoes with cement, he took his box of treats, his favorite coat, and inhaled Mira's air into his lungs one last time before he made his way to the door.

CHAPTER FOURTEEN

MIRA

SHE WALKED INTO THE KITCHEN, then out into the bakery, then back into the kitchen again. Pacing, she was pacing, clenching and unclenching her fists, her heart thundering louder than the actual thunder outside while raindrops started to slash against her windows. Why had she just let him go like that? Why did it all feel so wrong? When the low rumble of his Volvo driving away from her vibrated through her bones, panic made her knees weak. She'd messed up. She'd missed her chance. She'd hesitated and chickened out, and she'd never forgive herself for it.

But maybe... "Fuck it all!"

Shoving her feet into the nearest pair of shoes—which happened to be Ian's ratty black Vans at the bottom of the stairs that were a size too big—she raced to the door, wrenching it open so hard her grandfather's bell flew off its hinges and bounced off the ceiling, hitting the floor with a sharp *clang*.

Sprinting full tilt out into the rain, she shouted, "Wait! Cole, wait!" Her heart hurled itself against her ribs while she waved frantically at the back of his car. But he didn't slow. He didn't see her.

The sky opened up, rain plastering her hair to her face, sluicing down her arms as she dropped them to her sides, as she realized with a sharp twist in her belly that he was about to turn, that she was too late. Why hadn't she kissed him when she'd had the chance? Why hadn't she taken the risk when it was so obvious to her now that she'd regret not kissing Cole Sanderson for the rest of her natural born—

Brake lights flared as his car swerved to a stop. His door flew open wide, he stepped out onto the street, his hot gaze seared her cold, wet skin, and she broke into a run.

Shallow puddles erupted under his feet as he raced toward her, his lucky hoodie drenched and clinging to his shoulders. When they collided, his body was hard against hers, but his hands were impossibly soft as they slid over her cheeks. Under the downpour, his eyes searched her face while raindrops glistened like jewels between his lashes. Then his lips crashed into hers, and just like that, like the lightning lighting up the sky, like his name turning to ash between her fingertips, she burst into flames.

Raw, needy sounds tore from her throat as she slid her fingers under the back of his hoodie, desperate for the heat of his skin. His hand fisted gently in her hair, his arm looping around her back, hoisting her up until she hooked her ankles behind his hips—one of Ian's too-big shoes slipping off her foot to land on the street. She opened her mouth for him and moaned, almost in pain at the soft brush of his tongue over hers. As rain slipped between their lips, between their fingers and tongues, between her toes, Mira—who had never been so starved for another person—finally felt fed.

Lowering her carefully back to the ground when lightning flashed above them again, he said, "Jesus, Mira. We should have done that a long time ago."

As thunder rolled in the distance, she tilted her face up to his. "I'm proud of us for doing it at all."

A snowflake floated down, landing on his nose, followed by a few more in his hair, and then dozens, hundreds, fat spring flakes turning Main Street into a snow globe.

"Is it seriously snowing?" he asked, staring up at the sky, baffled as snowflakes turned his shoulders white. "Wasn't there lightning a second ago?"

Trying to blink through the flakes on her lashes, she explained, "Thundersnow."

"Huh. I thought that was a myth."

She grinned. "Just May in Montana."

"You're shivering." He wrapped his arms around her, tucking her head under his chin, brushing snow from her back and her ass, his hand lingering. "You should go back inside."

She let herself take a deep, slow breath in his arms. "And you should get on the road before this turns into an ice storm."

Even standing there freezing in the snow, it took several seconds before he leaned back, his hands still warm on her body, and kissed her one last time, as tenderly as she'd ever been kissed. Then he backed away, his eyes never leaving hers until he stepped on Ian's shoe. Bending down, he picked it up, brushed the snow away, then lowered onto a knee. "Nice Vans," he said, sliding the shoe back onto her foot.

"They're Ian's. I couldn't find any of mine, so it was either these or run out here after you barefoot."

Rising to his feet, he reached through the snow to cup her cheek, pained lines etched between his brows, around his mouth. "Damn, Mira. I wish..."

"I wish too," she said, bringing her fingertips to her lips, trying to hold the feel of his kiss there, to keep it from fading away.

Running a hand through his hair, flinging wet snow off his fingers, he said, "Go get warm. If you get a cold because of me, I'll never forgive myself."

He was wrong about the cold, because her skin was still so hot she was surprised steam wasn't rising from her arms. But he was right that she needed to go. She didn't want to, but anything was better than watching him drive away.

"You were the best wedding date I've ever had," she told him as snowflakes melted on her exposed shoulder, trickling down her back, making her shiver.

"I tried to tell you." He smirked, stepping back to reveal a black footprint on the street. Fresh flakes fell quickly, eager to fill it up, erase it like he'd never been there at all. "I am a blast at weddings."

He turned away, and when he reached his car, she forced her feet to carry her back to her door, to her bakery, to her mom, her son, her life. A very good life, but one without him in it.

As soon as she'd stepped up onto the curb, he called out, "Mira! Wait!" Spinning around, wet hair clinging to her cheeks, she found him standing beside his open car door, his phone in his hands, his camera aimed at her.

When he lowered his phone, revealing a smile brighter than the rays of sunlight already breaking through the clouds, he said, "I'm getting that one blown up. Life-sized."

Tucking her hair behind her ear, she decided to stay right where she was, watching him get into his car, close his door, and drive away from her while the snow stopped falling and the sun started shining.

CHAPTER FIFTEEN

COLE

ONE WEEK LATER

Her eyes finally closed, her tiny fingers loosening their grip on his shirt while he bounced her in his arms and the white noise machine whirred softly in the corner. He was about to lay Ruby down in her crib when the nursery door swung open and Becks strolled in, oblivious, talking loudly on her phone.

"Shh," Cole hissed, bouncing Ruby a few more times when she stirred at her mom's voice.

Ending her call, Becks whispered, "Sorry. It's not her usual naptime, so I thought maybe you two were just hanging out."

"She's been fighting it all morning." Placing Ruby in her crib the way a person would place a uranium core into a nuclear bomb, Cole watched her chubby arms flop down at her sides, her tiny chest rising and falling, slow and steady. "This is what they mean by sleeping like a baby. Look at her, on her back, no pillow, no blanket, out like a light. I'd need mountains of memory foam and at least two Ambien to sleep like that."

"I'm not sure I've slept since she was born." Becks reached into the crib, running her fingers lightly over Ruby's soft hair. "Not really." She turned to face him. "I did fall asleep at a red light the other day. It was nice, until a horn honked and some guy shouted, 'Move it, dumbass!'"

Leading his daughter out of the nursery, Cole said, "I was going to head into the studio, but I can wait a while if you want to take a nap."

"Can't," she said through a jaw-cracking yawn. "Have to work."

Cole frowned at the shadows under her eyes, dark circles that reminded him of the way Davis looked the day he'd left Red Falls, which reminded him of Mira. Not a stretch, since pretty much everything he'd done, seen, read, heard, or eaten in the last week reminded him of Mira.

"Dad?" Becks narrowed her brown eyes, the only part of his genetics Nancy's didn't edge out. The rest, her cropped auburn hair, defiant chin, five-foot-two height, those were all her mother. "You there?"

Brushing past her into the kitchen to turn on the baby monitor, he said. "Where else would I be?"

"I don't know. You tell me."

He opened the fridge and took out the box of last night's pizza, because, along with exhausted, he thought Becks might be hungry. "Want some?"

"God, yes. But don't change the subject. Ever since you got back from the wedding, you've been getting this weird, dare I say *dreamy*—"

"Dreamy?"

"—look in your eyes. What happened to you over there? Did you meet someone? Was it that woman you were dancing with?"

Cole nearly dropped the plate he'd just pulled out of the cupboard. "What?" How did she know about that?

"In Ashley's pictures. You're dancing with this hottie with black hair..." She stopped talking, taking in his wide eyes, his jaw, more than likely, on the floor. "Dad?"

The only thing he could think to say, the only coherent thought left in his mind at the knowledge that somewhere in the universe there were pictures of him and Mira dancing together, was "You follow Ashley on Facebook?"

"I've followed Uncle Madigan forever, so, yeah. Now I follow Ashley. You didn't see them?"

He cleared his throat, messed up his hair, scrubbed a hand over his chin stubble. "Uh, no. Can you...show them to me?"

"Suuure." She eyed him warily while he shoved two pieces of pizza into the toaster oven. "As long as you tell me who she is first."

Messing up his hair again, he pulled at his shirt collar. "She's just a friend. She's a baker. A baker friend. I mean, she's a friend who also bakes. She owns a bakery. She made the wedding cake. That's why she was there. For the cake."

Becks burst into laughter. "Did you honestly just call her a baker friend who also bakes?"

"What? Yes, she's a baker, and a friend—You know what? Giving your old man shit after he babysat for you all morning is a jerk move. Just show me the pictures."

Still laughing, she picked up her phone and opened Facebook.

Cole squeezed the edge of the counter in a death grip, his lungs seizing while Becks swiped her finger up the screen. "Just search for Ashley. It's faster," he said after she'd swiped four more times and there were still no pictures of Mira. "Click the little magnifying glass thingy."

"Chill, Mr. Eager. Found them."

If he were a lesser man, he would have swiped his daughter's phone out of her hands and run away with it. But he was a mature adult, so he waited with the patience of a flood while she swiped through too many pictures of Madigan and Ashley, Madigan's parents and brothers, Maude Alice, Davis, Clay, Sam, everyone. Everyone who'd ever existed in the entire world except for—

"Mira," he exhaled, devolving in real time to snatch Becks's phone and bring it close. Clicking on the picture, he expanded it, zooming in on the image of Mira in his arms on the dance floor, her head thrown back, laughter lighting up her face. He'd taken exactly twelve pictures of Mira while he'd been in Red Falls—including the one of her looking back at him right before he'd driven away, snow swirling around her like confetti—but he didn't have a single picture of the two of them together. "Can I have this?" he asked, transfixed by the way her hand wrapped around his, feeling the rush of her body against his all over again.

"My phone? That's gonna be a hard no."

Coming to his senses, bit by bit, he handed her phone back and said, "I meant the picture. Can you send it to me?"

"Or you could get on Facebook and send it to yourself."

The toaster oven dinged, the salt-spice scent of pepperoni pizza filling the air, and Cole pulled a face. "I hate Facebook."

"Because of Mom?" Becks guessed.

Nancy was all over Facebook. Back when he'd used the app, she was constantly in his DMs, commenting on anything he posted, being the worst reply guy ever. Instagram—which she'd been banned from for posting too many nudes during her "naturist" phase—was safer. "Maybe."

While Cole put the pizza on a plate and set it on the counter, Becks said, "You know, she hasn't come over in, like, a month."

"Have you talked to her?" He filled a glass with ice and water and placed it next to her plate. "You know how she gets when she's working on something." *Single-minded, self-centered, completely out of touch with the real world.*

Tracing a finger over Ruby's sleeping form on the monitor, Becks said, "No. She knows where her granddaughter is if she wants to see her."

"Speaking of people who might want to see Ruby..."

Her gaze slid from the monitor. "Seriously, Dad?"

"What? I'm only wondering how things are going."

"He's trying, I guess. But it's still weird." Pushing the monitor away, she said, "Sometimes I wonder if I'm too good at being alone."

Cole gave her a tight smile, because she wasn't wrong. Becks had gotten an apartment downtown with her friends the day she'd turned seventeen, too fed up with the Cole and Nancy shitshow to stay in their house a second longer than she'd had to. He'd missed her like a lost limb then, and having her back now made him feel whole again. He adored being a grandpa. He loved having these kinds of conversations with her that they'd never really had before. And yeah, he had to admit, he enjoyed feeling needed in some small way, when Becks had probably never *really* needed him in her entire, fiercely independent life.

But he also knew Ruby's dad was beating himself up about the choices he'd made after she was born—if the frequent phone calls, weekly flower deliveries, and daily Amazon boxes filled with baby toys were any indication. Cole half-expected the kid to show up in their driveway any day now wearing a sad brown trench coat with a boombox blaring "In Your Eyes" over his head.

"Josh messed up," he told her. "But I think he knows he messed up. I've got your back no matter what you decide, but I'm rooting for the two of you. The three of you, actually."

Pulling her plate closer, she said, "I know you are."

He leaned forward and kissed her forehead. In return, she picked up a piece of pizza, turned it toward him, and let him take a bite.

"Fuck! Hot!" he cried, fanning his mouth, the roof of which would never be the same again. "Blow on that before you eat it." Catching the time on the microwave, he said, "Well, if you don't need me, I guess I'll hit the road."

"Tell everyone I said hi," Becks said. Then she took a break from blowing on her pizza to add, somewhat grudgingly, "Even Mom."

"You bet," he told her, then, keeping his tone as breezy as a tumbleweed tumbling across the interstate, he swiped his keys off the counter, and added, "And send me Ashley's pictures."

"All of them?" Becks asked. "Or just the ones with your baker friend who's a baker?"

"Any of the ones I'm in." He winked at her. "I looked great in that suit."

"You could at least tell me her name," Becks called after him while he walked toward the door.

Turning back, thinking about his past and his future and wondering where he currently stood between them, he said, "Mira. Her name is Mira."

CHAPTER SIXTEEN

COLE

Turning into the Trax parking lot, he pulled up next to Nancy's black Escalade, took in the fuzzy red dice hanging from her rearview, and blew out a breath. He loved this studio. That's why he'd bought it over twenty years ago. Sure, there were nicer, newer, fancier studios in Seattle he could have invested in, but Trax belonged to them—the old guard, the eighties and nineties punk and rock bands. It was where all three Makers' albums were recorded. It was where he and Madigan carved their names into the bathroom wall when they were nineteen. It was where Becks grew up, learning to walk by cruising around the same big table where she did her homework when she got older. It was home. But it was Nancy's home too, and despite all they'd been through, he'd never been able to bring himself to ask her to go somewhere else.

While seeing her ridiculous hotel on wheels in the lot annoyed him, it also made him wish. He wished Nancy's Escalade was Mira's Element. He wished the danish he'd picked up on the way to the studio was one of Mira's tarts. He wished the busy interstates he drove on were quiet streets with quaint little shops and only two stoplights.

And this behavior wasn't new. Every night since he'd gotten home, he closed the door to his bedroom, flopped onto his bed, and *wished*. He wished he could text her. He wished he could follow her on Instagram. He wished he could have sent the "cute as hell" comment he'd drafted under her kitten cookies post this morning instead of deleting it. He wished he could talk to her, let her know he was thinking about her, hear her laugh, ask her more questions, be back in her world.

But he couldn't.

She hadn't reached out to him. She hadn't texted or liked his posts or followed him. And for some reason, he was convinced he needed to let her make the first move in reconnecting. She was busy. He wasn't. She had an entire bakery to run, a mom to look after, a son to raise. He had a temporary stint as a live-in grandpa, a studio that pretty much ran on its own at this point, and occasional drumming gigs. He also had a tendency to chase after things, after people, who only kept running. Even though he'd promised himself he'd stop, while he took the steps to the studio, he wished it was Mira's door he was about to open, Mira's face he'd see when he stepped inside.

"Did you bring one for me?" came the sultry, raspy voice *Rolling Stone* had once called "A whisper wrapped in barbed wire."

"Nancy," Cole said by way of hello.

Rolling her coal-lined eyes, she said, "When you pretend to be grumpy, it just makes me more obnoxious. You should know that by now." She wore tight black jeans, a sleeveless silver sequined top that glittered when she jumped down from the counter she'd been sitting on, and a cropped fur coat that hung off her shoulders. He thought it might be real. "What's in the bag?"

Not hungry anymore, he gave her his danish. It wasn't what he'd wanted anyway. What he'd wanted was buttery, flaky, and a day's drive away.

"Thank fuck," Nancy said, spinning away from him to knock on the window of the mixing booth where Benji—the lead singer of Stone's Throw who'd fronted the Makers during their last tour, and the co-owner of Trax after he'd worn Cole down to sell him a percentage—sat, pretending not to notice her. "Because Benji," she shouted through the glass, "that cheap-ass motherfucker, never gets the vending machines refilled!"

Glancing up from his board, Benji ducked his chin toward Cole, then raised a lazy middle finger at Nancy. Watching Benji chuckle behind the glass, listening to Nancy's chainsaw-after-a-pack-of-Marlboro-Reds cackle, Cole tried to laugh too, only achieving a limp huff through his nose.

Nancy scowled at him, unimpressed. "Come on, Cole." She fluffed out the shoulder-length hair she'd recently dyed from platinum blond to bright red. "We're just having fun. Remember fun? It's that thing when you don't take everything so seriously all the time?"

It used to thrill him, how Nancy was always turned up to eleven, always explosively alive in a way most people never were, always moving, creating, chasing after the next song or album or tour, giving him no choice but to chase after her. Now it wore him out. He didn't want explosions. He didn't want the chase. All he wanted at this point in his life was some peace and quiet. All he wanted was to be somewhere else, to be *doing* something else, only he had no idea what that something else was. Maybe it was to hop in his car and drive east, not stopping until he took the only exit into Red Falls.

Nancy's scowl softened a fraction. "Jesus, you look like I just shot your puppy. I was only giving you shit, Cole."

Signing deeply, he said, "I know, Nancy. I know."

PUSHING through the door after he'd spent the day booking recordings for next month, then cold-calling the lead singer of an up-and-coming punk band called the Sympathy Gags he was trying to convince to use Trax for their new album, Cole stood back as an enormous cloud of smoke rose into the sky.

Nancy sat sideways on the steps, taking up as much space as possible as she peered up at him through narrowed eyes. After taking another pull from her vape pen, she exhaled, scowling at the gray plastic device. "I fucking miss smoking. Know what I mean?"

"Yep." He'd quit when he'd turned thirty-five, but if someone invented a healthy cigarette tomorrow, he'd start back up in a heartbeat. "You're vaping now?"

"The guy I'm dating doesn't like cigarettes. I'm trying to"—she made a face—"compromise."

"Good for you," he said, because Nancy compromising over anything was substantial personal growth.

Tapping her right foot on the concrete—her only tell when she was feeling vulnerable—she asked, "How's the kid?"

"Which one? Your daughter or your granddaughter?"

"I am not old enough to be a grandmother," she grumbled.

"And yet..."

"Either," she eventually replied. "Both. I haven't been over there in a while."

"Ruby's doing great," he told her. "Growing like a weed. And Becks mentioned that this morning. You should come by, see Ruby again before she turns eighteen and moves out."

"Yeah, sure. Maybe." Her toes tapped faster.

"You should come see Becks too."

Under the overcast sky, her red hair glowed like a torch. "I wasn't sure if she wanted me there. She barely talked to me last time I visited. I think she's pissed at me again, even though I have no idea what I did wrong this time."

"She's not pissed at you," Cole said, settling into his well-worn role of mother/daughter relationship counselor. "She was probably just exhausted. Ruby was teething last month. It was a rough one for her." *And it's not always all about you, Nancy.*

"I'll try to find some time." She palmed her pen. "But it's been rough for me too. I'm busy recording an album, if you hadn't noticed. Speaking of which, I have something to ask you. You're not going to like it, but I think you should hear me out before you freak."

"Why are you about to ask me something that would make me freak? Don't we have boundaries for a reason?"

"Wow, Cole," she said with a sardonic edge. "Does it get lonely up there on that high horse? Do you get nosebleeds?"

He looked toward the sky, searching for patience up there between the clouds. "Fine. What did you want to ask me?"

"I'm going on tour next year."

"Congratulations."

"I need a drummer."

"Isn't Mikey from Gravel laying down drums for the album? Use him."

"Can't," she said. "He's busy. Therefore, I need a drummer."

"Well, you know lots of them."

"I don't want lots of them, Cole. I want the best. I want you."

After a beat, he burst into laughter. "Nancy, you can't be serious."

"Oh, but I can. Look, I know how badly you want to play some real shit again. In front of real crowds." Rising to her feet, she said, "Don't pretend you don't."

"The answer is—"

"I don't need an answer today." She pulled her fur coat up over her shoulders. "But you *do* need to think about it. If it wasn't me asking, what would you do? You owe it to yourself to be honest about that much."

"No," he said firmly. "No way." When he turned away from her to head toward his car, she called out, "Come on, Cole. You know you're only happy when you're drumming. You know you're dying to hear the fans screaming your name again. Tell me I'm wrong."

Was she wrong? Was that what was missing? Was that what would make him happy again? Or was Madigan right? Was he surrounded by his past, a past that kept trying to pull him back into it, keeping him from moving forward?

The answer came to him on the breeze. Not car exhaust, not Nancy's cloying vape clouds, but lemons and sugar.

Nancy was wrong. Because flirting with Mira, taking her to the wedding, dancing with her, kissing her, *that* had made him happy. Happier than he'd been in a very long time. Happier than he thought he might ever be again. *That* was what moving forward felt like. So why the hell hadn't he texted her yet?

Walking toward his car, unlocking it with a *chirp, chirp,* he turned back to his ex and said, "Come see your granddaughter."

While Nancy watched him with her head tilted and eyes narrowed, he slid into his seat and did what he'd been wanting to do all week, what he'd been telling himself he shouldn't do because he'd been scared. Pulling out his phone, he pulled up Mira's contact, and his fingers were sure, steady, not faltering once when he texted,

> Cole: I visited my former favorite bakery today and was neither grabbed nor kissed. Very disappointing. Zero stars.

He hit send, started his car, and drove home grinning.

CHAPTER SEVENTEEN

MIRA

Mira's phone flipped out of her hands, landing on the counter with a resonant *thud*.

"Mom?"

"Mira?"

Ignoring her son and her mother, Mira stared at the screen, at Cole's text. "He...texted me," she said to no one in particular, to the dust motes floating through the air, to the ether that filled the spaces between everything.

"Who texted you?" her mom asked, spraying cleaner on the glass of the cupcake display before wiping it clean.

"Cole Sanderson?" Ian suggested, not looking up from his math homework. "The wedding date?"

Retrieving her phone from the counter, Mira said, "Um, could you guys maybe—"

"We'll finish up here," her mom said. "Go talk to him."

Ian's head snapped up. "Wait, you're going to *text* him back, right?"

"No, I was planning on attaching a piece of parchment to a carrier pigeon," Mira replied flatly.

Pointing his chewed-up pencil at her, Ian said, "That would actually be preferable to calling him."

"What?" She tried to take her apron off, only to get caught up in the strings. "Why can't I call him? Jesus, what is *wrong* with this thing?"

"Let me help," her mom said, appearing at her side, setting down her rag and spray bottle. "You're tangled."

Walking to the door, turning the sign to CLOSED, Ian said, "You're just, like, not good on the phone."

"What are you talking about?" Mira asked, finally free of her apron.

"Well, dear," her mom said, "when you're nervous, sometimes you can get..."

"Yes?" Mira asked, incredulous. "What can I get?"

Her lips pinching in an apologetic frown, her mom said, "Chatty?"

"You talk too much about random shit," Ian stated with far less tact, hopping back up onto his stool.

"I do not talk about random shit."

"Hi, Cole," he said, pretending to be her. "I planted sweet pea seeds today. Don't you just love sweet peas? I get the seeds at Bud's every spring. They're so pretty. Do you like flowers? What's your favorite flower?" He turned his thumb to the ground and made a massive fart noise.

"Listen, pal." Mira jabbed her phone in his direction. "I only had that conversation with you this morning because it was too quiet in here, and sometimes getting you to say more than two words to me is like pulling teeth. But I know how to talk to men on the phone. I have great phone banter."

They only stared at her until her mom said, "Oh, sweetie."

"Fine," she relented, throwing a hand in the air. "I won't call him."

"You do whatever you want." Her mom squeezed her shoulder gently. "We're only giving you a hard time." Then she paused, blinked, took a step back, and it was like someone pulled a curtain down or pushed a cloud in front of the sun. It happened that way sometimes, a break in conversation, that vague look of confusion, a memory on the tip of her tongue, a memory slipping away completely. "Where did I put the spray bottle?"

"It's right here, Mom."

"Oh, of course," she said, picking the bottle and rag up from the counter. "I think I'll clean the cupcake display."

Ian's attention wandered back to his math homework.

"That one's good," Mira said quickly. "But the pie case could use some love."

One feature at a time—eyebrows, eyes, cheeks, lips—her mom's expression fell. "I already cleaned the cupcake display, didn't I?"

It was still so hard, resisting the urge to make light of the slip-ups, to downplay the significance of every lost moment. But since all her soothing and placating ever did was make her mom more upset, she finally realized she'd only been trying to make herself feel better. And so she stopped. "You did. You've got therapy in a couple hours if you want to take a nap after you're done with the pie case."

With a brittle smile, her mom said, "That's probably a good idea."

Because she needed it, Mira grabbed a chocolate chip cookie from the case on the counter. It was still warm, and it soothed her, holding it in her hand. "Okay, I'm going to go *text* him." Ian didn't bother looking up from his notebook again, but his lips quirked. "Wish me luck."

SHUTTING the door to her bedroom, she kicked off her shoes so hard one flipped into the air and landed on her bed, then she crawled into her window seat. After pushing the window open until the spring breeze cooled her overly warm cheeks and throat, she sat back against the wall and reread Cole's text. Flexing and straightening her toes, gathering her sparkling nerves, she typed out,

> Mira: Terrible service. On behalf of all inappropriate bakery owners everywhere, my sincerest apologies. I'm still waiting for your Yelp review for Glazed, btw.

Saying a silent prayer that something she thought might be moderately charming actually was, she pressed send. Then she waited, her heart rattling her ribs, her breath trapped in her lungs until it rushed out in a squeak when the texting dots popped up on her screen.

> Cole: Writing it now actually. "Great tarts, spectacular cookies, and the owner's lips taste like sugar."

She kicked her feet onto her windowsill.

> Mira: How are you?

> Cole: I'm good. How are you?

> Mira: Good.

Good? Shit, maybe Ian had been right. The temptation to start texting about flowers was nearly overwhelming.

> Mira: About to take Mom to therapy.

> Cole: How is Linda? And Ian? I'm bummed I never got a chance to meet them.

> Mira: Mom's good. Ian was just giving me hell about texting you back.

> Cole: Like any self-respecting 14-year-old should. What kind of hell?

Mira: He said I shouldn't call you because when I'm nervous, I "talk too much about random shit."

Cole: I like this kid. Smart-asses are my people.

Mira snorted.

Cole: Were you nervous to talk to me?

Sinking her teeth into her bottom lip, she texted,

Mira: A little. I wasn't sure if I'd ever hear from you again.

Cole: I've wanted to talk to you since the second I pulled away from your curb.

Mira: Really?

Cole: Yeah.

Three dots appeared, disappeared, then reappeared, the effect as thrilling as that drop tower Ian made her ride with him at the state fair last year.

Cole: I've got my new granddaughter. I've got my recording gigs. But all I can think about is Mira from Montana. And I look at this way too much.

Another text buzzed through, and there on her screen in black and white was a woman with wide eyes and dark hair falling out of a loose bun, wet strands clinging to her cheeks. The woman looked so alive, so vital, that it took Mira a long moment to realize it was her, staring back at him outside her bakery while the snow fell between them.

> Mira: I don't have any pictures of you.

She'd wanted to, nearly had several times, but saving screen shots of his Insta posts was a level of desperation even she wasn't willing to sink to.

> Cole: My daughter stole this one from Ashley's Facebook page.

> Mira: Facebook? Who's on Facebook anymore?

> Cole: Seriously, Mira. Marry me.

While an electrical current arced down her spine, pebbling every inch of her skin in its wake, she texted back a criminally understated,

> Mira: lol

> Cole: Hang on.

This next picture came through, and the world stopped spinning. They were dancing, Cole in his tux, her in her red dress, and the way he looked at her, his gaze hot on her throat as her head fell back...

> Mira: Who took that?

> Cole: Davis, I think. I vaguely remember spotting her with her phone pointed at us.

> Mira: It's amazing. I'll need to thank her next time I see her.

> Cole: I'm sending her a fruit basket.

She laughed out loud.

> Mira: What a night.

Cole: The best. Next time you need a wedding date, hit me up.

Mira: Deal.

Cole: Would it be okay if I texted you again? I won't call, especially if what Ian said about your phone game was true.

Mira: Omg

Cole: Only kidding, talking about random shit with you all night sounds pretty amazing.

Mira: Text me anytime you want.

Running her thumb up and down the side of her phone, refusing to overthink it, she added,

Mira: You can even call, because talking about random shit with you all night sounds pretty amazing to me too.

May 22, 6:14 pm

Cole: Hi Mira.

Mira: Hi Cole.

Cole: Want to hear something weird?

Mira: Always.

Cole: I was walking downtown today, and this man came up to me, pointed a three-pound sleeve of frozen ground beef at my chest, and said, "They told me you need this more than I do." Then he gave it to me and walked away.

Mira: Seriously?

Cole: Yep.

Mira: He just had a three-pound sleeve of frozen ground beef? Like just walking around with it?

Cole: That's the weird thing. He must have produced it from thin air because I definitely would have noticed if a dude was coming at me with a three-pound sleeve of frozen ground beef. I might have turned around, or at least dropped eye contact.

Mira: I think you met a bona fide meat magician.

Cole: If I hadn't been so shocked, I might have asked for his autograph.

Mira: Well, did you?

Cole: Did I what?

Mira: Need the three-pound sleeve of frozen ground beef more than he did?

Cole: I guess we'll never know. I gave it to Benji at the studio. He'll literally eat anything.

Mira: That is super weird. But you live in a big city. Doesn't shit like that happen all the time?

Cole: A complete stranger gifting me frozen meat? Far less often than you'd think.

. . .

MAY 23, 10:32pm

Mira: Hi Cole

Cole: Hi Mira

Mira: Did I ever tell you I'm scared of the dark?

Cole: I don't believe that came up in the two days we hung out.

Mira: I've been thinking about the time my stepdad took me to the Elktooth Caverns when I was ten. The tour guide led us down to this deep part of the cave, and with barely any warning, he turned off all the lights. It was so dark I couldn't see anything. I was so scared I couldn't move. Then the guide told us no matter how long we stayed down there, our eyes would never adjust to the darkness. I screamed so loud I lost my voice for a week.

Cole: That sounds traumatizing.

Mira: After they got me back up to the surface, they kindly invited me never to return. And I never did. But I was wondering how I'd feel if I went back to the caverns today. I still don't like the dark. I still have to sleep with twinkly lights in my room. But would it be as scary now? Or do some things stay terrifying no matter how old you get?

Cole: Maybe it depends on why you're scared of the thing you're scared of. Do you know why you're afraid of the dark?

Mira: Do we ever know why we have irrational fears? I mean, they're irrational.

Cole: Fair point. So nothing bad ever happened to you in the darkness?

Mira: Aside from some bad seven minutes in heaven sessions in middle school?

Cole: Ha! But we all had those, and we're not all afraid of the dark.

Mira: I don't know. Maybe in another lifetime I fell down a well.

Cole: Do you believe in reincarnation?

Mira: No. Do you?

Cole: I'm a nihilist. I believe in nothing.

Mira: Was that a Big Lebowski quote?

Cole: Uh, yeah. Probably past its prime, huh?

Mira: Big Lebowski is evergreen. The number of times I tell Ian every day that life does not stop and start at his convenience...

Cole: LOLOLOL

Mira: At least I'll never have to worry about going back to the caverns, since it was a lifetime ban.

Cole: Do you really think they'd remember you?

Mira: I made the local paper, and the news, and an NPR segment.

Cole: I guess we're both celebrities.

Mira: haha

May 24, 6:13am

Mira: Hi Cole

Cole: Hi Mira

Mira: Are you a morning person?

Cole: I didn't used to be. Now I'm up with the sun, especially with Ruby here. I'm sitting in the rocking chair with her right now.

Mira: Did she just wake up?

Cole: A few minutes ago. I love being the first one to hold her in the morning. Becks needs the sleep, plus Ruby is just so damn cuddly when she wakes up.

Mira: Warm sleepy baby.

Cole: The absolute best.

May 24, 12:24pm

Cole: Hi Mira

Mira: Hi Cole

Cole: I just followed you on Instagram.

Mira: I just followed you back so fast I sprained a finger.

May 25, 4:55pm

Cole: Hi Mira

Mira: Hi Cole

Cole: How are you?

Mira: I'm good. Did you do anything fun today?

Cole: I made a video for my channel with this twelve-year-old drummer from Alaska. She's unreal. How about you?

Mira: Nothing much. Worked all day. Went for a walk. Gave myself a facial.

Cole: Nice. I love getting facials.

Mira: You get facials?

Cole: Absolutely. I'm all about good grooming. What else do you like? Manis? Pedis? Massages?

Mira: All! All of the above! I just can't afford any of them anymore.

Cole: So you gave yourself a facial.

Mira: Never underestimate the importance of self-care, Cole.

Cole: I never would. Why do you think I started texting you?

Mira: ...

Cole: It's true.

Mira: fucking drummers

Cole: 😉

May 25, 8:49pm

Mira: Hi Cole

Cole: Hi Mira

Mira: Do you like living in Seattle?

Cole: Oh yeah. It's such a great city. And I love being so close to the water. Although, the rain can be a bit much sometimes.

Mira: The crowds don't bother you? The traffic? I think I'd feel hemmed in if I couldn't get away from people whenever I wanted to.

Cole: It's all I've ever known, so I guess I'm used to it. I actually get antsy if there aren't enough people around. If the streets are empty, I'm like, what happened? Where did everyone go? Is the world about to end? Are the zombies coming? It's unsettling.

Mira: I could go into the woods for a week with nothing but a tent and a book and be happy never seeing another soul the entire time.

Cole: Really? Who would help you if you got hurt or scared? What if you fell and broke something? What if you got eaten by a bear? Or a mountain lion? I heard they go straight for the face!

Mira: If I got eaten by a bear, I don't think I'd need any help.

Cole: True. Wait, aren't the woods dark?

Mira: It's a different dark, I guess. There are stars, the moon. And I bring lamps. Do you like to camp?

Cole: You may not believe this, but I've never been camping.

Mira: Never?!

Cole: Before you draw any conclusions about my soft city boyness, it's not the bugs or the dirt or anything like that. I would have loved to camp, but my folks were always gone, so they never took me. The Madigans weren't into it when I lived with them, so we never went. Nancy was vehemently opposed to anything that involved leaving city limits unless we were on tour. And Becks does actually hate bugs.

Mira: First of all, I would never draw conclusions about your soft city boyness. Because then you'd draw conclusions about my sheltered small-town girlness. Second, that makes me sad. Camping is the best. We go all the time. Or we used to. Now Ian's too busy hanging out with his friends every weekend, and the one time we tried with Mom a couple summers ago, she got super disoriented when she woke up in her tent in the middle of the night. I think it scared the shit out of her.

Cole: Mira?

Mira: Yes Cole?

Cole: Would you like to go camping with me?

Mira: I would love to.

Cole: Ok. I'll be right over to pick you up after I get some marshmallows.

Mira: I'll be waiting.

Cole: If only.

Mira: If only.

MAY 26, 10:42am

Mira: Hi Cole

Cole: Hi Mira

Mira: What are you doing?

Cole: Just put Ruby down for her morning nap. You?

Mira: Chilling for a minute between the breakfast and the lunch rush. Did you have a nice night?

Cole: It was actually kind of funny. Becks and I were hanging out after Ruby fell asleep, and she decided she wanted to watch a movie from back in our day. We started searching, and it was alarming how many of the movies we grew up on, movies I loved once, absolutely did not hold up.

Mira: It is sooo bad. What was wrong with us?

Cole: Seriously. I'm not sure we've ever fully examined the collective existential crisis of an entire generation looking back on the films that defined us and thinking, oh dear god no. The Toy? Soul Man? Turning trailblazing sandwich-artist Ally Sheedy into conformity Barbie in The Breakfast Club? And I'm pretty sure Long Duk Dong earned all of us a perpetual sitting in the corner to think about what we've done.

Mira: I tried to watch Revenge of the Nerds with Ian last year. We did not have a good time.

Cole: Yikes!

Mira: Banged my knee on the coffee table so hard lunging for the remote to turn it off I limped for three days.

Cole: Sacrificing your body to protect your kid. That's just good parenting.

Mira: Did you and Becks end up finding anything that wasn't a dumpster fire?

Cole: We did, actually. Say Anything. She'd never seen it before.

Mira: Ugh, that movie. So good.

Cole: I'd forgotten how much it affected me when I was younger. The first time I saw it, that moment when he shouts "I want to get hurt!" I felt understood in a way I'd never experienced before.

Mira: Lloyd Dobler. Heartthrob to End All Heartthrobs.

Cole: John Cusack in that movie finally convinced me I was bi.

Mira: Really? How old were you?

Cole: Seventeen, I think. We'd just started the band, I was dating Nancy, completely obsessed with Madigan, and getting off to Lloyd Dobler. And I was like, huh, maybe I'm not straight. Still took me a minute to say it out loud.

Mira: When did you come out?

Cole: Not until my thirties. Madigan knew, Nancy knew, my parents knew, even though they spent every second we happened to be in the same place at the same time trying to convince me it was just a phase or that I needed to see a shrink. Maybe because of that, maybe because things were different then, I don't know for sure, but it took me a long time to come out publicly.

Mira: Ian is bi.

Cole: He is?

Mira: Pan, actually. He says he's pan.

Cole: Has that been hard for him? I know times have changed, but I remember how chaotic and lonely I felt at his age.

Mira: Thank you for asking that. I wish I could say it's all been easy, but he's an openly queer kid in a small town in Montana, so it definitely hasn't. You're right, though. Times have changed. He has a lot of support from me and Mom and from most of his teachers. He's not the only out kid in his school either, so they have each other's backs.

Cole: That's amazing. I'm so happy he knows who he is and has friends who understand him. I'm happy he has you and Linda by his side. I'm happy he didn't have to wait until he was thirty-five to finally be true to himself.

Mira: I'm sorry it was hard for you, Cole. It's not fair. You deserved to be accepted. You deserved to be loved and supported, especially by your parents. I know it doesn't change anything, but I'm sorry that you weren't.

Cole: Well shit. I just got very emotional.

Mira: Need a hug?

Cole: Yeah.

Mira: *HUGS*

Cole: Feel better now.

MAY 27, 4:32pm

Cole: Hi Mira

Mira: Hi Cole

Cole: Where are you right now?

Mira: I'm in my bedroom.

Cole: ...go on...

Mira: lol. I'm sitting in the bay window in my room. It's my favorite place in our entire apartment, especially once the weather gets nice. I can hide in here, open the window, watch the cars drive down Main Street, smell the lilac bushes in the alley, sometimes hear the music from Jimmy's.

Cole: Sounds perfect.

Mira: Where are you right now?

Cole: Just stewing in my office at the studio. About to leave for the day.

Mira: Stewing? Something happen?

Cole: Nancy was at the studio all day. It always wears on me.

Mira: Do you two still get along?

Cole: Getting along was never really our thing. More like we couldn't stand to be together, and we couldn't stand to be apart. Or at least I couldn't. And now she's just here all the time being...Nancy. Trying to start arguments, dredge up the past, keep us entangled.

Mira: That sounds exhausting.

Cole: It is. I always had a blind spot when it came to her. I put up with a lot I probably shouldn't have.

Mira: How long were you two together?

Cole: On and off for about 25 years.

Mira: That is a very long time to be with someone who wasn't good to you. Are you okay?

Cole: I wasn't. I was kind of a mess because of her for years. But I'm finally seeing our relationship more clearly, the gaslighting, the way she withheld affection, her refusal to ever really commit to me or to our family. Even so, I try to at least be civil with her, because of Becks, because she uses the studio. But these days, I gotta say, I wouldn't mind having less Nancy in my life.

Mira: If Paul still lived in town, I'd probably hire a private investigator to follow him around just so I wouldn't accidentally run into him.

Cole: Haha. I wish!

Mira: But you can't avoid Nancy, because you've got Becks.

Cole: Yeah. But even if we didn't, Nancy is Seattle. She's everywhere here. There's no separating the two.

Mira: It's such a challenge, being surrounded by your past all the time.

Cole: That's funny. Madigan said something similar to me before I left Red Falls. And now I can't stop thinking about it.

Mira: Madigan is very wise.

Cole: That he is.

MAY 28, 9:53pm

Cole: Hi Mira

Mira: Hi Cole

Cole: I was thinking about you today. I mean, I think about you every day, but today in particular.

Mira: I think about you every day too (deleted)

Mira: Oh?

Cole: I was driving to the marina, and I realized, even though it's your heart song, I never asked if you'd been sailing before.

Mira: I've always wanted to, but I never have. People sail on Flathead Lake all the time, and it always looks so peaceful.

Cole: It's not always peaceful on the ocean, but I think you'd love it.

Mira: Remember how you said you've never camped? Don't judge me, but I've never dipped a single toe in the ocean.

Cole: *gasping*

Mira: I know.

Cole: How about you take me camping, and I'll take you sailing?

Mira: Deal.

MAY 29, 8:42am

Mira: Hi Cole

Cole: Hi Mira

Mira: If you could do anything in the world, what would you do?

Cole: Deep thoughts for so early in the day.

Mira: I've been up since 4:30.

Cole: Ouch.

Mira: #bakerslife

Cole: Hmm. I love owning a studio, but my YouTube channel is what really gets my motor running these days. So maybe doing something that helps get more kids involved in music. I'd also sail more. And I'd travel. What about you? What would you do if you could do anything?

Mira: I'd convince more businesses to move to Red Falls so downtown could thrive again.

Cole: That's amazing, and I'd love to see it too. But what would you do just for you?

Mira: I'd make wedding cakes.

Cole: Don't you already make wedding cakes? I seem to remember one recently that was sinfully delicious, especially that top tier.

Mira: *fans face*

Cole: *takes quick cold shower*

Mira: lol

Cole: So you'd make more wedding cakes?

Mira: I'd make only wedding cakes. It's surprisingly hard to break into the wedding cake market. Everyone goes to the big bakeries in Bozeman or Missoula. I get maybe one or two orders a year no matter how much I market.

Cole: Why wedding cakes?

Mira: At the wedding, you told me that Madigan and Ashley would remember my cake forever. That's it. Baking takes so much time and attention to detail and care, but whatever you bake is usually eaten and enjoyed and forgotten about.

Cole: I'll never forget your tarts.

Mira: omg

Cole: sorry

Mira: Don't be (deleted)

Mira: People remember their wedding cakes, they're moved by them. And designing one takes a level of creativity and originality and emotion I don't get to use every day. There are only so many tarts a woman can make before she burns out.

Cole: I hear you. There are only so many dramatic backing tracks a man can lay down for crime procedurals before he burns out too. I love drumming, but there is good drumming, bad drumming, and lightning running through my fucking fingers drumming.

Mira: You get me.

Cole: God, I wish (deleted)

Cole: I get you.

Mira: It's ironic too, because I don't actually like weddings.

Cole: You don't? Why not? I love weddings. Sometimes you meet the most interesting people...

Mira: That is very true. I don't know. I guess I'm just jaded. I've seen relationships end too many times to believe two people will stay together forever.

Cole: Ahh, you're a realist.

Mira: I suppose. What are you?

Cole: I am a hopeless dreamer. A die-hard romantic. A walking, talking bruise waiting to happen.

Mira: I think that's what I like about you the most (deleted)

Cole: Wait, you can't be that much of a realist. Didn't you tell me you have a wish jar?

Mira: I do. Maybe I'm a tiny bit of a dreamer too, although I burn all my dreams.

Cole: Why do you burn them?

Mira: It feels safer. Like I made the wish, but I didn't leave it out there. I made it, then let it go. If it comes true, that's great. But if not, I've already made my peace with it.

Cole: Hurts less that way?

Mira: Sigh. You're right. I'm a realist.

Cole: A realist with the reluctant heart of a dreamer.

Mira: The internal conflict is real.

Cole: haha I bet.

Mira: If money and time weren't issues, I'd travel more too. Maybe visit Seattle first.

Cole: Come dip a toe in the ocean?

Mira: Something like that.

Cole: I'm smiling pretty big right now.

Mira: Cole, I hope you have a lightning running through your fucking fingers kind of day.

Cole: Same, Mira. Same.

MAY 29, 9:32pm

Cole: Hi Mira

Mira: Hi Cole

Cole: Are you busy?

Mira: Nope. Just hanging with Ian watching TV.

Cole: How was your day?

Mira: Definitely not lightning fingers.

Cole: Uh oh. Did something happen?

Mira: Apparently my mom put the milk in the pantry instead of the fridge a few days ago, and Ian just found it. Because he's fourteen and into gross stuff, he unscrewed the cap and smelled it and made a huge deal about how nasty it was. Mom got upset because she thought he was making fun of her. I got upset because she started yelling at Ian, which is something she never would have done before all this started, and it just made me so sad and pissed off. And I hate when I get sad and pissed off about her because it makes me feel like a total asshole. I know she doesn't want to be changing like this. I know she's not doing any of this on purpose. Anyway, I was trying to protect Ian while also trying to calm Mom down, but I did a shitty job of both because I was too emotional. So they went to their rooms and slammed their doors. And I stood in the kitchen like a statue for ten straight minutes.

Cole: Fuck.

Mira: Yeah.

Cole: How are things now?

Mira: Mom hasn't left her room yet. But Ian's okay. We talked it out. But I'm kind of like…what's next? All the time. I live my life in a constant state of what's next? We're at this age where we have to worry about our kids and our parents at the same time, and it's exhausting.

Cole: These are definitely the worry-sandwich years.

Mira: Why didn't anyone tell us it would be like this? It's not like we're the first people in the history of time to get older.

Cole: It's actually pretty common. A tiny bit of preparation would have been nice.

Mira: Right? It's like getting older is this dirty little secret nobody ever talks about, which only makes everything about it harder. And don't even get me started on menopause. Nobody talks about that shit.

Cole: I think I saw a pamphlet in my doctor's office about menopause once. From, like, 1977.

Mira: Let me guess, they called it The Change.

Cole: Ha! I think they did. Eesh.

Mira: I read an article the other day that actually called menopause "taboo."

Cole: Tell me you're joking.

Mira: I wish I was.

Cole: Something half the population will go through is somehow taboo? Sure, that tracks. All men have to deal with is thinning hair and erectile dysfunction and there are fifty-thousand commercials a day for how to treat those. The most I've seen on The Change was a commercial selling ice pillows for hot flashes on late night TV.

Mira: Yep, men get a pill for everything. We get frozen hunks of gel.

Cole: So not cool.

Mira: Punny.

Cole: Thanks. I was kind of proud of that one.

Mira: Actually, the hot flashes haven't been terrible for me, but they come on at the weirdest, most inconvenient times. Like when I'm in line. Grocery store, movie theater, anything. If there's a line, I'm flashing. And when I'm nervous about something.

Cole: What do they feel like?

Mira: They're intense. Like someone sprayed bear spray all over my toes, then my thighs, then my chest, throat, cheeks. And then it's like a microwave melts me from the inside out. Like I'm just incandescent. My hair goes up into a bun, my clothes come off, and nothing gets done until it fades.

Cole: I don't know a lot about small towns, but isn't taking your clothes off in line at the grocery store frowned upon or...

Mira: Nobody's complained about it yet.

Cole: Send pics or it didn't happen.

Mira: lol. But it's a lot more than hot flashes.

Cole: Tell me everything.

Mira: Really?

Cole: Dead serious.

Mira: Okay, but you asked for it. First off, sleep is a total shitshow now. Every night, I'll almost fall asleep, I'll be so close, and then my brain goes "click," and I'm up again. Unless I take something, it's usually hours until I'm finally out. And I can't handle loud, banging noises at all anymore. They make my ears ring for hours, which sucks for a baker. I've had to get rid of all my metal bowls. My hair is thinning and won't get longer no matter how many biotin gummies I eat. I pee almost every time I sneeze. Oh, and I get my period for like one day whenever the fuck it wants. Sometimes every week. Sometimes I won't get it for months. It's like a fun little surprise. Is this TMI? This is totally TMI, isn't it?

Cole: Are you kidding? I'm taking detailed notes. Keep going.

Mira: Ian just asked what we were talking about. I told him.

Cole: What did he say?

Mira: He made a face, said something like "Yeuch," and went back into his room. Now I'm alone on the couch with my old lady menopause stories.

Cole: You're (deleted)

Cole: You're not (deleted)

Cole: You're not alone.

Mira: I don't feel alone (deleted)

Mira: Thanks, Cole.

CHAPTER EIGHTEEN

MIRA

STEPPING OUT OF HER OFFICE, Jen settled her hands on her hips. "What's your deal?" she asked, eyes squinty. "I haven't seen you smile like that in"—her lips, ironically, turned down—"I don't know, forever?"

Flipping her phone over, hiding Cole's last text telling her how Ruby had just spit up all over his shirt, Mira said, "I'm not smiling any more than I usually smile."

"Okay, this is not meant as an insult, but you're not really a smiler. And you *never* smile like that." She pointed at Mira's face, then at her phone. "Did you find a fun new game or something?"

Mira cleared her throat. "Um, yeah. I—"

"Babe, that was a joke," Jen cut in with a laugh. "You've been typing and smiling out here for Linda's entire session. Who are you texting? Did you meet someone?"

While Jen sat beside her on the waiting room couch, Mira admitted, "It's Cole."

"Wedding date Cole? Johnny Knoxville Cole?"

Mira nodded. "We've been texting for a week. Like, nonstop."

"Seriously?" Jen's eyes went wide. "What are you and the hot drummer texting about?"

Mira hadn't talked to anyone about whatever was happening between her and Cole. After a week of keeping it all to herself, she was champagne bubbling under pressure, and Jen just popped her cork. "Everything," she said, keeping her voice low. "Like, *everything*. All I want to do is text him. All day. All night. It's all I think about. I'm obsessed."

"I am loving this for you," Jen said with a wide, toothy grin. "But you're only texting? Not actually speaking?"

It wasn't for lack of wanting to. She'd hovered her finger over the call button no less than three times in the last few days, but she hadn't been able to make herself push it. "Not yet. I don't know, it seems like...a step."

"A step you're not sure you want to take with someone who lives so far away?"

"Right." She glanced down at her phone still face down in her lap. "Texting him this much already feels like I'm lighting the fuse that will eventually blow up my entire life. But calling him...I don't know. It's like tossing the match out and grabbing a blow torch instead."

Jen's head tilted. She'd straightened her hair today, and a silky red strand slid over her shoulder. "Why?"

Mira shrugged. "Because it couldn't work with him. I'm here. He's there. And not just a little bit here and there either. We're set. We both have situations we can't leave, even if we wanted to. I've got Mom and Ian. He's got his daughter and granddaughter and his studio. He loves the city. I love the mountains. I have a bakery to run. He's got strangers giving him frozen beef."

"I'm sorry, what?"

"Plus," Mira went on without explanation, "you know how I am. I don't do casual. I don't know how. I'd just get in over my head and get my heart broken again. You saw how long it took me to get over Paul. I don't want to go through that again."

"I get that," Jen said, tucking that stray strand behind her ear. "But maybe at our age, long-distance isn't so bad. You have each other, but you still have your own lives too. And it's not like he lives in another country. Seattle's only a day's drive away."

"A long day," Mira pointed out.

"But with him there and you here, there's nobody to get mad when one of you has to work late or spend all night at the barn taking care of a sick horse. Nobody to make you feel guilty because you've got too much shit to do to hang out and watch Netflix all day. Nobody stealing all the hot water because they insist on taking hour-long showers. Nobody to get embarrassingly wasted at your daughter's high school graduation."

Mira nudged Jen's shoulder, knowing she was talking about her estranged husband. "Have you talked to him recently?"

"Not for weeks. But I've heard he's been wearing a Scott-shaped indentation into one of the barstools at Randy's."

"Shit."

"Yeah." Shaking her own Scott-shaped indentation off, Jen said, "Look, I think I understand why you don't want to call him, but please tell me you and the drummer are at least sexting."

"Oh, all the time," Mira said, holding up her phone, tilting it side to side. "It's nothing but titty shots and dick pics in here."

"That's my girl."

When her mom returned from the bathroom, Mira tried to plaster a smile on her face, but her mom looked so tired, her skin thin and papery, her eyes sunken. She needed to get more sleep.

"Well?" she said. And even her voice sounded tired because the cognitive testing Jen put her through always took its toll. "How did I do this time?"

Jen motioned them back into her office. "Do you want the good news first, or the not so good?"

"There's not so good news?" A hollow pit opened up in Mira's stomach as she took a chair across from Jen's desk.

"Good news," her mom replied, taking the seat next to Mira, her hands clasped in her lap. "Always lead with the good news."

"For the most part, your results haven't changed very much since the last time I tested you."

"That's great news!" Mira said, awash with relief.

"But," Jen continued, "they have changed a little."

"What does that mean?" her mom asked. "Am I getting worse?"

"No," Jen said, but she said it like she wasn't sure, like there was a question mark hovering above her head. "Not necessarily. You're showing more difficulty with tasks that require divided attention. Some difficulty with dual tasking is a part of the normal aging process. For now, all it means is that you might have a harder time doing two things at once without making errors. Like following a recipe while having a conversation or balancing your checkbook while listening to the radio."

Or putting the milk back in the right place when you're on the phone with Maude Alice, Mira thought, then asked, "Is there anything we can do?"

"There's a lot we can do," Jen said with a reassuring nod that Mira only hoped worked on her mom, because it sure as shit wasn't working on her. "We'll address the deficit in your therapy sessions, and I'll give you both some recommendations on reducing distractions you can implement at home."

"More signs," her mom said on a somber exhale. "More strategies."

Mira hated this. She hated the way her fingers went stiff and cold when some new test result or difficulty with something her mom used to do with her eyes closed confirmed that her condition was progressing. She hated not knowing what would happen, how bad things might get, if her mom would wind up needing more help than she could give her, if she'd have to live as a long-term resident of this nursing home instead of only an outpatient, if someday she'd look at her but not know her, not know Ian, not remember.

She'd gotten lost hiking alone once, and the forest had been so thick she'd barely found her way out before sunset. That's what this felt like. Like they were in the woods, only this time, there was no out. There was only deeper, darker, colder.

"Thanks, Jen," she managed, pushing the words past the sharp lump in her throat. When her phone buzzed, she knew it was Cole without having to look, because the lump lost its thorns.

"I'll go get you those handouts," Jen said with a subtle nod toward her phone. "You've obviously got business to attend to."

Her phone buzzed again, and Jen's brow ticked up. "Important business."

"What?" Linda said, running a finger under her eye, drying a tear Mira hadn't even noticed. "Flirting with her drummer?"

Jen snorted.

Grateful for anything that lightened the mood, even if it came at her expense, Mira said, "It's a tough job, but someone's gotta do it."

PUSHING HER WINDOW OPEN, she crawled onto the seat and inhaled the thick, sweet scent of the lilac bushes in the alley. She hadn't had the time to conduct the *important business* of replying to Cole's text —a selfie with Ruby sleeping in his arms that had made her momentarily forget how to start her car—until now.

After dropping her mom off at home, then taking Ian to piano, then making dinner, then trying to help Ian with some pre-calc homework but only being able to provide emotional support, she was finally alone, in her room, holding her phone close like a security blanket.

She started a text, telling Cole about the therapy session and her mom's test results, but halfway through, her fingers stalled. Aside from Jen, Mira didn't talk to anyone about her mom. People in town asked her how things were going all the time, but she always kept her responses surface level. Anything more than that felt too much like gossip, and she never wanted her mom to hear something she'd said about her secondhand, well intentioned or not. So whenever anyone asked, her answer was always the same: she's fine, we're fine, everything is fine. But everything wasn't fine.

Finishing her text and hitting send made her heart pound and her palms sweat, but it also felt like a rebellion. Like she could finally let someone know, let *him* know, that she, Mira Harlow, stoic small-town baker, invisible woman behind the counter, the friend who rarely smiled but never cried, was really struggling. Like she might finally be able to scream out into the cool evening air, I AM NOT FUCKING FINE!

It only took a moment for his three dots to appear.

> Cole: I'm so sorry, Mira. How's Linda taking it? How are you holding up?

> Mira: She's okay. I'm less okay.

> Cole: Do you want to talk about it?

Slowly, one deliberate letter at a time, she let herself type out,

> Mira: I'm scared.

His response was immediate.

> Cole: I'm here.

A soft breeze carried her curtain away from the window, brushing the gauzy fabric over her bare toes.

> Mira: I'm drowning in what-ifs. What if she gets worse? What if I can't take care of her? What if something happens and I'm not there?

She didn't tell him all the other what-ifs, the ones that kept her up more often than her weird menopause shit, the ones that drilled themselves into her brain, intruding relentlessly on her only moments of peace and quiet night after night. *What if she forgets me? What if she forgets Ian? What if she becomes someone different? What if it's already happening? What if she leaves me too?*

> Mira: I'm trying to keep my head above water, but I'm kicking so hard under the surface right now my legs are giving out. I can't breathe.

> Cole: Do you feel like you're going through this all by yourself?

She clutched her phone. He'd cut into her, straight past her skin and her bones into her softest parts, the vulnerable parts she hid so carefully from everyone else. The thoughts that made her feel weak and selfish. The worries that hurt so much to say out loud, she never did.

Her eyes stung, because maybe she didn't have to hide these softest parts from him. Maybe he wouldn't judge her. Maybe he was safe.

> Mira: It's so lonely. I try not to involve Ian too much because I want him to have a normal, happy childhood. I try not to show how worried I am all the time because I don't want Mom to feel like she's a burden. I try to keep the bakery running so we can pay our bills. I try to make all the appointments and the lessons and help with homework and piano practice and therapy exercises. I try to hold it all together, and I just feel like I'm falling the fuck apart. Like I'm failing at all of it. Like no matter what I do, our lives getting harder and harder is just...inevitable.

She hit send, then waited. One second became two, then five, then thirty, but her screen only stared back up at her, her text sitting there in the void, unanswered, all alone, just like she was. She bit her cheek. Did she say too much? Was he judging her? Why wasn't he responding? Where were the dots? Where were the *goddamned dots?*

Her heart plummeted, falling like a stone kicked off a bridge, landing hard somewhere deep in her stomach.

And then her phone started ringing.

CHAPTER NINETEEN

COLE

HE'D BEEN the first to text, and he'd wanted to let her decide when they'd progress to calling. But she was hurting. He had to talk to her.

"Don't say anything," he said when she accepted the call. "You don't have to say a single word if you don't want to. I can do all the talking. But I didn't want you to feel like you were alone anymore."

"Cole. That's so...sweet." Her voice was quiet, thick with emotion, and finally hearing it again made him rub at the sudden ache in his chest.

"Well, I'm a sweet guy," he said, pretending he was cool, pretending the small sniff she took across the line didn't make him desperate to hold her, to beg Benji to let him borrow his private jet so he could race to see her. "Do you want to know what Ruby learned to do today?" he asked. Cute baby stories were always good for a distraction.

"I'd actually love that," she said softly.

"I was hanging with her while she did tummy time on her play mat, and all the sudden, she pushed her chubby little body up onto her hands and knees, crawled forward one step, and fell flat on her face."

"So relatable," she said with a laugh. "Is she okay?"

"She is. But she cried for ten minutes straight. You know, that type of crying where they start turning redder and redder, and you're like, 'Breathe, baby. Breathe!'"

"The kind that makes you cover your ears, because you know the post-cry scream will be deafening."

"That's the one. I couldn't tell if she was crying because she hurt herself, or because she was so mad she couldn't figure out how to crawl yet. Knowing Becks—and Nancy—it was the latter, because twenty minutes later, after trying so hard her face went from red to purple, she finally did this wonky army crawl all the way across the room to her little bookshelf. When she got there, she pulled herself up to standing and squealed with unbridled joy. Like that was all she'd wanted to do from the start."

"It sounds amazing, being a grandparent."

"It definitely is." After a silent moment, he held his phone closer to his ear, and asked, "Mira, is there anything I can do?"

Before she answered, someone with a scratchy voice that sounded like it hadn't been as deep as it was for very long said, "Mom?"

"Yeah, pal?" she said back, the sound muffled.

"Grandma can't find her glasses again. And they're not just on her head this time."

"Okay, I'll be right there."

"Do you need to go?" Cole asked. He'd known the call would end eventually, but he still wasn't prepared for how badly he didn't want it to.

"I'd better. Mom can't read without her glasses. And she can't sleep without reading."

"Me neither," he said, eyeing his readers lying next to the stack of books on his bedside table.

"Cole?"

"Yes, Mira?"

"You asked if there was anything you could do to help. Can we keep doing this? Talking? It helps."

He pumped his fist into the air, then realized maybe celebrating when she was having a rough time wasn't cool. But it was so hard to chill when it came to her, even though he knew he needed to. There were way too many unanswered questions to let his feelings run wild the way they wanted to. Were they only friends? Were they more? *Could* they be more? Did it matter?

Maybe they could never be more than this, whatever this was. But, *shit*, did Cole think he'd live forever? Did he think he'd have a thousand more chances to feel this thread tugging him toward another person so tightly it spanned six hundred miles without snapping?

"I'll call you tomorrow," he promised her, deciding it didn't matter at all.

"Hey, brother, help me out?"

Fishing the change from his morning coffee out of his pocket, Cole passed a folded wad of ones to the man sitting on the sidewalk and said, "Take it easy."

"Are you already hanging up on me?" Mira asked into his ear.

"Not yet, sugar," he told her with a grin.

Over the last two weeks, they'd talked at least once every day, usually twice. Once in the morning, then again before they'd fallen asleep, sometimes keeping each other up until he was more of a bleary-eyed wreck than Becks after Ruby decided two in the morning was a reasonable time to expect some breakfast.

But they'd done more than talking too. Yesterday, he'd sent her a shameless thirst trap while he'd been out sailing, shirtless and smiling in the sun, with the hashtag #ThatChristopherCrossLife. In retribution, she'd sent him a post-shower selfie, her hair wet, a white towel barely clinging to the swell of her breasts, her phone held high, angled so he could see down the line of her cleavage, the hashtag #Its-

NotFarDownToParadise taunting him without mercy. When they'd finally hung up last night, he'd been so worked up from her picture, and the way she'd teased him with a detailed step-by-step breakdown of how she liked to knead dough, he'd had to take care of himself before he could even think about falling asleep.

"But I'm almost at the studio," he said, looking up. Seattle was in its finest form, bright blue sky, big puffy clouds, the skyline sparkling in the sun, the snow capping Mount Rainier so white it was almost blinding. And then there was Nancy, vaping on the studio steps, wearing torn jeans and the remnants of a Misfits T-shirt he was pretty sure used to be his before she'd stolen it and turned it into a crop top. "So I'd probably better go."

"Talk to you later?"

"Absolutely."

Ending the call, schooling his features into something resembling neutrality, Cole approached his ex.

"You know that guy's going to use your money to get drunk or high, right?"

His jaw clenched. "Good morning to you too, Nancy."

She pulled on her vape pen, then blew out the smoke, charitably pointing it away from him. "Were you talking to that woman again? What's her name? Kara?"

"Mira."

"Right, Mira. *Mira, Mira, Mira.*" Her head tilted with each repetition. "What's your endgame here, Cole?"

He slid his phone into his back pocket. "Endgame with what?"

Her blue eyes rolled. "You've spent the last three weeks grinning at your phone like a gooey-eyed prepubescent boy. What, are you in love with her or something?"

"Nancy," he warned. "You have your shit, and I have mine. I don't ask about your life. I'd appreciate it if you didn't—"

"Fine, but I'm worried about you. Long distance isn't your thing."

"There's nothing to worry about. We're just friends. And what do you mean it's not my thing?"

Her eyes lit up, because that had been bait, and he'd just fallen for it. "You're a fixer, Cole. You freak out when you can't make everything good and lovely and perfect all the time. And it'll be too hard to make everything perfect for her when she's so far away."

"It's a little early in the morning for character assassination, Nance," he said, even though after spending literal decades doing everything in his power to fix their relationship before finally realizing it was irreparably broken, he couldn't say her take surprised him. But the nice puffy clouds, the lovely blue sky, the perfect picture of Mira in a towel on his phone, shrank his tolerance for Nancy's bullshit to a pinpoint. "Besides, don't you have an album to focus on instead of worrying about me?"

"Yeah, yeah," she said, brushing him off, because if Nancy was anything, it was unflappable. "Have you come to your senses about drumming for me?"

"Answer's still no," he said over his shoulder while he mounted the stairs.

"You'll change your mind," she singsonged, then stopped him in his tracks with "Oh, and by the way, there's a gift from your not-girlfriend in there."

He whipped back around. "A gift? From my not-girl—from Mira?"

Rolling her eyes for a second time, she grabbed his shoulders and spun him toward the door. He'd barely taken his first step into the studio when the sweetest scent he'd ever known nearly took him out at the knees.

Lemon, sugar, Mira.

Pink Glazed and Confused boxes crowded the big table, cupcakes, cookies, and, *good lord*, two entire boxes full of tarts.

"Overkill much?" Nancy bumped her shoulder into his. And then, lowering her defenses for half a second, she said with sincerity, "Happy birthday, Cole."

He stared open-mouthed at the bright pink boxes, splashes of color filling the typically dark studio with light. "She did this... for me?"

When he looked at Nancy, she looked away. "She must really like you or something."

Pulling his phone out, he flicked his thumb up the screen, found Mira's contact, and said, "Try the tarts, Nance. They're amazing."

"Bakery Goddess?" she mocked, looking over his shoulder at Mira's caller ID. "Seriously? So fucking cheesy."

While Benji eyed them warily from the table, a chocolate cupcake suspended in midair on the way to his mouth, Cole decided not to call Mira yet. Opening Instagram, he repeated, "Try a tart." And then, with a smile so smug he was almost ashamed of it, he added, "They'll change your life. They've definitely changed mine."

CHAPTER TWENTY

MIRA

THE DOUGH WAS soft as air under her palm, slightly sticky, almost velvety. She'd been worried she'd overworked it since she'd lost track of time while kneading, her mind preoccupied by the fact that Cole was about to walk into his studio, about to see the present she'd sent him. She was worried it was too much, too obvious, like a big pink sign saying, "Hey! I'm super into you!"

She'd never felt this way about a man before, not with Paul, not with her other boyfriends or crushes, not with anyone. It made perfect sense. It was so typically *her* that the first time butterflies swarmed in her belly, it would be for a man she couldn't touch, couldn't see, couldn't have—

"What are you doing?"

"Shit!" she shouted, slamming a hand over her pounding heart. "Don't sneak up on me like that!"

Ian's right brow hitched, his hair particularly unruly today, surrounding his head like a spun-sugar halo. "I knocked three times. I thought you were sleepwalking."

"Sorry." Putting the dough into a bowl to rise, she covered it with a proving cloth. "I must have spaced out for a minute."

"You've been doing that a lot lately," Ian said, his brow still popped. "Did you send Cole some tarts?"

"What?" How the hell did he know that? "I...don't know."

"You don't know," he echoed doubtfully.

She brushed her hands off on her apron. "Maybe. I, maybe... I might have—Why are you asking?"

"Because he just posted an Insta story from his studio with a shit-load of Glazed boxes."

"He did? When? Where?" She spun in a circle, patting down her pockets, leaving flour smears on her jeans. There weren't any mirrors in the kitchen, so she couldn't say with any certainty, but she was pretty sure her cheeks were currently flushed pinker than those boxes, heat prickling between her toes, surging up her thighs. "Where the hell is my phone?"

"Don't hurt yourself, Mom. You left it on the front counter."

Peeling off her apron, tying her hair up into a knot while a hot flash tore through her, she set the timer for the bread and walked to her son, flattening his hair until he swatted her hand away.

"I'm out," he said, heading toward the door while she snatched her phone from the counter and unlocked her screen.

"Where are you going?"

He fluffed his hair back up. "Brendan's. He made a new server last night."

"Oh. Okay. Great," she said absently while opening Instagram. "Sounds fun."

"Later, we're going to order two hundred pizzas and charge them to your credit card."

Looking up from her phone, she winked. "Save a slice of pepperoni for me, smart guy."

"Will do." When he opened the door to go, he nearly ran face first into Maude Alice.

"Hello, Ian," she said, looking extremely put together in slim yellow capris and a flowing floral blouse, her sleek, silver hair brushing the tops of her shoulders.

"Hey, M.A.," Ian replied, putting his earbuds in on his way out. "See ya."

"I hope he knows he's the only person I let call me that." She hooked her thumb over her shoulder at Ian while he started off down the sidewalk. "He's lucky he's so cute."

With deep regret, Mira turned her phone face down on the counter. "Don't let him hear you say that. The C-word has been permanently banned in this bakery." She fanned her face, the last few embers of her hot flash fading.

"Is that Maude Alice?" her mom called down from the stairs.

"Sure is!" Maude Alice called back.

"I'll be right down!"

Sniffing the air, Maude Alice asked, "What is that?"

"I'm making brioche for a grilled cheese special next week."

"Will it be done when we get back?"

"Should be," Mira said. "Want me to save you some?"

"Please. Thank you, dear."

Wiping down the counter, Mira asked, "How are the newlyweds?"

"As obnoxiously happy as you might imagine. I think Ashley has forgotten we have any chairs at Bluebird at all with how often she insists on sitting on Madigan's lap."

"Get a room, right?" Mira said with an airy laugh, wondering what it would feel like to have Cole's lap always available for sitting.

"They fly to Iceland in two days. I couldn't be more thrilled for my daughter, or for Madigan, but I think we're all looking forward to a little break from the constant public displays of affection. I'll take two of those, please," she said, pointing to the strawberry cheese danishes while her mom came down the stairs.

"Did Ian leave already?" her mom asked, turning the corner, wearing the same outfit she'd worn yesterday.

Mira bit down so hard something squeaked. She'd meant to, but after talking to Cole, she'd completely forgotten to go up and make sure her mom had changed. Hopefully Maude Alice wouldn't notice the small raspberry jam stain on her khaki pants or how wrinkled and slept-in her green shirt looked.

"He went to Brendan's. What are you two doing today?" Mira asked, ignoring the outfit, trying to forgive herself for not remembering to check, forgive her mom for refusing to allow signs in her bedroom, forgive a society that expected clean clothes every day.

"I believe," she started, turning to Maude Alice, her brow furrowed like she wasn't entirely sure, "we're going to a movie, right?"

Taking the pastries Mira handed her and placing them in her bag, Maude Alice nodded. "And then cribbage in the park."

It was a perfect day for it—warm, only slightly cloudy. After a huge storm had rolled through a few days ago, all the blossoms were off the trees, littering the ground like pink and white confetti. But the leaves had grown big enough to provide plenty of shade. "That sounds like fun."

"I'll be back for that brioche." Maude Alice winked.

"Me too," her mom said, following Maude Alice out through the door.

Mira watched them leave, waiting until they were clear of the bakery windows, then flipped her phone over to open Instagram.

The reel was short, Cole narrating while he filmed a shot of the studio, of her boxes on his table. And then he flipped the camera, his smiling face lighting up her screen. "And if you're ever in Red Falls, Montana, make sure to check out Glazed and Confused. Because these"—he held up one of her tarts—"are phenomenal."

When he bit into her flaky pastry, she couldn't hit the call button fast enough.

"Hey, sugar," he said, picking up on the first ring, his voice the starting shot sending goose bumps racing over her arms. "Have I ever told you that you're amazing?"

Her goose bumps grew goose bumps. "Not yet."

"You're amazing. How did you know it was my birthday?"

She flipped the OPEN sign to CLOSED, then leaned on the door, relieved Saturday was their short day. "I called Madigan."

"You did?"

"I knew it had to be soon, Mr. Gemini."

"Like I said, amazing."

"Happy birthday, Cole."

"What are you doing right now?"

She pushed herself away from the door as INXS's "Never Tear Us Apart" started playing through the speakers. "Just closing up."

"Are you alone?"

"I am. Ian's at a friend's, and Mom's out with Maude Alice."

"Do you want to mess around?"

Her eyes ratcheted so wide they stung. "Do I... Wait, what do you mean?" Because it sounded like he'd just asked her if she wanted to mess around, but maybe she'd misheard him. Maybe he'd only asked if she wanted to press a gown. Or dress a clown. Anything was possible! Her pulse pounded so hard between her ears she couldn't be sure.

"You know how we talked about trying to FaceTime?" His voice was so low and dark it seemed indecent that the sun was still shining. "I think we should. I want to. If you want to."

They'd been skirting around this step all week, their late-night conversations getting naughtier, the pictures they sent each other getting racier—especially that one she'd sent him only after he'd sworn up and down that he'd delete it after five seconds. But those were only words, only pictures. This would be different. This would be as close to having him here with her as she could get. This would be real...and really fucking hot.

"I want to," she said, not letting herself overthink it as she took off for the stairs.

"Where are you?"

"Running up to my room," she told him, already a little breathless. "Where are you?"

"At the studio. Locked in my office. Also alone, aside from your tart."

She tripped on the top step.

"You okay? I heard a thump."

"I'm fine," she said, her big toe throbbing. "But are you sure you want to do this now?" She stopped for a breather at the kitchen counter. "We can wait until you're home."

"My office is soundproof. The *Do Not Disturb* sign is up. Yeah, I want to do this now. I *need* to do this now."

She gulped. "Okay, but I need a minute. Can you give me a minute?"

FaceTiming meant he'd see her. FaceTiming meant she'd need to change out of her flour-covered clothes and wash her flour-covered face. FaceTiming meant he'd see her room!

"Make that five minutes," she said while her brain whirred through images of him alone in his office, his door locked, his lights dim, maybe already stroking himself through his jeans.

"Take as long as you need, Mira."

Mm-hmm. Yep, those were the slow, lazy words of a man stroking his cock all right. It was on. This was happening. This was fucking happening!

"See you soon," she said, ending the call before plowing through her bedroom door, her heart beating so fast she felt, heard, and practically tasted it. After peeling off her shirt and jeans, she turned in a frantic circle, surveying the chaos of clothes and shoes littering her floor.

Scooping shirts and bras and boots into her arms, she hurled them into her closet, shoved them into any drawer they'd fit into. Her head spinning, a cardiovascular event looming, she closed her eyes. *Calm down, Mira. Breathe. You are a fifty-year-old woman. You can do this. But you will not FaceTime him in your bra and underwear!*

She could put on a dress or wear that low-cut blouse she'd bought at the mall in Missoula that made her tits look fantastic. But in all the selfies she'd sent him over the last two weeks, he seemed to like her best when she was comfortable, casual.

Shucking off her bra—deciding bras were for people who didn't mess around over video chats in the middle of the day—she shoved it into a drawer she'd just stuffed full of random shit, then rooted around for her favorite black tank top. Opening the next drawer down, she found the pink shorts she never wore out, because while they were super cute, they were also super short. With trembling fingers and skyrocketing adrenaline, she slipped into the simple outfit she hoped like hell didn't give off mom-about-to-do-braless-yoga vibes.

Brushing the flour off her face in the mirror, then hiking up her boobs, she crawled into her window, blew out an enormous breath, and pulled up his contact.

"There she is," he said with a smile, leaning back in his chair, one hand curled behind his head.

"Hi." She waved at him, actually waved.

"Damn, Mira," he said, sitting up straighter, his eyes moving restlessly over her face.

"What?" She checked her tiny image in the corner of her screen for any flour smears she might have missed.

"I've missed you. I've missed your eyes, your lips, your everything. Pictures don't do you justice."

Forcing her breathing to slow, her focus to sharpen, she traced the straight line of his nose, the angle of his chin, the strong column of his throat, and said, "I've missed your everything too."

"You look amazing." His gaze dipped to her throat, her chest. "That top." His lower lip disappeared between his teeth.

While he took in her tank top, she took in his Cure shirt. "You wore that the first time we met."

Tearing his gaze from hers, he glanced down, reading the words scrawled across his chest: *Let's Go To Bed.* "You're right." His lips pulled into a smirk. "Ironic."

Her mouth went bone dry. "How do we do this? What happens next?"

"I need to see you. More of you. All of you. Will you show me?"

"You want to...see me?"

"I thought I could be cool," he said, scrubbing a hand over his face. "I thought I'd see you again, and I'd be able to act like a normal person. But there's nothing normal about how badly I want you, how badly I've wanted you for weeks, how out of my mind I've been for you since I pulled your zipper down in that walk-in freezer. It doesn't ease up. It doesn't let me sleep. I want you, Mira. However I can have you. So yes, I want to see you. I want to see everything you're willing to show me. Please."

And after that, not a single molecule of air moved through her lungs. Not a single shred of concern remained about how she looked or if her shorts were too short. All that mattered was only how badly she wanted him too. "Cole." It was all she could say, the only word she could manage.

"If this is too much, we don't have to keep going. We can just talk. We can do whatever you want."

"Whatever I want?"

Everything about him was fast, his wit, his fingers, his text response time, everything except this nod that was so slow, so carefully deliberate, that the dip of his chin might as well have been his hands tugging on her shorts.

Raising her phone, angling it down on the tank top barely containing her breasts, her shorts barely covering her thighs, she said, "I want to show you everything you want to see."

"Fuuuck." It was half said, half groaned. She could have lived the rest of her life in the sound.

"But I've never done anything like this before."

"What? FaceTimed?"

"Cole, don't make me laugh right now," she said, even though it was too late.

"I've never done anything like this before either," he admitted. "But I can't keep going on *not* doing it. I think about you every second of every day. I dream about you every night. Every time I walk past a store and see a cool piece of art or a soft, comfy-looking sweatshirt, I think *I wonder if Mira would like that*. Every day I spend recording or running the studio, scheduling sessions, having meetings, mixing tracks, doing things I should be paying attention to, things I should be caring about, all I do is watch the clock, waiting until I have a break so I can call you."

He was able to put all the feelings swirling around her chest into words in a way she couldn't, or at least wouldn't let herself. And maybe it was apparent on her face, how he'd touched her, how his honesty had warmed her skin enough to let her feel perfectly comfortable inside it, because he ran his hand through his hair, and said, "Sorry if I got too earnest there. It's just—"

"Can I show you something?"

His mouth opened, then stayed that way, his jaw slack, eyes ballooning while she slipped a finger under the strap of her tank top and slid it over her shoulder, exposing the upper curve of her breast, the fabric barely clinging to her peaked nipple. She watched his throat work through a swallow, his eyes glazing over.

"Is this what you wanted to see? Is this what you need, Cole?"

Again, slowly, as slowly as he ever moved, his chin dipped, his eyes never leaving the skin she'd uncovered for him. Even though people rarely walked through their alley, she pulled her gauzy curtain closed, keeping the moment safe, private, only for them.

Pushing the other strap over her shoulder, she kept her shirt up with her hand pressed between her breasts. "Do you want to see more?" she asked, brushing her fingertips over the top of her right breast.

He nodded, whispered, "Yes." It was intoxicating, the way his eyes drank her in, the way he brought his phone so close she saw the golden strands fanning out from his irises like sunflower petals, the thick sweep of his eyelashes when he blinked. "Please, Mira."

Removing her hand, letting her shirt fall from her left breast first, and then her right, she became a statue, motionless aside from her pulse pounding furiously in her throat, her phone trembling in her hand as the sunlight through the curtain lit her bare skin. When she forced herself to look up from her body to her phone again, she almost laughed.

His fist was at his mouth, his knuckle clamped between his teeth.

"Are you okay?" she asked, suddenly feeling far less naked, or at least less self-conscious about it. How could she be when he looked at her like he wanted to devour her?

"You're so gorgeous," he rasped. "So fucking gorgeous. I want to touch you. I wish I could touch you. I *need* to touch you."

Emboldened by his wet lips, his blacked-out eyes, his obvious, open arousal, she asked him, "How would you touch me, if you were here?" while trailing her fingers over her collarbone. When he only stared, she asked, "Would you touch me like this?" She ran her fingertips down her sternum, tracing over the swell of her left breast, her thumb circling, drawing close to her nipple but not touching it.

"Yes. Just like that," he told her. "If I was there, I'd find out how sensitive your nipples were. If they were as sensitive as your delicious neck. I'd find out if you liked it when I touched them, rolled them between my fingers, caught them between my lips, sucked them into my mouth."

Any question of if this was a good idea or not turned to ash in the searing heat coursing through her core, the tiny heartbeat pulsing between her legs.

"I'd lick them," he said as she moved her hand across her body, sliding her fingers over her right nipple. "I'd swirl my tongue around them, flicking the tip over—"

Her soft moan cut him short, her back arching away from the wall.

"Fuck, they're so tight. Your nipples need my mouth on them, don't they? My tongue. My teeth."

"Yes," she panted, more turned on than she'd ever been in her life, and he wasn't even in the room.

"What else do you need, sugar? Where else do you need my fingers? My mouth? Tell me."

It was almost too much, the tingle coiling tight in her core, the deep, incessant throbbing in her clit, the knowledge that if he was here with her, touching her, kissing her, he would be so, so good at it. "Are you sure you've never done this before?"

His laughter surrounded her like mist. "I swear it on my life."

"I need," she tried to say, but her throat closed up. "Cole, this is hard."

"Telling me what you want? Or my dick? Because I promise you—"

She burst into laughter.

"Let's take some pressure off," he purred. "Why don't I tell you what I want to do to you instead?"

Silently, her lips pinned between her teeth, she nodded.

"First, I'd graze my teeth over your nipples one at a time, then I'd lick them, then suck them one last time, leaving them wet and hard and greedy for more while I trailed kisses down your body. Would that feel good?"

"Yes," she said, closing her eyes against the ghost-like sensation of his mouth on her skin, her nipples so hard now they hurt.

"Then I'd settle between your legs, slide my hands up your thighs, my fingers under the hem of your shorts."

"Yes," she said again, raising her heavy lids.

"Place your hand on your thigh, Mira."

Like he'd attached strings to them, her arms and hands and fingers obeyed.

"Show me. Let me see."

Lowering the phone, she aimed her camera at the spot where she toyed with the hem of her shorts.

When he said, "Perfect. So perfect," the praise made her shiver. "Slide your fingers higher for me. Pull those sexy pink shorts to the side. Let me see."

Curling her fingers under the terry cloth fabric, she did as asked.

"Are you as wet as you look?" His voice caressed her skin, a feather brushing over the most sensitive parts of her. "Are you slippery?"

"I...don't know," she told him, her core going molten, her heart thundering. "Do you want me to check?"

He made a pained noise, and when she looked back up at her phone, he wasn't looking at her, not at her eyes anyway. With his gaze locked between her thighs, he said, "Pull your underwear out of the way, sugar. I have to see you. Please. *Please*, Mira."

It was that second *please* that undid her, the needy rasp across the line. Sliding her finger beneath the elastic of her underwear, she pulled it to the side, exposing herself fully to him.

"So pretty," he said, his pupils blown. "So pink and swollen and wet. I want to taste it."

Desire shuddered through her. "Tell me what to do."

"Take off your shorts and your underwear. I need to see everything."

Lifting her hips, she pushed her shorts and undies down her legs, letting them slide from her feet to the floor. When she positioned the phone between her legs again, when he said, "Closer, Mira," it felt almost obscene, watching his tongue sneak out to wet his lips, seeing what he saw in the corner of her screen, seeing herself spread out for him, hearing someone who sounded like her ask, "What should I do next?"

"Touch yourself. Touch yourself and pretend it's me. My fingers. My mouth." He hummed deep in his throat. "Show me how you like it."

She hadn't been this wet in literal decades, her fingers sliding between her lips, her head landing on the wall behind her with a soft thud when the slippery tip of her middle finger reached her clit.

"Is that how you like it?" he asked when she started stroking herself lightly, drawing tiny circles. "Slow and sweet? Or do you like it faster? Harder?"

She wasn't going to survive this. She was going to come so fast and so thoroughly she'd simply cease to be, drifting through the formless void forever. But it was too late to turn back now. "Faster. I like it faster."

"That's what I thought. Don't hold back, Mira." While her circling gained speed, while she added the pressure of a second fingertip, he said, "Imagine my mouth is on you now. Imagine I'm licking you, flicking my tongue over you, grazing your clit so gently with my teeth."

All light in her room narrowed to a pinpoint, every sound except his voice sucked into the vacuum of sensation as pleasure built at the base of her spine, spreading out through her stomach, curling her toes.

"I'm going faster now," he said, and her fingers responded, moving swiftly, feverishly, sacrificing rhythm for speed. "I'm swirling, sucking, sliding a finger inside—"

Catching her cries in her throat, she only allowed herself a quiet, strangled moan as her body tensed, ecstasy blazing through her veins, pleasure shattering her into a million pieces, each one flying away before floating slowly to the ground like the apple blossoms off the trees after the storm rolled through.

"So good," he said from somewhere in the distance. "So perfect." And then, sharply, "Oh, you have *got* to be kidding me."

Her eyes popped open. "What?" She raised her phone to her face, suddenly acutely aware of her nakedness.

"Madigan's calling on the other line."

"Right now?" she blurted out, struggling to regain control over her legs, her arms, her hands, yanking the straps of her tank top up as quickly as she could, like Madigan was somehow about to join their FaceTime sex call. "Can you call him back later?"

"I would. I absolutely would. But he almost never calls me unless it's important. Shit, he's calling again."

Despite the pleasure still melting her muscles and making her thoughts mushy, she said, "But it's your turn."

He laughed, but it was more like a groan. "I'm so sorry, Mira. But I should really take this. Believe me, I don't want to. Missing out on aftercare so I can talk to my best friend with a raging hard-on was definitely not on my agenda today."

Now she was laughing too. "Call me after?"

"Count on it."

"Wait," she said before he ended the call. "Happy birthday."

"Best present I ever got," he said, and then he winked. "And I don't mean the tarts."

When he ended the call, she slid her curtain open an inch, letting the sun shine on her skin. Her body was warm, her core pulsing, her heart soaring. But little by little, second by second, she and her heart came back down to earth, gravity returning, doubling, tripling.

It was too quiet. It was too quiet because Cole was gone. Because he'd never really been there at all. She was still alone, and as much as she wanted to convince herself the sudden, oppressive silence closing in all around her was tolerable, no big deal, completely fine, she couldn't. Because it wasn't fine. *She* wasn't fine.

Was this where they were heading? Was this what a long-distance romantic relationship would be like with him? FaceTime orgasms followed by missing him so much it caved her chest in, crushing everything vital beneath it? Would it be worth it? Would it be enough?

As a fluffy white cloud moved overhead, passing in front of the sun, her shoulders sank, because she didn't have an answer.

CHAPTER TWENTY-ONE

COLE

Cole was beside himself, inconsolable, not only because he'd just watched Mira come for the first time, but because her pleasure at her own fingers instead of his had opened a gaping hole in his chest he had no idea how to describe, let alone how to fill.

"Hey, Mad." It was miraculous, but he sounded almost normal, not at all like a man who'd just been completely and utterly destroyed by a muffled cry.

"Cole." Madigan's uncharacteristically tense voice was a bucket of ice water over Cole's head, and his pants. "Have a minute?"

"What's wrong?" He stood from his chair. "Is it Ashley? Davis?"

"No, no. They're fine. Everyone is fine."

"You don't sound fine, Mad. What's going on?"

He sighed, and Cole would have bet every penny he owned that he was running his knuckles through his beard. "You know how Ashley and I are about to go on our honeymoon?"

"Yeah," Cole said. "In a couple of days, right?"

"That was the plan. But now it looks like we might not be able to go at all."

"What? Why?"

Mad sighed again, even deeper. "The entire time I've owned Little Timber, I haven't spent more than a few days away at once. The only reason I thought we could take three weeks off was because Brian agreed to come back to Red Falls while we were gone to look after the home for me. But he just called."

It was strange, the buzzing sensation building beneath Cole's sternum. "Okay."

"His horse threw him this morning, and he broke his hip. He's in the hospital now having surgery. I don't have anyone else to watch over the guys. Nobody else I trust. So I don't think we can go."

"Oh, man."

"I've been trying to stay calm and positive for Ashley, but I need to let somebody know how absolutely devastated I am. I hate to admit it, but I'm so burnt out. So is Ashley. And this trip was supposed to be our time to reset, to find enthusiasm for our jobs again, to recharge. I hadn't realized how much I'd needed that time until I found out I couldn't have it anymore."

The buzzing grew, spreading until it tingled over his shoulders, down his arms, arcing into his "lightning fingers," he said out loud.

"What fingers?" Mad asked.

Thinking so hard on the fly that reason had no chance of catching up, Cole said, "What if someone else could watch Little Timber for you while you were gone?"

"Who? There's nobody else," Madigan said. "Clay's unavailable. I even called Huge Harvey, but he's too busy with his dogs."

Sure, he didn't know the first thing about working with recovering addicts and alcoholics. And if someone asked him what Madigan did every day, what he'd be expected to do, his blank stare would be heard around the world. But he had a friend who needed his help, an absurdly flexible lifestyle, and a heart beating out one word over and over and over: Mira, Mira, Mira. "What about"—he cleared his throat, tugged at his shirt collar—"me?"

"You?" There was no trace of the outright shock Cole expected, which was encouraging. "You'd...be able to?"

"It's only for a few weeks, right?" Cole scratched his head. "Benji can hold Trax down. And Ruby and Becks are doing great these days. I'm definitely available. Unless you don't think I have enough experience—"

"You'll be perfect," Madigan cut in, excitement and relief kicking his deep voice up a register. "You're funny, a great listener, and the guys already love you. Are you serious? You'd really do this for us?"

On his right shoulder, the reasonable, responsible Cole whispered that now would be an excellent time to come clean and confess that while he was thrilled to help Mad and Ashley out so they could get the break they needed, he was entire fucking galaxies more jacked to have a legitimate reason to see Mira again. But the louder—and much hornier—Cole on his left shoulder convinced him it wasn't necessary. "I'd be honored. You two deserve a honeymoon, and I've got the time." *And I get to see Mira. I get to see and touch and hold Mira.* Even if it was only for a few weeks, he'd take it. He'd take whatever he could get. "I'll be there as soon as I can."

WALKING THROUGH HIS DIM, quiet house, Cole made his way down the hall to the nursery. He tapped his fingertips on the door, then pushed it open a crack, finding Becks in the glider nursing Ruby in her arms.

"Can I come in?"

"Sure, Dad." Sensing something in his expression—excitement, fear, joy, sadness to be leaving them...so many fighting for supremacy he couldn't begin to guess—she frowned up at him. "What's up?"

Lowering himself to the floor, leaning back to rest against the crib, he reached out and rubbed Ruby's tiny foot. "Something's come up. I have to leave for a few weeks."

"Where are you going?" She kept her voice level for Ruby's sake, but he still heard the concern in it.

"Madigan and Ashley need someone to watch Little Timber while they're on their honeymoon. I offered to help them out."

"You're going back to Red Falls? Wait"—her head tilted—"isn't that where your baker lives?"

Since she already had him pegged, he didn't bother trying to deny it. "Yep."

One corner of her mouth hitched, followed quickly by the other. "What a coincidence."

"Mm-hmm," he murmured.

"What amazing luck."

He pressed his lips tight. "Sure is."

"Some might even call it serendipity."

"You done?"

"Yeah," she said, nudging his knee with her toes. "I'm done."

"I feel bad leaving you two." He curled his fingers around Ruby's leg. "She'll be twice this big when I get back."

When Ruby unlatched, Becks passed him the baby so she could pull up her shirt and zip up her hoodie.

"Will you be okay here alone?" Cole asked, reaching into the basket beside the glider for a burp cloth, throwing it over his shoulder.

"Yes," Becks said firmly. "We will be fine. Josh has been begging to come by more lately anyway. And I think I might actually be ready to let him. Don't worry about us for a second."

"And there's always Nancy," he suggested while patting Ruby's back.

Becks's scowl spoke volumes. "That's the nuclear option."

"But it's still an option."

"Dad?"

"Yeah, honey?" Ruby's head fell heavily on his shoulder, her mouth open into a tiny *o* as the milk coma took her out.

"I know you don't talk about her, your baker, your Mira."

My Mira, he thought, that buzzing in his chest returning, intensifying.

"But ever since you got back from Montana, you seem so much happier." Leaning forward, she squeezed his fingers. "I just want you to be happy. Whatever that looks like for you, okay?"

He wasn't entirely sure what she meant by that, but the mist blurring his vision kept him from asking. One more earnest word, and he'd need to take a box of Kleenex with him on the road. "Thanks, Becks."

"When do you leave?"

"I'm packing now. I'll probably start driving tonight, stop somewhere along the way. Madigan needs a day or two to show me the ropes before they fly out."

Taking Ruby back into her arms, then placing her in her crib, Becks kissed her fingertips and pressed them gently to her daughter's forehead. She turned to Cole, offered him a hand to help him to his feet, and threw her arms around him. "We'll miss you," she said, then added, "But not that much."

With a watery laugh, he squeezed her back. "Noted."

"I mean we'll survive. This is a really great thing you're doing. I'm excited for you."

"Yeah, it'll be nice to help Madigan. He's always helping everyone else all the time, and he deserves a break."

Pulling back, she smiled up at him, and said, "I wasn't talking about Madigan."

CHAPTER TWENTY-TWO

MIRA

Taking advantage of the quiet Sunday-morning calm, Mira tapped a green colored pencil against her lips, frowning at the veiny leaves she'd finished outlining around the base of a four-tiered cake. The wedding cakes in her sketchpad were only for fun, possible ideas for the future, except for this one, which was destined for the trash can. Her head wasn't in it, too filled with Cole's night-dark eyes devouring her body, his low voice rumbling over her skin.

It had been hard, coming to terms with her loneliness after he'd said goodbye yesterday, but not masturbating to the memory of him before she'd fallen asleep—and then again when she'd woken up— had been even harder. She still wasn't sure what they were doing, what she could handle, but she couldn't deny the way she wanted him, so badly she wondered if she'd need to come again to get any real work done today.

Her phone buzzed, the devil she'd just imagined pleasuring herself to popping on her screen. Setting her pencil down, she stole a moment to enjoy his caller ID pic, his sun-kissed cheeks, the sparkling blue water behind him, the stark white of his sail. But after the third ring, she took the call.

"Mira Harlow," she said, "owner of Glazed and Confused and recent haver of spectacular FaceTime orgasm. How can I help you?"

His laughter was a soft breeze, tickling her neck. "Morning, sugar. How are you today?"

"I'm good."

"What are you up to?"

"Hanging out, sketching, daydreaming." About cakes. About him. About both at once, smearing frosting over every inch of his naked body. She was in so much trouble.

"Sounds perfect."

Walking out into the bakery, she put the phone on speaker, set it on the counter, and started looking through her orders for next week. "How are you?"

"I am fantastic. You'll never believe what just happened to me."

"Did it involve a sleeve of beef?"

This laugh was much louder. "That is actually really, really funny."

Leaving herself a note to order more cherries, she said, "Well, are you going to tell me?"

"I will, but first, when's the last time anyone told you how beautiful you are?"

Yep. She was definitely going to have to masturbate again. "You. Yesterday."

"Are you blushing?"

"No," she lied, placing a hand over her flushed cheek.

"You are. I can tell."

"You can not."

"Can too."

"How?"

"I can hear it in your voice," he told her. "I can almost see it. That pink cheek you're trying to hide behind your fingers. And I love it when you wear your hair up like that."

Her hand floated up to touch her high pony. "My hair? How—"

"I remember wrapping my hand around that ponytail once. And I like that sweatshirt too."

She looked down at her favorite gray sweatshirt.

"You were wearing it the last time I saw you."

Her heart reeled back, then launched itself into her throat. "Cole?"

"Mira?"

"How do you know what I'm wearing?"

There was a smile in his voice when he said, "Magic."

She glanced around the bakery, like he might be hiding behind the hot cross buns. "What's going on? Are you..." Leaning across the counter to look out through the windows, she stumbled sideways, the planet shifting on its axis. "Oh my god."

"Hey, sugar." He waved once, smirking at her, existing ten feet away from where she stood. He was here. He was *here*, leaning against his Volvo, his eyes hidden behind his sunglasses, his legs crossed at his ankles.

She couldn't speak. She couldn't move. She could barely breathe.

With his phone still pressed to his ear, he stepped up to her door. When he slid his sunglasses into his hair, his lips curving into a full, unguarded, life-altering smile, her hand flew up to cover her mouth.

"Can I come in? The sign says CLOSED."

She only stared at him, unblinking, her eyes stinging.

"Mira?"

Lowering her hand, she rasped, "How?" every molecule of air rushing out of her lungs at once.

"Let me in." He placed his palm flat on the glass. "Please."

Evidently, please actually was the magic word, because like a spell had been broken, she lurched to life, rounding the counter and sprinting for the door. It was locked, and she fumbled the bolt, trying to turn it the wrong way at first before finally sliding it free. She yanked the door open, the poor bell flying off its hinges again, and then she was in his arms.

He was in her bakery, in her town, and she was in his arms.

She took his face between her hands, his soft stubble tickling her palms, the heat of his skin and firmness of his bones almost convincing her she wasn't dreaming. "How are you here?"

While his gaze searched her face, his hands surveyed her body, sliding over her hips, pressing, squeezing, like he was making sure she was real too. "It can wait," he ground out a split second before he cupped her neck, brought his lips to hers, and kissed her.

She thought she'd been so careful, that she'd meticulously committed the strength of his lips, the soft slide of his tongue, his minty taste to memory, but the Cole in her mind was in shades of gray compared to the technicolor Cole in her arms.

Backing her up step by step, he took her ass in both hands and hauled her up onto the counter, breaking their kiss only long enough to slur, "Madigan needs someone to watch Little Timber while they're on their honeymoon," so fast she barely understood a single word. And then he was kissing her again, and it didn't matter what he'd said. It only mattered that he was warm and solid and *here*.

Wrapping her legs around his waist, she slid her fingers into his hair, knocking his sunglasses off his head. When they fell to the floor with a *clack*, they looked down at his glasses curling around her broken bell, looked back at each other, and then they smiled the kind of smiles reserved for children opening birthday presents, skydivers jumping out of airplanes, hikers summiting Everest.

Coming reluctantly to her senses, she said, "Did you say you'll be watching over Little Timber?"

He nodded. "It seemed like a good idea when I offered, but now I think I might be pretty screwed."

Your lips to god's ears, she muttered inwardly.

"I'm not Madigan," he continued while she hooked her heels behind his hips, wondering what it would feel like to run her tongue along his collarbone, over the ridges of his throat. "I have no idea what I'm doing. The men will probably eat me alive. But I had to come." He cupped her cheek. "I had to see you again."

"You'll be amazing," she told him, not entirely sure what they were talking about anymore, barely caring when he pulled her hips forward, his hard length pressing into her through her thin leggings.

"Is anyone home?" he asked, kissing her shoulder, her neck, his hand sneaking under the hem of her sweatshirt.

While his fingertips slid up her side, she struggled to say, "Ian's... playing at church. Mom's at...water aerobics," dazed by the softness of his lips, the hardness of everything else. "Gone for a little more than...an hour."

He pulled back, and when his thumb grazed the underside of her breast, when he said, "I can work with that," she nearly lost consciousness. "Is there somewhere we can go?" He angled his head toward the very large, very see-through windows. "To talk?"

"So *that's* what they call fucking in your fancy big city."

"Please," he scoffed, pulling her off the counter while she clung to him. "Everyone knows 'talk' means oral. Now point me to your room so I can *talk* to you until you forget your name."

"This door," she said, sucking on his earlobe while he pushed her door open.

"You sure you want to do this?" He kicked the door closed behind them, pushing the lock button. "We really could just talk."

He set her feet on the ground, and she said, "I'm sure. Are you sure?"

"Never been surer of anything."

Grateful that yesterday Mira had cleared her clothes and shoes from her floor, she kicked off her flats, grasped the collar of his soft, plaid shirt in both hands, and froze. "Cole?" she said, staring at his chest. "Are these...pearl snaps?"

His smirk was the single sexiest thing she'd ever seen in her entire life. "Montana enough for you?"

Biting her lip, about to make all her secret cowboy fantasies come true, she popped his first snap, and then his second, then the rest all at once.

"Nice technique," he said while she slid his shirt off his shoulders, letting it fall to the floor, letting her gaze trace the soft swirls of silver blond hair between his pecs, down the line of his stomach, leading into his boxers.

"I've always wanted to do that." When she reached for his pants, fumbling for his button, he covered her hands with his, stilling them.

"Can we slow down for a second? Only one," he promised when she actually whimpered. "I just want to look at you."

Raising her head, she met the rich depth of his eyes and knew he was right. She needed to look at him too, feel him, breathe in the sun-warmed scent of him and hold it in her lungs.

After a moment, he dropped his forehead to hers. "I've missed you."

"How long?" she asked, running her hands over his shoulders. "How long do I have you for?"

"Three weeks."

"Three weeks," she echoed. It was longer than she'd let herself hope for, but she knew how time worked, how it moved, how three weeks could feel more like three days.

Sinking to his knees, he gazed up at her through his long lashes. "But right now, we only have an hour."

She pulled her sweatshirt over her head and hurled it behind her where it landed...somewhere. Glancing down, relief raced through her. It wasn't her best bra, but at least it wasn't neon yellow.

But when he hooked his fingers into the waistband of her leggings and said, "Take that off too," the bra could have been covered in bright purple starfish and she wouldn't have cared as it flew through the air to join her sweatshirt somewhere in the void. And like his existence here in her room hung in the balance, like if she looked away for a single moment, he'd vanish, she watched him intently as he slid her leggings down her thighs.

"I still can't believe you're here," she told him, brushing his hair off his forehead with her fingertips while he knelt in front of her in faded jeans and nothing else, about to strip her naked, about to take off her—"Oh, fuck," she gasped when he skipped a step, pressing his open mouth over her through the thin cotton of her underwear. His mouth was hot, his tongue wet, his finger sneaking under elastic, sliding through her, then inside her with slippery ease.

She grasped his head, holding him close while fighting to stay upright on trembling legs. He was good, so good, *too* good while a second finger joined the first, his tongue dragging over her clit, soaking her underwear, blurring her vision. Sliding his fingers back out, he used them to pull her underwear to the side. "Hmm," he murmured appreciatively. "It's even prettier in person."

"Cole," she gasped when he licked her without the fabric barrier between them, when he sucked her, grazed his teeth over her just like he'd said he would yesterday, like she'd fantasized about him doing this morning. She was so close, already hovering on the edge of release, pain and pleasure building, swirling. "You have to stop."

"I do?" He looked up, his mouth still hovering over her wet, sensitive skin as she watched his tongue slide over her one last time with excruciating slowness.

"I usually only come once," she said, pushing his head away before pushing her underwear down her legs and kicking them off. "I want you inside me when I do. I want you to feel it."

Rising to his feet, he said, "That might be the sweetest thing anyone has ever said to me," and they laughed. Until she reached for the button of his jeans again, releasing it and his zipper enough to slide her hand inside. Then he wasn't laughing anymore.

He was hard as steel under her fingers, his crown round and slippery and perfect. She tried to push his jeans down with her other hand, but he said, "Wait a sec." Reaching into his back pocket, he pulled out a shiny foil square and twirled it in his fingers.

"You had a condom in your back pocket?"

The left side of his mouth quirked, his left shoulder rising and falling at the same time. "Hope springs eternal."

Grabbing his face, she kissed him fiercely, then said, "Come on, Cole. We both know I'm a sure thing."

Thank god putting a condom on was like riding a bike, because it had been a minute. But after dropping to her knees, she rolled it over him like a pro. When she gazed back up at him, desire, lust, need, all of it threatened to ruin her life, because his head was thrown back, his throat long, abs tight, his hands fisting in her hair while she cupped him gently. Then she stood, spun him toward her bed, and pushed him down until he sat on the edge. Climbing up with him, she straddled him, needing him with such raw intensity it shuddered through her bones.

"Are you okay?" he asked, his hand sliding up her side. "You're shaking."

"I'm okay." Arching her back when he cupped her breast, his thumb brushing over her peaked nipple, she didn't say it, she tried not to even think it, but the thought came anyway: *I'm just happy.*

With her eyes locked on his, her heart caged mid-beat, she reached between them, held him steady, and sank slowly onto him, savoring every hard inch, cherishing the warmth of his body, the grip of his hands on her hips, the rumble of his low groan as he filled her. When she finally took him in fully, coming to rest in his lap, they shared a breath, shuddering and deep.

Wrapping his arms around her, he whispered, "This feels good," his lips brushing over her ear, his hand sliding up her back to cradle her neck. "It feels right."

Remembering those words he'd said to her while they'd danced at Jimmy's, she let her smile hover above his skin before dropping her lips to his shoulder. She could have stayed that way forever, holding him while his hands roamed over her back, her thighs, while he told her how good she felt, that he'd dreamt of having her this way, being inside her like this. But they didn't have forever. They didn't even have an hour anymore.

The realization must have hit him too, because as his mouth slid along her neck, his hands slid over her ass, grasping, holding her steady while his hips rolled. Then he kissed her, his tongue teasing hers while he swallowed her needy noises.

The sex was unhurried, languid, slow as dripping honey, the kind of sex that felt amazing, even though it rarely got her there. But there was something about the way his hands moved to her hips, the way his fingers held her down while he thrust up into her, his perfect, unchanging rhythm while he kissed her lips, her neck, scraping his teeth over her shoulder, that brought her to the edge again so quickly she had to tell him, "I'm close." When he leaned back to cup her breast, guiding her nipple toward his mouth, she warned, "Cole, I'm really close."

"Do you want me to slow down?" he asked while he thrust into her again. "Or do you want to come now?"

The question, the way his tongue swirled around her nipple after he'd asked it, the way he covered her tight peak with his mouth and sucked, didn't help her situation one bit. "I'm...not sure I have a choice."

"Mira?" he asked, a little demanding while his teeth grazed the swell of her breast.

"Now," she said. "Now, please."

His hand slipped between their bodies, his thumb finding her clit, pressing down, and she stifled her moan into the soft heat of his shoulder. But it wasn't until his thumb started moving, finding its own rhythm, circling faster and faster, that her vision went hazy, pleasure pulling tight in her belly, pooling between her legs, sparking up the length of her spine until all she saw was light.

He didn't say a word, only held her tighter, his thumb slowing while she collapsed against him, her body slack and pulsing from the intensity of her climax. Caressing her back in soothing strokes, he let her savor every moment of ecstasy without chasing his own.

"Christ," she breathed against his neck after the aftershocks of her orgasm finally faded. Leaning back, her vision focusing on him little by little, she noticed his clenched jaw, his furrowed brow, his closed eyes.

"Cole, I'm good," she told him, kissing the furrow smooth. "I'm so good. It's your turn now—"

Before she knew what was up or down, she was on her back, with Cole looming above her. Slipping a hand under her knee, he bent her leg up and slid into her again, so slowly she had to bite her cheek against the acutely sensitive agony of it.

He bent to kiss her, his tongue caressing hers while his hips found that same honey-slow rhythm that made her eyelids sink. But when he broke the kiss, she forced her eyes open, fighting the current of sensation tugging her under, making herself pay attention, making herself focus on the band of golden caramel orbiting his pupils, not letting herself miss the way he stared at her, like he was paying attention too.

His breathing changed first, his exhales catching in soft, delicious grunts. Then his jaw clenched, his forehead creasing again as his chin dipped toward his chest. When she slid her hands down his hips, over his ass, when he changed his angle and she moaned, it snapped whatever leash he'd been keeping on himself. Hoisting her leg higher, he snapped his hips, moving faster, harder, driving into her so deeply she had to reach back and push against her headboard so Joe Strummer wouldn't get banged off the wall.

There had been thoughts in her head at one point, about her mom, Ian, the man on top of her and what it meant that he was here. Too many thoughts, all of them too loud, but she had no idea where they'd gone. Right now, she was blank, empty, only one thing filling her. Him.

Or maybe there was something else there too, an ache swirling low in her core, tingling, glowing like embers in a fire, making her eyes close, her toes curl more tightly with every thrust—

The groan vibrating through him yanked her back from the second-orgasm ledge as he tensed, jerked, and then collapsed into her arms. While his cock pulsed inside her—and even that felt phenomenal—she stared up at the ceiling, wondering what the hell just happened, or almost just happened.

"Mira," he whispered between her breasts while her thoughts spiraled. "That was amazing."

"Mm-hmm," she murmured, patting his back weakly, her head spinning, heart pounding. Maybe it was a fluke, a lucky few thrusts, a one-off response to the emotions of the moment, a weird menopausal hormone spike. It wasn't that Cole touched her the way she liked to be touched, kissed her the way she wanted to be kissed, worked her over exactly the way she needed with his perfectly hard, perfectly round, perfectly thick, "Beef sleeve!"

"What?"

"Oh...my...god," she said as laughter stole her breath. "I think I just got the joke."

His head raised. "What joke?"

"When I asked you about the sleeve of beef. You said it was really, really funny. Because you knew—"

"I'd hoped," he corrected. "I only hoped I'd be giving you my—"

"Meat?"

They were both laughing now, and it was fine. Everything was fine. She was fine. He was fine. The sex had been...fine. And when these three weeks were over, when he had to leave her again, she would be fine then too. She had no other choice.

CHAPTER TWENTY-THREE

COLE

Swiping his sunglasses up off her floor, he hooked them into his shirt collar before picking up her bell. Dinging it back and forth, he asked, "Do you want my help hanging this back up?"

Propping her elbows on the counter, she cupped her face in her hands and shook her head. "I got it."

He sauntered toward her, and when she reached for him, grabbing his shirt in both hands, he said, "This feels familiar," smirking for the split second she gave him before her lips met his.

"What the what?"

Wheeling around, Cole met the measured, unimpressed stare of the lanky teenage boy with big curly hair who'd just walked through the door.

"No bell," Mira muttered behind him, then louder, "Ian, this is Cole—"

"Sanderson," Ian said. When the kid's eyes narrowed, he looked so much like Mira, Cole couldn't help but smile, which only made Ian squint harder. "You're back in town."

Feeling more than a little like he was the teenager trying to win the approval of a parent in this situation, Cole held out his hand and said, "Nice to meet you, man. Your mom tells me you can really play."

Ian's handshake, Cole thought, could use some work. "I'm okay, I guess."

"Cool, cool."

Ian responded with a microscopic shrug.

"Super cool," Cole added...for some unknowable reason, and the exchange was so awkward he couldn't blame Mira for snorting.

"Cole's helping Madigan out at Little Timber while he and Ashley are on their honeymoon," she explained. "He'll be here for a few weeks."

Shifting his gaze between them—no doubt sensing that Cole had just done very inappropriate things to his mother—Ian said, "'Kay."

Taking mercy on all three of them at this point, Cole turned to Mira, slid his hands into his pockets, and said, "I guess I'd better get going."

"Oh, wait." She dove behind the counter, popping back up with a chocolate chip cookie in her hand. "One for the road?"

He cocked a brow. "The perks keep coming."

With a groan, followed by an uncanny approximation of a cat throwing up, Ian said, "I'm going upstairs." And then he was gone, his rangy legs taking him far away from his mom and the weird stranger flirting with her in their bakery. It struck Cole then, with a cookie in his hand and a sharp twinge in his heart, that he didn't necessarily want to be a stranger here.

After watching Ian disappear up the stairs, Mira said, "You're probably going to be pretty busy up at Bluebird?"

It was both a statement and a question, not that Cole had an answer. "Maybe. Probably." When he'd thought about it on the drive over, he'd envisioned a camp counselor-type situation. Like he'd be Bill Murray from *Meatballs*, cracking jokes and rousing the men with inspirational speeches. *It just doesn't matter!* and all that. He was also one hundred percent sure that assessment was cataclysmically naïve. "I don't know if I'll have to stay up there all the time or not. I'm going over all the details with Mad as soon as I leave here."

"I make deliveries to Bluebird sometimes," she told him. "I've been wanting to go more often, show my support for Little Timber in a more *meaningful* way."

"I see." He leaned against the counter. "Can I place special orders?"

"Of course," she replied. "Do you want my private menu? It's pretty exclusive."

"Not something you give out to every Tom, Dick, and Harry?"

"Certainly not any Dick."

When she blushed, he brushed his fingers over her cheek and said, "Mira Pink. My favorite color."

Her blush deepened.

"I'll call you later," he said, pulling his sunglasses out of his shirt and sliding them on.

"You'd better."

He leaned in to kiss her cheek, then laughed deep in his throat when she grasped his face and corrected his course, taking his mouth instead.

Every time Cole pulled into Bluebird's parking lot, the mountain looked a little different. Today, aside from the snow still clinging to its peak, it was covered in bright, velvety green grass. When he stepped out of his car, he was so taken by the view he almost missed the gigantic dog barreling toward him.

"Ugh, Murph," he grunted, widening his stance so Murphy didn't knock him onto his ass. "Good to see you too," he managed while the dog attacked his face with big, fat licks.

"Murphy, get down! Cole, I'm so sorry. Murphy! Down!"

"It's all good, Ashley," Cole said, scratching the dog's neck, trying to avoid his slobbery jowls because *damn* the dog had some jowls, and some slobber.

"Come!"

Even though both Cole's and the dog's heads whipped around at Madigan's command, only Murphy dropped to all fours and trotted up to Mad's side.

"Why does he only listen to you?" Ashley asked, frowning up at Madigan, who only shrugged, then kissed her head. And it was apparently answer enough, because she stepped away from her husband to wrap Cole in a hug. "I can't believe you're doing this for us," she said. "Thank you. Thank you. Thank you."

"It's nothing, honestly. I'm just happy to be here." As soon as the words left Cole's lips, Madigan crossed his arms, his head tilting, eyes narrowing the same way Ian's had, making Cole wonder if he had I JUST GOT LAID stamped across his forehead.

Letting him go, Ashley said, "I haven't actually taken a vacation in"—her lips twisted thoughtfully—"I can't even remember. Not since Davis was a kid."

"That's outrageous," Cole said, tapping his fingers on his thighs, his nerves suddenly jangling. "I just hope I won't fuck things up while you're gone."

Taking his turn to give Cole a hug, complete with a hearty, bordering on painful back slap, Madigan said, "You'll do great," out loud, followed by, "Did you see Mira?" in a whisper only Cole could hear. "You smell like cookies."

Shit. "Well, you smell like a ski chalet at Christmas time," Cole countered, sniffing Madigan's beard.

Mad huffed a laugh. "Fair enough." Backing away, giving Cole a tight smile, he said, "Let's get you set up. We've got a lot to go over and not a lot of time."

WHILE COLE WALKED down the path to the cabins, the resinous tang of the surrounding pines sharp in his nose, he tried to pay attention when Mad said, "I tend to keep a pretty loose schedule. But you might want to firm things up to make it easier on you."

He'd been waiting for it to hit, the reality of what he was about to take on. Now that he was here, putting one foot in front of the other with the mountain looming large in front of him, it finally arrived with the breath-stealing force of an Andre the Giant body slam. "What would be in a schedule?" he asked, stumbling over a tree root. "Like classes or something?"

"No, but a group would probably be a good idea."

Cole stopped walking, wiping his sweaty palms off on his jeans. "What's a group?"

Noticing his lack of forward progress, Madigan turned around, his brows knitting. "Are you okay?"

Trying to calm his racing heart, Cole said, "I don't think so."

Madigan's footsteps crunched over pine needles, his hand landing on Cole's shoulder. "I promise this isn't as hard as it seems. Especially since the guys are all busy cutting trails for the mountain bike course. Mostly, you'll help them organize their day, keep them on task, and listen when they have something to say. That's it."

"That's it?" Cole was dubious.

"That, and the drug tests, of course."

He groaned.

Madigan's hand squeezed. "They're only once a week now, and the guys know when to expect them. The most important thing you need to do is care, Cole. We can't fix them. We can't save them. They have to do that on their own. But we can care about them, listen to them, support them, keep them safe. Can you do that?"

Murphy trotted off ahead toward the clearing, and Cole said, "I can do that." But when he met Madigan's unyielding blue-eyed stare, he sensed that the conversation, the moment, was about to get real.

"Listen," Madigan said, "I know you might have some," he

paused for effect, "distractions while you're here. Of the cookie-scented variety."

"Mad, I—"

"I understand. Believe me, I do. I'm the last person to tell you not to do what you need to do when it comes to your personal life. But I have to know that the guys will be your top priority while I'm gone. They need stability, someone they can count on to be there when they need them, someone who puts them first." He dragged his knuckles through his beard. "I know this is asking a lot from you, and if it seems like it's too much, Ashley and I can adjust. Iceland isn't going anywhere."

"Well, it's pretty much made of volcanoes. So you never know."

"I'm serious," Madigan said. "Just say the word, and we'll cancel."

If Cole was being perfectly honest with himself, he wasn't sure he was up to the task. What he was sure of, though, was that his friend needed him, and he wasn't going to let him down. "I've got this. I won't be perfect"—he placed his hand over his heart—"but I promise to treat Little Timber like it's my own."

"You don't need to be perfect. In fact, most of these guys wouldn't trust you if you were. You only need to be consistent and genuine, and you need to know the rules."

"Rules?" Cole blinked. "What rules?"

While a slow grin slid across his face, Madigan tilted his head toward his cabin and said, "Come on and find out."

"RULE NUMBER ONE: We don't use." Leaning against the kitchen counter, Cole scanned the Little Timber House Rules written in black Sharpie on white poster board hanging on the bathroom door of Madigan's old cabin. "That one makes sense, obviously. But no swearing? Seriously?"

"Rule number two is surprisingly important," Madigan said,

counting the folded towels in the bathroom closet. "With a group of guys who are generally unskilled at getting their point across, communication degrades to nothing but *fucks* without it."

"That should have been our band name. Nothing But Fucks."

Madigan snorted.

"Rule number five: We don't have guests or overnight visitors without approval." Tapping his fingers on the counter, Cole said, "I bet that one leads to some awkward conversations."

"You have no idea."

He could, though, have an idea. "What do I do if one of the guys wants a visitor?"

Opening and closing the top dresser drawer, Madigan said, "I have a list of approved visitors. If someone isn't on the list, call me. I'll have my phone with me at all times. But as long as they're on the list, they're good."

After reading rule number eleven—We don't break our host's stuff—Cole pushed himself off the counter. "What happens if they break a rule? Is there a punishment? I'm not, like, a disciplinarian." A punk to his core, Cole only had one rule in his house: Always question authority. He'd even had an agreement with Becks when she was growing up that he couldn't put her in timeout or ground her unless he was able to convince her *why* her actions deserved the punishment. It wasn't an easy way to parent, but Becks got the lesson to never follow anyone blindly. And she'd learned to argue like a courtroom lawyer.

Madigan slid the middle drawer closed. "If anyone breaks the first rule, call me immediately. For the other rules, some repercussions are necessary. Otherwise, chaos reigns. But you can get creative with it. I've made them find a poem that resonates with them and read it out loud in group. Or make friendship bracelets for the rest of the men; that's a fun one. And if all else fails, there's always bathroom duty."

Cole shuddered bodily, the idea of making grown men scrub

bathroom floors because they said the word *fuck* offending him deeply and on multiple levels.

Ignoring his appalled expression, Madigan opened the bottom dresser drawer and said, "The new guy, Thom, is on laundry shift this month, so he'll take your clothes to the lodge once a week. But you've got plenty of towels, and Ashley put a second set of sheets in this drawer."

"I can do my own laundry, Mad."

"Up to you. But don't make the mistake of discounting how important it is for these guys to have duties and expectations. A sense of purpose can be hard to come by, and boredom is not our friend."

"That makes sense."

"So." Turning to face him, Mad stood to his full height, those three extra inches he had on Cole feeling more like a solid foot. "What questions do you have?"

What questions *didn't* he have? "Davis and Maude Alice will be here the whole time, right?"

Madigan nodded. "Mace left for summer camp last week, and Shannon's taking some time off, but Davis and Maude Alice are here. Davis is out mountain biking right now, otherwise I'm sure she'd be chatting you up already. Maude Alice can help you with the home, but Davis can't. She's not on the contract and hasn't signed the confidentiality agreement. And"—he ran a hand through his hair—"it's complicated, because of Kev. Speaking of which, I don't know what it is yet, but I think something's going on with them."

"Things seemed...strained between them at your wedding," Cole admitted.

Mad nodded. "It all started when Clay left. Clay and Kev were roommates. They were close, and I think Kev relied on Clay as his emotional support more than he'd realized. He's been quieter, more withdrawn since Clay moved back home. Whenever I ask him how he's doing, he says he's fine, but I don't know. I'm sure whatever's going on with him and Davis will work itself out one way or another.

But relationships can be tough on addicts, especially for someone like Kev."

When Madigan sat on the edge of the bed, Cole sat beside him.

"Kev has not had an easy life," Madigan continued. "His history, his parents..." He shook his head. "But he's always happy, or at least he's trying very hard to *look* like he's always happy. Sometimes, with guys like Kev, they end up doing and saying whatever they think everyone around them wants them to do or say so they'll stay under the radar. Sometimes, it's what they did so they could use without anyone catching on to them. Sometimes, it's how they learned to survive in bad homes. Either way, I'm worried there's something beneath the surface that Kev hasn't dealt with yet, and by smiling and laughing and pleasing everyone around him, he's convincing us not to look too hard for it."

In some deep, barely conscious way, Cole understood that more than he wanted to.

"Hopefully I'm wrong," Mad said. "But I worry. It's hard to stay clean when an addict has feelings they're refusing to feel. The emotions, the memories, they tend to find a way out, and when they do, no matter how many coping mechanisms I might teach these guys, I can't compete with the way drugs erase"—he waved a hand through the air—"everything. I've never been sure what kind of relationship Kev and Davis have, whether it's romantic or they're only close friends. I think it's possible they aren't sure either. But if they're getting serious, if she's making him feel things—"

"He might be pulling away, just so he doesn't have to."

Mad nodded. "I've tried to talk to him about it, but he's like Fort Knox. And he refuses to try therapy because he insists there's nothing wrong."

Remembering his attempts to talk to Davis at the wedding, Cole thought Kev wasn't the only one of them locked up tight. "I'll keep an eye on him," he said, even though he wasn't entirely sure what to look for.

"I know you will." Madigan clapped a big hand over his knee.

"You know, it's hard leaving the home, but it helps knowing it's you looking after it for me."

The hand on Cole's knee turned heavy as lead, the hours and days he'd fantasized about spending with Mira vanishing, replaced by group sessions and bathroom buckets. Because this was a big deal, being here. Watching over these men was a huge deal. And he would not let them or Madigan down. "I'll do my best."

"It's all we can do." Standing from the bed, Madigan leaned back against the dresser. "And by the way," he said, his lips twitching beneath his beard, "you don't have to be on the premises twenty-four hours a day, and you don't need my permission to have overnight guests."

He really was a mind reader.

"Just make sure to let Davis and Maude Alice know if you're leaving and when you'll be back."

"Are you sure?" Cole asked, trying to hide his excitement, his odd, horny guilt. "It's not a problem if you need me to be here and only here."

"You should definitely be on-site during working hours, especially while they're on the trails. But if you tell me that you'll put the guys first, and that you'll be here for them when they need you, that's all I need to know."

Rising to his feet, Cole looked his best friend in the eye, and with every ounce of sincerity in his body, said, "You've got my word."

CHAPTER TWENTY-FOUR

COLE

"Don't forget to drink your water!" Cole called out over the droning buzz of weed whackers while wiping a veritable river of sweat off his brow. "Don't want to get dehydrated!"

As if in agreement, Murphy whined up at him before resuming his limp-tongued panting.

"Yes, Dad!" Thom called back, his grin wide and toothy.

Killing the motor on his weed whacker, Tex walked over to Cole and said, "You should probably take your own advice. You're looking a little...red."

Cole felt more than a little red. He felt like he'd spent the entire day with his face nestled in Satan's armpit. "Thanks, Tex."

"Maybe we should all take a break." Sam's not-so-subtle nod in Cole's direction made it clear who he thought actually needed the breather.

"Yeah," Kev said, taking his CUBS hat off to fluff his curly blond hair. Putting the hat back on, he tugged on the brim. "The shade's looking awfully good right about now."

"I know I could use a rest," Stanley added, pointing up at the sun. "Sure is a scorcher today."

If he wasn't so busy trying to decide if the pulse pounding in his throat or the spots swirling in front of his eyes required a 911 call, Cole might have laughed at the guys doing everything they could to keep him from croaking on his first day.

"A break sounds great," Cole said, following the guys toward a shady spot under a tall ponderosa. "I'm not used to all of this—"

"Altitude?" Sam asked.

"Sun?" Tex suggested.

"Socializing?" Thom offered.

"Work," Cole admitted before one of the guys hurt themselves trying to avoid calling him out on his sad tolerance for manual labor. As carefully as possible, he lowered himself to sit on a blanket of pine needles. "It'll probably take me a minute to adjust." *Or all the minutes.*

"No kidding." Tex fanned his face with his cowboy hat. "After the first couple days out here clearing trails, I could barely walk."

Joining Cole on the ground, Kev said, "I got so sunburned, I looked like a lobster."

"You should have seen the gnarly blister on my big toe." Without warning, Thom plopped down between Kev and Sam and yanked off his shoe and his sock. His nose crinkled while he studied the toe in question. "You can still kind of see it."

"Get your nasty as—your nasty foot away from me," Sam snapped, holding back his swear word while he plucked a dandelion head off its stem and hurled it at Thom's face. "We're trying to *keep* Cole from passing out, not give him no other choice."

Kev laughed softly to himself, his knee bouncing in its cross-legged position.

Thirstier than he'd ever been—maybe thirstier than *anyone* had ever been—Cole threw back his head and guzzled nearly every drop of his water. One by one, the guys turned to look at him with varying levels of concern.

When Sam asked, "You okay there, Boss?" Cole choked so hard water erupted out of his mouth.

"P-please," he spluttered while Tex slapped his back a little too hard, "do not call me that."

"Call you what?" Kev asked, his mouth turned down. "Boss?"

Cole shuddered. "Yeah, no. No Boss."

"What should we call you then?" asked a neck-craningly tall man with dark brown skin everyone called Ace even though his name was Frank. "Big C?"

"Sticks?" Tex suggested, explaining, "Because he's a drummer," when the other men frowned at him.

"Seattle Slim?" Sam chimed in, making Thom snort.

"Cole. Just Cole."

"Okay, Cole." Thom stared him down while putting his shoe back on. "I'm curious. What made you decide to come all the way out here to babysit a bunch of addicts?"

While the rest of the men gave him their undivided attention, Cole, suddenly much more uncomfortable than only from the impending heatstroke, said, "Madigan needed help. He's my friend. That's all there is to it." That was so *not* all there was to it, but he wasn't about to tell these relative strangers that he had a hopeless, probably ill-advised crush on the town's baker and would have done just about anything to have a reason to see her again. And now he was thinking about Mira again, missing her, wanting her, imagining her naked body sprawled out on his bed in ways he should not be imagining while he was surrounded by other people. But it couldn't be helped.

He hadn't had time to see her at all yesterday, too busy introducing himself to the men, sitting in on their morning group, walking the trails they'd be clearing with Madigan, getting a crash course on the ins and outs of running Little Timber—including the sordid details of bathroom duty.

"Yeah, but you're getting paid at least, right?" Stanley asked after using his shirt to dry his face. "For your time?"

"Paid? No. That thought never crossed my mind," Cole replied honestly.

"Wow," Kev said, his blue eyes flaring. "You're a really good friend. That's, like, so admirable." He tugged the brim of his hat down again. "I've never had a friend like that. I've definitely never *been* a friend like that."

Knowing the thought that appeared in his head—*Isn't Davis that kind of friend for you?*—should absolutely not make its way out of his mouth, Cole only said, "Thank you, Kev," even though he wanted to say so much more.

Breaking the suddenly heavy mood, Tex jumped up, settling his cowboy hat back onto his head. "We'd better get back to work if we want to make it to the stake before quitting time."

Cole held up a hand, shielding his eyes from the sun beating down over Tex's shoulder, making a mental note to wear his sunglasses tomorrow. "The stake?" he asked. "What stake?"

Pointing downhill, Tex said, "See it? Down there?"

Dread crept along Cole's spine as he followed the path of Tex's finger to a tiny red stick poking out of the ground, literal light-years away from where they were now. "That thing?"

"Yep. That's our goal for today."

While Cole bit back a groan, Sam said, "Let's get cracking," rising smoothly to his feet. "I've got a phone date with Izzy and Sara tonight."

On his first attempt to stand, something twinged in Cole's back, the sinister kind of twinge that could mean nothing, or it could mean trying to get out of bed in the morning would remind him of his own mortality. Taking mercy on him, Kev held out a hand and pulled him slowly to his feet. Once they were standing eye to eye, Kev said softly, and with a raw honesty that made Cole want to grab the kid and hug him for a solid minute, "I mean it. Madigan's lucky to have a friend like you."

Cole was chatty by nature, but he couldn't think of a single thing to say to that. Or maybe it wasn't that. Maybe it was that he couldn't think of the *right* thing to say. This moment felt like it needed a *right* thing, and he didn't have it. So he clasped Kev's shoulder and squeezed instead.

ONE HAND BRACED on his royally pissed-off lower back, the other holding his phone so he could text Mira, Cole staggered toward his cabin.

> Cole: No wonder Madigan's so stacked these days. One day in and my soft city-boy ass is broken.

He pushed through his door, making doe eyes at his shower, imagining how good the steady, hot stream would feel on his neck, back, shoulders...

> Mira: I guess I didn't think about the manual labor aspect of the job. They're clearing the mountain bike trails, right?

> Cole: Yep.

> Mira: Woof.

> Cole: You can say that again. But why did I, a fifty-four-year-old man, feel the need to try and keep up with a bunch of mostly twenty and thirty-year-olds today, you ask?

> Mira: I didn't ask, lol. But go on.

> Cole: The answer is, because just yesterday, I was one of them. In my head, anyway.

Groaning, he squeezed the boulder that had taken up residence in his left shoulder ever since he'd decided he could pull lodgepole saplings out of the ground with his bare hands like the other guys.

> Mira: Well, be careful. I happen to like your soft city-boy ass. Hmm, maybe it just needs to be rubbed. I'm pretty sure I have some Tiger Balm around here somewhere...

She was driving up tonight, bringing him a "special delivery," which, at this point, he actually hoped included Tiger Balm.

> Cole: If you find it, bring it. I can barely move. Not to be presumptuous, but you don't mind being on top, right?

> Mira: Hahahaha. Poor baby. See you soon.

CHAPTER TWENTY-FIVE

MIRA

THE DRIVE UP to Bluebird took much longer than the usual thirty minutes, her thoughts racing ahead of her while she clutched the steering wheel. Thoughts like: *Should I have worn my red under-wear? Does my breath smell okay? Why don't I have any mints? What the hell am I doing?*

Cole had only been in Red Falls for three days, and her life was already in complete upheaval. She barely functioned, focus a thing of the past. Her thoughts were consumed by the sense memory of Cole's mouth between her legs, his hand cupping her neck, their bodies entwined, skin sliding against skin. It was so bad she'd forgotten to put sugar in the cupcake batter this morning, baking two dozen bland bread balls that now RIP'd in the trash can. Everything had happened too quickly. Cole was in Seattle, then he was in her bakery, in her arms, in her bed. And then he was gone again.

If it hadn't been for the faint soreness she'd woken up to yester-day, that dull *you've finally had sex again* throb, she could have convinced herself that none of it had actually happened. The problem was, as much as she tried—and she'd tried, all day yesterday, most of the day today—she couldn't quite convince herself that doing it again was a terrible idea. She was almost there, so close to calling him and telling him they shouldn't turn the next three weeks into a secret spring fuckfest. Not only because he'd fuck and run. Not only because after all the years she'd spent searching—despite thinking she'd found it in Paul and learning the hard way that she'd been wrong—she knew she'd never find another man as great in text, wonderful on the phone, phenomenal in person, and spectacular in bed as Cole. But mainly because she still had a life to live, a son to parent, a mom to care for, a business to run, and a sinking suspicion that all those things would be substantially harder to do while she was also trying to sneak off with him like a sex-crazed teenager.

But after he'd texted her one single question this morning: *Can you get away?* all the reasons why she shouldn't hook up with him as much as possible while he was here evaporated like mist.

Pinching her cheeks in her rearview while the big wooden Blue-bird Basin sign loomed to her left, she tried to wrangle her thoughts and concerns into something coherent she could share with him. As soon as she parked her car where Cole had suggested—near the woods at the far end of the lot—dinner-plate sized dog paws slammed against her window.

"Hey, Murphy." The dog only panted at her through the glass. "Can I get out?"

Once he dropped back down to all fours, his mouth open and tongue wagging, Mira pushed her door open and climbed out, inhaling deeply when her feet hit the gravel. It always smelled amazing up at Bluebird, like the clean bite of snow or musty rain or, like today, sun-warmed pine.

After giving Murphy's head a good scratch, she walked to her passenger door and pulled out the basket of goodies she'd brought for Cole and the guys. Slinging the basket over her shoulder, she whispered, "Be strong, Mira," and started down the path leading to Cole's cabin.

"Mira?" she heard him say after she knocked on his door.

"Yep."

"Hey, sugar. It's unlocked."

The skin on the back of her neck pebbled. None of her partners had ever given her a nickname. She'd always thought she didn't inspire them. She just wasn't a sweetheart or a darling or even a honeybunch. But *sugar*... She loved it, the way it rolled off his tongue, the way it heated her cheeks, the way it made her feel sweet.

Pushing the door open, she froze in place, not prepared in any way, shape, or form for the view that greeted her.

Cole stood outside his bathroom in nothing but a towel wrapped around his waist, a smaller towel scrubbing his hair, and a smile.

"Uhhh..." She stalled out, finding it surprisingly difficult to remember the intricacies of the English language when confronted with a half-naked Cole.

Nodding at her basket, he said, "You really brought us treats?" He walked back into the bathroom, the words "You're amazing" trailing behind him, reeling her into the cabin like a lasso wrapped around her waist, a hook in her mouth.

"It's only some muffins and scones," she said, waving a dismissive hand while he did whatever he was doing in the bathroom, while she tried not to obsess over whether that towel was still slung around his hips or not. She set the basket on top of the dresser and looked around. His cabin was small but warm, cozy as a magazine cover. "Oh, and Tiger Balm."

"You brought it?"

"One does not offer to bring Tiger Balm and not bring it."

Still shirtless, still in his towel, he ducked his head out of the bathroom. "I'm not joking this time, Mira. Marry me."

She gave him a smile, but the one he gave her back was a religious experience. Angels wept, harps trilled, choirs sang, her nipples hardened.

"I meant to shower earlier, but then I ended up passing out on my bed. I'll be out in a sec. Make yourself comfortable. Did you have a good day? How was Linda's therapy session?"

This was the thing, or one of the things, that made him so unfairly irresistible. He paid attention. He remembered the days Ian had piano, when her mom had her therapy, whenever Mira had a big order she was working on or when she had to get up extra early to make sourdough. It was too much. Things could not go on like this. They just couldn't.

"Cole," she said, sitting down on his couch, wringing her hands in her lap. "Can you come back out here?"

"I'm still not dressed."

"It won't take long, but I need to tell you something."

Walking out of the bathroom, he stood in front of her with that damn towel clinging to his hips while he wiped stray bits of shaving cream from his face. "What's up?" He looked so cute, so vulnerable, with his clean shave and wet hair and bare chest dusted in silver-blond curls, that if she didn't get this out right away, she feared she might melt into the couch.

She couldn't melt. She needed to be strong, firm, unmoving as the mountain behind them. But she wanted to be nice about it too. First the carrot, then the stick.

Digging into her basket, she pulled out one of her gifts, tilting the bottle of golden liquid from side to side. "I think you should stay in your towel."

"Is that?" His eyes swelled. "Massage oil?"

"You said you were sore."

He tossed the hand towel he'd been using to wipe his face clean into the bathroom. "If I thought I'd ever be able to get back up again, I'd go to my knees and kiss your feet right now."

Now for the stick. Gathering her nerve, and whatever willpower he hadn't already charmed out of her with his smiles and broad shoulders and flat abs charitably covered with enough over-fifty skin sag that she didn't feel too self-conscious about her own, she said, "But first we need to talk about what's going on here, between us." *Like adults*, she thought with a determined nod of her chin.

His head tilted. "Okay." He said it calmly, carefully, like he was tiptoeing into a minefield. "Should I sit?"

She motioned to the edge of his bed, placing him directly across from her but at a distance safe for talking instead of kissing. Once he sat, however, he spread his legs, that damn towel sliding open over his thigh, exposing his knee, and she realized he was still too close. Across the room on one of the kitchen bar stools would have been better, or out on the porch, or in Idaho.

With her hands clasped in her lap, her posture so upright Ian's piano teacher would've been impressed, she said, "I was surprised when you showed up the other day. In a good way," she added when his shoulders fell a fraction of an inch. "But now that I've had some time to think about things, I just want to be clear about what we're doing...with each other. So there's no confusion."

She paused, and while he waited silently for her to continue, a single drop of water slid from a wet curl down his neck, between his pecs. Tearing her eyes away from the southern journey the drop made toward the white cotton edge of his towel, she said, "If you want to keep doing this, hooking up, we need to be clear that it's just sex."

He sat up a little straighter.

"We're obviously attracted to each other, but you still live in Seattle. I'm still here. It doesn't make any sense to involve emotions in this."

"You don't want emotions." He didn't ask this; he stated it, his eyes staring steadily into hers.

She pulled her hair over her shoulder, wondering why this conversation that had seemed perfectly reasonable when she'd had it with herself in the car now felt wrong, somehow. "It's just, we're friends. Over the last month, you've come to mean a lot to me." It felt a little clinical, a smidge understated, a lot like horseshit. "But we've both been through some stuff. I've been hurt before. You've been hurt before. And I just don't want us to end up hurting each other. We only have a few weeks. I can't go anywhere. And it's not like you'll ever move here." Her laughter was uneasy. His silence was deafening.

Clutching the massage oil bottle so tightly she was worried it might explode in her fist, she said, "So, we're only good friends having sex, right? Consenting adults taking advantage of a unique situation?" She probably didn't need to ask, since it was probably all he'd thought they were doing in the first place. "No feelings. No weirdness. No attachments. Unless you don't want to have more sex. Which is fine too."

Aside from his left eye twitching once, he only stared at her for several long, nerve-racking moments. Finally, he said, "I understand. And I definitely want more sex."

She slumped in relief, burying her face in her hands. "Thank you. That was awful."

"Awful?" There was a faint trace of laughter in his voice. "I thought you did great. You stated your case clearly and provided sound reasoning, all while offering me no-strings orgasms. A+ execution." Graciously saving her from having to overthink everything she'd just said to him, he opened his legs a bit wider, wide enough to fit her, and said, "Come here."

Even though she'd had him inside her less than forty-eight hours ago, she was anxious, uncertain while she rose to her feet. She'd put it there herself, insisted on it, but with each step toward him, the gap between them stretched out long, like a shadow.

But then his arms wrapped around her waist and tugged, his forehead pressing into her stomach. His clean, soapy scent surrounded her, and she realized there was no gap. There was only Cole. The same Cole who'd sent her pictures of flowers and sunsets because he thought they were pretty. The same Cole whose voice had been the last thing she'd heard before falling asleep almost every night over the last several weeks. "Are you still sore?" she asked, running her fingers through his soft, damp hair.

Gazing up at her, he said, "I'm not sure I've ever been in this much pain in my entire life."

She gave him a pitying look. "Then lie down on your stomach. Let me make you feel better."

Slowly, still holding his towel around his waist, he rolled over, sucking air in through his teeth while he crawled up the bed until he collapsed onto his pillow. Turning his head to the side, he grunted, "Ow."

"Can I straddle you?"

Only one corner of his mouth was visible, but when it curled, she felt his full grin all the same. "Mira, I could be at death's door, and the answer to that question would still be a resounding yes."

Grinning too, she climbed on top of him, carefully bracketing his legs with hers. Flipping open the cap, she poured a small amount of massage oil into her palm and rubbed her hands together. When she touched her fingertips to his skin, he flinched.

"I never knew clearing trails could make a person's skin hurt."

"Is it too much?" she asked. "Do you want me to stop?"

"Not if the world was ending."

Running her hands slowly over his shoulders, between his shoulder blades, she told him, "You have a very nice back."

"Thank you," he mumbled into his pillow.

"You have a nice front too."

He laughed softly.

"How do you stay in such good shape? What do you do?"

"Nothing much."

Her hikes and yoga classes and terrible YouTube tabata workouts collectively gasped. "Seriously?"

With a chuckle that vibrated through her hands on his back, he said, "Fucking drummers, am I right?"

"I guess drumming is pretty hard work," she conceded.

"Fame and fortune aren't the only perks of the job." He craned his neck, peering up at her over his shoulder. "There's also strength, stamina, dexterity…"

While the way blood shot to her core wasn't gentle, the way she pushed his head back down to his pillow was. "Aside from overdoing it, sexy rock god, how was your first day alone with the guys?"

"I think it went okay. They were all nice to me, even though I'm fairly clueless. Fuck, that's amazing," he groaned while she ran her thumbs up and down his neck.

Moving to his shoulders again, squeezing, she winced. "I think you have rocks in here."

"I know. It's so bad."

"It's a good thing you texted me to come over." His skin was so warm it made her warm everywhere she touched him—her hands, her thighs, between her legs. "You needed someone to take care of you."

After a quiet moment while she tried to soften his knotted muscles, he asked, "How long do I have you tonight?"

"I should probably head back in a few hours."

"Hmm" was all he said, but the way he said it was so dirty, so filled with promise, that heat coursed through her veins. Seriously, she was on fire.

"Is it hot in here?"

"It's definitely hot," he purred. "You should take off your shirt."

"You want me to take off my shirt?"

"It's all coming off eventually, sugar."

Another surge of heat flared over her skin, between her toes, her breasts, up her throat. And if her body chose this particular moment to have a hot flash, she was going to lose her shit. After unbuttoning her blouse and slipping it off her shoulders, though, her internal temperature cooled to a low simmer.

"What happens in a few hours that you need to be back for, if you don't mind my asking?"

Returning her hands to his back after pouring another few drops of oil into her palm, she said, "It's shower night."

"Shower night?"

"For Mom. She forgets to shower unless we remind her. Usually, she's okay with the schedule, the reminders, but sometimes, out of nowhere, she gets really pissed about it and yells at me for treating her like a child. I always try to be home before she goes to bed on shower nights so Ian doesn't have to be the one to remind her. I hate it when she loses her temper with him. She never used to."

"Can I ask you a question?" he said while she turned her attention to his lower back, digging the heels of her palms into the bars of iron along his spine.

"Sure."

"I know you had a dad and a stepdad, but you've never told me where they are now."

"My real dad lives in Florida, last I heard."

"What...happened?" he ground out when she hit a particularly tight spot.

"I guess family life wasn't for him. He took off when I was five. I don't remember him much. I only remember my mom completely redecorating the house we lived in at the time. She let me paint my bedroom pink, and I'd thought it was so cool, having a pink room and my mom all to myself."

"And your stepdad?"

She let herself smile, even though there was some deep sadness behind it. "Deadhead Fred. He was a great guy, total hippie goofball with long hair and a fantastic laugh. He used to take us camping and fishing—"

"And to terrifyingly dark caverns."

"That too," she said, surprised Cole remembered. She shouldn't have been. He remembered everything. "It always seemed like Fred and my mom were happy together. But then he got a job out of town when I was Ian's age, and that was that. I guess dealing with a grumpy teenager wasn't how the wind blew him." The words lodged themselves sideways in her chest. "I've talked to him a few times since then, but I haven't seen him in years."

"You don't think Fred leaving was your fault, do you?" Cole

asked, looking back over his shoulder at her again, a tiny pillow line creasing his cheek.

"I definitely did at the time." While she slid her knuckles up his back, she wondered if she still did. "It's not out of the realm of possibility. People leave over difficult things like that, like having to help raise a hormonal teenager who isn't theirs." *Or help take care of another person's parent.* "It happens."

Settling back down on his pillow, he said, "I guess that's true. Both my parents checked out once I got old enough to start talking back. Did Linda ever tell you what actually happened with Fred? I bet there's a story there."

"No. She never talks about either of them. Even before she started having memory problems, she never mentioned them."

"What is it with boomers?" Cole asked. "They'd all rather sleep in a bed made of live snakes than open up about anything."

"They're allergic to it," she said. "The only way my mom ever tells me anything is after half a bottle of wine."

"Speaking of dads, you said Paul wasn't Ian's, right?"

Running both hands down the expanse of his back, she said, "No, definitely not. I've actually never met Ian's dad."

"Huh. That must have made the conception challenging."

She laughed. "I used a sperm donor."

"No shit?"

"No shit. I've always wanted a kid, and I was thirty-five and not getting any younger or any less single. I thought about asking a few of the men in town if they'd be willing to donate, but that seemed like it might have turned into too much of a hot tangle. So I found a donor I liked, and I just...did it."

Smiling into the pillow, he said, "I love that."

She set back in on the tight bands between his shoulder blades. "All I know about Ian's donor is that he was thirty-two at the time, had blue eyes and brown hair, and was a concert pianist."

"Strong genes," Cole groaned as she dug her knuckles in. "Mira, your hands are magic."

"Yeah?"

"World class. It's almost like you knead for a living."

"I'm glad you like it, but I've saved the best part for last." Tugging gently on the towel still wrapped around his waist, she said, "Hips up."

Without hesitation, he raised his hips so she could slide the towel out from under him and drop it to the floor.

"Unngh," he grunted when she put her kneading skills to use on his adorably round butt.

"Too much?"

"No. Maybe. I don't know. Don't stop."

She didn't, sliding her hands down his hips, up and over the curves of his ass, taking time to study the way his low back dipped, the way his shoulders fanned out, the tattoo of a bird skull over his right shoulder blade. "Is that your only tattoo?"

"Mm-hmm," he managed, somewhat pained, while she worked on his upper thighs. "It hurt too much to ever get another one. I almost passed out."

"Soft city boy."

When he reached back and pinched her calf, she squealed. But then his fingertips stayed, running up and down the length of her leg, and he said, "I'm not very *soft* right now."

She rolled her lips together, then asked, "Does that hurt, too?"

"No, that definitely doesn't hurt. Mira?"

"Yes, Cole?"

"When's the last time you got a massage?"

She paused for a moment, thinking. "Honestly, I don't think I've ever gotten a—" She was on her back before she finished her sentence, Cole's lips on her lips, his tongue in her mouth, his cock hard and heavy between her legs. And then, like she was a rag doll he liked to play with, he flipped her onto her stomach.

"My turn," he said, and mischief danced through the words. She felt her bra clasp spring free, her hips raised into the air, her button unbuttoned, zipper unzipped, pants and underwear peeled from her legs. She heard the click of the oil cap, and then his hands were everywhere.

The oil was warm and slick, his hands strong and sure moving over her skin, squeezing her shoulders, cupping her neck, his thumb and fingers working out tension at the base of her skull she hadn't even known was there. "That feels so good," she said, her muscles unwinding a lifetime of tension under his long fingers, her skin loose and tingling.

"I might not be a baker, but I'm no slouch at kneading."

"If you want a job"—she moaned when he pressed his thumbs into her lower back—"you're hired."

His soft laughter raised the hairs on her arms, and then he kissed her between her shoulder blades, his hands gliding over the sides of her body, fingertips grazing the outer curves of her breasts. "This tattoo," he said against her skin. "I have dreams about it."

His lips followed the path of Ian's song, kissing along her spine. The tattoo stopped at her low back, but Cole didn't, dragging his tongue down her crease, taking her ass in both hands and squeezing, kissing, nibbling.

She writhed beneath him, need and desire spiraling through her, swelling like a storm as he pushed her knee out to the side, opening her up to him.

His fingers found her first, sliding between her lips, bringing the wetness he found there forward to draw slippery circles around her clit. "Is this what you had in mind, Mira? Is this what you came here for?"

"Yes." It felt wrong, admitting that. But she couldn't deny how much she wanted him, needed him. He had her too exposed in this position, spread out for him, too open to not tell him the truth. Yes, she was here for sex, for his hands, his body, his lips and his teeth and, *oh god*, his tongue.

He licked a searing path along her inner thigh, then hoisted her hips up. "Or did you come here for this?" Before she could answer, his tongue slid through her entrance, higher, pressing, licking, swirling around the sensitive skin of her hole.

It didn't matter, her insecurities, her fears, because with the low, heavy buzz already building in her core, she knew he was about to make her come so hard she could be stranded in the desert for days, and she'd take this climax before she'd take water.

"All right, one-orgasm-wonder," he said, his finger abandoning her clit to slide inside her. "Should I finish you off like this? Or when I fuck you?"

"Like this," she gasped while a second finger stretched her, filling her. "Please."

Pulling his fingers out, he pushed her knees apart, rolled onto his back, and slid beneath her.

What followed would exist in her memory as a hazy, ecstasy-induced fever dream in which she'd be fairly certain he'd grasped her hips and pulled her down onto his hot, open mouth. But it would be impossible to say. She'd need a functioning brain to remember this orgasm with any accuracy. And with his fingers and his tongue working her over in perfect unison, with her hips grinding helplessly against him while she buried her moans in his pillow, there wasn't a single working neuron left in all the land.

She was already hovering on the edge, but when he crooked his fingers inside her, when he pressed her clit between his lips and sucked, when he found every single spot that lit her up like she'd painstakingly drawn him a diagram, she was gone, flung far away from this cabin, from this town, from this planet. White heat uncoiled in her belly, whipping through her limbs as the orgasm built, swelled, hovered so long she nearly cried out until it finally broke over her, pleasure pulsing in its wake.

Her arms didn't work. Her legs were useless. Her body didn't belong to her anymore. It was all his. And there was something exhilarating but also terrifying about it, the surrender, the inability to think or plan or care about anything except the deep brown pools of his eyes when he flipped her over, wiped his mouth with the back of his hand, and said, "I changed my mind. I want to be on top."

CHAPTER TWENTY-SIX

COLE

ONLY SEX? She wanted them to only have meaningless, emotionless, robot sex?

The fuck we will.

He'd told her he understood, but that didn't mean he agreed with her. Because he didn't. At all. He was already a proud resident of Emotionland. He'd popped a tent after Madigan's wedding, built a house when she'd sent him tarts, and dug out a football field–sized bunker when she'd led him into her bedroom. And now? *Fuck it.* He was running for mayor.

Even though he'd promised himself he wouldn't do this again, chase after someone who seemed intent on staying an arm's length away, he couldn't help it. At least Mira had good reasons to keep her distance. She was protecting herself, being realistic, being smart. Three things that he was, admittedly, terrible at. He didn't care. She might be worried they'd end up hurting each other, but he wasn't. He knew she'd never hurt him, not like Nancy had. And he'd cut off his own hands before he'd ever hurt her.

Maybe she couldn't see a future for them romantically, but he could. He didn't know what that future looked like yet, but he knew it existed. And he had a little less than three weeks to convince her it existed too. Starting right now.

If sex was what she wanted, then sex was what she'd get. He could hardly be blamed if he made sure it was the best sex of her life.

While Mira came down, her eyes still half-closed, her fingers soft on his hips, he leaned over and rummaged in the nightstand for the box of condoms. Fishing one out, he tore the wrapper with his teeth and rolled it on like he was going for a world speed record. The last thing he wanted was to rush this moment that still felt stolen with her, but he knew if he gave her too much time to unwind, it wouldn't feel as good. And he needed her to feel good. He needed to keep her as close to the edge as possible, whether he could push her over it again or not.

Settling between her legs, he lined up with her entrance, and while her heels hooked behind his waist, while he pressed his hips forward, stars exploded in front of his eyes, constellations, galaxies.

"Mira," he groaned, dropping his head because holding it up was impossible. "You feel so good." This was such a colossal understatement it bordered on an outright lie. *Good?* A fresh shave felt good. A warm bath felt good. Being inside Mira Harlow fucked him up. It rearranged his atoms, altered his molecular structure. He knew somewhere in the back of his mind that he'd destroyed his body today, but right now, he felt no pain.

While he slid out, then back in, drawing whispered moans from her throat, she dragged her fingernails up his back, took his face in her hands, and kissed him. Her mouth was soft when he kissed her back, her tongue even softer, tempting him to stay there, buried deep inside her, cradled in the warmth of her thighs.

Not yet.

Breaking the kiss, he slid his hand up her ribs to cup her breast, backing out enough to guide her nipple toward his lips, suck it into his mouth. When he swirled his tongue around the hard tip, grazed her tight, pebbled skin with his teeth, her back arched off the bed.

Taking advantage, he released her breast to slip his hand underneath her, spreading his palm flat against her lower back, holding her tightly while he thrust into her, deep and hard.

"Cole." His name was a whispered plea on her lips while she hitched her leg over his hip, improving his angle, letting him find a new depth inside her.

"Is it good, sugar?"

"Mm-hmm," she moaned, and he couldn't decide if the lines diving between her brows were from pain or pleasure. He was about to ask if he should slow down, if it was too much, when her hands sliding over his ass, urging him on, answered his question.

There was music in the way they moved together, a rhythm, each note driving him closer and closer to mindless, formless ecstasy. If he didn't know better, he could have sworn she was right there with him, her head thrown back, her lips parting, breaths ragged. But he was no rookie. He wasn't about to ruin whatever she was feeling by asking her about it. Now was not the time for words, only his hips moving and her hands pressing and his mouth finding her neck, kissing and licking, savoring the sweet taste of her skin in that sensitive valley behind her ear.

She shuddered, her fingernails digging into his back, her inner muscles flickering, and as much as he might have wanted to, he couldn't hold back. He bit down gently on the sacred spot where her neck met her shoulder, and as she cried out his name, a storm of pleasure barreled through him, making him glow like neon.

He groaned, her name on his lips, his hips still moving, animated by some deep, primal part of his brain that had evolved to believe this climax was more important for the survival of the human race than eating, drinking, even running from lions.

It lasted forever. It ended too quickly. Refusing to be anywhere now but buried deep inside her, warm between her thighs, he relaxed into her arms, regaining his bearings while she pressed soft kisses into his hair.

He wanted to tell her things, words preparing to dive off the tip of his tongue, words like *amazing* and *beautiful* and *life changing*. But as his mind cleared, he remembered why he couldn't say those things. *Only sex. No emotions.* He'd behave. For now. And because it was right there, tempting him like a cherry glistening on top of a sundae, he turned his head to the side and took her nipple back into his mouth.

Her arms falling to the bed, she exhaled, "Christ," a benediction offered up to the ceiling.

He released her nipple, then asked, "Did you? Again?" while gazing up at her. He didn't want to make a big deal out of it, but it kind of felt like she had, and he was gathering data, learning what she liked, what worked, what didn't, what he could do better next time.

She threw an arm over her eyes, her lips curving into a grin that didn't quite answer his question. "It was so good."

"Yes," he told her, pushing up to kiss her again, "it was." Pulling out reluctantly, he kissed her one last time, then rolled to the side, heading into the bathroom to throw the condom away. "Funny story," he said when he returned to the bed, slinging her slightly limp arm over his waist, letting her nestle into him. "I found that condom in a box in the nightstand. Randomly."

"Didn't Madigan stay in this cabin before he moved into the lodge with Ashley?"

"That he did. You know the old saying, friends who share condoms... I forget how the rest of it goes."

Her laughter brushed across his chest.

"Speaking of condoms. We don't have to use them, if you don't want to."

Her head popped up like a meerkat from its hole. "What?"

"If you like them or something, that's fine with me. But we don't have to—"

"I realize my most fertile days are behind me, Cole. But I know two women who got pregnant in their fifties. No thanks."

Now it was his turn to laugh. "I'd never doubt your fertility. But you're in the clear. I got a vasectomy years ago. Right after Roe v. Wade was overturned."

"You..." She blinked at him, her green eyes wide and breathtaking. "Are you serious?"

He smirked, said, "Human rights are nothing to joke about, Mira," then squirmed when she pinched his side. "I've been tested recently too."

"Okay," she said, considering. "But I haven't been tested in years."

"Would you want to?" he asked. "Get tested for me? If not, it's fine. We can keep using condoms. Whatever you want." *Whatever you want for this no-strings sexcation where my heart is absolutely ready to fall out of my chest and into your hands, and my cock is literally dying to feel you bare.* "I'm cool with it either way."

Running her fingertips over his chest, she said, "I'll stop by the clinic tomorrow."

For a long moment, they only stared at each other, the muted light from the bedside lamp casting her in gold. He reached up, tucking a stray strand of hair behind her ear. "Mira," he said softly, "you are so beautiful."

It was too much. He saw it immediately in the way her eyes went wide, feel it in the way her shoulders stiffened.

"I'm sorry," he said. "I didn't mean—"

She rolled onto her back, away from him, leaving a cold patch along the entire right side of his body. "I should probably go. It's getting late."

Shit. "Finally," he said, trying to lighten the mood he'd accidentally darkened. "It's way past my bedtime."

Turning her head, she smiled at him, and he successfully resisted the urge to roll back on top of her, kiss her forehead, her cheek, her mouth, but barely.

"Oh, wait." She crawled off the bed to dig in her basket. Watching her, staring openly, he appreciated that she didn't seem uncomfortable being naked in front of him. He'd live his entire life without a stitch on if it was socially acceptable. And she looked so mouthwateringly sexy.

"Hey, Mira?"

Still searching through the basket, she said, "Yes, Cole?"

"Would it be all right if I objectified you for a second?"

Her head rose, her eyes sparkling. "In what way?"

"It's just," he dragged his gaze down to her toes and back up again, "your body is fucking phenomenal."

Turning back to face him, and with a heaping dose of sarcasm, she said, "Really?"

Did she think he was joking? "Yes, really."

"Which part?" She waved a hand over her thick, luscious thighs. "The cellulite?"

He sucked his lower lip between his teeth. "Fuck yes."

Her hand moved to the soft curve of her stomach. "Maybe these stretch marks?"

He moaned. "So hot."

She took her breasts in both hands, raising them slightly. "Or these, that used to live up here? But now?" She dropped them, letting them bounce.

"Your tits might be my favorite part. It's a toss-up between your tits and your big, beautiful ass."

The Mira Pink flooding her cheeks made him wish he could grab his phone and take her picture. "You're making me blush."

"You're making me hard." He tried to sit up, then winced because the post-sex euphoria was wearing off and moving fucking hurt.

Shaking her head at him like he was the saddest little over-achiever she'd ever seen, she turned around again, giving him one last view of her world-class booty. When she found what she was looking for in her basket, brandishing the red tin of Tiger Balm in her hands like a game show host, he almost wept. "Mira, you're seriously saving my life right now."

Twirling her finger in the air, she motioned for him to roll over, climbed back onto the bed with him, and said, "Tell me where it hurts."

My shoulders, my back, my heart. Since he couldn't say that last part, not yet, he told her, "Everywhere," because it was at least partially true.

CHAPTER TWENTY-SEVEN

MIRA

"Three?" Jen's eyes ratcheted so wide, Mira half expected a cartoon *boi-oing* sound effect. "Three times?"

"Yep," Mira admitted before knocking her entire espresso back in one bewildered go. When Cole had made her come twice in his cabin last week, she'd worked very hard to chalk it up to more luck. Then it happened again in his car parked in the woods a couple days later, and then again the other day in her bed—and then her shower—before Ian got home from school and her mom got back from afternoon tea with Maude Alice. But last night, when she brought him fresh strawberry shortcake and he decided to put the whipped cream to much better use, she realized there wasn't a pot of gold big enough to take the blame for three orgasms.

"Jesus." Jen picked absently at her chocolate chip scone. "I don't think I've ever come three times in a row. Two is practically miraculous. But three? That's sainthood-level boning. Is he just walking around with a golden halo around his head and his balls clanging together like cowbells?"

It was a good thing Mira had already swallowed her espresso, or Jen might have wound up wearing it. "What?"

"You know," Jen said, laughing. "Like rams. The hottest ones who get all the ewes strut around with these big, dangly balls all day."

"Hot rams? Are you watching that farm dating show again? Because I don't think that's a thing, even for sheep."

Jen only shrugged, brushing red curls off her shoulder before breaking off a corner of the scone and popping it into her mouth.

"Cole wouldn't necessarily be clanging his cowbell balls together anyway, because"—she bit her cheek, embarrassment drawing her shoulders toward her ears—"I'm not sure he knows how hot of a ram he is."

Leveling her with a confused stare that slid into suspicion, Jen chewed, then swallowed as the music faded. The silence between one song and the next lasted so long Mira almost faked a cough to break it. But just as the steel drums of "Jane Says" chimed through the bakery speakers, Jen asked, "Why would Cole not know? Surely you're not implying—"

"I'm having silent orgasms," she blurted out as quickly as she could, the verbal equivalent of ripping off a Band-Aid. "And don't call me Shirley."

Jen's lips didn't so much as twitch at the joke. "What in the world is a silent orgasm?"

"It's when you come, but silently," Mira explained, although it seemed fairly self-explanatory to her.

"Okay," Jen said slowly. "Let's try again. Why in the world are you coming silently?"

"I don't know!" Mira flung her hands into the air. "I wish I did. Because I'm sure he knows. I'm sure he can tell." There was no way anyone who fucked like he did, anyone who was as attentive and skilled and *creative* as he was, wouldn't sense when their partner was coming apart at the seams. "I told him I only come once, because I usually do. And when I almost came twice the first time we were together, I kind of brushed it off. But then, the next time, I did come twice, and when he asked me about it, I froze up. I didn't answer. And now we're, like, stuck there. Like it's this multiple-orgasm elephant in the room. He doesn't ask, I don't tell, and the whole thing has become so weird I can barely stand it."

"Huh," Jen said with a deep, contemplative pout.

"Yeah," Mira concurred. She knew how it sounded. She knew how it felt. Like she'd tried to protect herself by making the smart, mature, adult decision to keep their relationship purely physical, and the universe had laughed hysterically and said, "Great plan! Here's three weeks of the most amazing sex you'll ever have. Good luck!"

"So, what's keeping you from just...starting to get louder?"

Mira leaned forward, because even alone in her bakery with her best friend, she could only whisper the truth. "I'm scared, Jen. I feel like I have to be quiet. Like if I admit out loud how good everything with him is—"

"Reality might bite?" she offered.

Mira nodded miserably. "But I was going to try to talk to him about it last night. I really was. And then *boom*."

Sitting back with a deep, knowing exhale, Jen raised three fingers.

"Three fucking orgasms." As dramatically as possible without hurting herself, Mira collapsed against the counter, dropping her head onto her folded arms, because it was about to get so much worse.

She'd gotten her test results back that morning, and while they couldn't celebrate their condom-free lifestyle right away since her chaotic period had decided to start in the middle of the night, even the delusional part of her that believed she'd reached black belt status in the ancient art of stealth orgasms knew there was no way she'd sneak another one past him while he was bare. Her traitorous clit, absolutely no help at all, throbbed at the thought.

"This is interesting," Jen said. "I know lots of women who have complicated relationships with orgasms, but this one might take the cake."

"You're not helping," Mira groaned into her arms.

"Do you want my help?"

Raising her head, Mira said, "Please."

"You should tell him."

"But it's too good, Jen."

"I think we've clearly established that."

"No, I mean it's *all* too good. Not only the sex." Sure, she'd written *multiple orgasms forever* on a scrap of paper and burned it into her wish jar after she'd gotten home from his cabin last night. But that hadn't been the only wish about Cole she'd turned to ash. There was also *always feeling warm* and *laughing myself to sleep.* "It's everything. And I can't have everything."

"Why, though?" Jen asked, suddenly serious. "Why can't you have everything?"

"Because he's leaving in two weeks. Because I can already tell how much it's going to hurt when he's not here anymore."

Reaching across the counter, Jen squeezed her fingers. "Why can't you still be together, though? I know long distance isn't ideal, but it kind of sounds like he might be worth it."

"I don't think I can do long distance. I've got too much holding me here. He'd always have to come visit me. He'd always have to be the one making the trip, making the effort, leaving his life so we could be together. It would be completely unfair, and I don't think I could ask someone else to do that for me. Jen, what are you doing?" Mira asked while Jen leaned over the counter, looking to Mira's right side, then her left.

"I'm trying to find the chains holding you behind that counter. They must be invisible or something, because I don't see them."

"Hysterical."

"I'm serious, Mira. You have always been someone who makes sacrifices so that everyone else in your life is safe. Remember in fifth grade when Timothy Green started following me home and pushing my face into the snow, and you dropped out of the school play to walk with me every day so he'd leave me alone?"

"That guy was such a prick."

"Still is, if you ask me," Jen said. "Being good at selling RVs isn't a personality trait, dude."

Mira nodded her agreement.

"My point is, you're always looking out for everyone else. But you're allowed to look out for yourself too. You're allowed to have a life."

Jen might have been right, in some ideological sense, but she didn't understand. Mira wasn't being a Good Samaritan, a good mother, a good daughter, because of some altruistic sense of duty. Her interests were completely selfish. If she ever decided to put herself first, and something happened when she wasn't there, the guilt would crush her.

"Speaking of having a life," Mira said, whipping the conversation around the nearest turn. "How are things with the firefighter?"

Jen's sigh was audible. "That mercury is, sadly, no longer in fucktrograde."

"What happened? I thought you two were having fun."

"We were, at first. But I think he's too young. Or maybe I'm too old. And"—her shoulder hitched—"you know."

"Scott?" Mira guessed, because even though Jen's estranged husband had made his bed and was now sleeping—or drinking—in it, she knew Jen still missed him.

"One thing they never tell you when your marriage falls apart is that no matter how bad it got, no matter how miserable the last few years might have been, it's really hard to pretend the twenty amazing years that came before them never existed."

Before Mira could respond, her phone chimed on the counter, her screen lighting up.

"Who is it?" Jen asked, looking sideways at Mira's caller ID. "Is it the G-spot whisperer?"

"No, his ringtone is 'I Will Always Love You.'"

Like a broken mailbox, Jen's mouth flipped open. "You gave him his own ringtone? And it's *that* song?"

"It's not what you think," Mira said, waving off her concern. "It's only his heart song."

"His what what?"

Accepting the call, Mira said, "Glazed and Confused. How can I help you?" in her overly chipper bakery phone voice.

"Hello," a woman said over the line. "My name is Beth Montgomery, and I'm an aide for Senator Jon Richardson."

"Is it election season again already?" Mira asked Jen with a hand over the phone.

Jen shook her head, finishing off her scone.

"We always vote for Jon," Mira told Beth Montgomery. "Thank you and have a nice—"

"Wait, this isn't a political call," Beth said. "I'll only take a moment of your time, I swear."

"Okay." Mira was still dubious, but she didn't want to be rude to some staffer who probably spent most of her day having people treat her like shit. "What can I do for you?"

"I'm not sure if you know this, but Senator Richardson is a big fan of music, especially 1990s alternative rock. There are grunge band posters all over his office, and the break room, and the staff bathroom. So much flannel."

"That's...interesting," Mira said slowly, not entirely sure how to respond to that random factoid about a state senator.

"Who is it?" Jen whispered. "What's happening?"

Mira held up a finger while Beth Montgomery said, "The other day, a man named Cole Sanderson, he was apparently the drummer for a '90s band called the Markers—"

"Makers," Mira corrected the twenty-something sounding woman, her interest in the conversation abruptly sparked.

"Oh, right. Sorry. The Makers. Anyway, Mr. Sanderson posted a reel on Instagram about your bakery. Senator Richardson saw the reel and visited your website. Are you still making wedding cakes?"

Mira burst into laughter. "Is this a prank? Did Cole put you up to this?"

"No, ma'am. Senator Richardson would like to know if you still make wedding cakes."

Mira blinked.

"What is it?" Jen whispered louder, leaning in to try to hear the conversation.

Putting the call on speaker, Mira set her phone on the counter between them.

"I realize this may seem like a strange call," Beth said with a nervous laugh. "But the senator's daughter is getting married next month in Bozeman, and he is very interested in having your bakery supply the wedding cake. He thinks your cakes are"—she cleared her throat—"'fun, flirty, and original.'"

Jen's hand flew to her mouth, covering her snort.

"He said that?" Mira had a hard time imagining Jon Richardson with his cowboy boots and his flattop haircut and his big farmer's shoulders hopping off his tractor to call her baked goods *flirty*.

"Verbatim. He doesn't like being misquoted. But he does like promoting small businesses in Montana. He also said something about tagging Mr. Sanderson in a social media post with the cake to get 'another degree closer to Eddie Vedder.' I don't remember his exact wording, so please don't quote him—or me—on that."

"She does make wedding cakes," Jen said, leaning in. "Beautiful, amazing, one-of-a-kind wedding cakes."

"That's great." Beth sounded more relieved than anything else. "If you accept the senator's offer, we'll include QR codes that link directly to your bakery on all the dessert napkins. We'll also post professional pictures of the cake across all the Senator's social media platforms as well as on his website. It will be great publicity for you."

Raising her stunned gaze from her phone, Mira stared at Jen, who beamed back at her while bouncing on her toes. This was enormous, monumental, gargantuan, the biggest opportunity she'd ever had or would probably ever get.

"Unfortunately, we're in a time crunch, and the senator needs an answer"—Beth cleared her throat again—"'in two shakes of a lamb's heinie.' His words. Are you interested?"

"Yes!" Mira and Jen shouted at the same time.

"Fantastic. I'll text you the senator's daughter's contact information. She's expecting your call. Have a great day, and don't forget to vote Jon!"

The call ended.

Jen's eyes flared wide.

Mira shouted, "Holy shit!" Then she ran around the counter and grabbed Jen by her arms, and they jumped up and down like two tweens who'd scored Taylor Swift tickets.

"I can't believe it," Mira said.

"I totally can. But I need to stop jumping."

"Why?"

"Because I just peed a little."

"Me too," Mira said, crossing one leg over the other and squeezing.

Pushing his way through the door, Ian muttered, "Gross."

She really needed to fix their bell.

"I gotta go." Jen kissed Mira's cheek. "The new gelding won't train himself."

"Is Madigan still thinking about teaming up with you for equine therapy for Little Timber?"

"I think he's still firmly in the pre-contemplative phase. But it would be cool."

"So cool," Mira agreed.

"Congratulations, Mira," Jen said, then added in a whisper, "To celebrate, why don't you break your vow of orgasm silence?"

Mira snorted.

After Ian gave Jen knucks on her way out the door, he looked at Mira, narrowed his eyes, and asked, "You're smiling. Is this a Cole thing? Are you going to smile like that all the time while he's here?"

Mira walked around the counter again. "Will it just ruin your life if I do?"

"Totally," he deadpanned, taking a seat at the counter, setting his backpack down. "It's...kinda nice. You don't smile much normally."

She nearly tripped over her own feet. *Do not overreact. Do not freak out. Do not make it a thing that your teen son said something nice to you, because if you do, he may never do it again.* "Actually, I got a gig making a wedding cake for Jon Richardson."

"The senator guy? Isn't he already married?"

"It's for his daughter."

Without looking up, too busy rummaging through his bag, pulling out his notebook, his pencil, Ian raised his left hand for a high five. "Cool," he said while she slapped it.

Their heads turned slowly toward the stairs when her mom came down them, then Mira jerked to attention when the rhythm of her steps faltered. "You okay, Mom?"

"I'm fine," she crooned, rounding the corner. "Just need to pay better attention."

It was brief, but the look Mira shared with her son was one they'd honed since her mom moved in: a nonverbal "Should we be concerned?"

"Be careful, Mimi," Ian said, his shoulders tense until she ruffled his hair and said, "Oh, don't worry about me."

It was all her mom wanted, for them not to worry, for everything to be normal, the way it used to be. It was also the one thing they couldn't give her, because what if she fell down the stairs? What if she broke a hip or an ankle or hit her head? What if she left the oven on while she was baking? They had to be vigilant.

"Did I hear you shouting earlier?" her mom asked. "Did something happen?"

Opening his math book, Ian said, "Mom scored a wedding cake job for Senator Richardson's daughter."

Her mom clapped her hands together, her eyes clear and bright. "That is spectacular news! When? How much are they paying you? Did you negotiate?"

Mira laughed. "I have no idea. I forgot to ask."

Her mom clucked her tongue. "Of course you did. Well, this is worthy of a celebration. Cards? Pizza?" And when she suggested, "Maybe your new boyfriend can come. I'd like to meet him," Mira coughed into her fist.

"Yeah, Mom," Ian said with a sideways grin. "Let's invite your *boyfriend*." He might as well have said "fuck buddy."

She was an easy target. Moms were always easy targets, especially when they had fuck buddies. But her mom was trying not to laugh, and Ian was smiling, and it all felt so good, she didn't even mind. "First of all, he's not my boyfriend. We're only friends."

Her mom and Ian exchanged doubtful glances.

"With...some benefits," Mira admitted grudgingly. It seemed like too much, like a step reserved for people in a relationship, but the idea of Cole in her apartment, with her family, sitting at their table, laughing over pizza and cards, celebrating with them, maybe too much would be okay for one night. It would be a PG night anyway, since her geriatric hormones had decided to pussy-block her. "Fine, I'll invite him. But you two have to behave. No talking shit under your breath or making inappropriate jokes, okay?"

"Who, us?" Her mom stepped to Ian's side until they looked like the family portrait of innocence.

"We would never," Ian said, his mouth open in feigned outrage. "How dare you, Mother?"

Letting this *Mother* slide, Mira walked to the door, flipped the sign to CLOSED, then paused at her reflection in the window, barely recognizing the woman smiling back at her.

CHAPTER TWENTY-EIGHT

COLE

THE LOG COLE sat on was hard and bumpy, and a knot dug ruthlessly into his ass, but it was downright pleasant compared to the way all ten men stared at him, scratching their heads or clearing their throats, waiting for him to act like he knew what he was doing.

"So..." He glanced around the clearing where they sat, relieved the weather was nice enough to have this meeting outside since having all the men in his cabin—which he was pretty sure still smelled like sex and whipped cream—would have been a bridge too far. "Welcome to Cole's first Little Timber group session."

In the ensuing silence, a magpie squawked.

"Is there anything anyone wants to talk about today?" Madigan had told him the group sessions were typically unstructured, and that he always tried to encourage the men to choose the topics, guide the conversations. Cole figured he could handle that. What he couldn't handle, however, was ten pairs of eyes locked on his, waiting, like they expected him to know what to say next. "Anyone?" he asked while Murphy whined up at him. "Bueller?"

Looking horrified, Thom turned to him and asked, "Was that a *Ferris Bueller* joke? In this year of our lord?"

"It was," Cole said, trying not to laugh at the equally alarmed expressions the other men gave him. "And there's a lot more where that came from if I'm the only one who talks during this group. So help me, guys. Help me, help you."

"Not *Jerry Maguire*!" Sam cried. "If you tell us we complete you, I'm out!"

"I did warn you," Cole said with a grin.

When Stanley said, "I think I've got something," the laughter around the circle faded, the men lapsing into what seemed to Cole to be a practiced kind of silence. "I've, um, been having a lot of cravings lately." He folded his hands in his lap. "I was watching TV yesterday, and this Cuervo commercial came on and, I don't know. It messed me up."

"Do you want to talk about it?" Cole asked.

Slipping a hand into Murphy's scruff after the dog trotted over to flop down by his side, Stanley said, "That's what I drank. Tequila. Most of the time, I feel okay. But sometimes, either after seeing a commercial like that, or sitting outside on a nice evening, or even when I smell the same wood polish the bartender at my usual place used, I miss it so much I'm not sure I'll keep being able to resist it once I'm done here."

"What do you miss about it?" Tex asked, adjusting his hat.

"Everything, I guess."

"Can you come up with something specific?" Sam held up a finger. "Just one thing?"

"I can try." Stanley's lips flattened under his round nose and deeply set hazel eyes. "I guess I miss the way the tequila looked, smooth and slightly thick, like the bartender was pouring liquid gold into my glass. I miss the smoky smell, how it stung my nose. I miss the way it burned my throat when I knocked it back."

A thoughtful "hmm" came from one of the guys. Cole wasn't sure which one.

"I miss the way I felt so much...*less* after I had a few drinks," Stanley continued. "Like all the stress and worry faded away, and I could finally relax. I don't know how to relax now. Shoot, I even miss the feel of the barstool I used to sit on." He twisted his shoulders side to side. "It had a real easy swivel."

"Um-hmm," Tex murmured, nodding sagely.

"Yep," Sam concurred, as if they'd both reached some secret conclusion.

"What?" Stanley asked. "Why are you nodding at me like that?"

Sitting to Cole's right, plucking at a piece of bark on the log beneath him, Kev said, "It's called euphoric recall."

"What's euphoric recall?" Stanley asked before Cole had a chance.

"It's when you only remember the good parts about something," Tex explained.

"You, like, romanticize them," Sam added.

"So you get all these cravings and longings for something that's bad for you, because you only remember how good it felt once upon a time," Tex said. "Because drugs, alcohol, sex, unhealthy relationships, they all feel good at first. There's a reason we become addicted to them."

Cole squeezed the back of his neck. *Unhealthy relationships.* Was that why he'd gone back to Nancy over and over for the past three decades? Because he'd wanted to experience the good parts of being with her again so badly that he gave himself amnesia for the bad?

"It's harder to remember the whole story," Tex continued. "But when we get a craving, we have to play it all the way through. From the euphoria of the high to the reality of the low. The fights we had when we finally stumbled home, the hangovers, the withdrawals when we couldn't get that next fix, being on edge all the time."

"Letting everyone down," Stanley said softly. "Letting myself down. Feeling sick. Feeling ashamed." When he looked up again, his eyes were clear. "I'm not going back there."

"That's right, brother," Tex said, leaning over to squeeze his shoulder. "Always play it through to the end."

Gong-like. That was the only way Cole could describe how Tex's words reverberated through his bones.

"You okay, Cole?" Ace asked, his long legs crossed in front of him. "You look a little like a fish I caught last summer."

Realizing it was gaping, Cole closed his mouth. "Sorry. I'm just wondering where this advice has been my entire life, that's all. Did Madigan teach you all that?"

With a wry grin, Tex clicked his tongue. "He's more than just a pretty face."

Deciding to wait until he was alone to lapse into a full-fledged existential crisis, because it was possible he'd never once played anything in his life through to the end, including coming back to Red Falls, Cole said, "Does anyone else have anything they want to talk about?"

Sam took a deep breath, then blew it out through his lips. "I'm nervous." While the rest of the men settled down again, waiting quietly, Sam explained. "I'm leaving Little Timber next month, and it's kind of freaking me out. I definitely don't want to stay here forever. But the idea of leaving is..."

"Heavy?" Stanley suggested.

Several of the men grunted their agreement.

"Yeah," Sam said. "And it's not that I'm worried about using again."

Heads whipped up, even Murphy's.

Raising his hands, laughing, Sam amended, "Okay, I'm not *only* worried about using again. Look, I know things won't magically be perfect with Izzy and Sara, but I'm ready to put the work in. So that's not what's keeping me up at night either. It's more like..." He looked up to the sky. "It's hard to describe."

Cole, who had a thousand words for every emotion he'd ever felt, wondered if there was something in the water in Red Falls that made people clam up. Sam, Davis, Kev, Mira—who'd literally pushed him out of her bakery the other day after he'd held her hand over his heart in the shower and told her, "It beats a little faster when I'm with you."

"This is a safe space, Sam," Stanley said. "If you want to talk about it, we're listening."

"It's just... It's embarrassing."

"Aww," Thom crooned. "Are you worried about not being able to sleep without Tex in the next bed over?"

Elbowing Thom in the ribs, Kev said, "Don't be an idiot."

"Thom may be an idiot," Sam said evenly, "but he's not completely wrong. Obviously, I don't need Tex sleeping next to me every night, even though it's been nice, like summer camp. But it's little things like that. Mundane, everyday things. I'm gonna have to go grocery shopping, open up a bank account, pay my bills, get a job. Actually *go* to that job, like, consistently. I wasn't very good at that stuff before, and when I think of the responsibilities waiting for me out there, the stress involved in just existing as a sober, functioning member of society, I'm freaking terrified. What if, even after all the tools I've learned here and all the strategies Madigan's taught me, it's still too much?" His huffed laughter lacked any humor. "What if I just suck at real life?"

After a beat, Ace said, "So what if you do?"

Sam frowned. "What if I suck?"

"Yeah. What if you went back to real life with the mindset that it was okay to suck at it? Maybe it's okay to be overwhelmed by having to pay bills and hold down a job. Maybe it doesn't mean there's anything wrong with you if it's all really hard at first. Maybe sober, functioning members of society are just better at messing up than we are. Maybe they're more"—Ace scratched his chin thoughtfully— "*forgiving* of themselves."

Half the men nodded, the other half stared at the ground.

"We're gonna let people down," Ace continued. "It's inevitable. And letting them down by forgetting the eggs at the grocery store is a hell of a lot better than letting them down by using again. For people like us, just forgetting the eggs is, like, progress. We should celebrate it."

After a moment of silence, Sam made an explosive sound, his

fingers flinging into the air. "I need to build a shelter for that insight bomb."

"Sometimes," Tex said, "I wonder if one of the reasons we became addicts is because we're all so scared of the same thing."

"Failing?" Cole guessed.

Every man nodded this time, until someone asked, so quietly the wind nearly swept his words away, "But what if that's all we'll ever do?"

Kev's question landed like a blow, and Cole opened his mouth to ask—*more like beg*—Kev to elaborate, to let them in, give them a tiny hint about whatever was making him withdraw so hard it created a vacuum around him. A vacuum that was sucking Davis in too while she and Kev tiptoed around each other, the distance between them stretching farther and farther each day. But then his phone buzzed.

He silenced the call. And when his phone buzzed again, he wondered if he should answer it. What if it was Becks? Or Madigan? He'd sacrifice a big toe to put Madigan on speaker right now. Mad would know what to say. He'd know how to keep Kev talking.

Buzz, buzz, buzzzz.

"If you need to get that"—Tex pointed his chin at Cole's shorts—"go ahead. We can keep things going here."

Pushing himself up from his log, Cole said, "Sorry, guys. I'll only be a second." He turned away from the men, pulled his phone out of his pocket, and smiled at his screen. It wasn't Madigan. It was Mira.

"Hey, sugar," he said, keeping his tone light while the hairs on the back of his neck flicked up one by one. Mira hadn't actually called him since he showed up in Red Falls, only texted. He wasn't sure why, but these days, he always expected bad, or at least significant, news whenever anyone called him.

"Hi," Mira said. "Are you busy?"

He glanced over his shoulder at the men, at Kev picking silently at his log again. Whatever the moment was, whatever Kev might have been about to say, it was over now. "I'm never too busy for you. What's up?"

"Are you sure? I can call back. Are you with the guys? Are you working? Shit. You're working, aren't you?"

"I'm on a break. Is everything okay?" he asked, her rapid-fire speech doing nothing to restore his sense of calm.

"Yeah. Everything is good. Amazing, actually."

"Funny," he said, stepping farther away from the guys. "That's exactly what I've been telling myself since I rolled back into town."

When she laughed over the line, he was back in Seattle, lying in his bed, remembering how tightly he'd pressed his phone to his ear all night long so he wouldn't miss a single word she'd said, a single breath. And while she told him about her call with the senator's aide, he grinned so wide he probably earned a new wrinkle.

"It's all because of you," she told him. "If you hadn't posted that reel, he never would have seen me."

"Nah, sugar. That was all you. If you hadn't done something so sweet for me, there wouldn't have been a reel to post."

"Is there any chance you might be free tonight?"

He ran his tongue over the tip of his left canine. "I mean, I'd planned on hitting you up after work."

"Um, instead of getting laid, how does a night of pizza and cards sound?"

"Good?" he ventured, wondering if this was some sort of bizarre trick question. "I love pizza, and I'm great at cards."

"We were going to celebrate tonight. And my mom wants, we all want, Ian too...and me." She groaned, then said all at once, "Would you like to come over tonight for dinner and cards with me and my family?"

Either the sun chose that precise moment to break through the clouds, or it had always been shining down on him, and he'd only noticed it now. Either way, every inch of his skin warmed by a few degrees. "I'd love to."

"You would?" She sounded genuinely surprised, which genuinely surprised him right back. Because how could she not see it? How could she not tell how far gone he was for her? It wasn't like he was trying to hide it. Well, maybe a little. But that was only because he still wasn't sure if she felt the same.

Despite how it looked, he really was trying to be more careful with his feelings, hold them closer to his chest instead of pinning them right out there on his sleeve. But while the guys were afraid of failing, Cole had whatever the exact opposite of that was. He was almost pathologically optimistic, diving headfirst off every cliff because there was no doubt the water would be deep enough, warm enough, safe enough.

He only had two weeks left in Red Falls, so of course he'd love to spend the night eating pizza and playing cards with Mira and her family. He'd spend an entire day sitting in uncomfortable plastic chairs at the DMV, getting two-for-one root canals, staring at taillights in never-ending rush hour traffic, anything, if it meant he'd be doing it next to her.

His head knew this was dangerous territory, that he was falling too hard, too fast. If he followed his craving for something real and lasting with Mira all the way through to the end like Tex had said, maybe he'd be able to see all the ways they wouldn't work out, maybe he'd agree with her that they needed to keep things between them surface level. But his heart was incapable of looking into the future. It was too busy running to the edge of the nearest cliff and diving.

"What time do you want me, and what can I bring?"

CHAPTER TWENTY-NINE

MIRA

Renee, Senator Richardson's daughter, had been somewhat vague on the phone about what she and her fiancé Amy wanted for their wedding cake. Aside from three tiers of lemon chiffon, they wanted it to look "Artsy, but not pretentious. Unique, but not annoying. Sweet, but not pretty." When Mira had asked them to send her some pictures of the kinds of cakes they liked, Renee had told her, "We've looked on your website. We trust you. Have fun with it."

She'd spent the last two hours since their phone call sketching, not "having fun" with anything. Maybe it was the pressure, but she couldn't get the images in her head to obey and jump to the page.

She'd kept the sound turned up on her phone all day, not wanting to miss Renee's call, so when her screen lit up with sunny Cole on his boat, Whitney sang, "And Iiii-eeyiii will always love youuu."

"Hi Cole," she said after silencing her phone again. He definitely didn't need to know she'd Whitneyed his ringtone.

"Hi Mira. I'm here."

Dropping her pencil onto her sketchpad, she walked into the bakery and gave herself over to the full-bodied sigh that only Cole standing outside her door—flowers in one hand, a bottle of red in the other, and a smirk curving his lips—could give her.

But then she refortified. If she let him become her in-person source of full-body sighs, of skin-pebbling excitement, of heart-aching relief, then once he went back home, once she spent every night alone in her window again, listening to the echoes of Jimmy's jukebox, surrounded by the clothes currently trapped in her closet that would be re-strewn all over her floor, she didn't know if she'd be able to stand it.

His head tilted while he watched her unlock the door, brow creasing like he heard every thought she was trying to keep trapped between her ears.

"Hey," he said when she let him inside. "Are you okay?"

Not answering his question, because she was perfectly fine, she took his flowers and his wine and set them on the counter. "Thank you for these," she said, then she took his shirt in her hands and urged his lips to hers. Because this was what they did. This was the agreement. This was what she could stand.

Wrapping her up tightly in his arms, he kissed her like the world was ending, which was exactly how she needed to be kissed. When she started walking backward, he followed her through the hall and into the kitchen, spinning her around after he closed the door behind them, pressing her up against it.

Her hands slid up the back of his shirt while he hitched one of her legs up over his hip, palming her ass.

"Where are Ian and Linda?" he asked, trailing kisses down the side of her neck.

"Upstairs."

Humming against her collarbone, he said, "So fucking you right here on the kitchen table would probably be a bad idea."

"Unfortunately."

"That's a shame." Dragging his lips from her skin, his hand from her ass, he kissed her temple, then turned around, reaching into his jeans.

"What are you doing?" she asked.

"Just adjusting myself so your mom and kid don't get an eyeful of erection bulge."

While she fought the urge to reach inside his jeans and take care of his bulge no matter how many people were waiting for them, he started turning back to her, stalling out halfway. "Holy shit, Mira." He walked to the table where she'd been sketching and spread her drawings out carefully. "Are these for the senator's daughter?"

"No," she said. "Not yet, anyway."

He slid the sketch she'd just been working on closer, the one with lace and pearl detailing piped to look like embroidery. "They're amazing."

"None of them are quite right. Something's missing." She just wasn't sure what. "I have time, though. It'll come."

Leaning over, he studied the cake with hand-painted lupine and wild roses. "The only thing missing is the magazine cover these cakes should be gracing. You'll need to hire more staff to deal with the orders you're going to get after all those people see what you can do."

"Cole, that's"—she placed a hand over the sudden tightness in her throat—"such a nice thing to say."

"Can I have one of these? If you're not going to use them."

"You want one of my cake sketches?"

"I want them all. But I'll settle for one." He turned to face her. "If you're okay with it."

She could only imagine how red her cheeks were, how many splotches decorated her throat. "I'm okay with it—"

"The pizza's almost here!" Ian called from the top of the stairs. "You want me to come down and get it or what?"

"Nope!" she shouted, grinning at Cole while he smiled back at her, feeling like they'd just gotten caught doing something scandalous even though they were only looking at cakes. "We'll get it!"

Kissing her quickly, Cole said, "I want this one," pointing to the lupine and wild rose sketch.

"If you want it"—she kissed him back—"then it's yours."

"Are those the rules now?" His hands found their way to her hips. "Because there are all sorts of things I want—"

The knock at the front door cut him off, which was probably for the best. Spinning him around, she nudged him out of the kitchen. "You can tell me all about them later."

"Believe me," he warned, "I will."

"You must be Cole," her mom said, rising from their tiny table in their tiny dining area, her salt and pepper hair brushed and curled, her favorite coral lipstick freshly applied. She was wearing a lovely pale blue linen blouse Mira had never seen before. Maude Alice must have taken her shopping.

"It's so nice to meet you, Linda." Cole leaned in for a hug while Mira walked to the kitchen to put his flowers in water. "But I hope I'm not crashing your party tonight."

"Not at all. We both wanted to meet the man making Mira smile more than she has in years. Isn't that right, Ian?"

"Mimi," Ian grumbled. "Awkward."

Glancing over his shoulder at Mira while she uncorked his wine, he said, "Is that so?"

Mira pursed her lips, bit her cheek, did everything she could not to smile back at Cole, thus proving her mom's point. "Who wants pepperoni?"

"Me," Ian said, his thumbs flying over his phone screen. "Four pieces please."

"Mom, do you want some wine?"

Cole popped up from his seat. "I can help with that. Linda? Wine? It's red."

"Is there any other kind?" her mom asked.

"Not in my world," he replied with a grin so warm Mira's heart simmered.

"Only a small glass for Mom," she whispered when Cole joined her in the kitchen. "She can get a little loopy if she drinks too much."

"So can I," he whispered back, leaning in close enough for his lips to brush over the shell of her ear. "I'll keep all our glasses light, so nobody feels singled out."

It was such a simple, thoughtful gesture that, in her experience, most people wouldn't have thought to make.

"And can I chip in for the pizza?" He reached for his wallet. "I think I have some cash."

"No," she told him. "Absolutely not. You're my guest tonight."

"Okay, then I guess I'll just have to find another way to pay you back." He slid his hand to her ass, then smacked it.

At Mira's shocked chirp, her mom turned in her chair. "You okay in there?"

"Sorry," Mira said, raising an incriminating brow in Cole's direction. "The pizza's hot." Holding his stare, she sucked her finger into her mouth, sliding it back out with a small *pop*, because two could play at the being-inappropriately-horny-in-the-kitchen game. "I think I burned myself."

Eyeing her lips, rolling his own together, Cole backed out of the kitchen and brought the glasses of wine to the table.

"Music?" Mira asked after passing out the pizza and taking her seat.

Cole had just raised his glass to his lips when Ian suggested, "How about the Makers?"

Coughing on his wine, Cole said, "Good one," holding his fist out to the side for Ian to bump.

There was a split second where Mira's breath caught, when she worried Ian might leave Cole hanging, but she exhaled when their knuckles touched. Ian, she thought, might have even smiled.

Her mom cleared her throat. "Alexa, play the album *Graceland*."

Holding his fist out toward her mom now, Cole said, "Fantastic choice." Their knuckles bumped as "The Boy in the Bubble" started playing, and Mira rose from the table.

She'd only wanted to grab some napkins, but she listed, forced to steady herself on the kitchen counter while her head went fuzzy, the room spinning. She hadn't had more than a sip, so it couldn't have been the wine. She finally felt relaxed, so it couldn't have been her normal daily intake of stress. But there was something about her mom and her son and...her Cole together in her apartment, sharing this space with these people she cared about so deeply. He *fit* here, she realized. He clicked into place like the most unfair puzzle piece, the kind that belonged right in the middle of the puzzle, so once it was gone, all you'd ever see was the empty space it left behind.

She knew this thing with him was temporary. She'd never leave Red Falls. And even on the off chance that he'd be willing, she'd never ask him to leave Seattle, leave his daughter and granddaughter, his friends, his sailboat and his studio and the endless opportunities his life there afforded him that she couldn't begin to compete with. But watching him nestle himself comfortably between the people she loved most in this world, heartache, both wonderful and terrible, spread through her entire body until it was everywhere all at once.

Finding her phone on the counter, needing to talk to someone, to tell at least one person what she knew was true, she sent Jen a text.

> Mira: I think I'm in trouble with him.

In a split second, Jen texted back.

> Jen: Yeah, babe. I know.

CHAPTER THIRTY

COLE

"Bullshit!" Linda shouted, and when Ian turned over his cards, proving that he did, in fact, have three aces, she cried, "Cheater, cheater, pants on fire!"

"That's not a saying, Mimi. It doesn't even rhyme. And I didn't cheat." Ian cracked his knuckles. "I'm just really, really good."

Cole had come in last, because while he might be good at cards, he sucked at lying. But he didn't care. After spending the past week trying to be Madigan, it was nice to be away from the mountain, away from the constant worry he might do or say the wrong thing, and just be himself.

"You're a card shark is what you are," Mira said, nudging Ian gently on the shoulder while he checked something on his phone. When he frowned, she asked, "Brendan?"

"Yeah." His lips twisted. "It's okay, though."

"You can go, buddy."

"Are you sure? I don't have to."

Cole recognized this dance all too well, the kid's social life calling while they were supposed to be having family time. He always used to let Becks go too.

"I'm sure. Have fun."

Rising to his feet, Ian fluffed his hair and said, "Um, that was fun. Cole, you should come over more often or something."

Cole held his hand out, and Ian picked up on the dude-cue, slapping his palm twice, then sliding out until their fingertips hooked together and snapped. "I'd love to. Maybe we could even play together sometime. You'd absolutely crush on my YouTube channel."

"Seriously?" Ian's eyes popped. "But, wait... You've never heard me play."

Cole cut his eyes toward Mira. He didn't know if he'd be busting her or not, so he kept his mouth shut.

"I sent him some of your videos," Mira admitted with a preemptive wince. "Don't be mad."

"You're really fantastic," Cole said. "Super talented."

"Um, thanks." Color flashed high on Ian's pale cheeks. "I guess." He rounded the table and gave hugs to Mira and Linda. Then he was gone the way teenagers go, quickly and with little fanfare.

While Cole picked up the cards and slid them back into their box, Mira asked Alexa to play Washed Out, and Linda took a sip of her wine.

"Tell me about your family," Linda said while the chill music transformed the mood in the room to something more thoughtful. "You have a daughter, right?"

"And a granddaughter. Becks and Ruby. Ruby just turned six months old today."

"You missed it?" Mira asked with a gasp.

Giving her a reassuring smile—because was she worried about that? Was she worried he'd been here with her for the milestone?—he said, "It's okay. I FaceTimed with Becks this morning to celebrate." Picking his phone up off the table, he opened his *Ruby* folder, showing them the screenshot he'd taken of her stuffing a chocolate chip pancake into her mouth during their call.

"Oh, she's adorable," Linda said. With Cole's help, she flipped through a few more pictures before pausing on the selfie of Ruby sleeping on his chest, the one he'd sent to Mira what felt like ages ago now.

Pointing at Mira, Linda said, "I think I have a picture of your father holding you like this somewhere. Although"—her lips pressed tight—"I can't for the life of me remember where I put it."

"Most of the old pictures are in storage," Mira told her. "But we can go to the unit tomorrow and get them if you want to."

"No, no. It's all right." Linda looked at the picture again before handing Cole's phone back to him. "She's perfect."

Cole laughed. "She also wails like a fire engine."

"Do you remember how loud Ian used to be?" Linda asked. "He was colicky," she told Cole, quietly like it was a secret, tapping her fingernails on her wineglass. "He'd screamed bloody murder from dinner to bedtime."

"We had to take turns walking him back and forth down the alley." Mira shuddered. "In the dead of winter."

"Back then, there was a laundromat in the empty building across the street, and the owner called the cops on us. Twice."

"I forgot all about that," Mira said, shaking her head. "Honestly, I think I've blocked a lot of that time out. It was one of the hardest things I've ever been through." She looked at her mom, her throat working through a swallow. "I have no idea how I would have gotten through it alone."

There was a weight to the moment, to Mira's words, and Cole felt it like a current tugging on his boat, changing his course. Turning to Linda, he asked, "What was Mira like as a baby?"

Linda's eyes lit up. "Oh, a lot like she is now. Quiet, thoughtful, sensitive."

"That's so not true," Mira said, sitting back in her chair, bringing her glass of wine with her. "You told me I didn't sleep through the night until I was one. And I used to steal all the chocolate chip cookie dough from you and Gramps."

Linda waved a hand through the air. "That was when you were three. Everyone's an asshole when they're three."

"I'd thought I might have to hire a young priest and an old priest for an exorcism when Becks was three," Cole concurred.

"You were a very easy baby." Linda reached over to squeeze Mira's hand. "An easy kid. An easy teen. A wonderful daughter. I've never been so proud of anyone or anything, except maybe for Ian."

Mira's eyes shone then, sparkling like gems. And when she said, "I love you, Mom," with a broken warble, Cole suddenly felt too involved in this conversation that seemed like it should exist only between them. Rising from his chair, he said, "Let me get the dishes."

"That's not necessary, Cole."

Collecting Linda's plate, he told her, "It's the least I can do."

Gazing up at him while he took her plate, Mira said, "Thank you," and he wanted to kiss her then, kiss away that sadness in her eyes. But he only nodded and retreated to the kitchen.

While he washed and dried the dishes, he listened to Mira and Linda talk, he listened to them laugh. He watched them drink their wine, Mira's hand sliding over her mom's, Linda's head shaking back and forth as she swiped a knuckle under her eye. He listened to the music drifting through the apartment and felt moved. The song was about fate being a guide. Fate had brought him here, and he was grateful.

When he returned to the table, Linda finished what remained of her wine, then said, "I'm afraid it's past my bedtime."

"Already?" he asked, holding out his hand, helping her to her feet.

"Sleep is hard to come by, sometimes," she said with a yawn that felt forced. "And I actually feel tired tonight. Remind me, Cole. How much longer are you here?"

"Two weeks," he told her.

"That's not long at all, is it?" Holding his gaze, she patted his arm. "Good thing Seattle isn't very far away."

In that moment, he became transparent as glass, like she could see his heart beating beneath his ribs, her daughter's name scrawled all over it. "Good thing," he agreed.

After saying good night, Cole slid into his seat again while Linda made her way to her bedroom. But the moment her door snicked shut, Mira's head dropped into her hands, her shoulder shaking.

"Mira? Are you okay?"

In the silence, the quietest sob he'd ever heard escaped between her fingers.

"Hey, hey, hey." He slid his chair next to hers, close enough to rub her back. "What's wrong?"

"What am I...going...to do?" Her voice was shattered, and he realized that even though they'd talked about real things, hard things, even though he'd teared up more than a few times during their phone conversations—*no big surprise there*—she never had. He didn't like it, Mira crying.

"Come here," he said, pulling her onto his lap, holding her while she wept so silently the only sign of it was the wet spot her tears left on his shirt.

"What will I do?" she asked the safe space between his neck and shoulder. "What will I do when she's gone? When she leaves like everyone else?"

Everyone else? He supposed it made sense, after her dad, and then her stepdad, and then Paul, that she felt abandoned, left too easily. Well, good or bad, he never left anyone easily.

Sliding an arm under her knees, cradling her against him, he rose from his chair. While she clung to him, he carried her into her bedroom. After closing her door behind them, he placed her on her bed, slotted in behind her, curled his body around hers, and waited, letting her cry, not speaking. Not leaving.

"We never talk like that anymore," she said softly after several minutes. "But we used to. We used to talk like that all the time. We'd have these long conversations about parenting, about life and religion and politics over a glass of wine after Ian had gone to sleep. I hadn't realized how long it had been. I hadn't realized how much I'd missed them." A deep breath shuddered through her. "I hadn't even realized they were gone."

He pressed a kiss to her spine, right over the first note of her tattoo.

"She was so lucid tonight. She was so *Mom*. And every time she wakes up like this, I know I shouldn't, but I always wonder, is she getting better? Has this all just been a bad dream? Are all the doctors wrong? Are we the lucky ones?"

Wrapping his arm around her waist, he pulled her close.

"But then she'll get confused again, she'll forget. She might not even remember that tonight happened. Tomorrow she might, but in a month? A year? These memories that mean so much to me and to her, they might just...vanish." She bent her knees up, hugging them tightly to her chest, and Cole slid his arm around them too. "It's always been us. After everyone else left, we always had each other, me and Mom. And I feel so selfish, but I don't think I'm strong enough to watch her leave me too."

There was nothing to say to that, nothing that he thought would help, so he didn't try. He only held her, running his thumb over her wrist, letting time pass. Eventually, her shoulders relaxed as she released her knees, took his hand in hers, and pulled it up to her lips.

"I'm sorry I'm falling apart," she whispered into his knuckles. "I know this isn't our deal. You don't need to stay here with—"

"Fuck our deal," he said. "Respectfully."

"Cole, I'm serious."

So am I, Mira. "It's okay. Sometimes we have to fall apart. Life does not stop and start at our convenience, right?"

The tiny laugh she huffed made his heart ache.

"I'm not going anywhere," he promised. "If you need to cry, I'm here. If you want to talk, I'm here. If you want to stare at the wall in silence, I'm here. Whatever you need tonight, I'm here."

Her lips were soft on his skin, but her fingers squeezing his were cold. "I think I have to tell you something," she said. "But I'm worried you're going to think I'm weird."

"Okay," he said with a half smile.

"It's just, *ugh*, this is so embarrassing, because what I'm doing, the way I'm acting when we're together, it makes no sense. It—"

"Is this about the secret orgasms?"

Rolling over to face him, her mouth set—ironically—in a little round *o*, she said, "You know?"

"Of course I know." She might be able to stifle her moans well enough, but she could never hide the way her cheeks and her tits flushed red, the way she gripped him when she came. "I can feel it."

She groaned, burying her face in his chest.

"What's wrong?" He brushed a hand over her hair.

"What's wrong?" she repeated in an unnerved rasp. "I'm having silent orgasms. I have no idea why. And you've known the whole time!"

He couldn't help but smile. "I just figured you didn't want to jinx it. Like when the Mariners are on a streak or your record is climbing the charts. You don't talk about it. You just keep your head down and hope for the best."

Clearly, she didn't want to laugh, but she did anyway, and he loved the sound. Then she looked up at him again, her eyes pleading. "But it's not okay. It's not okay, because *I* am not okay. It's just, you're too good. You're too good in bed. You're too good in...me." Cupping his cheek, she said, "You're too good, Cole. And it scares the shit out of me. It scares me so much I'm having silent orgasms. What kind of weirdo does that? I mean, nobody in their right mind does that. But that's the thing. I'm not in my right mind when I'm with you."

He hadn't been in his right mind since he first laid eyes on her, but even if the sensation felt phenomenal to him, it made a solemn kind of sense that it might not feel that way for her. And maybe that was the thing, the stop sign she kept trying to erect between them. He was ready for the challenge of moving heaven and earth to be with her, and she already had so many challenges that adding one more to the pile might make it all feel insurmountable.

He didn't want to be another hard thing in her life, another obstacle she needed to overcome. He didn't want to be insurmountable for her. He wanted to be, in every possible way, mountable.

"I meant what I said, Mira. I'm not going anywhere unless you tell me to go. If it feels good being with me, then let it feel good. Let me make you feel good. I *want* to make you feel good." *More than you'll ever know.* He kissed her forehead, brushed his fingers over the shaved hair above her ear. "I don't care much for people who are in their right minds anyway. I'm here for the weirdos." He grinned at her. "So let's make some noise."

Like a ray of sunshine, her answering smile pierced the darkness in her room. Then she grabbed his face and pulled him into a kiss. His body responded, his arm snaking around her waist and tugging her across the bed, his fingers hauling her leg up over his hip, his tongue sliding between her lips.

"Shit," she bit out, breaking the kiss.

"Shit?" That wasn't the response he'd been hoping for.

"I forgot to tell you I got my test results back. I don't have any STIs."

Frowning, he asked, "Isn't that a good thing?"

"It would have been, but then I got my bullshit asshole period this morning."

He blew out an unimpressed breath. *If she thinks that will stop me...* Kissing her top lip, and then her bottom lip, he said, "Sugar, if you need to be fucked, I have no problem fucking you while you're bleeding." He kissed her eyelids, one at a time, both still puffy, still red. "We can do, or not do, whatever you want. Whatever you need."

"I want to be with you." She watched him while he took her hand in his, kissing her fingertips one by one. "But I'm bloated and crampy and, honestly"—her eyes misted over again—"just really sad."

"Have you taken any ibuprofen?"

"No. I probably should. I'll go get some."

"I got it," he said, grasping her hip, holding her still when she tried to roll away. "Where is it?"

"Kitchen. Cupboard over the sink. And thank you, Cole, for everything."

After giving her a soft kiss, he padded into the kitchen, filling his palm with two Advil and a glass with cold water. Slipping back into her room, kneeling on her bed, he fed her the Advil one by one. Then he put the glass of water on her nightstand, rolled her onto her side, and nestled in behind her again. When she grabbed his hand and tucked it back under her chin, he kissed her shoulder and said, "Mira?"

"Yes, Cole?"

Breathing in her sugary, citrus scent, he said, "You make me feel scary good too. I just thought you should know."

In the quiet stillness of her room, while her body relaxed in his arms, his mind did the opposite. He wanted to stay with her all night, to let her sleep in and make her breakfast in bed, and if she was up for it, silently fuck her senseless so she could start her day loose and smiling. But he had to get back to Bluebird. Besides, she'd let him hug her, cuddle her, hold her while she fell asleep. He'd take the win.

Emotions: One. Meaningless robot sex: Zero.

He kissed her neck one last time before pulling her covers up over her shoulders and tucking her in tight. Unable to bring himself to wake her up to say goodbye, he thought about sending her a text, but he couldn't find her phone and didn't want to risk the notification noise in case it wasn't on silent. Luckily, he found several torn scraps of paper and one of those multicolored pens next to a book of matches and a jar full of ashes on her dresser. Her wish jar.

Clicking on the pen's black tab, he wrote *You're beautiful when you sleep. Call me later*, and only paused for half a second before adding *Love, Cole*. Folding the paper in half, he placed it on her nightstand, hoping this was a wish she wouldn't burn.

Stepping through her door, he doubled back, remembering something. It was dark in her room, and she hated the dark. Walking over to her window, the same window she'd sat in countless times when they'd texted and talked, and that one time they'd FaceTimed, he reached down to where the cord dangled along her wall, and then he plugged in her string of twinkly lights.

CHAPTER THIRTY-ONE

COLE

AFTER SPENDING so much time on the mountain clearing trails, not only did Cole no longer need to slather his neck and back in Tiger Balm at the end of every day, but he could almost keep up with the guys all the way until they reached the day's stake. When he wasn't busy cutting down trees, he led groups with Murphy, helped Maude Alice cook for the men, went on walks with Davis, saw Mira whenever possible, and went to sleep exhausted but also happier than he had any right to be. But nothing made him as happy as Ruby's face on his phone.

"How is she so much bigger? I've only been gone for two weeks!"

Chewing on her pappy, Ruby produced a string of drool that landed on her shirt, then squealed.

"I guess that's what happens when all you do is eat and sleep," Becks said, flipping the camera back to herself. "How's it going over there? You crushing it?"

"Not sure I'd go that far, but it's going well." He sounded more confident than he felt, faking it until making it even though everything seemed to be going smoothly. The guys worked hard, passed all their drug tests, hung out reading on their porches or talking around the fire pit Cole dug out in the clearing between the cabins—after asking Madigan if it would be okay and receiving a "Why haven't I ever thought of that?" text in response. It had all been relatively easy, surprisingly quiet. "I haven't had to give out bathroom duty once."

Her face pinched. "What the hell is bathroom duty?"

"Long story," he said, waving her off. "How are you two? Has Nancy come by yet?"

"Yeah. Briefly the other day. It was...fine."

"With your mom, sometimes 'fine' is the *best we can hope for*," he cooed when Becks flipped the camera back to Ruby, who'd started blowing raspberries. "I need to kiss those pudgy cheeks!"

"How are things with the baker?"

Even Ruby sensed the weight of that question, settling down to stare at him intently with her huge caramel eyes while she popped her pappy back into her mouth.

"They're good," Cole answered quickly, keeping his voice level.

"Good? Is that all? Because I saw your Instagram post of her bread racks the other day, and then the one of her hands kneading dough, and that last one of her looking out the window of your cabin with her hair up in a ponytail and the sun hitting her just so..."

He scratched his head.

"Dad." Becks flipped the screen again so he could see how serious she was, bordering on dire. "I'm not sure if you know this or not, but your Instagram appears to be deeply, deeply in love. Have you spoken with it recently? Done a welfare check?"

While it was true that he and Mira had been having a *lot* of fun lately, he still had his work cut out for him when it came to anything more than that. He'd thought they'd had a breakthrough last week, but after he'd tucked her in and driven back up to Bluebird, she'd woken up in the middle of the night and texted him to apologize for "breaking their rules," telling him if he needed to take a step back from her, she understood because she was "a mess, and her life was complete and utter chaos."

It had taken every ounce of self-preservation left in him not to drive right back down the mountain, run up her stairs, take her face between his hands, and tell her, "No, I will not be taking a fucking step back from you." But after a few deep breaths, he texted back.

Cole: Without chaos, there would be no stars in the sky. See you tomorrow.

"It's not like that," he said, lying to his own flesh and blood. "We're only—"

"Friends?" Becks guessed. "Tell that to your story yesterday of the sun setting over Bluebird with the song 'Lips Like Sugar' playing in the background. Felt like I was watching the end of an elder-emo rom-com."

He'd shot that video after he'd gotten back from spending an hour steaming up her Element's windows, parked in the woods halfway between Bluebird and Glazed, the ridges of her floor mat still indenting his knees, her taste still sweet on his tongue.

"You're reading too much into it," he said. "I *am* an elder-emo rom-com." When the doorbell rang across the line, he stiffened. "Who's that?" he asked, his instinctual dad fight-or-flight response kicking in. He never liked it when they were alone. "Check the doorbell camera. Don't let anyone you don't recognize in."

"Dad, you must chill," she said. "It's just Josh. I gotta go."

"Josh is coming over again?" It was the third time in the last week, not that he'd been checking their doorbell cam too. "Are you two doing better?"

Flipping the screen back to Ruby, Becks evaded the question with "Say goodbye to your grandpa. Love you, Dad."

"Becks, wait!" But it was too late, and Ruby was too damn cute. "Bye-bye, little angel," he said, waving at the phone. "Grandpa will see you soon. Tell your mom to talk to me about your dad, okay?"

Ruby squealed so loud it echoed between his ears long after Becks ended the call. Staring at his silent screen, sitting in the rocking chair in his silent cabin, Cole felt suddenly so alone he could barely breathe. He missed Becks and Ruby so much it hurt. But he also knew the next time he'd get to see them, he'd only trade missing them for missing Mira. The realization made him sink helplessly into the cushion beneath him. But he didn't have time for existential sinking. Today was a day off at Little Timber. And that meant he'd spend all afternoon monitoring visitations.

While he rocked forward to stand up, his phone buzzed again.

"Hey, Benji," he said, making his voice light, pretending he hadn't nearly been swallowed whole by a rocking chair.

"Cole? Jesus, man. You sound like shit. You sick or something?"

Apparently, he hadn't done a very good job. "I'm good. Just got done FaceTiming with Becks and Ruby."

"Ah, yeah. Homesick, right?"

That wasn't quite it. Cole missed his family, but he wouldn't call the weight pushing on his shoulders homesickness. Because, as clearly as he'd ever felt anything, he felt at home here too. "Something like that."

"Funny thing," Benji said. "I might be able to help you out with that."

Cole straightened. "What do you mean?"

"You know that band you've been trying to get to use Trax?"

He slid to the edge of the rocking chair. "The Sympathy Gags?"

"Apparently, they just go by the SyGs now."

"Cute."

"Well," Benji continued, "I saw them the other night, and they were fantastic. I talked to them after the show. I didn't think they were into using Trax at all, probably because they were ridiculously stoned. But they called me yesterday, then they came by. They're actually interested. They loved our, quote, 'old-school vibes.' They want to start recording next week."

"That's amazing!" This was the type of break they'd been waiting for, that Cole had been pushing for. Getting the new Seattle punk scene to give them a chance.

"There's only one problem. They want to meet. Tomorrow."

"Okay," Cole said. "The service up here isn't fantastic, but I can drive into town to do a Zoom—"

"That's the thing. Apparently, they don't Zoom. Or use social media. Or cell phones. The lead singer used a pay phone to call me, and I wish that was a joke. They think 'technology is the end of civilization as we know it.' They want to meet in person, otherwise they're going to go somewhere else."

"Can't you meet with them?"

"I offered that. They want you."

"Me?"

"The one and only."

Getting to his feet, needing to pace, Cole said, "Shit, Benji. I can't meet with them tomorrow. I'm here for another week. They won't give me a week to get back?"

"They wanted to meet today. I had to beg them to give us until tomorrow. Look, I can send the jet in the morning and have you back in Red Falls by dinner. This is huge for us, Cole. I'm sure Madigan will understand."

Tomorrow was another off day for the guys, and there were only a few visitations scheduled. If there was ever a time when Cole might feel okay asking Maude Alice to cover Little Timber by herself, that would be it. He'd have to clear it with Mad first, but a trip back to Seattle, only for a day, just to show her how easy it could be to visit him there...

"Can I bring someone with me?"

COLE COULDN'T TELL who was more exhausted after the visitations, him, the guys, or Murphy after he'd spent the entire day running from cabin to cabin, meeting and greeting everyone who'd come to the mountain. Walking up the lodge steps after getting an unexpect-edly enthusiastic thumbs-up from Madigan to take the day off tomorrow—especially after he'd confessed his hope that Mira would come to Seattle with him—Cole filled Murphy's bowl with food and fresh water, then made his way toward the kitchen.

"Maude Alice? Davis?" he called out. "You home?"

"Back here," Davis answered.

When he opened the door to Ashley's office, he slowed, the hairs on his neck rising one by one.

Davis stood staring out through the window, her arms crossed, her shoulders drawn in so tightly the ridge of her spine poked through her shirt.

"Everything all right?" he asked. "You look—"

"Do you want to know something?" she said to the window, so quietly he had to strain to hear her. "Despite what people might think, Kev and I have never been intimate. Not physically, anyway."

While Cole stepped into the room, Murphy pushed through the door, trotting over to sit at Davis's side. Raising a fuzzy brow, the dog fixed Cole with an expression that said, "Here's your chance, pal. Don't blow it."

"Oh?" Cole eventually said. It wasn't poetry, but if it kept her talking...

"We've been together, or whatever you want to call what we've been, for over six months, and we've never even kissed. He said it was because of Madigan's rules, because he wanted to keep things simple while he was learning how to stay clean."

Cole wasn't sure how to respond, but for some reason, no matter what, he knew he needed to get her away from that window. Because whatever she was looking at down there, it was sucking the life out of her right before his eyes. "Do you want to sit down?" He took a step toward her. "We can talk about it."

Turning to look at him, tears standing in her eyes, and like she hadn't even heard him, she said, "But we used to at least hold hands.

He used to hug me, touch me. We used to be close. We used to *feel* close." She blinked a tear down her cheek, then swiped it away while she faced the window again. "I've tried my hardest to support him. But that's all I feel like I'm doing now, just *being* there for Kev. And every day, it feels more and more like it doesn't matter, because he's just...gone."

Gingerly, he edged closer, trying to look past her through the window.

"I love him, Cole. I've never loved anyone before, but I love him. I know it in my bones and my skin, my hair, all these parts of myself I never realized could hurt this badly. And maybe he did once," she said as another tear slipped free, "but I don't think he loves me back anymore. I've been spending all day, every day, wondering how I can fix this. But right now"—her finger rose, trembling, pointing at the glass while her jaw clenched—"the only thing I'm wondering, is who the *fuck* is that?"

Staring down through the window, following the line of Davis's finger, Cole whispered, "Shit," before he could stop himself.

In front of the trees, at the foot of the path leading back to the cabins, Kev stood with his arms at his sides, leaning in close and talking in what looked like hushed tones to another woman. A woman with long blondish hair and pale, reedy arms who reached out, cradled his neck, and pulled his forehead toward hers.

"You know who she is, don't you?" Davis's voice cracked, her eyes hollow, empty.

Of course Cole knew who she was. Murphy hadn't been the only one who'd made sure to meet all the visitors today. But he couldn't tell Davis that the woman was Thom's sister without his permission.

"I do," he told her, and his heart sank. "But I can't—"

"Right." She laughed, but it was nothing but pain. "More rules." Finally leaving the window, she walked to her mom's desk and sat slowly in her chair.

Cole's heart wanted to respond in the same way it would have responded to his own daughter hurting. He wanted to comfort Davis the same way he'd comfort Becks, to hug her, make her dinner, take her sailing, try and make everything better as fast as possible no matter what it took. But Davis wasn't Becks. He wasn't the one who could fix this, if anyone could. "Have you tried talking to him about how you feel?"

Her shoulders rose and fell. "Sort of, but it's hard. I think I'm scared that if we finally admit out loud that something's wrong, whatever we do still have together won't survive it. Not that it's surviving now." She gazed up at him. "What's wrong with me, Cole? I used to be stronger than this. I'd never let anyone shut me out like this before I met Kev."

Sitting down across from her, he reached out, taking her hand in his. "It's different when you really love someone, and all you want, more than anything in the world, is for them to love you back." A shiver crawled across his neck at his own words. Like by trying to help Davis with hers, he'd inadvertently voiced his own insecurities.

When he'd called her after getting the okay from Madigan, he hadn't been surprised by Mira's hesitance to join him in Seattle. He'd been more surprised that she actually agreed. But now, the quiet but persistent part of him that wondered if he was doing it again, loving too hard, going all in on someone without making sure they felt the same, suddenly became uncomfortably loud.

"I know what you're thinking," Davis said, cutting in on his dismal thoughts that were likely not at all what she suspected. "It's the same things my friends keep telling me, to protect myself, to be willing to let him go if he keeps refusing to open up. They all make it sound so easy, but they don't understand. Nothing about this is easy."

"Davis, I'm not going to say any of those things. I'm literally the last person to give advice about fighting for a relationship that might not be worth fighting for. I did it for most of my life."

"How did you know when to stop?" she asked, her desperation grabbing his heart and squeezing. "How did you know when it was time to give up?"

"I'm not sure I ever really knew," he answered honestly, another shiver gripping his neck. "But I think, eventually, I realized it hurt more to be with Nancy than it hurt to be without her."

She stared at him for a long moment, and when Murphy grumbled across the room, she said, "I don't think I'm there yet." Allowing herself a single chin wobble, she wiped her eyes dry. "I'm probably overreacting anyway. Kev and that woman out there are probably just friends."

"I'm sure they are," he lied, not actually sure of anything.

"Thanks, Cole." She smiled at him, but it was only by definition. "Thanks for listening. I can't talk about Kev with Mom or Madigan. Mom is...*Mom*, and Madigan and Kev are too close, too complicated. Don't tell Madigan I talked to you, okay?"

"I won't," he promised her. He wouldn't tell Mad about Davis, but he wondered if he should tell him about Thom's sister. She was on the list, and even though she'd looked a little strung out when she'd showed up this afternoon, Cole had figured she was safe. But if she knew Kev, if they had a history, maybe she wasn't.

Rolling her neck, downshifting so suddenly Cole felt the lurch, she said, all business, "You probably came up here for a reason. Did you need something?"

With what she'd just told him, what they'd just seen through the window, the answer to that question felt a hell of a lot heavier than it had ten minutes ago. "I have to leave tomorrow. Only for the day," he added when her gaze snapped to his. "There's a band that wants to use the studio, and I need to meet with them. I've already told Mad, but I wanted to make sure it was okay with Maude Alice, and you, before I left."

Her mouth opened, then closed, then she said, "I see. I'm sure Grandma won't mind watching Little Timber."

"Davis." He held her stare. "I don't have to go. If you're worried about—"

"We'll be fine." And then, because she was just like her grandmother in that nothing much got past her, she asked, "Are you going alone?"

LIPS LIKE SUGAR 281

"No," he admitted. "Mira's coming."

"That's good." Davis nodded. "Really good. A chance to show Mira a bit of your world. It's not like Seattle is a million miles away, right?"

He'd heard this sentiment before. He'd said it to himself. But the longer he stayed in Red Falls, the farther away Seattle felt. He'd do his best to convince Mira she could have an easy place in his world, but more and more, after their evening walks through town, having dinner with her at charming little restaurants, spending time with her family, unwinding to the slower pace here, he wondered if his world was what he wanted anymore. "I'm going to try" was all he could say.

"Are you seeing her tonight?"

"I was. But I don't have to. We can hang out if you want, maybe go for a hike to watch the sunset? It's gorgeous out." It was a blissfully cool evening after a string of ninety-degree days, and while it was true that he'd gnaw his own hand off if it was stuck in a trap to see Mira tonight, he wanted to make sure Davis was okay. Besides, he could always sneak out later when everyone else had gone to sleep, throw pebbles Romeo-style at her window, scramble up her fire escape and into her room...

"A hike's not a bad idea," she said. "I need to think. Or maybe I need to clear my mind." She shrugged, attempting a genuine smile. "Maybe both. But you should go see Mira."

"You don't want company?"

"Thank you, but no. I think I need to be alone." Her smile died before it stood a chance. "I should probably get used to it, right?"

He wanted to say something helpful, something profound and wise that would keep her from making the same mistakes he'd made, or at least let her know she wasn't alone if she decided to make them anyway. But if someone had said something like that to him when he'd been in her shoes, he wouldn't have listened to them. He only ever listened to his heart. So he pivoted to his never-fail strategy for making Becks feel better, hoping it would work on Davis too. "Can I bring you back some pastries from Glazed? Mira made huckleberry danishes this morning."

"Oh, sure," she said, placating him now. "That would be great."

Gaining his feet, he walked to the window. "She's gone. Kev must have gone back to his cabin."

"She might not be on the mountain anymore," Davis said behind him. "But I think we both know she's not gone."

CHAPTER THIRTY-TWO

MIRA

"Are you sure you'll be okay?" Mira asked, looking nervously between her mom and Ian. "I don't have to go."

"Oh, yes you do," her mom said, playing solitaire at the dining room table. "A sexy, single man offers you a free trip to Seattle on a private jet, you go."

Her mom calling Cole *sexy* was not on her Sunday morning bingo card, but she couldn't disagree. He was sexy. He was also sweet and kind, and he did things like tuck her in and plug in her twinkly lights. It had made her think about his wedding speech, how someone could be the light for someone else when their world went dark. She'd wondered if he could be that person for her.

"You're only gone for the day," Ian said from the couch, his thumbs clicking over his remote. "I think we can handle it."

It wasn't that Mira thought the bakery would burst into flames the second she buckled up in Cole's passenger seat. It wasn't that she hadn't left her mom alone for an entire day before. And it definitely wasn't that Ian couldn't fend for himself. But she'd never left the state. Because she didn't do things like say, "See ya!" and zip off in a private jet for the day. She was too busy dunking her feet in cement and chaining herself to every responsibility within a twenty-mile radius.

So why shouldn't she go? What was she actually risking? She knew what she was risking by not going: a chance to meet Cole's people, see his life, maybe have sex on a private jet. It was also a chance to see if *she* could actually visit *him* every once in a while, if the ability to see him wouldn't always depend on him leaving Seattle, if they could really make something out of this relationship she was more and more tempted every day to call it a relationship. Out loud. To other people. To him.

It wouldn't be easy. It might not work out. But nobody in her life had ever once asked her to stop living because of them. That was something she was doing all by herself. Maybe she could take a chance. Maybe they could find a balance. Maybe she could be his light too.

A car horn honked twice, each one a shot of adrenaline skyrocketing up her spine.

"Your chariot awaits," her mom said, waving Mira over for a hug, telling her when she leaned in, "And don't worry about us for one minute. We will be just fine."

Smiling down at her mom, then kissing Ian on his head, Mira decided to believe it.

"Wow," Mira whispered, popping her head out of the jet to a crystal-clear view of Mount Rainier, its snowy peak rising above a thin layer of haze like a diamond hovering in the sky.

"Amazing, right?" Cole asked, joining her on the airplane stairs.

"It was too cloudy to see it the last time I was here."

Sliding his sunglasses on, he said, "Not a cloud in the sky today." He slipped an arm around her waist and smiled down at her. "Absolutely gorgeous."

She leaned in for a kiss, but a second before their lips met, a red convertible with the top down came screaming around the corner.

"That would be Benji," Cole said, then he kissed her anyway, so deeply that if he wasn't holding on to her, she might have fallen down the stairs.

"Get in!" The stocky white man behind the wheel sported a pair of aviators, a trucker hat that said E=MC HAMMER, and a braided goatee. "Cole, we gotta go! Hi, Mira!"

"Hi, Benji!" she called back, following Cole down the stairs, sliding into the back seat of the car despite Cole doing everything he could to convince her to ride shotgun.

"How was the flight?" Benji asked her in the rearview. "Smooth, I hope?"

Watching a corner of Cole's mouth tip up in his profile, Mira said, "It was perfect," not mentioning the part of the flight she'd spent on her knees between Cole's spread legs, her lips wrapped around him while his hands fisted in her hair. "Super smooth."

As Cole turned to wink at her, his cheeks flushed, Mira couldn't keep the guilty grin from her face. Her first time on a private jet had been invigorating, the text from Ian waiting for her after they'd landed—telling her they were all still alive—had loosened the tightness in her chest, and the sun shining above her now warmed her skin. Maybe she really could do this. Maybe *they* could really do this.

When they arrived at his studio, chills bloomed, tingling at the base of her neck, racing down her arms. This was Cole's place, his home. The weathered stone steps they took were the same steps the Makers had taken when they made their first record. The door Cole opened for her was the same door he'd walked through the first time as a business owner. Mira knew that feeling well, how empowering it was to have a place that belonged to her, where she was able to share what she loved with everyone else.

"Welcome to Trax," he said with pride, leading her into the space she'd seen so many times on his Instagram stories but never in person. There was a long table to her right she remembered seeing covered with her birthday present Glazed boxes. Windows looking into four recording booths lined the walls. One of the booths was filled with the drum set she'd watched Cole play on countless times. Posters of Bowie, the Cure, the Ramones, Patti Smith, and—

"It's the same one I have over my bed," Mira said, pointing at the poster of Joe Strummer smoking a cigarette hanging on a door marked CONFERENCE ROOM, the FERENCE crossed out with black duct tape. She looked closer at the poster, noticing the signature followed by a little star. "But, of course, yours is signed."

"Mad and I saw him with the Pogues when we were on tour in the UK in the early '90s," Cole said, his breath soft on her neck before he kissed her there.

"That must have been an amazing show."

"We got backstage." He gave her a small grin. "Lifetime achievement."

"And now they're both gone, Joe and Shane."

With a sigh, he said, "Far too soon."

"They're already here," Benji cut in, taking Cole by the elbow, leading him away from Mira and toward the *con* room.

"Make yourself comfortable," Cole told her before he followed Benji through the door. "There are some couches upstairs, or you can hang down here. I shouldn't be more than an hour."

Taking a seat on one of the chairs at the big table, hearing Cole's excited voice through the door as he introduced himself to the band, feeling weirdly free and absurdly happy, Mira pulled out her phone.

> Mira: I think you're right. I have been chaining myself in place.

> Jen: Oof. I said that, didn't I? That was a bit harsh of me.

> Mira: It was true, though.

> Jen: How's Seattle?

> Mira: Gorgeous.

Jen: I'm proud of you.

Mira: I'm proud of me too.

"You must be the bakery goddess."

"Jesus fucking Christ!" Mira shouted, nearly leaping out of her skin.

"Jumpy," Nancy said with a wolfish grin as she plopped onto the chair next to Mira's. "Didn't mean to scare you."

"You're"—Mira's throat spasmed—"Nancy Hayes." If she'd been starstruck when she'd first met Cole, it didn't hold a candle to the wide-eyed, speechless paralysis of sitting a foot away from *the* Asyd Nancy.

When Nancy extended her hand, miraculously, Mira took and shook it. "I'm... Yes, I'm the...bakery goddess." It was unsettling, meeting someone she'd admired so much as a teenager yet felt so wary about now because of how she'd treated Cole. Maybe that was why her brain had decided to say those words. It was confused, caught off guard, short-circuiting. "I'm Mira. Mira Harlow."

So much pure, vibrating electricity sparked off Nancy she could have powered a small city. Her shoulder-length red hair glowed around her head, her blue-eyed stare piercing straight into Mira's soul. "Benji didn't tell me you were coming back with Cole today." Her eyes narrowed. "That little shit. He's never trusted me. Not that any of Cole's friends ever have. Guess I can't blame them." When she leaned forward, the cinnamon scent of her gum hung in the air between them. "So tell me, Mira Harlow. Are you hungry?"

Telling her the truth, because Mira suspected this woman could look straight through the center of the earth and spot a lie told by someone on the other side of it, she said, "Starving."

SHE'D WANTED to text Cole that she was heading out with Nancy to get coffee and snacks, but she didn't want to interrupt his meeting, especially if the guys in the band were as technophobic as Cole had made them out to be. Besides, she figured they'd be back before anyone knew they were gone. But apparently the meeting had wrapped up early, because as soon as she left the coffee shop with some horrifically sugary whipped-cream concoction Nancy practically demanded she try, her phone buzzed with,

> Cole: We're already done. We nailed it.
> Where are you?

When she texted back that she was out with Nancy, his dots appeared and disappeared no less than four times before he finally sent,

> Cole: Blink twice if you need help.

She laughed, but the truth was, she was fine. Despite intimidating the holy living shit out of her at every turn, Nancy had been nothing but pleasant.

When they finally returned to the studio, the con room was empty, Benji was behind the counter clacking away on his computer, and Cole was nowhere to be seen. But he could be heard.

"Someone's letting off steam." Nancy angled her head toward the recording booth, where Cole wailed on his drums. "I don't think he liked that I borrowed you."

Stepping closer to the window, close enough to watch his muscles flex, his wrists flick, his eyes close while he raised his face toward the ceiling, Mira said, "He's amazing."

Nancy turned to face her. "I'm not sure how much Cole has told you about me, but I'm really not a bad person."

Mira had no idea what to say to that, so she didn't say anything.

"I'm not necessarily a good person," Nancy added with a small laugh. "But Cole is. He's one of the best humans to ever walk this planet. I thought only drumming made him happy these days."

And then, like his ears were burning, Cole opened his eyes and noticed them through the window, and when he looked at Mira, his face lit up with a heart-stopping smile.

"Obviously, I was wrong," Nancy said. "It's the worst cliché, and I'm making myself sick saying it, but I just want him to be happy. He deserves it."

"He really does," Mira said, and when Nancy walked away, she turned the doorknob, stepped into his booth, and closed the door behind her.

Dropping one of his drumsticks, he waved her over, tapping on his knee while he kept playing with the other. The entire scene was so absurdly sexy she actually swooned, this close to putting a hand to her forehead and sighing. Instead, she crossed the room, sat in his lap, cupped his neck, and kissed him while he twirled his drumstick in the air.

"What is that?" he asked after they pulled apart, staring down at the foamy drink still in her other hand.

Bringing the straw to his lips, she said, "Give it a try."

He took a sip, then made a face. "Jesus, that's awful."

"Nancy made me get it. I think she was punking me."

"Nah." He pulled her deeper into his lap. "She loves that sugary shit."

"And you?" she asked, brushing her thumb over his soft bottom lip, drawn to that tiny freckle under his eye like a kitten to a ray of sunlight. "What do you like?"

"Don't you already know?" Leaning forward, kissing her behind her ear, making her shiver, he said, "You're the only sugar I need."

CHAPTER THIRTY-THREE

COLE

HER HAND WARM IN HIS, Cole led Mira back to Benji's convertible after he'd told Cole that not only could he borrow it for the day, but after how well he'd sweet-talked the band into recording at their studio, he could "fucking have it, bro!"

Looking up at the perfect blue sky, he said, "I wish we had time to go sailing."

"Maybe next time," she suggested, squeezing his hand, and his heart skittered to a stop.

"Yeah?"

When she nodded, her cheeks glowing, jumpstarting his heart, he said, "Definitely next time." Then he pulled her into a soft, lingering kiss. "But today"—he brushed a windswept curl from her forehead—"how would you like to meet my granddaughter?"

Her smile shone brighter than the midday sun. "Are you kidding? Yes, please!"

Forty-five minutes later, pulling into his driveway, Cole wondered how much of his life he'd already wasted sitting in Seattle traffic. When he undid his seat belt, he looked at Mira, and aside from her mouth slowly sliding open, her eyes going wider and wider as she stared at his house, she didn't move a muscle.

"Mira?" He waved his hand in front of her face. "You okay?"

"Yeah," she said absently. "It's just... Your house..." She turned to face him. "Cole, it's enormous."

"It's not that big," he said. But when he looked at the sprawling two-story cedar house now, it did seem like more than he needed. "I picked it up at a very good time to buy houses in Seattle." He slid a hand over her cheek, hungry for any excuse to touch her. "Does it bother you that I have money?"

"Does it bother you that I don't?"

He shook his head, and in case that wasn't enough, added, "No. That would never bother me."

"Okay." She leaned into his touch.

"Okay." He brushed his thumb over her soft skin, that string between them tugging on his chest, like the *okays* they'd just said to each other were about more than money, more than this day, more than the week he still had left in Red Falls, just...more. They should, he realized, probably talk about that, what that *more* could mean, what it might look like, what he wanted it to look like.

"Come with me," he said, releasing her seat belt, because whether they needed to or not, now wasn't the time for that kind of conversation. "It's almost naptime. We don't want to miss her."

THE SENSATION of seeing Ruby after not seeing her for two weeks, not smelling her baby powder scent, not feeling her fuzzy hair against his cheek, was like the warmest blanket wrapping tightly around him. "She's huge!" he cried, lifting her into the air until she squealed. "And is that another tooth?"

"Just started coming in a couple days ago," Becks said.

"Amazing." Gazing into Ruby's eyes, he told her, "You get more and more amazing every single day." When he turned to Mira, her expression was pained, almost heartbroken. But the look passed so quickly he decided he'd imagined it. "Would you like to hold her?"

While Mira held his granddaughter, Becks filled them in on everything he'd missed over the last two weeks: the new teeth, how many times Ruby had fallen trying to stand without holding on to something, how she'd been sleeping better, eating better. It was indescribable, the mixture of pride and love and relief twisting Cole's chest. Because even though his help might have been necessary after Ruby was born, even though Becks might still want him around, she didn't actually need him anymore.

Watching Mira bounce Ruby on her knee, one of her raven curls twined through Ruby's chubby fingers as she laughed at something Becks said, Cole wondered, for the first time in a very long time, what did *he* need?

"I'm so happy you flew over with Dad," Becks said, giving Mira a goodbye hug after she'd finished putting Ruby down.

"I am too," Mira said, then she glanced between them and asked, "Can I use your bathroom before we go?"

After Cole pointed Mira down the hall to the guest bathroom, he pulled Becks into a hug. Or tried to, but she stopped him with a hand on his chest.

"It's not only your Instagram that's deeply in love, Dad."

"What do you mean?" he said, pretending he didn't know exactly what she meant.

"You're gone. You're simping so hard."

"Becks, what the hell is 'simping'?"

"You've already bought the house, haven't you?"

"I have no idea what you're talking about."

She removed her hand from his chest, only to point her finger into it. "In her little town, you've already picked out the house you're going to buy."

He scoffed. "No." *Because it isn't even a house.*

"Does she know?" Becks asked, setting her hands on her hips. "Have you told her how you feel? Does she feel the same? Please tell me you've talked about it."

Not about to tell his daughter all they'd actually talked about was robot sex, he said, "We will."

"When?"

"Today. Tonight. I don't know. But I'll talk to her."

"Do you promise? Promise me, Dad. This isn't like your other partners since Mom. This is different. I can tell. I can't watch you get hurt again."

Suddenly, his mouth felt like he'd been sucking on cotton for the last hour. He hadn't thought about what this might look like to Becks. Probably like he was actually shouting, "I want to get hurt!" right in front of her. "It's not like that," he said, not entirely sure which one of them he was trying to convince. "We're taking things slowly." *Lies.* "We're being very open with each other." *More lies.*

Rubbing two fingers up and down the bridge of her nose, she relented. "Okay, fine."

But when the bathroom door swung open down the hall, she grabbed his shirt, locked eyes with him, and said softly but fiercely, "You deserve to be loved. Head over heels, no compromises, no second-guessing loved. And anyone who offers less than that is not worth giving your heart to." She threw her arms around his waist, and all he could do while his heart thumped and Mira walked their way was hug her back.

CHAPTER THIRTY-FOUR

MIRA

WITH A SMILE on her face she didn't think had faltered once in the last hour, Mira floated across the plane and into her seat.

"How was your day?" Cole asked while he took the seat across from her.

"Wonderful," she told him. "Amazing. Phenomenal."

With a gleam in his eye, he said, "Same."

Then, like they'd choreographed it, they both pulled out their phones.

"Davis says everything's still fine at Bluebird," he said.

Rolling her eyes at the text back from Ian telling her to "stop bugging" them, Mira said, "Mom and Ian are good too."

"Good evening," the pilot intoned over the speaker. "Please put your phones on airplane mode and keep your seats in the upright position with your seat belts fully fastened until we reach safe cruising altitude and I've turned the seat belt sign off. We might have some early turbulence."

Mira checked her phone one last time before putting it on airplane mode, then tried to settle in as the plane started its taxi to the runway. But she couldn't settle. She was antsy, agitated, overly warm, her skin heating one degree at a time when Cole's jaw muscles flickered as he peered through the window, when he tightened his seat belt with an efficient tug, when he turned to her, catching her stare, his throat bobbing through a swallow as she licked her lips.

Every bit of Cole in his world, his competence in the studio, the way he loved his daughter and granddaughter, even the way his corded forearms flexed while he worked the stick in Benji's convertible—or maybe especially that—had served one single purpose: making her so turned on she could barely see straight. And now, confined to her seat, she wondered if she should give him a taste of his own medicine.

"I guess we're stuck here for a while," she said, glancing down at her seat belt, then flicking her gaze back to his. "All tied up."

Cole's eyes darkened. "I guess so."

"Is it warm in here?" she asked him, skating her fingers along her collarbone. "I'm kind of hot."

He cleared his throat, his eyes following her fingertips as they dipped between her breasts. "Maybe you're having a hot flash."

"Maybe so." She leaned forward until her seat belt cut into her hips, giving him an unobstructed view down her shirt. "You know the only thing that works when I'm having one of those?"

His fingertips tapped at light speed on his seat belt buckle. "Remind me."

"Please prepare for take-off," the pilot said.

"Believe me," Cole rasped, his legs spreading wide. "I am."

Slipping out of her shoes, she grasped the hem of her shirt and pulled it over her head. When she tossed it onto the floor beside her, Cole asked, "Does that feel better?" his eyes midnight black, his gaze devouring her body.

Gathering her hair up off her neck while the plane's acceleration pushed her back into her seat, she hummed. "A little. But I'm still so hot."

Cole groaned, taking his hand off the seat belt buckle to palm himself through his jeans.

"Maybe"—dropping her hair, she reached around her back for the clasp of her bra—"I should take this off too."

When they launched into the sky, Cole said, "I think that's a good idea."

"But what if the pilot comes out?" she asked, lowering her hands, pouting innocently. "I don't want to get into trouble."

"She won't come out. She wouldn't dream of it. Mira, please," Cole begged, shifting in his seat. "I'm so fucking hard right now."

"Well, then I should definitely keep it on," she teased. "I wouldn't want to make you uncomfortable."

"I'm not uncomfortable," he said to her breasts. "I'm perfectly comfortable. I've never been so comfortable in my entire life."

With a small laugh, she reached back again, unclasped her bra, and slid the straps off her shoulders one at a time. Tossing her bra near her shirt, she said, "Ahh, that's so much better."

His hands made fists as he ground out, "How long does it take to reach safe cruising altitude?"

Fluttering her lashes, she gazed down and said, "Oh, look. My nipples are hard."

"Fuck my life."

"They're so hard." She arched her back. "Cole, they're aching."

"Maybe you should touch them," he suggested in a strained voice, running a hand roughly over his stubble.

"Like this?" she asked, circling two fingers over her right nipple.

"Yeah, like that." He bit his lower lip. "You can pinch them a little too. If you want to."

"Pinch them? But won't that hurt?"

He scrubbed both hands over his face now. "No, it won't hurt," he said through his fingers. "Just don't do it too hard."

She made a show of pinching her nipples, softly at first, then a little harder, twisting gently. "You're right. That does feel good.

Really good. I wonder if this would feel good too?" Cupping her right breast, she lifted its warm weight, brought her tongue to her nipple, and licked it.

"God help me," he said harshly, shifting in his seat again. Raising his gaze to the console above her head, he warned, "God help *you* when that light goes off."

"Why?" she asked, sliding her other hand between her legs. "Are you going to do something to me?"

When he opened his mouth to respond, two dings rang through the cabin. The seat belt light clicked off, and Cole was on her, his lips around her nipple, sucking hard, his fingers rolling her other nipple between them, making her moan.

When she reached for her own buckle, he grasped her wrists in his hands, holding her still. "Don't you dare," he growled. "That comes off only when I want it to."

If Mira wanted to object—which she didn't—she couldn't find the words, her head dropping back to her headrest when his dove between her legs.

"Shit," she hissed, burying her hands in his hair, bucking while he kissed and licked her through too many layers of fabric.

Raising his head, he hooked his fingers into the waistband of her pants and, with a wicked grin, said, "You were teasing me, weren't you?"

"I—"

With a swift tug, he pulled her pants down over her hips, effectively cutting off any flimsy excuse she might have come up with.

When she jerked against the seat belt holding her down, he gave her a warning look, then pulled it tighter, making it so snug it was just shy of painful. Now she could barely move, couldn't escape the white-hot sensation of his fingertip ghosting up and down her seam. "Hmm," he hummed. "Should I tease you back?"

She was so keyed up, so turned on, that all he'd have to do was lick her once, and she'd come. But, like he knew exactly how close she was, he pulled his finger away, not touching her, only staring between her legs for a long moment, long enough for her to calm down, just a little, just enough. Then he gazed up at her and, with steady, unwavering eye contact, said, "No, I don't think I should," and pushed a finger inside her, and then another. While her legs fell open and her eyes fell closed, he surrounded her clit with his lips, sucking and licking and swirling his tongue while he pumped his fingers in and out of her so quickly she had to bite her fist to keep from screaming.

Through the heavy haze of release, she felt her buckle click free, strong arms wrapping around her, lowering her carefully to the ground. When she forced her eyes open again, she was on her back, Cole tense and hovering above her, heat pouring from his body into hers.

"I'm sorry, but I can't wait," he said, rising up to kneel between her legs, unbuttoning his jeans, releasing his zipper, his hard cock tenting his boxers until he pushed them down. Stroking himself once, then twice, he said, "I need you, Mira. I'm out of my mind."

Reaching around his hips, she urged him closer, because she needed him too. His weight, his firm muscles, his warm skin sliding against hers. While their gazes locked, he braced himself on straight arms, and she reached between their bodies, guiding him into her.

Sliding deep in one even thrust, he moaned, dropped to his elbows, kissed her neck, her throat, her jaw, his hips setting a brain-scrambling rhythm. It was all so blisteringly hot. She wouldn't have been surprised if they'd steamed up the airplane windows. But then something changed. Like flames giving way to glowing embers, the fire between their bodies simmered, his thrusts slowing, his hands rising to cradle her face between them, his lips lowering to hers. He kissed her deeply, his hips rolling sweetly, his hand leaving her face to slide reverently down the side of her body, and pressure swelled behind her eyes.

"Cole," she gasped, curling her fingers into his lower back, trying to get him to speed up, to thrust harder, because what he was doing, it wasn't fair. This, his forehead pressing lightly against hers, his steady, hooded gaze searing her skin, his soft kisses brushing over the corners of her mouth, this wasn't sex. This wasn't their deal. This was making love.

"Please, don't," she said, tears gathering under her closed lids. She'd thought she was ready, but she was wrong, because the only thing coursing through her now was fear. The day with him had been wonderful, one she'd never forget, but it didn't change their situation. They needed to talk about things, so many things, before they could take this step, before she could let him give himself to her like this. Before she could give herself back. "Please."

He raised his head, staring down at her, pleading, "Mira."

"I can't. Cole, I can't."

His hips stilled. "Do you want me to stop?"

"No." A single tear leaked from the corner of her eye, sliding down her temple, dropping off her earlobe. "I don't want you to stop, but we can't. Not like this. I'm so sorry. But I'm not—"

"Shh," he soothed, his thumb brushing over her temple, drying the path her tear had taken. "It's okay. I should have told you first, how I felt. How I *feel* about you."

Another tear streaked into her hair. She wanted him to say it. She wanted to say it back, because she felt it. She felt it in every single cell in her body. But she couldn't. Not without a plan. Not without knowing what would happen next. This trip had worked out, but what about the next one? What would happen if there wasn't a next one? If her mom got worse and she really couldn't leave her? She didn't need all the answers, but she needed some. Otherwise, she was floating, and this was all only a dream. They could have sex in a dream, but the first time they made love, she didn't want it to be a dream. She wanted it to be real.

"Please don't cry, sugar," he said with a wry smile that didn't reach his eyes. "There's no crying in airplane sex."

She exhaled, a small laugh, then sniffed.

"We don't have to talk about it now." Sliding out, he thrust into her again, harder this time, and relief washed over her with the force of it. "But we do need to talk about it. Eventually."

Wrapping her legs around his waist, pulling him tight, she said, "Okay." When he bent to kiss her, she knew he deserved more than her okays, more than her tears and her hesitance and her fear. But right now, okay was the best she could give him. And because he was more than she would ever deserve, he gave her no reason to believe okay wasn't enough.

Sometime later, they helped each other get dressed, smiling, laughing as they rushed into their seats, buckling up when the pilot turned the seatbelt light on during their initial descent. Although everything seemed fine, Mira knew it wasn't. She hadn't meant to, but she'd damaged them tonight. He was right. They needed to talk. She needed to tell him how she felt, what she wanted. All she had to do was open her mouth. But she couldn't.

Tomorrow. She'd tell him tomorrow.

The second their wheels hit the runway, they both took their phones off airplane mode and waited. He smiled at her, and she tried her hardest to give him a genuine smile back, but then—

Buzz.

It was a text from Ian, and then—*buzz*—another, and another—*buzz, buzz.*

While she stared at her phone, three more texts buzzed through, and her vision went white around the edges. Why were there so many messages? Ian never texted her this many times. Had something happened?

Buzz, buzz, two more, each one an extra heartbeat, another stone lodged in her stomach. While she'd been out pretending she could have a different life, living in a dream, had the people in her real life been hurt?

With trembling fingers and a cold dread sinking into her bones, she opened the first message.

Ian: Mom?

Ian: You there?

Ian: We need help.

Ice flooded her veins, nausea roiling in her belly. They needed help. They needed her, and she wasn't there.

Ian: Are you still in the air?

Even though the plane hadn't stopped moving yet, she unclasped her seat belt, about to stand, about to run to the door when she read the next message.

Ian: Where's the cheese grater?

The cheese grater?

Ian: Do we have any pizza sauce?

Ian: What about pepperoni?

Ian: What temperature should we set the oven to? We don't remember.

Ian: Never mind. We figured it out.

Ian: We just used pasta sauce.

Ian: Sorry for bugging you.

Ian: Can you pick up some ice cream on the way home?

Ian: Love you.

Collapsing back into her seat, she dropped her phone into her lap, dropped her face into her hands, and tried to catch her breath. "They're okay," she said, relieved tears welling while the plane finally came to a stop. "Thank god, they're okay." She wiped the blur from her eyes. "I'm going to have a long talk with my son about sending me multiple mundane texts about dinner when I'm on a plane. But they're okay. They're..." She trailed off, going silent as every drop of blood drained from his face.

"Cole?"

His eyes were glued to his phone, his knuckles turning white around it, hands shaking.

"What's wrong? What happened?"

Looking up, his expression terrifyingly blank, he only said, "It's the guys," before his hand rose to cover his mouth.

CHAPTER THIRTY-FIVE

MIRA

June 29, 8:32am

> Mira: Hi Cole

June 29, 8:36am

> Mira: Just wanted to check in. I hope you're okay.

June 29, 8:40am

> Mira: I'm thinking about you.

June 29, 11:44am

> Mira: I can't imagine what you're going through. But I'm here if you need to talk.

June 30, 2:37pm

Mira: Do you need anything? Can I help in any way?

June 30, 2:41pm

Mira: I miss you (deleted)

June 30, 6:49pm

Mira: I'm trying not to be worried, but I'm really worried. Please just let me know you're okay (deleted)

Mira: I miss you.

July 1, 10:12am

Cole: I'm so sorry I've been MIA. I've been doing everything I can to keep the rest of the guys calm and on the premises, and there's so much I can't talk about. I've barely slept since we got back, but Mad's here now. He thinks he knows where they went and we're trying to make a plan to get them back. I'll call you when I can. I miss you too.

AFTER PIPING another fine-line vein on a fondant leaf, Mira stood back, frowning at the third trial wedding cake she'd baked in the last three days. None of them looked the way she wanted them to, but at least she had something to keep herself busy, considering the bakery had been completely dead and her brain so painfully alive her entire head buzzed.

She'd received that one single text from Cole yesterday morning, and then nothing. She was trying to be calm, patient, but the silence was breaking her. Even Jen hadn't known what to say, what advice to give her aside from "fuck every duck!" when she'd told her what had happened, what little she knew, only that two of the men had left Little Timber while she and Cole had been in the air. Only that Cole had been so devastated, so completely inconsolable he could barely speak. Only that he'd dropped her off at the bakery before peeling out like he was racing against a fire threatening to burn everything he was supposed to keep safe to the ground. Only that she'd flown into her apartment and hugged Ian and her mom for ten solid minutes because they were okay, because she wasn't, and because she couldn't hug Cole.

Frowning at the not-right wedding cake she needed to get right by next Saturday, she untied her apron, hung it on the hook in the kitchen, and took the tray of lemon poppyseed cupcakes she'd baked earlier in the day out to the bakery. When she rounded the corner from the hallway, the tray wobbled in her hands, all twelve cupcakes nearly toppling to the floor before she set it down on the counter. Because there he was, standing outside her door.

A dark, formless sky that hadn't quite threatened rain had hovered over Red Falls all day. And Cole, the hood of his lucky hoodie up, his shoulders hunched, his head hanging, looked so cold all Mira wanted to do was get him into her arms and warm him up. But when she opened the door, when he looked up at her with gaunt cheeks and sunken eyes, she stumbled back, letting him inside.

"Are you okay?" she asked, following him toward the stairs before he turned back to face her. "Cole, are you—"

"No." He pushed his hood down. "I am not okay."

"Can I get you something? A coffee? Water? Do you want to sit?"

"I should go—"

"Go? You just got here."

"—back to Seattle."

Her heart stopped. Time stopped. "W-what do you mean?"

"Madigan's here. He"—his voice broke, and a knife sank into her side—"got the kid back. So I should go."

"When?" she asked, grasping at her throat, trying to keep it from closing up entirely.

"Now."

"Now?" The knife twisted. She wasn't ready. They were supposed to have another week.

"Mira, you wouldn't believe the things I've seen." He shook his head, his eyes shot through with tiny red lines like the veins in her leaves. "The way he looked..." He brought his fist to his mouth, his eyes misting.

"Can you sit?" she asked, because if he didn't sit, if he kept standing there like a man waiting for a feather to take him down, it was going to break her. "Please, let me take care of you. Let me get you something to—"

"I've been thinking, thinking, thinking," he said, staring at his feet, maybe at nothing. "I've been trying to figure it all out, put all the pieces together, figure out how we got here." She wasn't sure he was talking to her anymore. Not until he met her stare. "And no matter how much I try to wrap my brain around it, around us. I can't make it work."

"Us?" She reached out, grabbing the counter so she didn't fall through the floor. Was this it? Was this how they ended? He thought it couldn't work just when she'd finally started to believe it could.

"Life is so short," he said, taking a step toward her. "So fragile. We take so much for granted. We think we'll have all this time, so we wait and wait and wait. But we don't have time. The only thing we have is right now, and even that's gone before we know it."

He wasn't making sense. He was distraught and not thinking clearly. She needed to talk him down, talk him into giving them a chance. But first, she needed him to sit. "When's the last time you slept?" she asked. "Or ate?"

"I don't think I realized how lonely I was, how *alone* I was"—he took another step toward her, but he was still so far away—"until I met you."

"Then why are you leaving?" she asked, her skin shrinking around her bones until she could barely breathe.

"I don't want to leave, Mira. I don't want to be away from you for a second longer than I have to. I don't want to lose you."

She couldn't stand it anymore, the distance between them, the space pushing them apart. Willing her body to move, she crossed the room, taking his face in her hands and lifting his head when it dropped to his chest, her eyes burning when his cold hands rose to cover hers. "I don't want to lose you either," she told him, holding his head steady, making him focus on her. "Please don't leave yet. Stay here. Stay with me for a few more—"

"You don't understand," he said fiercely, his fingers curling around hers, his focus suddenly sharp as glass. "I don't want to leave you. Ever. I want to be with you. I want to be here, with you. Always."

Always? She slid her hands out of his, lowering them to her sides. "What?"

"I want to fall asleep with you, wake up next to you."

She stepped back. "Cole, this is—"

Every step she took away from him, he took another toward her. "I want to see you every day, hold you, touch you, run my fingers through your hair. I want to have breakfast with you every morning and make you dinner every night. I want to cuddle with you in our comfy clothes on Sundays. I want to stand in line for you at the grocery store so you don't have to have a hot flash. I want to exist in your world, and not just over the phone."

There was something wrong with her heart. It hurt too much, each beat more painful than the last. "Maybe we should...slow down for a second."

"I don't want to slow down." He took another step, so close now she smelled the sea. "I don't want to wait. I want to be here, in Red Falls—"

"Cole, stop."

"Why, Mira?" He brushed his fingers over her cheek, wiping away a tear she hadn't felt fall. "Why should I stop?"

She'd been waiting for him, ready to tell him she wanted to try, to see if they could have a real long-distance relationship. But what he was suggesting, leaving his home, his studio, his family, his entire life, for her?

"I just think we should talk about things first." Things like the sacrifices he'd be making, the losses he'd suffer, that look of pure love in his eyes when he'd held his granddaughter in his arms, the way he'd resent her when he realized how much he'd given up to be with her. The way it would destroy her when he'd eventually decide he'd given up too much. "I think you've been through a lot, and we need to just take a breath and talk this through."

"There's only one thing to talk about." Grasping her hand, he placed her palm on his chest. Unlike hers, which hurled itself so hard and fast against her ribs her shirt vibrated from the force of it, his heart beat steadily, slowly. "I might look like shit right now." His lips inched into a muted smile. "In fact, I'm sure I look like shit right now. But I'm not delirious. My mind is clear. My heart knows what it wants." Brushing his thumb so softly over hers it ached, he said, "Does yours?"

CHAPTER THIRTY-SIX

COLE

COLE KNEW COMING to see her in his current state was a risk. But after watching Madigan walk a pale and stumbling Kev to his truck to take him to the hospital, after not seeing or talking to Mira during the three days of pure hell they'd all just endured, it was a risk he had to take. Because something happened to a person when the narrow, meandering path they'd been following blindly for years finally straightened, showing them there was a purpose to continually putting one foot in front of the other, a meaning behind the countless steps they'd taken. Something happened when that person looked up to see their future reveal itself like a mountain rising from the fog. Something happened when they realized that future didn't exist without Mira Harlow in it. They were given no other choice but to let her know it as soon as humanly possible.

"Talk to me," he whispered into the space between them. "Please, say something." He was ready for this, ready to be with her, but she had to be ready too. "Tell me you want this, Mira. Tell me to stay."

With a sharp inhale, a shuddering gasp, she pushed him back a step. Then she wheeled around, buried her face in her hands, and said, "You can't move to Red Falls for me."

"The fuck I can't."

She turned back to him, her eyes shining like sea glass. "You can't leave your entire life, your granddaughter, for me. I would never ask you to do that. I would never *tell* you to do that."

"Why not?"

"Because!" she cried, throwing her hands into the air.

"That's not an answer, Mira."

"Look, I care about you, Cole."

"You *care* about me?"

"I think you're a very special person."

Special? Jesus, did he have this all wrong?

"But I think this is all moving way too fast. We haven't known each other long enough to—"

"Don't," he said, barely believing his ears. "I know you, Mira. I know you as well as I've ever known anyone. I know you like cats more than dogs. I know you're secretly obsessed with yacht rock. I know you love the smell of lilacs in the evening and rain in the morning. I know you sleep with twinkly lights, and your closet is full of dirty laundry. Yeah, I know that too," he said when her eyes went wide. "I know you smell like lemon-flavored icing, even though you prefer strawberry. I know you give yourself to everyone around you and never ask for anything in return. I know you've felt abandoned before, and that probably makes you scared. I know you love your family, your bakery, your town, your life."

"But you love those things too," she insisted, her chin quivering. "You love your studio, your boat, your daughter, Ruby. I know you think you care about me, but you're emotional right now."

"I'm always emotional," he said. "I'm an emotional person. And I don't only *think* I care about you. You're all I think about. It's you, Mira. It's all you. All you have to do is tell me you feel the same." He ran his fingers down her arm, over her wrist, curling his hand around hers. "You don't even have to feel all the way same. I'll take half. I'll take half of what I feel for you. It'll be enough."

When she didn't say anything, he felt the silent ticking of time like a hand pushing him back, slowing him down, shaking him until his head cleared. Not even half. She didn't even feel half the same. He thought she did. He'd been so sure. What was it the guys told him? Always play it through to the end? He hadn't done that. He hadn't thought any further than the next minute ahead of him.

Play it through, Cole. How would this end? After he poured his whole heart out in the middle of her bakery, after she wouldn't pour even half her heart out back, how would this story end? With him doing everything he could to make it work with someone who maybe didn't want it to? With him alone again with his heart breaking over and over and over?

"I'm sorry," she said, tears filling her eyes. "But we can't. Not like this."

He dropped her hand, his jaw clenching so hard something popped, and he just cracked. "Fuck!" he shouted up to the ceiling. "What is *wrong* with me? Why do I keep doing this to myself?"

"Doing what?" she asked, frantic. "Cole, what—"

Taking her face between his hands, holding her emerald gaze while it threatened to break him apart, he said, "Why do I keep falling in love with people who refuse to love me back?"

"That's not fair." She blinked, and tears streamed down her face. "That is not fair. I never said that."

"I know." Gently, he brushed her tears away with his thumbs, because this wasn't her fault. "You didn't."

"Cole, please." She grasped his wrists. "Please don't leave like this. I'm not saying any of the right things."

"It's okay, sugar. It's okay." He brought his forehead to hers. "But I have to go."

"No." She threw her arms around him, kissed his jaw, his cheek, the corner of his lips. "Not yet."

Sliding his hand under her hair to cup her neck, he pulled her mouth to his and kissed her like it was the last time he'd ever have the pleasure, knowing it very likely was. Breaking the kiss before he was anywhere near ready, the salt of their tears mingling on his lips, and because it was too late now to protect either one of them from the truth, he said, "I love you, Mira."

Her mouth opened, her eyelashes wet, eyes red and swollen, but then she closed it again. And that was that.

He let her go, then walked away, both desperate to get out of her bakery and also hating every single step that took him closer to her door.

"Wait."

His heart dared to pause between beats. Would she say it back? Would she make that leap with him? But when he turned around, she wasn't looking at him anymore. She was behind her counter, grabbing a pink box from the display case, handing it to him.

"What's this?" he asked, staring at the box with some hope, like it might hold the secret to fixing all the things he'd just broken.

"It's a cupcake. You need to eat. I need you to eat." She massaged her throat, working through a swallow, and punched him in the gut with "Please let me know when you get home safe."

He couldn't say a word, not a single syllable, because if he did, he'd disintegrate right there in front of her. So he only nodded, wiped his cheeks with the back of his hand, and walked out of her bakery, pulling his hood back up against the cold, gray sky.

Halfway out of town, he asked his Bluetooth to call Becks.

"Dad? Where the hell have you been? I've left, like, twenty messages."

"I know, honey. I'm sorry. I'll tell you what I can when I get home."

"You're coming home? I thought you had another week?"

Squeezing his steering wheel so hard it would leave dents, he said, "Yeah. But I'm not...needed here anymore."

"What happened? You sound terrible. Talk to me."

Trying his hardest not to cry alone in his car to his daughter, he said, "Things with Mira, they didn't..."

"Oh, Dad. Oh, no. I'm so sorry."

"I gave her my heart." He cleared the thickness from his throat, staring at the pretty pink box on his passenger seat. "And she gave me a cupcake."

"Come home," Becks said. "Just come home, and we'll work through it all together."

"Okay, honey. I'm on my way."

CHAPTER THIRTY-SEVEN

MIRA

"Zombies are more alive than you are these days."

Mira would have glared at her son, but he was right, and she didn't have the energy. "Thanks."

It had been a week since she'd last talked to Cole. Since he'd texted her that he'd made it home safely, and she'd replied with an inexcusably pathetic *thank you for letting me know.* Deleting the: I miss you. The: I'm sorry. The: Can we please talk?

No wonder he'd left. No wonder he hadn't reached out again. She'd broken his heart. She'd broken her own heart. But she'd been right. He was offering to give up too much. Even now, even after a week, even after the lump in her throat had gotten so big she'd made Jen look at it with some weird flexible scope she'd shoved down her nose, Mira still didn't think she'd made the wrong choice. No matter how much she loved him, no matter how much it killed her not saying it back, no matter how hard it was to eat or sleep or, apparently, function more convincingly than the walking dead, she still would never tell him to leave his life for her.

She'd been alone before. It wasn't like it was anything new. But she never remembered it hurting this bad.

"Cake looks good, though," Ian said, and she appreciated the attempt to make her feel better. "Is that the one? Or can I eat it too?"

"Dunno," Mira said, scowling at the cake she'd spent all day decorating. "Whatever."

"Isn't the wedding, like, tomorrow?"

She only groaned.

"Uh, Mom?"

"Yeah," she replied, plucking a pink frosting rose off the cake and popping it into her mouth. At least sugar still tasted good.

"I'm, um, sorry about Cole." She looked at Ian in time to watch his narrow shoulders rise and fall. "I liked him."

Thunking her elbows on the table, rubbing the ache throbbing behind her temples with her fingertips, she said, "Me too, bud."

"I'm going to Brendan's," Ian said. "I...think he might be my boyfriend now."

Her head whipped up. "Really?"

Ian nodded, and if his hair hadn't been so outrageously in need of a trim, Mira knew she'd see the tips of his ears turning pink.

"That's great, pal." Tilting her head, she asked, "Do his parents know? Are they cool?"

"I think they knew before we did. Yeah, they're cool."

For the first time in seven days that felt more like seventy, Mira smiled. "I'm so happy for you guys."

"Thanks." He pointed at the cake. "Can I have one of those flowers? Or two?"

Waving her hand at the cake, she said, "Take whatever you want. It's not the one."

As soon as Ian left, a Glazed box filled with the cake's entire top tier in his hands, Mira plopped onto a chair at the kitchen table and stared into space. It was her new favorite pastime, just staring, vacant, motionless, like a zombie.

"I'm worried about you," her mom said, walking into the kitchen and taking the chair beside her. "Who will take care of me if you go catatonic?"

"I haven't been doing a good job lately, have I?" Mira said, running her fingers over a tangled mass in the back of her mom's hair. "We need to brush it."

Feeling the tangle for herself, her mom sighed. "It's only hair." She pointed her chin at what remained of the wedding cake. "This one's not right either?"

"No," Mira replied, monotone, defeated. "Nothing's right."

Tapping her finger on her lips, her mom said, "It's very neat. Very tidy. Very pretty, but very tidy."

"Hmm," Mira huffed. "I guess."

"But sometimes, daughter, life is messy."

"You think I should make a messy cake?"

"No, I think you should make a beautiful cake. But sometimes it's the things that don't line up perfectly or fall right into place that move us the most. Sometimes it's the mess that makes life beautiful." Picking up another rose from the cake, holding the frilly red decoration between her fingertips, she said, "I think if I'd known that when I was your age, I wouldn't have told Fred to leave."

Mira coughed, choking on air. "You wouldn't have what?"

"Ended things with Fred," she replied calmly before taking a bite of the rose.

"But you didn't end things with Fred," Mira insisted.

Her mom looked confused, but it wasn't the blank, empty confusion of forgetting what she was talking about or what the next step of a recipe was. "Of course I did. Remember, he'd taken that job in Colstrip? He was still coming home most weekends, but everything was so tense between us I could barely stand it. I think I worried too much, missed him too much, maybe resented him for leaving us, even though I knew he couldn't find a job here, and I refused to leave Red Falls. I think, eventually, I decided it was all too hard, too messy, so I ended it before it could get any worse. Before he started to resent me too." Her gaze drifted back to the cake. "I shouldn't have done that. I should have tried harder. I shouldn't have been so scared."

"Mom," Mira said, her entire life reorienting itself, like she'd woken up with her head on backward. "I always thought he left us. I thought he left...because of me."

"You did?"

Her nod was robotic.

"Oh, Mira." She grasped her hand. "Why would you ever think that?"

"I don't know. I guess because I was around Ian's age and grumpy and probably a pain in the ass to be around. And he'd stopped taking me camping and hiking. And when you're a teenager, you think everything is your fault." Words poured out of her like water from a dam she'd spent a lifetime plugging up with her fingers. "And we never talked about it. He never told me what happened. You never told me what happened. All both of you ever said was that it didn't work out, or that sometimes love wasn't enough, or some other Hallmark card country song bullshit that always felt like you'd just decided not to tell me the truth."

"Listen to me, Mira," her mom said, squeezing her fingers so hard her bones whined. "It was *not* your fault. If it was anyone's fault, it was mine. It's no excuse, but Fred broke my heart when he moved away. But he was a good man, not like your father," she said hotly. "I never looked back after I finally told him to hit the road."

"You kicked Dad out too!" Mira cried, wondering if this was some sort of Mandela effect thing, the Berenstein/stain Bears of childhood divorce.

"Of course I did. Didn't you know that?"

"No," she said, shaking her head, "I did not. You never told me anything about Dad. I always thought—"

Her mom sat back in her chair with a *whoosh*. "You thought they both left us?"

WHAT MIRA HAD THOUGHT, as a matter of fact, was that she'd somehow driven them both off. "I did."

"Oh, sweetie, no. Your father needed to go, and the only reason I don't regret every year I spent with that man is because without him, I wouldn't have you. But Fred thought you hung the moon. I should have told you that. I should have been more considerate of you and your feelings. These days, we'd all be going to therapy after a divorce. But back then, things were different. Back then we just tucked it all away." She raised a shoulder. "And life went on."

"Life went on," Mira echoed numbly. Was that what her life was doing now? Going on? Because it sure as shit didn't feel like it.

"But I should have told you," her mom repeated, giving Mira's hand another squeeze before letting her go. "And I am so sorry I didn't. I am so sorry you thought any of it was your fault."

Hot tears filling her eyes until they were all she could see, Mira said, "Mom, why is it all so hard?"

"Because if life was easy, we'd all be insufferable assholes."

Mira gave her a watery laugh.

"Sometimes I think the only perk of possibly losing my mind is that I won't remember all my mistakes."

"Mom, please don't—"

"I hope you'll make fewer mistakes than I made," she went on. "Have fewer regrets." She looked at the cake one last time. "I hope you'll have the courage to find the beauty in life's messes. I'd like that for you."

And with that, she left Mira alone with a heavy silence, an aching heart, and an uninspiring cake. Slowly, Mira's mind slipped back to the day Cole had been in the kitchen with her, when he'd kissed her against the door, asked for one of her sketches. When he'd held her later that night while she'd cried, then tucked her in, plugging in her twinkly lights so it wouldn't be dark when she woke up.

No, she wouldn't make fewer mistakes than her mom. She wouldn't have fewer regrets. She wasn't courageous. She was scared and guarded and overthought everything, and because of it, she'd probably be alone forever. Without multiple orgasms, without laughing herself to sleep, without ever being tucked in again. Without Cole.

"Fuck," she whispered harshly as fresh tears blurred the cake in front of her, smearing frosting flowers, bleeding blue into pink into red. She blinked her tears free, and there it was.

Sometimes it's the mess that makes life beautiful.

Not bothering to wipe her eyes dry, Mira slid the clean and neat and perfectly wrong cake out of the way. Grasping her sketchpad, she swiped the nearest colored pencil off the table, decided to search for the beauty in the mess, and started drawing.

"CAN YOU SLOW DOWN?" Jen shouted, doing her best to hold the cake steady in the back of the Element. "I'm not an octopus. I don't have six arms."

"Sorry." Mira let her foot off the gas. "Wait, did you say *six* arms?"

"This is your best work yet." Jen beamed like a headlight in the rearview. "Everyone's gonna love it. Your phone'll be ringing off the hook! It's so beautiful, nobody will even want to eat it! But they will, of course. Because it's cake."

Mira did her best to beam back. This was everything she'd ever wanted, her literal dreams coming true, but her beam was a flickering fluorescent at best. "I hope you're right," she said, trying to sound like she cared, like she wasn't still checking her phone every ten minutes in case the one person she did care about texted or called or, *shit*, she'd take liking one of her Instagram posts at this point.

"Here we are," Jen squealed. At least she was excited.

Mira put the Element in park, turned her back on the big white tent in front of them, and said, "Jen, thank you for coming with me. The cake would probably be all over the car if I had to do this by—"

"Shh." Jen gave her head a shake. "You'll jinx us. You know that saying, don't count your chickens until the cake is on the table."

"I...do not know that saying," Mira said, then nodded. "But I like it."

Gingerly sliding the cake box out of the car, Mira took one side and Jen took the other, then they recited, "Don't trip, don't trip, do not fucking trip," all the way up the grassy hill until they reached the tent.

After they unboxed the cake and set it carefully on its stand, Jen stepped back. "It's perfect, Mira," she said, her chin wobbling. "It's perfect, because it's so *not* perfect." Turning away from the cake, from its pale-blue buttercream, its textured, almost chaotic strokes of green and purple and pink frosting creating a watercolor portrait of a meadow in springtime, but one you could reach out and feel with your fingertips, Jen said, "I'm so proud of you, Mira. Because you don't usually do this. My life is a love letter to catastrophe, but you don't usually let yourself be...not perfect."

Since she'd stopped denying that she routinely worshiped at the altar of perfection after the conversation with her mom, Mira said, "It was kind of liberating."

"It's kind of stunning."

Wheeling around at the deep, friendly voice she'd only ever heard on the radio or the news, Mira said, "Senator Richardson. Good morning." She shifted her gaze to the young women with him, one under each big arm, both in gorgeous silk pantsuits, one ivory, one burgundy. "You must be the brides."

"I'm Renee," the petite brunette on the senator's right said, reaching out for Mira's hand and shaking it. Stepping out from under her dad's arm, Renee moved closer to the table, examining the cake for a long moment, squinting, tilting her head to one side and then the other before saying, "Amy, I can't even *deal* with this right now."

Mira's heart made a break for her throat. "You don't like—"

"I know, right? It's the most incredible thing I've ever seen," Amy said through a thick warble.

With a surprisingly strong grip, Renee took hold of Mira's arms. "We didn't want a wedding. We were just gonna go to Vegas, until

Dad asked us to stay and get married here." When she looked at the cake, her eyes went glassy. "And now, I'm so glad he did." Swinging her gaze back to Mira's, she squeezed her arms so hard it hurt. "You get us."

"You really do," Amy added, still nestled into the senator's side. "It's amazing. Thank you, Mira."

Clearing his throat, Senator Richardson said, "I always trust my instincts. And my instincts told me you would give my daughters exactly what they wanted. I hope Glazed and Confused gets a big bump from this. And whatever you do"—he winked—"don't forget to vote."

"Yes, I will. I mean I won't forget. I will vote. For you, of course," Mira spluttered, blinking the sting from her eyes while she watched them walk away toward the catering table. Spinning on her heel, she shared a silent scream with Jen, then a slightly less silent laugh-hug, until Jen tensed, stiff as a board, and whispered, "Oh shit."

"What?" Mira asked, turning in the direction of Jen's wide-eyed stare.

"The cake is phenomenal," said a tall, pale man with nearly black hair swooping perfectly over his forehead.

"Paul?" The cake splitting in half so purple doves could fly out of it would have been less of a shock. "What are you doing here?"

Shifting her gaze between them, Jen said, "I'm gonna go check out"—she looked around until she found something plausible—"that fountain over there. Good to see you, Paul."

"You too, Jen," Paul said, his eyes locked on Mira's until he leaned toward the cake to get a closer look. The gesture reminded her so much of Cole, the way he'd studied her cake at Ashley and Madigan's wedding, the way she'd always felt plugged into an electrical outlet whenever he was near, the way she hovered around zero watts without him. "This is amazing."

"Thanks," she said. "But why are you here?"

Paul huffed a laugh. "I'm not stalking you, if that's what you think. It may not be as small as Red Falls, but Bozeman is still pretty small. The senator hired my company to do the digital displays." He waved a hand at one of the three large screens surrounding the dance floor in the middle of the park. "They're actually pretty cool."

"Oh, right," Mira said, giving him a bubbly laugh, or at least trying to. "What are the odds?"

Paul's smile seemed far too genuine. "Will you be sticking around?"

"Jen has to head back. So do I," she added quickly, even though she didn't actually have anything to do except more zombie-ing around the bakery.

"I see."

"Where's Chrissy?" she asked.

"She'll be here soon. Where's Cole?"

The question landed like a sledgehammer. "Oh, um," she hedged while the ground beneath her feet vanished. "We're...not together anymore."

"Really? That's too bad."

"Ha!" she barked. Then she said it again, but softer when someone carrying a couple of folding chairs looked their way. "Ha! Let's not pretend you're upset about it. You thought he wasn't good for me, remember? You thought a long-distance relationship with a drummer wouldn't make me happy. Well, guess what?" *I will not cry. I. Will. Not. Cry.* "It did!"

"Mira, I'm sorry." To his credit, he did look contrite. "I shouldn't have said that."

"Well, you did."

He ran a hand through his perfect hair and blew out a breath, then admitted, "Believe it or not, I was jealous, because you did seem happy. Then I realized it was shitty of me to be jealous of your happiness when I'm happy too. But," his jaw muscles flickered, "I always thought it would be me making you happy."

"What?" Mira scoffed. "If you wanted to make me happy, then why did you leave?"

"I...didn't," he said. Each millimeter his frown deepened, each small shake of his head, reeled the ground back up to her feet. "The way I remember it, you ended things with me, not the other way around."

"That's not," she started to say before he stepped closer to her, his hand swinging forward before returning to his side, like he was considering reaching for her but thought better of it.

"That's what I wanted to tell you at Ashley and Madigan's wedding, when we were out on the deck. But, I don't know. It didn't seem like the right time." His fingers flexed at his sides. "That's not true. Honestly, I chickened out and acted like an ass. I'm sorry about that too, by the way. I've felt like shit since the wedding. But I need you to know that I *never* wanted to break up with you."

The park around her spun, the entire world lapsing into silence. "Paul—"

"Because I was crazy about you," he went on despite the very real possibility that she was going to pass out. "I would have done just about anything to stay with you. And when I saw you here today, I had to tell you. I had to say something."

"But it's not true." Her palms itched. "None of that is true. You left me. You moved on."

"Because you told me you'd be too busy for a relationship. After you said—no, you *decided*—it would be too hard on us, too hard on me, to try and stay together when you'd be so busy running the bakery and taking care of your mom, that's when I left. You shut me out, Mira. And sure, okay, you never technically broke up with me, but I can take a hint."

Inch by inch, Mira's jaw dropped until it found a home in the grass at her feet.

"I never wanted to leave you. But it felt like you didn't want me to stay. I realized, after I left, that I shouldn't have given up so easily. I should have fought for us."

Her mom's words banged between her ears like drumbeats. *I should have tried harder. I shouldn't have been so scared.*

"But I was kind of devastated, and it all felt like it was too late. Like your mind was made up."

"Too...late." Her throat spasmed.

"Are you okay? Shit, Mira. You're really pale. Do you want to sit down? I can get you a chair."

He was still talking, but she barely heard him. Because it was her. It wasn't Paul. It wasn't Cole. It was all her.

Paul had wanted to stay, but she'd pushed him out of her life. Cole wanted to be with her, and she'd pushed him out too. Was she so afraid of ending up alone, so convinced everyone would leave her, that she didn't even give them the chance to prove her wrong? Was it some sort of hereditary emotional damage handed down through the generations? "Jesus, I'm just like my mother."

"Whoa," Paul said, his eyes comically wide. "I did *not* say that."

"Cole told me he wanted to move to Red Falls. He told me he loved me. He put his whole entire heart in my hands"—she swayed on her feet—"and I shoved him out the door with a fucking cupcake as a parting gift!"

Paul's horrified grimace was the indictment she deserved. "A cupcake?"

Doubling over, she braced her hands on her knees and tried not to throw up.

"It's okay," he said in a soothing voice. "It's going to be okay. It's—"

Hauling herself upright, she grasped the lapels of his summer weight jacket and shook him bodily. "Is it too late? Tell me it's not too late."

"How long ago did he leave?"

"Ten days." Was that all? It felt like a lifetime.

"It's not too late," Paul told her. "I waited months. Although," he reconsidered, "the cupcake might be a tough one to get over."

"Don't make fun of me. I'm in the middle of a full-blown existential crisis right now."

"It's not too late, Mira. But do me a favor. When you do talk to him, when you tell him how you feel, don't hold anything back. Not only does he deserve it." He tucked a strand of hair behind her ear. "But you deserve it too."

Giving him a quick, tight hug, she said, "I'm so sorry, Paul. For everything. But thank you. Thank you, thank you, thank you." She pulled back, wiped her eyes. "I gotta go."

"Yeah, you do. But make Jen drive. You're a mess."

"Ha!" She didn't even care who looked at her now. "You're right! I am a mess!" Walking backward toward her car while a thousand-watt smile shot across her face, she shouted, "But sometimes it's the mess that makes life beautiful!"

CHAPTER THIRTY-EIGHT

COLE

THREE DAYS EARLIER

Staring at the sketch of Mira's cake he'd hung on the recording booth wall the day after he'd gotten back, because, apparently, he was a masochist, Cole asked, "How's Davis?" into his phone. "I text her every day, checking in, but she doesn't reply very often. And when she does, it's only a sentence or two."

"She doesn't say much to me either," Madigan replied, sounding indescribably exhausted. "But Ashley and Maude Alice have mobilized around her. They're trying to keep her busy, not giving her much down time. But she's not okay. She's so...vacant. It was a trauma, seeing Kev like that. She needs time to process it. I wish she hadn't followed us. I wish I'd noticed her car and made her turn around."

"Even if we had, nothing would have kept Davis from coming," Cole assured him. "We would have had to chain her up in the basement, and she *still* would have found a way out."

"You're probably right. But I'm worried sick about her."

"Me too," Cole said, and then, hesitantly, "How's Kev?"

After a deep sigh, Madigan said, "I keep reminding myself that it could be worse, but it's hard. I pulled every string I could, called in every favor anyone has ever owed me to keep him out of jail. He'll do at least a month in rehab, and then... I don't know."

"I'm so sorry, Mad."

"Not the first time, won't be the last. But yeah, this one hurts."

"I should have been there," Cole said, finally giving voice to only one of the many regrets kicking relentlessly around his head since he'd gotten back from Red Falls. "I shouldn't have left. I shouldn't have let Thom's sister onto the property when she looked the way she looked. I should have told you immediately that they knew each other."

"No, Kev's the one who should have told me he knew Thom and his sister. He should have told me they used to use together. That part, at least, is on him."

"I still feel like it's all my fault," Cole admitted.

"I get it. I wake up every morning with my brain trying to convince me Kev only left with them because I was gone." The rasp of his knuckles against his beard through the phone made Cole wish they were having this conversation in person. They both needed to hug this one out. "Truth is, he would have found his way off the mountain one way or another no matter where we were. It's addiction. This is just what it does. Relapse is, unfortunately, a normal part of recovery. But"—he sighed—"you already know that."

Cole nodded, remembering Mad's relapses, remembering how awful they were, but also how he came through each one a little bit stronger. Maybe that would happen with Kev too. "Will you take them back?"

"Not Thom." Madigan's voice held a cold anger Cole had never heard from him before. "When I admitted him, I had a gut feeling he didn't actually want to get clean. Now I wonder if he'd had this whole thing planned from the jump. I'd take Kev back, but I don't know how everyone else here will feel about that. It's complicated."

Picking up a drumstick, twirling it absently, Cole could only say, "Yeah."

"But enough about me. Have you talked to her?"

"Who?" Cole asked, pretending he didn't know exactly who Mad meant.

"Seriously, Cole?"

"I've tried," he relented, scratching his head with his drumstick. "But I can't figure out what to say. You know when you get something so wrong you don't even understand how it happened? Like, you look at yourself in the mirror and think, 'You really messed that one up, dipshit'?"

"Well," Madigan said with his patented knowing tone, and Cole braced himself for the lesson he knew was coming. "Sometimes things feel wrong when, really, they're just unfinished."

Sometimes, he hated being right.

"You should call her."

"Yeah." Cole set his stick down across the floor tom. "Maybe."

"Cole?"

"Yes?"

"What's Mira's love language?"

"Come on, Mad," Cole groaned. "That's a low blow."

"Tell me."

Sitting back on his stool, staring up at the ceiling, he surrendered. "It's Physical Touch."

"That's what I thought. Call her."

It wasn't that he didn't want to. He did, more than anything. But it wasn't that easy. "I gotta run. Love you, man."

"Love you, too, brother."

STEPPING out of his booth an hour later, Cole glanced around the silent, empty studio, fighting off the eerie sensation that while he'd been recording backing tracks for *CSI: Something or Other*, everyone else in the world had disappeared, leaving him alone forever. "Hey?" he called out. "Anyone here?"

"Just me," Benji grumbled, popping his head out from behind his computer at the front desk, rubbing his eyes.

"Late night?"

"Out with the SyGs again. I'm getting too old for this shit."

Cole almost laughed at the forty-year-old, and he would have, if laughs weren't so hard to come by these days. "Talk to me in fourteen years. Have you seen Nancy?"

"Yeah, she was here. She walked in, took one look at you in the booth, shook her head, and walked back out."

"Huh." Cole had no idea what that meant but figured it probably wasn't good.

"It was weird, not gonna lie. Any chance you want to take a shift tonight? The SyGs want to go to this experimental witch house show that doesn't even start until two in the morning." Benji's groan was pained. "I think they might, just, live like this. Like, every day."

"We certainly did."

"How? How the fuck did we do that? I feel like I've been punched in the throat."

"I honestly have no idea," Cole said. "But I don't think you want this"—he ran a hand over his face, down his drab clothes, pointing out his sad, miserable...everything—"as Trax's PR guy right now."

"Maybe we should actually hire a PR guy. Someone young."

Cole nodded. "That's not a bad idea."

"I've got a lot of good ideas," Benji said, tugging on his goatee braid. "I think we should have a meeting about them sometime. Officially."

"Officially?" Cole asked.

"Well, over a beer."

"Ah, an official beer meeting. I was gonna ask if I needed to reserve the con room, maybe bring my lawyer."

"You're an ass."

He wasn't wrong there. "Let's do it. Tomorrow night? Tell the young punks you'll be busy?"

After a few clacks on his keyboard, Benji looked up and said, "It's on my calendar. And Cole, I'm, uh, I'm sorry, man. She seemed like a good one."

"Thanks, Benji." Cole knew he was a walking, barely talking, wide-open wound right now, but hearing everyone around him apologize for it, for the mess he'd made of everything, made him desperate to snap out of it. He needed something to help him move on, something to remind him of who he was and what he wanted, especially since what, or who, he really wanted didn't want him back.

Dragging his phone out of his pocket, he punched out a text.

Cole: Hey Nancy. Can we talk?

It was odd that Nancy hadn't responded, since she usually texted back the second he'd pressed send. But when he pulled into his driveway, seeing her Escalade sprawled sideways in front of the garage, taking up so much space he couldn't park in there even if he'd wanted to, he realized why.

Walking through the door, tossing his mail and his keys down on the counter, he followed the sound of voices to the nursery and knocked on the door.

"Oh look," Nancy cooed to Ruby when he opened the door. "It's grumpy Grandpa."

"Ha ha," Cole deadpanned, unable to hide his grumpiness even long enough to prove Nancy wrong. Because she wasn't wrong. He was grumpy, and sad, and miserable. And he had no one to blame but himself. He was the one who willingly entered a sex-only relationship, caught every feeling imaginable, and just assumed Mira had too.

Sitting cross-legged on the floor with Ruby while they stacked colorful plastic blocks on top of each other, Nancy squinted up at him. "Not to be too blunt, but you look like shit."

"Thanks, Nance," Cole said, sarcasm dripping from every word.

"Mom, don't swear in front of the baby." Becks handed Ruby a red block. "I don't want her first word to be a chain-smoking curse."

Nancy rolled her eyes. "I don't smoke anymore, and...sorry, fine. I'll *try* not to swear."

"It's actually good you're here, Nancy." Cole leaned against the crib.

"It is?" Nancy and Becks asked at the same time, equally dubious.

"Yeah." He cleared his throat. "I wanted to talk to you. To both of you, actually."

"Oh god." Nancy looked horrified. "Are you sick or something? You're sick, aren't you? I cannot handle that type of shi—*stuff* today."

He raised his hands. "No, I'm not sick. Calm down."

"Well, we're of the age," Nancy said distantly. "For beekeeping and heart disease. And like I said, you look like...poop."

Accepting a very slobbery blue block from Ruby, Becks stacked it on top of the other slobbery blocks and asked, "What did you want to talk to us about?"

Cole rolled his neck, preparing himself for the punishing gravity of the words about to leave his mouth. "Nancy, I want to take the gig. I'll come drum for you on your tour."

"You what?" Becks cried, which made Ruby cry. "Oh no, baby," she soothed, scooping Ruby into her arms. "Shh, it's okay. Grandpa's just being ridiculous."

"I'm not being ridiculous," he said while Nancy assessed him, her eyes narrowing by degrees. "Your mom needs a drummer, and I need a break from Seattle"—*and everything else*—"for a while."

Giving him a look he couldn't begin to decipher, Nancy said, "Wow, Cole. That's amazing. Thank you."

"You're wel—"

"But," she cut across him, letting the moment stretch, "I'm going to have to pass."

"What?" he blurted out, some good old-fashioned outrage coursing through him.

"You're not hired." Nancy picked up a light blue block, pointed it at him. "Sorry, Cole. But I don't want some mopey, lovesick puppy dog who'd be wishing he was somewhere else the entire time shi—*pooping* all over the mood in my tour bus."

Mildly offended, he put his hands on his hips, and said, "That's... I wouldn't...poop—"

"Dad, come sit with us." Setting Ruby back down near her blocks, Becks tapped the floor beside her. "We need to talk to you about something too."

"We?" he asked, suddenly suspicious. "What do you mean?"

While Nancy stared a hole straight through him, Becks said, "We've been waiting for you to come home."

"You've been waiting..." He reeled back. "Wait, what's happening here?"

"Don't freak, Dad. But this is an adorable baby-assisted intervention." She patted the floor again. "Sit."

Gingerly, and not only because his knees objected to anything faster, Cole lowered himself to the carpet. Picking Ruby up when she crawled to him, he said, "I don't need an intervention. I'm fine. I just need something to do."

"You're not fine," Becks said. "You're a mess. You went to Montana, fell in love, and came home empty-handed."

"Not true," he pointed out, thinking of the cupcake going stale in his fridge, because while he couldn't eat it, he couldn't bring himself to throw it away either. "Look, it's not that complicated. I told her I loved her, she gave me a goodbye cupcake, and that's that. It's a tale as old as time."

Nancy and Becks shared a look, then Becks said, "Dad, I love you, but is it possible you might be minimizing a little bit? I think it might help if you told us what actually went down. Specifically."

Relenting, partly because he knew they'd get it out of him eventually and partly because he needed to get it off his chest, he told them the whole story, every sad, painful, disastrous detail. When he was done, when he looked up, he found Becks and Nancy staring at him, their eyes wide, their mouths hanging open, like he'd just told them he'd love it if his teeth started falling out. "What?" he said, shrugging the shoulder Ruby wasn't currently drooling on.

"Just so I'm clear," Becks said at length. "You got off the airplane, left suddenly, didn't talk to Mira for three days—three days she probably spent worried sick about you. Then you showed up out of nowhere looking like literal death warmed over, and instead of debriefing and giving yourself, and her, time to come down from the emotional shit show you'd just gone through, you told her you loved her for the first time ever, and, like, ultimatumed her into telling you to dump your entire life and move to a different state for her?"

Having it all laid out there like that with such brutal efficiency, the only thing Cole could say was "I mean..."

"Did I do this to you?" Nancy asked, still staring, unblinking. "Did I mess you up this badly?"

"Probably," he replied in pure, baffled exasperation.

While Nancy winced, Becks continued. "I'm trying to imagine what that situation might have felt like for Mira. And all I can see is, here comes this man who has an amazing life he'd just spent an entire day showing off to her, offering—in what could easily have been perceived as a sleep-deprived fugue state—to leave it all behind to be with her, but only if she asked him to. And when she didn't, because who in their right mind would? He just...left."

It always surprised him, how hard certain words could hit, and Becks's aim was devastating.

"If you want to be with her, then be with her," Becks said, taking Ruby from his slack arms. "But you need to do it for you, because *you* want to take the risk. Because you see a life for yourself in her world. You can't expect her to make that choice for you. It's too much pressure. For anyone."

"Even for me," Nancy muttered.

Becks's voice turned soft, her brows sliding together. "You told me Mira is the type of person who always puts everyone else first. I hate to say it, but I think you just walked out on her because of it. Because *everyone*, in that moment, also included you."

Burying his head in his hands, reality crashing over him like one of those waves that dragged him under and kept him there until he was disoriented and desperate for air, he said, "You're right." He'd thought he was being careful, trying to protect himself, making sure she was on the same page before packing up his U-Haul. He'd just never considered she might have been trying to protect him too. He never considered how unfair it was to expect her to tell him to stay, not only because of the shape he'd been in, but also because he'd only given her half the story. "No wonder she gave me that fucking cupcake."

"I agree," Becks said, covering Ruby's ears. "But that really is enough swearing around the baby."

When he raised his head to give her an apologetic look, Nancy asked him, "So what are you going to do now?"

In the few milliseconds it took for the answer to form in his mind —while his heart kicked at his ribs and blood pumped hot through his veins for the first time in days—the image of his life existing in hers hovered before him. It had been there for a while, exactly what he'd wanted to do and how he'd wanted to do it, only he'd skipped the step of actually telling her about it. But there it was, meaning, purpose, Mira. The whole story, beginning to end, good, bad, and everything in between. And he wanted it all.

Looking at Nancy, then at Becks, then at precious little Ruby, Cole smiled.

CHAPTER THIRTY-NINE

MIRA

SHE'D WANTED to call Cole, or at least text him, after she'd gotten home from the wedding, but she hadn't been ready. She'd needed time to get the words right, to make sure that when she was finished spilling her heart, he'd know exactly how she felt, exactly what she wanted. Because, apparently, this was not one of her skills.

But today, sitting in her window, the warm breeze carrying the scent of freshly cut grass, she unfolded a scrap of paper, and wrote slowly, carefully, *He will know how much I love him.* When she opened the wish jar and held the paper out in front of her, she paused before flicking her lighter. This one, this wish, she wouldn't burn. Because this wish wasn't a wish. It was a plan.

Closing the jar, folding the paper in half and tucking it into her bra, she picked up her phone, opened her contacts, then paused. It was faint, just barely audible, but the wind must have been blowing the right way today, because she heard the unmistakable lilt of music floating down the alley from Jimmy's. Her skin pebbled, the hairs on her arms floating upward as the strings, the guitar, and then the voice sang to her about paradise..

It had to be a sign, a massive cosmic fist bump, that right as she was about to call Cole, someone played "Sailing" on the jukebox. Then, another sign, her phone lit up like a firework in her hand.

As Whitney began to belt, both of their heart songs playing at once, his face bloomed right in front of her eyes, and maybe the scrap of paper nestled over her heart was a wish after all.

"Hello?" she said, her voice raw, throat tight.

"Hey sugar—What was that?"

"Shit! Nothing!" she shouted, swiping her phone up from where she'd dropped it on the floor, because hearing him call her sugar again fried every single pathway between her brain and her muscles. "Hi, hello. Hi."

"Hi."

"Hi." This was going very well. "How are you?"

"I'm good," he said. "How are you?"

"Good. I'm good." *Just keep talking. Don't hang up. Don't leave.*

"I was thinking," he said while Christopher Cross serenaded her, "about what I told you before I left." He must have been outside, walking somewhere, the sound of his feet crunching over gravel tickling her ears.

"You were?" She tried to swallow, but only produced a dry gulp.

"I meant what I said, when I told you I loved you. Because it's true. I am so madly in love with you it's almost embarrassing. And I never get embarrassed."

She stopped breathing.

"But I forgot to tell you a few other things too," he went on, oblivious to her current state of suspended animation. "I forgot to tell you how much I loved your bakery, your family, your town, being so close to Madigan." *Crunch, crunch, crunch* went his feet. "I forgot to tell you how much the traffic in Seattle had started to bug me, how much the rain had been getting me down, how I was starting to find more and more excuses not to go into the studio, how ready I was for a change. I forgot to tell you how excited I was about this idea I had. I should have told you these things."

Reaching inside her bra, she pulled out her wish, unfolded it, reread it to herself, listened to the words *"Just a dream and the wind to carry me. Soon I will be free."*

"It wasn't fair of me to expect you to just know what was going on in my head," Cole told her while a car drove by. "It wasn't fair to expect you to ask me to leave everything behind to be with you, when I hadn't let you know that my life, my future, my home, was already here." *Crunch, crunch.* "Right here, right across the street, right down this alley." *Crunch.* "Right next to these lilac bushes. Right under this window."

She held her hand over her mouth, and when her phone fell to the floor this time, she didn't bother picking it back up. She didn't need to, because he was there, right there, standing in her alley, just below her window.

"Mira? Are you still there?" he said into the phone. He must have ended the call and tried her again, because "I Will Always Love You" blared from her floor.

"Do you have that set as my ringtone?" he called up to her when she shoved her head out her window. His smile was so wide and beautiful and messy and perfect it made her sob through her fingers.

"How?" she managed through a ragged breath, and then, "Wait, was this you?" She pointed at the sky, like the musical notes were something tangible they both could see and hear and touch.

"I was hoping to use Madigan's boombox, but he didn't have this tape, and his tape guy was out of town. So I asked Jimmy. He actually started playing it on repeat ten minutes ago. But I couldn't hear it. I had to double my bribe to get him to turn it up."

"I'll send him some cookies," she said, her eyes misting over until his beautiful face blurred.

He responded with only two words, two words with an entire lifetime of hope behind them. "Come down."

"I'm coming," she said, briefly considering climbing out her window and down the rickety fire escape just to get there faster. She raised her hand, palm out. "Wait for me. Don't leave. Don't leave again."

He raised a hand too, using it to cover his heart. "Mira, I'm not going anywhere."

Racing down the stairs, missing the last two and landing so hard her mom shouted "What on earth!" from the kitchen, Mira threw the door open—the poor bell didn't stand a chance—and gasped at Cole's Volvo parked across the street, a moving trailer hitched behind it.

She looked around, spun in a circle, her heart racing, his wish still clutched between her fingers. And then he was there, walking out of her alley, his hand still over his chest. "Hi, Mira."

Swiping her tears away, she replied, "Hi, Cole."

They stood apart, at least a few feet separating them, but it felt more like a mile. She hated the distance. She hated the part she'd played in putting it there. "I was about to call you," she said in a rush. "When you called me, I was just about to call you."

"You were?" His hand fell to his side. "What were you going to say?"

"I—" *It's now or never, Mira.* "I was going to tell you that I was scared. When you came back, when you said you wanted to stay here for me, I was so scared. But I never wanted you to leave. I should have tried harder to make you stay. I should have told you exactly how I felt." She blinked, and a tear tracked down her cheek. "I don't want to be scared anymore. I want you, Cole. I want you here, with me, always. I want to go to sleep with you every night and wake up with you in the morning. I want you to tuck me in. I want you to play cards with my family. I want to bake for you every day."

"No cupcakes," he said, and she laughed, like really laughed.

"You are the most wonderful man I've ever met. You're selfless and generous and kind. You remember things nobody else would. You give everything you have to the people you love. You put yourself out there with your arms open wide over and over again, even when you've been hurt, and I don't know if you realize how rare that is, how much your refusal to let the world get you down spreads like sunlight to everyone around you." She took a step toward him, pulled by that magnetic force that drew her inexorably in one direction, her favorite direction: due Cole. "I am so sorry if I made you feel like you weren't enough for me. You were. You *are*. I just didn't think that I would be enough for you. I didn't think I deserved someone like you. But I don't care if I deserve you or not. I want you. I need you. I love you." She watched his fingers flex, his jaw muscles tick. "You said you keep falling in love with people who don't love you back."

"I shouldn't have said that," he told her. "You were right. It wasn't fair. I was overly emotional and under slept—"

"But that's okay. Because I love you when you're overly emotional. I love you when you haven't slept. I love you when you care so much that you say all the things I've been too afraid to say. I love you, Cole, and not only by half. I love you with my whole entire heart."

"Mira," he whispered harshly, eating the remaining distance between them to take her face between his hands, pull her close, and kiss her. And, *god*, she'd missed his lips, his strong fingers, his warm body against hers.

"I love you," she said again between kisses, grasping the back of his shirt, her wish crumpling in her hand as she breathed in sunshine. "I love you so much I had to get my throat looked at."

He tried to say something. Probably "What's that?" But she kissed him again before he could, and he kissed her back, so deeply the world around them went silent, still. Until Ian grumbled, "Get a room," walking hand in hand with Brendan up the sidewalk toward the bakery.

"Hey, Ian," Cole said with a nod in her son's direction. "Thanks for not blowing my cover."

Ian nodded back, hiding a half smile before disappearing inside.

"He saw me when I first got here," Cole explained at her quizzical expression, taking her hands in his. "I thought I might have to bribe him to keep quiet, but he's a good kid." He turned her right hand over, noticing the crumpled bit of paper in her palm. "What's this?"

Giving him the paper, she watched him unfold it, smooth it out, read the words she'd written. "He will know how much I love him."

"Ever since I was a kid," she said, brushing her fingers over his cheek. "I've burned all my wishes. But I didn't burn this one, because it's for us. And I was going to make it come true no matter—"

Now it was his lips doing the interrupting, his tongue silencing hers while his hands cupped her face, her wish pressed between his palm and her cheek.

"Come with me," he said after he broke their kiss. "I have something to show you."

Taking her hand and leading her across the street to the storefront that used to be a laundromat, he pulled a set of keys out of his back pocket. Sliding the key into the lock, he turned the knob, pushed the door open, and said, "Welcome to Trax Montana."

"Trax what?" she asked, stumbling over the front step.

"Montana," he repeated, reaching out for her elbow, steadying her. "This is my new studio."

Taking in the empty space, the plain white walls, the bare hardwood floors, the fantastic windows, she said, "Are you renting this or—"

"I bought it. Three days ago."

"You...bought it?" Pinpricks of light danced through her vision, everything around her growing still, more vibrant. Every detail of the space, of Cole standing in it, his hair a little messy, jeans hanging low on his hips, white V-neck barely tucked in on one side, so clear in her mind she knew she'd remember this moment forever. "You bought this store, right across from mine?"

"Mm-hmm," he answered calmly, running his finger through the dust along the front windowsill. "Needs some love, but it's pretty sweet, don't you think?" When he finally turned to face her, when his lips quirked, she silently expressed her deepest and most heartfelt gratitude for whatever force in their random universe ushered him through her bakery door, into her life, her heart. "Someone once told me there wasn't anywhere in Red Falls for kids to take music lessons.

And I thought that was a real shame. The arts are important to a community, Mira."

"But what about your studio in Seattle?"

"Sold it to Benji, most of it anyway. I'm still part owner until he's ready to buy me out all the way. But it's what he's always wanted."

"What about Becks?" she asked. "And Ruby?"

"It's okay, sugar," he said softly, probably sensing her growing distress. "I gave Becks the house, and part of the studio deal was monthly use of Benji's jet. Someone needs to teach that man how to negotiate."

She wanted to laugh, but her brain was too busy trying to spiral in chaotic circles. "What about your boat? Your sailing. There's no ocean in Montana."

"Really?" he said, feigning confusion. "Huh, shoot."

"Cole, be serious. You love your boat."

"There might not be an ocean, but there are a lot of lakes. I'll either leave her in Seattle or bring her here. Haven't given it too much thought." Taking a step toward her, he said, "To be honest, there's only one thing I've given most of my thoughts to."

She brought her hand to her throat, expecting that same painful lump when she swallowed. Only this time, it wasn't there. "What's that?"

His eyes glittered as he slid an arm around her back and tugged. "What kind of twinkly lights I should get for you upstairs in my bedroom."

"You'd live over here, too? Right across the street?"

"Thought I would." Taking her hand in his, swaying her side to side to a song that wasn't playing, he said, "You've kind of got your hands full over there. I figured it might be nice for you to have a place you could sneak away to. We could have sleepovers."

Her wish hadn't been enough, not by a mile. His wish for them had been so much better.

"You see, Mira. I was kind of lonely in Seattle." He held her close, the heat of his body finally making her warm again. "I was a bit aimless, lost. I thought, *Maybe I need a change.* I thought, *Maybe if I move to this little town in Montana, I'll meet someone.* Maybe at a bar, or at a concert."

"A concert," she said while pressure built behind her eyes. "And after the concert, maybe we had a once-in-a-lifetime first date."

He kissed her forehead with a smile on his lips. "The next day, maybe I found you on Instagram. Maybe I followed you."

"Maybe I followed you back so fast I sprained a finger."

"Maybe we started DMing."

She blinked her tears free. "Maybe I gave you my number, and we started texting."

"Maybe I got the courage to call you."

"Then I got brave enough to FaceTime you."

"And then, slowly," his fingers threaded through hers, "we became..."

"Us," they said at the same time.

And as she stared into his eyes, he asked, "So, what do you think, Mira?"

With her cheeks wet and her heart so full it might burst, she said, "It feels right."

He took her hand, pressed a kiss into her palm, and said against her skin, "It always has."

She kissed him again, then pulled away, and while he dried her tears with his thumbs, he frowned down at her and asked, "So what was that about getting your throat looked at?"

"Whatever it was"—she slid her fingertips under the hem of his shirt, flattening her palms on the warm expanse of his back, easing him close again until his arms surrounded her—"it's all better now."

"I love you," he whispered into her ear, each word a shiver across her neck as he held her the way he always held her, like she was precious to him, like she was necessary.

Trying her best to hold him so that he'd know how precious he was to her, she said, "I love you too."

After a moment, with his cheeks flaring pink, his grin almost bashful—which was exceptionally adorable on a fifty-four-year-old man, he said, "I did some unpacking before I came to find you."

She raised a brow, looked around. "You did? I don't see anything."

"Well, it was really only one thing. I did *an* unpacking. It's upstairs."

Sliding her hands over his shoulders, up his neck, she sucked her lower lip into her mouth and dragged it out slowly between her teeth while he watched. "What is it?"

Grasping her ass, he hauled her close and said, "My bed."

EPILOGUE

Cole: Hi Mira

Mira: Hi Cole

Cole: Can you get away?

Mira: Ian just offered to clean up for me, so upside is I can. Downside is my son might be possessed.

Cole: Lol. I'll be waiting.

Watching her door like a hawk, Cole waited for Ian to flip the sign to CLOSED while he flipped his keys around his finger. He'd made sure that neither he nor Ian—who'd started teaching piano at the studio over the summer—had any lessons scheduled for the afternoon, because he'd wanted Mira all to himself. He'd also given a definitely not-possessed Ian twenty bucks to clean the bakery today, but what Mira didn't know wouldn't hurt her.

It had been three months since he'd moved to Red Falls, and like he did almost every day, he wanted to celebrate. The studio was filling up, Ian helped him run the scheduling, his boyfriend, Brendan, was actually a whiz at bookkeeping, and Cole was still getting decent recording gigs from his regular clients. He drank coffee with Mira every morning, had lunch with her every day, made love to her as often as possible, tucked her in every night, either at her place or his. He even took Linda to her therapy sessions when Mira needed to run errands or go for a hike or get the facials and massages he liked to buy for her because self-care really was important. He'd wanted, more than anything, to make her life easier, and he hoped that he had. He hoped he'd made the insurmountable feel mountable. But today might be a stretch.

When Ian finally flipped the sign, giving Cole a thumbs-up through the window, he held his breath. Then her door swung open. She emerged into the afternoon sun in the form-fitting blank tank dress he loved peeling off her, and he jumped into action.

"Hey, baby," she said when he greeted her at his door, using the pet name that always made his knees weak, the one she'd bestowed upon him the first day he met her and started using for real after he surprised her in her alley.

"Hey, sugar." He shoved his keys into his back pocket, giving his shaking hands something to do. "How was your day?"

"Looong," she moaned, falling into his open arms. "I was up at three making the Sampson wedding cake."

"Poor thing," he said, not really meaning it, because the senator's daughter's wedding had done exactly what they'd hoped it would do, and now Glazed and Confused was swimming in wedding cake orders. He kissed her head. "Feel like doing something fun?"

Glancing up at him through her lashes, a sparkle in her eye, she said, "Yes. You should put your readers on, and we can play naughty teacher again."

That did sound good. Maybe they should just do that. *Focus, Cole.* "I was thinking more like getting out of Dodge. Wanna go for a ride? I'll drive."

"A ride? Where to?"

Hopefully not to the evening news. "Remember when we talked about going back to the caverns?"

"Yeah," she said warily. "I remember."

"I think we should go. It's a gorgeous afternoon, and you said you wanted to try—"

"Let's do it."

"Yeah?" he said, leaning back, the resolve blazing in her emerald eyes knocking the wind out of him. "You sure?"

"No." She gave him a smile. "But let's do it anyway."

"That's my girl."

"THIS PLACE IS AMAZING!" He pointed to the tubes of rock sliding down the walls, the strange, lumpy formations rising from the ground like mineralized snowmen. "Everything's so smooth and shiny."

"It's so hot down here," Mira said by his side, her hand clutching his in a death grip. "So humid. Are you hot?"

"No," he replied, because while it was humid, it was pretty chilly. But then he noticed the line of people walking the path in front of them. "It's a line," he whispered into her ear. "And you're nervous."

"Ugh." She twirled her hair up into a bun. "Fucking hot flashes."

Taking full advantage, he brushed his lips over her exposed neck and whispered, "Just don't take all your clothes off, okay?" But when she reached around him to squeeze his butt, he twisted out of the way. "Ah, ah, ah," he scolded, tilting his head toward the family lagging behind them, finding a plausible explanation for why he didn't want her hands on his ass, at least not yet. "There are children present."

Grabbing his elbow, her face suddenly paling, she yanked him close. "I think we're almost there, just around that corner. That's where they turn off the lights."

"You remember it that well?" Cole asked, squinting down the walkway, because it all looked the same to him: subterranean, gloopy, like goblins carved themselves a tiny city out of rock.

Staring up at him, squeezing his hand with cold, trembling fingers, she said, "I don't know if I can do this."

"Do you want to leave?" It would mess up his plan, but he could adjust.

"I don't know. I'm freaking out." She fanned her face. "And I'm so hot."

"You can say that again."

"Cole, be serious."

Sliding his hand over her cheek, he said, "Maybe this will help." And then he kissed her, with tongue, for ten solid seconds, giving it everything he had.

When he pulled away, she looked a little dazed, color rushing to her cheeks, Mira Pink. "I guess we're not worried about the families anymore?"

He turned, catching the wide-eyed stare of what looked like a five-year-old boy, and winced. "Oops."

"Actually, that did help. Thank you." She took a breath and blew it out, then jumped in place a few times, like a boxer warming up for a fight. "I can do this."

Nodding, he repeated, "You can do this."

"If you'll follow me this way, folks," the tour guide called out, "we'll go into the deepest parts of the cavern. Once we're there, we'll turn off the lights for thirty seconds so you can see what it's like to be in total darkness, the kind your eyes would never adjust to."

"At least they warn you about turning off the lights now," she muttered.

Holding her close, Cole walked with her around the corner, her face tucked into his chest, her arms cinched around his waist. "Are you ready?" he asked her.

"No."

"Need another kiss? I'm happy to feel you up real quick too, if you think that'll help."

At least she laughed, until the tour guide said, "Here we go, folks. Thirty seconds. See you on the other side."

The lights went out, one at a time, until only a single yellow bulb buzzed along the wall. When that flickered off too, Cole had to admit it was pretty damn disconcerting, the complete absence of light, of sound as everyone in the cavern seemed to hold their breath at once.

"I'm right here," he said into Mira's hair as she burrowed into his side. "I've got you." After a moment, her arms relaxed, and even though he couldn't see her, he felt her looking at him.

He'd been counting in his head, *twenty, nineteen, eighteen, seventeen.* He didn't have much time left. "Are you okay?"

"I'm okay," she said. "Because you're here." Squeezing him tighter, but not in fear, she whispered, "You're my light when the world goes dark."

His wedding speech. She remembered. Either his chest shrank, or maybe his heart swelled, but there wasn't enough room left for all the love inside him. "I'll always be here," he told her. And then he reached into his back pocket, pulled out the ring she definitely would have felt if he'd let her grope his ass, and held it in front of her, his fingers trembling so hard he only prayed he wouldn't drop it.

Six, five, four...

When the lights flared back to life, nearly blinding him, he looked down at Mira and grinned. "Doesn't closing your eyes just make it darker?"

With a self-deprecating laugh, she opened her eyes, then gasped when she saw the ring, her eyes misting over while she watched him sink to his knee, her chin wobbling when he told her, "You made it, sugar."

"Cole?" she said, her voice cracking.

"I thought it might be memorable to do it like this." He glanced around. The tour guide—who was more than happy to take Cole's twenty bucks to give him a little extra time on this part of the tour—

gave him a wink, while everyone surrounding them watched on, covering their mouths or their hearts, holding their own loved ones close. "But I didn't realize there would be so many people watching."

Mira laughed. So did everyone else. But then he caught her stare, the tear slipping down her cheek, and the world around them disappeared, the way it always did when she was this close to him.

"I thought this moment would be meaningful, significant. Because we've both had to overcome our fears in order to find our way to each other," he explained, the simple violet sapphire set in a vintage platinum band glinting under the artificial lighting. "I thought that when the lights went out, I'd feel...different somehow. But I don't feel different. I guess I didn't need to bring you all the way to this strange, dark cave, because I could have done this sitting at your counter having coffee with you, or walking with you through the streets in town, or dancing with you to the jukebox at Jimmy's. Because, Mira Jean Harlow, every moment when you're by my side is meaningful. Every laugh, every touch, every breath I'm lucky enough to share with you is significant. Every single second I spend with you becomes my new favorite memory."

Across the cavern, someone sniffled.

"I know you don't care for weddings, so we can just stay engaged forever if you want—"

"I want a wedding," she said quickly, her tears streaming. "I want a huge wedding with everyone I've ever known, all their relatives, and their friends, and their friends' friends. Everyone!"

Cole laughed, even though his eyes stung. "Mira, sugar, I love you. I always will, and I want you and everyone else to know that. I've already asked you so many times. I meant them, each one, and I mean it now too. Will you marry me?"

Bending over, she took his face in her hands, smiled through her tears, and said, "Fuck yes, I'll marry you!"

While the entire cavern erupted into cheers, Mira helped him to his feet, and he slid the ring onto her finger. When he met her stare again, she cupped his cheek, and told him, "Every second I spend with you becomes my new favorite memory too. But"—she gave him a watery grin—"it's gonna be pretty hard to top this one."

She kissed him then, and as he stood in that hidden place carved out by time, surrounded by whistling, cheering strangers, holding the woman he would have moved all the way to the moon for in his arms, Cole thought, *Hell yeah.* Because this moment was meaningful, it was significant, and it would be very hard to top. Good thing he had the rest of their lives to try.

~THE END~

For a bonus scene where Mira takes Cole camping, click HERE.

Cole and Mira's PLAYLIST

ACKNOWLEDGMENTS

Cole and Mira took me for a ride with this book. It wasn't a fast book, but I think most of that had to do with me not wanting to let these two go. I love them both so much, and writing their story felt like riding a roller coaster that just kept climbing and climbing until it hit the damn sun!

Mira is inspired by so many women I know who are in their late 40s/early 50s and just working so hard to hold it all down that they don't believe they have the time, or deserve to take the time, to find love again. I knew she needed someone who would make her life easier, who would meet her where she was and say, "I see your life. I understand your life. And I am all in!" And Cole was the right man at the right time with the right...everything to help Mira see that she was allowed to fall in love again. I mean, how could she resist? He's Cole Fucking-Drummers Sanderson!

Older people are largely absent from the media we consume outside of the role of parent or grandparent or plucky upstairs neighbor. Those depictions tend to be so surface level they're practically transparent. I write these stories because I think it's important to realize that older people are all still learning, still growing, still fucking up and sometimes making terrible choices, still deeply emotional, deeply flawed, outrageously immature at times, still having sex, still falling in love, and still worthy of being main characters. Romance readers age up, so romance stories should age up too.

As always, it takes a village to publish a book. And I can't thank my village enough. Especially Sarah T. Dubb, Angela Wren Crocker,

J Calamy, Livy Hart, and Heather Williams for being the most amazing beta readers. An enormous thank you to Kate Clayborn, Sarah MacLean, Nikki Payne, Anita Kelly, Jessica Joyce, Erin Hahn, Alicia Thompson, Lauren Morrill, Karen Booth, Regina Black, Denise Williams, LB Dunbar, Destany @book_halfunread, and Kara @mzkarareads for your support.

Thank you to my agent, Katie Shea Boutillier, for finding me.

Thank you to Aljane Compendio for continuing to rock my character art. Thank you to Beth at VB Edits for catching my oopsies.

Thank you to my beloved husband, my amazing son, my dogs, my sisters, my parents, my friends, and Johnny Knoxville.

And as always, thank you, from the bottom of my heart to everyone who has taken the time to read this story. It means the world to me.

ABOUT THE AUTHOR

A Montana transplant hailing from the suburbs of Chicago and about twenty other places, Jess K Hardy is a lover of mountains and snow, long nights and fireplaces. She has been a sandwich artist, a student, a horse trainer, a physical therapist, a wife, a mother, and also a writer. She writes contemporary and speculative adult romance.

ALSO BY JESS K HARDY

COME AS YOU ARE (BLUEBIRD BASIN BOOK 1)
THE CURSE OF NONA MAY TAYLOR
THE 7 RULES OF MOVING ON

Made in United States
Troutdale, OR
12/04/2024

25758170R00206